Henry T. Johns

Life with the Forty-Ninth Massachusetts Volunteers

Henry T. Johns

Life with the Forty-Ninth Massachusetts Volunteers

ISBN/EAN: 9783337268008

Printed in Europe, USA, Canada, Australia, Japan

Cover: Foto ©Andreas Hilbeck / pixelio.de

More available books at **www.hansebooks.com**

LIFE

WITH THE

FORTY-NINTH MASSACHUSETTS

VOLUNTEERS.

BY

HENRY T. JOHNS,

Late Private Co. C, Forty-Ninth Mass. Vols.

RAMSEY & BISBEE,
PRINTERS AND BINDERS,
WASHINGTON, D. C.

To the Children

OF MY

Comrades Living and My Comrades Dead.

THAT the noble record of your fathers may be accessible to you, I issue and dedicate to you this second edition of "Life with the Forty-Ninth Massachusetts Volunteers."

Every year, as you more clearly comprehend the importance of their work, you will more proudly remember that you are sons and daughters of VETERANS; of men who, all of them,—the surviving as well as the "fallen brave,"—dedicated their ALL that their country should realize the best hopes of mankind. YOUR children will also read this humble volume, and a noble pride of ancestry will inspire them to noble living. Some of your blood and name will bring forth this book at the next Centennial, proud to turn to the rolls and exhibit there the names of their patriotic ancestors.

Most of it was written in our different camps; much of it on the perilous edge of battles on slips sent to the rear to be forwarded to my wife in case I should be selected as one of the "fallen brave." I could not improve on it; so, except the correction of a few errors, it is just the book your fathers read and prized.

The plates of the portraits of the officers have been lost or destroyed; not a few of those officers are dead; so, as all cannot be reproduced, I reluctantly send forth this volume without any portrait, except that of Col. Bartlett, which was fortunately preserved.

I am, affectionately,

Your fathers' comrade,

HENRY T. JOHNS.

Boston, Mass., Aug. 1, 1890.

PREFACE.

The "Forty-ninth Regiment, Massachusetts Volunteers," sprang from Berkshire. This, their record, is written for Berkshire readers. If it shall, in after years, enable my comrades to recall the events and some of the emotions of our soldier-life; if it shall tend to unite us in sympathy; if it shall present to our friends a fuller view of our deeds and experiences, and bring out more vividly the merits of our "fallen brave," I shall be satisfied.

Writing it has been to me a "labor of love." I have written fully and earnestly of the principles underlying this struggle; otherwise I have confined my pen to our regimental life as it came within my observation and experience. It would be sad to believe those *principles* were no part of that *life*.

My chief regret is, that fuller *data* did not enable me to do justice to all our dead.

The engraving of Colonel Bartlett, one of the best evidences of the skill of the leading engraver of New York, A. W. Ritchie, needs this remark: On applying for a photograph, from which to obtain an engraving, the Colonel sent me several, taken in different styles, by different artists, at different times. I selected the one that was used because I deemed it the best one, and because it was suggestive of the wound received at Port Hudson, a memorable part of the most memorable day in our history.

I have written this "Life" in the form of "letters," thus making it less didactic and stiff than had I observed the historic style. Necessarily the "first person" is much used, perchance so much as to render liable the charge of egotism. In describing our battles, I have dwelt at length on my own actions and feelings, believing the *personalness* thereof would convey to my readers a better idea of such scenes than merely general descriptions. What is a battle, but the aggregate of individual deeds and emotions? If pride, in being allowed to share in our honorable career, occasionally crops out, I can only say in extenuation, "out of the abundance of the heart the mouth speaketh."

Hoping this hurriedly-prepared volume will keep fresh the memories that gather round the "Forty-ninth Regiment, Massachusetts Volunteers," and do something, however little, to inculcate those principles of which our military life was but an outgrowth, I send it forth to fulfill its mission.

HENRY T. JOHNS.

PITTSFIELD, MASS., *May* 1, 1864.

LETTERS.

LETTER 1.

HINSDALE, MASS., *August* 10, 1862.

MY DEAR T.

Like many others, I am almost decided to enlist. A large class, about the time of the bombardment of Sumter, forgetting their physical weakness, enlisted. In those grand days (and despite all our mismanagement and repulses, the days have been growing grander ever since), when God seemed to be saying to our internal foe, "Thy days are numbered, and thy kingdom is taken from thee," the weak felt strong, so that "one" almost imagined he "could chase a thousand, and two put ten thousand to flight." Alas! they fill our hospitals, or lie in lonely graves on the Peninsula. When victories, "like angel visits, few and far between," illumined the horizon, I have had no special promptings to join the army; but there has never been a signal defeat, that I have not felt the old half yearning, half conviction, that so nearly led me to enlist in the spring of 1861.

As we recede from the seven days' fight before Richmond, we get a clearer view thereof, and are compelled to call it a fearful reverse. True, there were splendid exhibitions of Northern valor, and that 's all we have gained. Had we so entirely forgotten our past, did we think we had so degenerated, that such battles, with their slain, were necessary to convince us and the world that valor was an heirloom of freemen? Wisely has the President called for three hundred thousand more men, and now his call for three hundred thousand *more* looks so much like being in earnest, that it calls out the hopeful earnestness of the nation. The country needs the men, and I, for one, feel that no longer can I say "Go!" but "Come!"

But a serious thought arises : "Have I a right to take human life?" To be slain seems not half so fearful as to slay. Grant that war *can* be right and the matter is settled, for never was war holy if *this* war be not holy. Fully have I considered the matter, and I am grounded in the conviction that, under certain circumstances, war is not only not wrong, but an imperative duty we owe to God and man.

God commanded the Jews to go up to battle against the heathen nations that inhabited Canaan. *That* forever settles the fact that war is not *inherently* wrong, for though a holy God may *allow* sin, he never *commands* it to be done. To say that that was under the old dispensation does not affect me ; for, no matter what the circumstances, God would never *command* or *encourage* that which is essentially wrong, that which is in opposition to His own nature. True, a thing not wrong in itself, may become wrong to us, if divinely prohibited. Though the genius of Religion is opposed to all violence, and will ultimately subdue the spirit of war, yet neither is there in the Old nor New Testament any direct or clearly implied prohibition of War. When John the Baptist was asked by some Roman soldiers what *they* should do to inherit the kingdom of heaven, he did not

say, leave " the army," but among other directions,
"be content with your wages," wages received as soldiers. He knew full well that some of them were at
times sent on unhallowed enterprises, but he doubtless
considered the army as the armed police of the empire,
often unjustly employed, but a necessary part of that
machinery which protects the good and weak from the
assaults of the evil and strong. The Saviour and His
disciples fellowshipped with soldiers, and acknowledged
them as Christians. True, war ushers many souls into
eternity unprepared. God does this often in individual
and collective cases, and we do not impugn Him.

Nothing can be more certain than that God is a God
of *government*. We believe that every thing material is
bound by laws. Is man alone left to his own impulses
and to anarchy? The most ancient history, that of the
Old Testament, teaches us that the Creator established
governments among men. His rulers had the right to
use the sword under certain circumstances. The theoc-
racies of early days were followed by the institution of
civil government, which has been declared to be " ordained of God." Now, the sword is necessary to uphold
government. Sad it is, but it is true. Man is dealt
with as he *is*, not as we hope he *will be*. A man steals;
an officer tries to arrest him; he resists that officer, who
uses violence, even unto the death of the offender. Now,
that is not a death punishment for *theft*, but for an attempt to undermine government itself. Let him succeed, let a thousand others succeed unresisted, and
where is the safety of property? That safety once gone,
and our very support depends on our brute strength;
so *might* becomes triumphant, and for the weak there
is nothing but injury and death. A man commits an
assault, an ordinary assault on another. Let him alone,

let all such alone, and where is order? where is society? where is government? All swallowed up in anarchy. Human life is valuable, but national life is yet more valuable. Human life may be sacrificed, perchance unjustly, with comparatively little injury to society; but the destruction of a nation's life brings untold woe. If government, that divinely ordained institution, can not be maintained without sacrificing human life, then the axe must descend. Now right here, in the right to take the life of those who would overthrow society, lies the war-power.

If individual life is worthy of defense, national life, on which so much of the happiness of living depends, is more worthy. Thus it seems to me, that revelation and reason alike teach the duty of war. Neither is this incompatible with the idea of peace. Peace is not non-resistance to wrong, but rather the quiet enjoyment of our rights. Wherever a right is assailed. *there* is war, though never a gun or a soldier is called into service. That nation which tamely bears wrongs that may be righted does not half as much for the cause of peace as they who rise against oppression with the old war cry, "Resistance to tyrants is obedience to God."

These are some of the reflections leading me to believe I could engage in war with an untroubled conscience. I give you results, not processes of reasonings. If ever I go into battle, I may forget those processes; but while I hold fast to the conclusion to which they have led me, my eye will not pity, nor my arm spare an armed rebel. Where men get in the way of human progress, I would remove them by gentle means; if they resist and are obdurate, let the triumphal car go on, for the rejoicings of the saved will drown the groans of the lost. The rebels *have* got right in the path of God and freedom. They refuse to move: let sword and cannon do their mission. Openly or blindly, every Union soldier is doing God's work. Let our foes succeed, and not only will we be draped in mourning, but the best part of humanity will be sharers of our sorrow and despair. The leaven of Protestantism, of liberty, and of education will permeate the *world* if we succeed. Anti-slavery men may fight with an intense enthusiasm, if they believe that the end of this war will find our flag, stripes all hidden by stars, waving over never a master or a slave ; but he who takes a fuller view of the dealings of Providence with this nation, and has faith in the Divine mission imposed on it, will scarcely need the inspiration of that belief (and it is great) to continue the contest till victory or death. While African slavery is sure to go under the waves of this aroused ocean, future historians will scarcely recognize it as one of the blessed fruits of this war, so rich and full shall be the clusters of blessings that our success shall give to the world. *That* alone is worth a nation's blood and treasure ; but comprehensive must be the memory that can recall the the "first fruits," when enjoying the full harvest. The *world* will meet to enjoy the "harvest home" purchased by the blood and treasure of hundreds of thousands of Americans.

LETTER II.

HINSDALE, MASS., *August* 29, 1862.

MY DEAR L.:

This evening I enlisted, thus deciding the contest of months. My health and strength *may* prove sufficient for the duties I have just taken on me. I enlisted under the call of August 4th, for volunteers for nine months, deeming that wiser than to join a three years' regiment.

The whole county is absorbed in the raising of troops. The draft was postponed till August 15th, and then to September 3d. If the war continues we must resort to the drafting system. It is the fairest and surest way of raising men. Conscription is the everlasting root of a nation. And, when party feeling is comparatively inactive, a draft could be easily enforced ; but, if we wait till that feeling puts on some of its old activity (and even now there are signs thereof), draft and anti-draft will become political tests. Then the strength of our government may be put to its severest test. The people quietly allow their *property* to be taken for the use of the nation ; if they will also submit to the forced seizure of their *persons* for the same end, none will dare say that there is not strength in a republican form of government.

It is a pity that the last call of the President was not for three years' men. Out of New England, they are raising but few nine months' regiments. I feel quite confident that it will not work well. Nine months is

too small a period to imbue men with a soldierly pride.
Let a few months pass, and they will begin to say, "in
four or six months our time will be out ;" and when
that is the case, the longing for home will weaken their
attachment to the army. The sick, soon expecting to
be discharged, will not brace up against disease, as if
they knew that they had to serve for nearly three years
more. These regiments, unless placed in the Army of
the Potomac, will scarcely see any dangerous service
till near the expiration of their nine months ; and it
is but human nature to take greater care of ourselves
when we are about closing up a perilous business, than
when the peril fills up years of our future.

To stimulate volunteering, we have adopted the system of paying bounties to recruits on being mustered
into the United States service. A town votes so much
bounty to each recruit, expecting that the State will
assume the debt as in the case of aid paid to families
of soldiers. Those bounties range from $50 to $150,
often increased largely by the selfishness or patriotism
of private individuals. I suppose no intelligent man
really admires this bounty system, yet it has been
started, and we must adopt it, or lo! the draft! It
brings out a good deal of selfishness. Men come from
towns where they offer small bounties, and enlist where
they can secure larger ones. Some carefully conceal
physical defects till they are mustered in and paid, and
then are discharged for disability, while others desert
as soon as they pocket their bounties. Few would object to seeing *them* receive the full penalty of the law—
death ! Strange as it may sound to you, after the
above, yet it is true, a better class of men are enlisting
now than ever before. Go through the county, see
the comfortable homes they are leaving, learn their po-

sition and reputation in community, and you must stultify your common sense before believing that greed of money influences them. Some of the best of the county have enlisted. Better remain not behind. If any selfishness alloyed their patriotism, it was dread of the draft, and to a proud-spirited man the idea of being a conscript in a nation of volunteers is repugnant to every feeling of self-respect. I believe we will raise the needed number. Surely it is a *needed* number when President Lincoln formally refuses to receive negroes as soldiers, and is laboring to colonize them. Strange what mad crotchets will sometimes invade the brain of sagacious men. Colonize four millions! Remove four millions of laborers from a country that needs nothing as much as working men! Refuse half a million of soldiers, and then make frantic appeals to men to hurry to the country's rescue! Old Abe will see his mistake ere long. I believe he sees it now, but fears that public opinion is not ready for the correction of the error. Statesmen should lead, if necessary *drag*, public opinion up to the right. Still the negro can bide his time. He has begged for the privilege of fighting ; the time may come when, with large bounties in our hands, *we* may beg *him* to join our ranks. Too numerous ever to be removed, God will give them the opportunity to secure our respect and their rights. With no nationality to fall back on, with their own swords they must earn a share in that of ours. The innocent cause of this great rebellion, they will yet become potential in crushing alike it and its prolific parent—their curse, slavery.

LETTER III.

Hinsdale, Mass., *September 8, 1862.*

My Dear L.:

Though you are absent from old Berkshire, the home of your youth, and with the people of which you are so well acquainted, I know your new home has not dethroned the old from your affections; so I will gratify you by writing at length concerning Berkshire men and events, only promising that all I communicate will savor of war; for, in common with us all, the war absorbs nearly all my thoughts, feelings, and actions.

War meetings for the raising of troops are more numerous than ever. The best of it is they are successes. We have filled up our quota of three years' men. Week before last was a memorable one for Pittsfield. On Thursday thereof a monster meeting was held in the Park, and there, where our Revolutionary fathers gathered in the morning of this struggle, many of their sons volunteered to continue and close up the old contest between aristocratic usurpation and popular rights. How history repeats itself! how little there is new under the sun! Change dates and names, and you can imagine Cavaliers and Puritans to be the actors, instead of Yankees and Southrons. We fight no new battle. It is only another phase of the old contest, old as human governments. A truce to this digressing, which, though one of the privileges of letter-writers, I will not further avail myself of now. At the Park were gathered the wealth, the bone and sinew of the land.

Messrs. Bowerman, Colt, Emerson, and others spake burning words to the people. Many of our wealthy citizens came forward to do, by their purses, what they could not do or would not do by their right arms. They did not *then* fill up their quotas. On the following Saturday, at noon, nearly all places of business were closed, and the work of volunteering went on with some success. Saturday night found them yet deficient. The draft was to commence the coming Wednesday; our brothers, outnumbered on the Potomac, were loudly calling for help, and it was decided to continue the effort on the morrow, the Sabbath day. In the quiet of a New England Sabbath evening they secured the requisite number of men. A holy day was appropriated to a holy purpose. How foolish ! how wicked ! the remark, that moral character has nothing to do with the efficiency of the soldier. The solemn enthusiasm of *that* hour, carried into the battle-field, would render any army invincible.

What fatality is opposed to our success ? We ask with our President, " Is it possible that God is on the side of the rebels ?" No! He wants to be on *our* side, and will be openly when we are willing to make this a war of ideas. Though superior to the enemy in everything. save knowledge of the country where the seat of war is located, we find that, after eighteen months of the most prodigal expenditure of men and means, we have made but little real progress. True, we have had some success in the *radical* West, but the nation, the world, looks on the Army of the Potomac as the representative army. It is so. Say what we may, all valuable as are the services of the Western commands, the progress of the war is wrapped up in the army just scattered, if not beaten, near Washington. By it we judge; by it

we are judged. The two contending armies of the respective Capitals must strike the decisive blow. I am
aware that the improved and enlarged facilities of travel
have rendered obsolete the idea that London is England, that Paris is France, that the Capital is the nation,
yet none ever dreamed of calling *them* victors whose seat
of government was assailed or endangered by an enemy.
Why this comparative unsuccess? Simply because we
have not been possessed of any great inspiring *idea*. We
have the fixed determination never to surrender our national unity, and "the Constitution and the Union"
for a rallying cry, but we need something more. Liberty, which is the life-blood of the Constitution, and
the jewel enshrined in the Union, has been studiously
kept out of sight. Bayonets think in these days, and
they *feel*, if they cannot logically *see* the difference between appeals to the *body* and to the *spirit*. Love of a
mere written instrument, or a civil organism, has but
little influence in making men

"Their Fatherland's befriender,
By life and blood surrender."

Yesterday, the Thirty-seventh left for Dixie. Under
the old elm, Dr. Todd made a farewell prayer. Though
he was heard by few, it was a solemn scene. We knew
they were bound for the Potomac, and that the exigen-
cies of the times were such that they might be rushed
into battle before another Sabbath day.

There are few more solemn, subduing scenes than the
departure of a regiment for the seat of war. Many of
the men assume a levity that poorly hides their own
sadness, and as poorly comforts those who are to remain
behind. Mothers, wives, children, were there to bid,
to look, the last adieu. Many a mother then pressed

her aching head into silence, and heroically struggled
to fasten in her boy's heart the memory of a farewell
smile. Kind, but vain mockery! To many wives, the
measured tread of that thousand men, marching from
home and life, seemed to be over their own hearts.
They felt *they* were nearing a day when there would be

> "A blush as of roses
> Where rose never grew;"

and though they were not deficient in the spirit of self-
sacrifice, nor heedless of the glory of the strife, yet the
farewell was with

> "Ah me! This glory and this grief
> Agrees not well together."

When the cars started, there was the usual cheering
given by the soldiers as evidence of their cheerfulness,
and taken up by those who had no very near friends
leaving. Those who had emptied hearts and homes for
their country's sake, fearing it might be — forever —
cheered not, but gazed on the receding train till out of
sight, and then turned sorrowfully homeward, to bear
alone the suspense of months, while their loved ones
should enter into scenes whose novelty and excitement
would lift up their sadness. Not *all* the brave go to
war. Saving the physical privation, exposure, and suffering endured by soldiers who are really loved, their
lot is enviable in comparison to that of the lone women
of our land.

> "Heroic males the country bears,
>   But *daughters* give up more than *sons*.
> Flags wave, drums beat, and unawares
> *You* flash your souls out with the guns,
>   And take your heaven at once.

But *we*, we empty heart and home
Of life's life — love !   *We* bear to think
   You're gone, to feel you may not come,
To hear the door-latch stir and clink,
   Yet no more *you*,— nor sink."

LETTER IV.

CAMP BRIGGS, MASS., *September* 15, 1862.

MY DEAR L.:

The first week of camp-life is over. Of course, you want to know all about it. The encampment is styled as above in honor of Brigadier-General Henry S. Briggs, son of the late ex-Governor, G. N. Briggs. Our homes are tents, called A or wedge-tents. They slope from the ground to the ridge-pole, being five and a half feet high, six feet wide, and seven feet deep. Six form a family circle. Did you ever try sleeping with five full-grown men, with most of your clothes on, in a bed six feet wide? If so, you know *that* involves lying "spoon fashion," and when one turns, all must turn, else some vigorous remarks will convince you that you are encroaching, not on the territory, but on the body of your neighbor. The weather must be very bad indeed, if we do not hail as a godsend the detailing of one or more of our family to "stand guard." *That* has some drawbacks, for, when his two hours of guard-duty are over, and just when we are beginning to enjoy the luxury of expansion, he returns, and a wet bed-fellow is sometimes the result; and if he oversleeps himself so as not to hear the guard-call, we have a visit from the corporal of the guard, who, after divers hallooings and shakings, succeeds in waking us all up, *the right man last.*

Sixteen of these tents are used by the enlisted men of each company, being eight on each side of a street some twenty feet wide. The streets are designated "A," "B," "C," after the names of the companies occupying them. The first street to the right is occupied by Co. A, it having come into camp first, and named accordingly. The next by Co. B, and so on. We have placed evergreen bushes around our tents, giving quite a home-like, a sylvan look to the encampment. Our streets are kept scrupulously clean. They run nearly east and west. To the rear is a line of cook-houses, to be used when we are furnished with rations raw, instead of rations cooked, as we now are. A trench five or six feet long, two wide, and one deep, with a crane made of green saplings, serves for the cook-stove of each company. Beyond these are sinks for depositing slops, rarely used, for our shrewd farmers, having no Jewish aversion to pork, are on hand glad to purchase all the refuse of the cook-houses. Often milk graces the tables, the cooks having learned that alchemy that transmutes slops into good, rich milk. Yet further east are places, sometimes within and sometimes without the lines of sentinels, reserved for *meditation*.

To the west of the company streets, and at right angles with them, is the grand promenade of the camp. On the western side of this avenue are located the tents of the Line Officers, captains and lieutenants, opposite severally to their respective company's streets. Each captain is entitled to a tent, as also are two lieutenants. Unless unsociable, they are generally placed so that one will be in the rear of the other, the front one being used for office, sitting-room, and parlor ; the other for bed-room. Do not imagine that the officers are doomed to the penalty of living in wedge-tents. *They* have wall tents, which are nearly seven feet square, running up at the sides about five feet, and thence to a ridge-pole some ten feet from the floor. So, you see, *they* can live, having room for comfortable beds or berths, chairs, and tables. Over these tents are spread flies, increasing the protection from the rays of the sun and from rain. To the rear of them, a little to the north, is to be the *sanctum sanctorum;* the tents of the Field and Staff Officers, or " Headquarters," before which a succession of unlucky wights must separately stand on guard that there be no profanation of military dignity.

Our regiment is to be known as the Forty-ninth Massachusetts Volunteer Militia. We hope to make the "Forty-ninth" a historic name worthy of the glorious old commonwealth.

We have now three companies, A, B, and C, in camp. With regard to lettering the companies, first come, first served. If lettering went in accordance with the dates of commission, " B " would be " C," and " C " would be " B." Co. A is called the "Allen Guards," for many of them once belonged to that organization. It was named after the Hon. Thomas Allen, of this place, who has been a very liberal sponsor. From the Allen Guards have already issued several companies in different regiments, dating from the first war-cry to this last call. I know not how many privates have gone from it, but it has furnished the service upward of twenty commissioned officers. I think Co. A will preserve unimpaired the honor of the name. They encamped in Burbank Hall from the 3d to the 7th inst. When the Thirty-seventh had left, they marched into Camp Briggs, a pleasant contrast to the gloomy hall. They number, all told, one hundred men. Though not large, they are rugged and healthy, and will stand the wear and tear of army life better than the six feet giants

who never bend till they break. Being so nearly the
same size and partially uniformed, and having had
some little drilling, *they* are our veterans. Some of
our best young men, who know nothing of hardship
and privation, are with them. Their average age is
twenty-two years, eight months, and eleven days. Their
average height is five feet, seven and one-tenth inches.

They are well officered. Israel C. Weller, of the firm
of Isham & Weller, flour dealers, is captain. He will
make a good one. He served as sergeant with the
three months' men under Captain (now General) Briggs,
and at the time of his election was a lieutenant in the
Allen Guards. He is well posted in military matters,
and having a fondness therefor, will make a superior
officer. To his own men he will always be, in thought
if not in words, *Is.* Weller. I shall watch Capt. Weller's course with some curiosity. He has before him
a much harder task than if his men were all strangers
to him. They like him, and while he is free with
them, they obey him very readily. I fancy he will
continue the same cheery, lively spirit, but I mistake
the man if he will ever allow familiarity to degenerate
into insolence or disobedience. He is twenty-two
years of age

George W. Clark, a finisher in Pittsfield Woolen
Mills, is the first lieutenant. He is a stranger to me,
but he *looks* the officer, and is very highly spoken of.
He is twenty-eight years of age.

Frederick A. Francis, of Sternsville, aged twenty-
seven, is the second lieutenant. You know him, and
will readily believe that he will make a popular and
efficient officer. So gentlemanly, with such a winning
voice, men will receive punishment at his hands more
readily than favors from some others. Neat and tasty

in dress, with pride of carriage, he makes an attractive appearance, and I prophesy a good report of him when comes the time to prove our soldierly qualities. By the by, the post of second lieutenant is just the easiest and pleasantest in the regiment. He has but little responsibility, and almost nothing to do with administering discipline. He can discharge his whole duty and yet play the gentleman, winning the good will of those who would curse him had he the sterner duties of a captain to fulfill.

Co. A is very fortunate in having for its orderly George Reed, one of our three months' men. He was a printer in the *Berkshire Eagle* office, and very highly respected. The post of orderly or first sergeant is almost as responsible as that of captain, with none of *its* privileges or honors. He is the business man of the regiment. If a detail is to be made for police, guard, or any other duty, *he* selects the men, and on him fall the anathemas of the shirkers and of those who may be really, though innocently, overtasked. If punishment is to be inflicted, he is the agent of that punishment. If the captain is censured for the uncleanliness of the men or quarters, he comes back on the orderly. Living with the soldiers, he must yet keep up the dignity of the officer, so that his numerous commands will be obeyed without the interference of his superior. The neatness, discipline, general efficiency of a company depends as much on the first sergeant as on the commander. Give a company a good captain and orderly, and you may be sure they will be worthy of the service. I send you a copy of the company roll. As you run your eye over it, you will see there is excellent material in it, warranting me in saying that some of the best young men of the town are there. They start well, being all united. As four-fifths of the men are from Pittsfield, she has all the officers, and none feel aggrieved thereat.

Co. B came into camp on the 7th and 8th instant. It numbers one hundred and two stalwart men, among whom are the pride of many homes and the respected of many communities. The *morale* of this company is very high. By reading over its roll, you will see the names of those who never left their homes and prospects save at the promptings of duty. Their average age is twenty-six years, three months, and seven days, and height five feet, eight and nine-tenths inches.

Charles R. Garlick, of Lanesboro, one of the firm of H. G. Davis & Co., dealers in dry goods, is captain. I have almost no acquaintance with him. He is very gentlemanly, dresses well, and is considered a prompt, active business man, of great value to his company. I think he will be an excellent disciplinarian and a reliable officer. He owns to twenty-six years of age.

Charles W. Kniffin, aged twenty-six years, merchant of West Stockbridge, is first lieutenant. He is a man of unusual personal popularity, and certainly very much of the gentleman. In common with others, I am prepared to prophesy a brilliant career for Lieut. Kniffin.

Robert R. Noble, aged twenty-two years, is second lieutenant. He is a son of R. Noble, Esq., of Williamstown, and was for six months a sergeant in Second Massachusetts Volunteers, from which regiment he was discharged on account of ill-health. He was the first volunteer from Williamstown. He acted as drill-master to Co. E, of the Thirty-seventh Massachusetts, receiving the praise of Col. Edwards. He is a good type of Young America, active, intelligent, self-confident. He loves military, and makes a fine drill-master, putting *vim* into the exercises, thus making them attractive to the men. As the other officers have had no military experience, Co. B has shown excellent judgment in raising young Noble from the position of a private to that of second lieutenant.

Orton W. Jennings, of Beckett, is the first sergeant. His looks denote intelligence and promptness, indispensable requisites for the orderly of a company. The men speak highly of him. I wish I was able to give you the names of those households from which two or more have gone forth to the war. Some have sent their all—husbands and sons—leaving none behind save the aged and the women. Abraham Rosseter, of Richmond, has three sons, his all, in this company. It is easy to write that sentence, but it is a wonderfully suggestive one. It speaks of an aged couple in their loneliness (perchance of lonely wives) following their boys in prayer and thought through all the temptations of the camp and the dangers of the field, stopping awhile as in fancy they hear, amid the groans of the dying, voices all too familiar to them. Who can tell their need of leaning upon the Great Father of all for strength to sustain them in their weary waiting for *them* who may never return !

> There were sad hearts in a darken'd home,
>   When the brave had left their bower ;
> But the strength of prayer and sacrifice
>   Was with them in that hour.

We turn from Co. B, otherwise known as "Pomeroy Guards," in compliment to Robert Pomeroy, Esq., of this town, and introduce to your notice Co. C, called "Berkshire Guards," to which I have the honor to belong.

It consists of ninety-three men, some of whom are equal in morality and intelligence to any in the regiment. Their average age is twenty-six years, four months and twenty-six days. Their average height is five feet, nine and five-seventh inches. For size, we will be apt to wear the palm.

Charles T. Plunkett, son of Hon. T. F. Plunkett, is captain. He is a splendid specimen of the *genus homo*, being six feet, six inches high. As he is but twenty-two years of age, he may have reached his height (it is to be hoped so), but not his full growth. He can hardly be called spare or stout, but every way a well-built man. Give him two or three years of war life, and you may hunt New England over for a better specimen of a soldier. He was engaged in the manufacturing business at South Glastenbury, Conn., and was a member-elect of the Connecticut legislature. Bright seemed the opening world to him, but, leaving all the comforts and luxuries of wealth and of high social position, he has taken on himself the duties and hardships of a soldier. He steps in his new position with ease, and if not suddenly stricken down by rebel bullets, which his commanding stature will invite, we believe he will do honor to the family name. He has a brother who went out with the 37th as a lieutenant.

Daniel B. Foster, of Cheshire, is our first lieutenant. He is thirty-four years of age, and has in him many of the qualities that make an efficient and popular officer.

By a combination not unusual at elections, Pittsfield has not only the captaincy of our company, but also the second lieutenantcy in the person of William W. Wells. He is thirty-five years of age, and possessed of considerable ambition and energy.

John R. Camp holds the delicate and responsible potion of first sergeant, which we hope he will occupy to his honor and our benefit. You may not be aware that in these nine months' regiments the men elect the commissioned officers, who, in turn, appoint the non-commissioned officers. Thus, a duty of no ordinary importance devolved on us. When we consider the power entrusted to officers, how that power may be abused, that our happiness, almost our lives, are in their hands, it seems but right that we should have the privilege of choosing our own commanders. Yet I know not if it were not wiser to have them appointed by the Governor. True, with him "kissing goes by favor;" but he could choose as wisely as we could, seeing that we were called upon to vote for officers before going into camp and becoming acquainted with the candidates. Could elections be deferred till after an active campaign, we *might* vote more wisely.

If, under the present system, the men choose unwisely, they will have none to blame but themselves. Poor satisfaction, to write "fool" against your own name.

LETTER V.

CAMP BRIGGS, MASS., *September* 22, 1862.

MY DEAR L.:

On Monday last, the 15th inst., Co. D, raised mainly in Barrington, came into camp. It is not too much to say that a better company never joined any regiment. It has a large number of farmers and farmers' boys, and also an unusual number of intelligent business men. In every respect, it is an honor to old Barrington. It numbers ninety-eight men, averaging in age twenty-five years, five months and five days : and in height, five feet, seven and one-fifth inches.

Its captain is Samuel B. Sumner, a son of Hon. Increase Sumner, of Barrington. He is a man of thirty-two years of age, one of our rapidly rising young lawyers, a graduate of Williams College, an ex-State Senator, and a poet and orator of no mean pretensions. I believe he has had considerable militia experience, and therefore is presumed to be competent to fill the duties of the majorship of the regiment, for which position report has already nominated him. He is shrewd and politic, and will make few blunders. All will like him.

Joseph Tucker, of Great Barrington, is first lieutenant. He was originally named for captain, but when the company roll was partially filled, Mr. Sumner enlisted, and Lieutenant Tucker assented to him as their

captain, believing, as all do, that the promotion of
Captain Sumner would soon make way for another
commander of Co. D. Lieutenant Tucker is a son of
George J. Tucker, Esq., Register of Deeds for this
county, and also County Treasurer. He comes from a
good family (not considered a despicable thing even in
Democratic Massachusetts), and is counted a fine fellow and an estimable man. He is a lawyer by profession.

The second lieutenant is Samuel J. Chaffee, originally from Connecticut, but recently connected with
some of the mills in Berkshire. He is active, intelligent, and very popular. He is a man of earnest convictions and great independence; one, we may prophesy, who will do his duty, regardless of fear or favor.
The orderly sergeant is James K. Parker, who, I believe, has been in the service before. Co. D. is an
able company, ably officered.

Wednesday, September 17th, Co. E made its appearance. The *very best* of the young men of Southern
Berkshire come with it. Among them are students
from Harvard and Yale, besides ministers and embryo
doctors and lawyers. A nation is rich indeed that has
such sons to call to her defense; richer still when those
sons promptly answer her call, that the principles that
have made her great and glorious may be maintained,
and become the heritage of the world. The material
of Co. E is such that we can safely predict for *it* an
honorable career. They number one hundred and two
men, of an average age of twenty-six years, and height
of five feet, eight and one-quarter inches.

They are commanded by Horace D. Train, a physician of Sheffield. He is forty years of age, pleasant,
and evidently used to good society. He is considered

a very good physician of the Homœopathic school. If our surgeons shall belong to the same school, we will have in him one more than the standard number ; if not, Dr., *alias* Captain Train, will have to practice on the sly. Then, commend me to him rather than to the tender mercies of the heroic school.

Robert T. Sherman, of Egremont, is first lieutenant. He is twenty-five years of age, an excellent machinist, and an impulsive son of Green Erin; a splendid fellow to lead in a forlorn hope, He will make an efficient officer.

H. Dwight Sissons, mechanic, of New Marlboro, occupies the position of second lieutenant. He is twenty-five years of age, unobtrusive, faithful, intelligent, and popular. He will wear well. You can count on him with but little fear of disappointment. Their first sergeant (we always call them orderlies), Moses H. Tuttle, is a young man of twenty-two years, a graduate of Yale College, and comes from an excellent family. The men like him, and confide in him. Captain Train showed excellent judgment in selecting so worthy an orderly to have the supervision of as worthy men as ever enlisted under any banner. You remember after the battle of Marathon, each officer was requested to state which of the officers was most deserving of praise. Each man wrote himself down as that worthy one, and Themistocles second. Ask the members of each company which are the two best companies in the regiment, and nearly every man would call his own company the best, and E the next best. By this, we really unanimously place E at the head of the list. The future will show if they realize the promise of the present.

Co. F came into camp on Tuesday, September 16th. They number ninety-eight stalwart, respectable, steady men. I judge them mainly by their appearance and reputation, for as yet I know but little concerning them. They average in age twenty-five years and seven months; in height, five feet, seven and one-half inches.

Benjamin A. Morey, druggist, of Lee, is captain. He is a man of forty years of age, stern in looks, but really genial in life, a generous friend, a decided foe. He was a lieutenant in the Thirty-first Mass. Vols,, and bears the name of a strict disciplinarian. Of course, that does not give him a *popular* start, but the experience of an active campaign will teach us how to appreciate the value of *discipline*, though it may occasionally be irksome to us.

Edson T. Dresser of Stockbridge, holds the position of first lieutenant. A desire to aid in the quelling of this unholy rebellion drew him away from his class at Williams College to enlist as a common soldier. He is worthily popular, and having the benefit of the experience of his colleague, will make an efficient officer. He is twenty-two years of age.

With the second lieutenant, George H. Sweet, aged twenty, farmer, of Tyringham, I am not acquainted. He is a gentlemanly looking young man, but rather too delicate for the duties that lie before him. *Will* often supplies the absence of *muscle;* it may with him.

John Doolittle, merchant, of Monterey, is the orderly of this company. He is twenty-six years of age, and will, I think, creditably perform the peculiar duties of his position. No company starts more favorably than Co. F. In a hundred little things, as well as in large things, will they see the benefit of commencing their military service under the command of one who has had some experience in soldier life.

On Friday, the 19th inst., ninety-nine fine, robust

men, forming Co. G, were added to our rapidly increasing number. Mainly drawn from manufacturing communities, they may not have the steadiness of our farmer boys; but what they lack in that trait, they make up in vivacity. Their average height is five feet, eight inches ; their average age is twenty-three years, two months and two days.

Their captain is Francis W. Parker, aged twenty-seven, printer by trade, and, I believe, for awhile connected with the *Adams Transcript*. As they have but just entered our prolific family, I am able to give you but a brief account of him and his associate officers.

Robert B. Harvie, of Williamstown, is first lieutenant. He is a young man of twenty-one years, painter by trade, and has the appearance of having much energy and vim. He looks like the lamented Colonel Ellsworth, and is a splendid specimen of physical mankind. He will make a popular officer.

The second lieutenant is Henry M. Lyons, a spinner in Phillips's Woolen Mill, at South Adams. He is twenty-three years of age, active, and intelligent. He has a brother a sergeant in the same company. George Southwick, of Adams, is the orderly.

On Thursday, the 18th, Co. A was mustered into service for *three* months [he meant for *nine* months] by Captain H. G. Thomas, of the 11th Regular Infantry. The process is the examination of the rolls, and then the mustering officer walks along the lines of men and examines them. At some he merely glances ; others he tries by running and otherwise testing their wind and strength. There is no appeal from his decision ; and as he walks along there is a great expanding of chest and rising to the fullest height on the part of small men, while those who fear they have teeth not adequate to the eating of hard bread and the tearing of cart-ridges, need no injunction about talking in the ranks. After he has thus examined them, throwing out whom he pleases, with uplifted hands and uncovered heads they subscribe to the following oath :

" You do solemnly swear that you will bear true alle-giance to the United States of America, and that you will serve them honestly and faithfully against all their enemies or opposers whatsoever, and observe and obey the orders of the President of the United States, and the orders of the officers appointed over you, according to the rules and articles for the government of the ar-mies of the United States, for the period of nine mouths. unless sooner discharged ; that you will receive the pay, rations, and such clothing as may from time to time be allowed. So help you God !"

After swearing in the men, or, in other words, con-stituting a company, the officers are mustered in. Com-panies B, C, D, E, and F were mustered in on the nineteenth, and G on Sunday, the twenty-first. At these musterings, a few were rejected, and some of them for seemingly insufficient reasons. It was a cause of mortification and sorrow to them. Some, already tired of soldiering, refused to take the oath. They were put under arrest, but soon released. They could not legally be held, for the enlistment papers they signed read : "We promise to serve for nine months *from the time of being mustered into the service of the United States.*" Law will not *compel* a man to take an oath ; and, until he *is* sworn, he can not be mus-tered into the service.

We are no longer a body without a head. On Satur-day, Captain William F. Bartlett assumed command of this post. He belongs to the Twentieth Massachu-

setts Volunteers, and last April lost a leg at the siege
of Yorktown. His appearance denotes much of intelligent energy, and his gentlemanly manner, his soldierly bearing (for he looks the soldier even on crutches),
and our sympathy with him in his great loss have made
him at once a universal favorite. We can not afford
to despise these sudden likings. Soldiers, having their
individuality absorbed in the mass, their independence
in submission, are somewhat like children, and reach
conclusions, not by deductions of logic, but by their
surer intuitions.

Lieutenant Francis has been appointed as acting
quartermaster. Lieutenant Noble is our acting or post
adjutant, and an excellent one he makes, too. He
takes pride and pleasure in his duties, and any one can
see that he enjoys his position. If these prove permanent appointments, it will be promotion for them, as
adjutants and quartermasters have the rank of *first*
lieutenants. The adjutant is the business officer of
the regiment, having supervision, under the commandant, of all affairs save those belonging to the quartermaster's and medical departments.

Thus, you see, we are getting into running order.
At present, everything runs smoothly. Pomeroy and
Springstein feed us. It is said that they get forty cents
a day for each man. If so, they certainly have a lucrative job. Our living is good, but we are so recently
from home that we find fault with it. It seems strange
to us to have butter but once or twice a week, and to
be confined to what we have always considered the
merest necessaries. Happy soldiers! if *this* does not
prove the buttered side of our living. Tolerably flushed
with money, we supplement our meals at the sutler's
stand, which is placed so conveniently near the tables

as to lead to the conclusion that the profits of the former are in an inverse ratio to the superfluities of the latter. We march to the tables in military order—there, order ceases ; our tin cups and plates make excellent table bells to attract the attention of the waiters. When any luxury (?), such as butter, cheese, or cake, makes its appearance, it is greeted with three cheers and a tiger, and honest criticism leads to groans when we notice any great deficiency. Men are detailed each day to help in the culinary department. It is not conducive to a vigorous appetite to watch the minutiæ of that department , but one thing is certain, the detail of cooks always *come back* with clean hands. The officers have a mess of their own, where, at five dollars pe week, they find that position does not merely mean honor, but increased comfort also.

The drum calls us up about sunrise, that most witching time for sleep. No parleying up we get, springing from our planks like Minerva from Jupiter, ready armed and clothed. Our hasty ablutions over, we attend roll-call, and generally drill an hour before breakfast. After breakfast, our streets are cleaned up, and at 8 A. M. we have guard mountings. The guards appointed the previous morning are substituted by fresh ones, who are divided into three parts, called reliefs. Each relief serves two hours on duty, and has four hours for rest, or, as we call it, "two hours on and four hours off." We are furnished with rusty firelocks, and a true soldier never allows his gun to touch the ground. There are few such among us yet, and you might observe some of the sentinels lying down several feet from their guns, which, supported by the bayonets, gracefully present their butts to the sky. We mean to be obedient, but soldiering *here* seems so much like playing that we can not make serious work of it.

Under no circumstances must a sentinel give up his gun but to an officer of the guard. Some officers find no little sport in getting guns away from verdant, confiding ones, and walking off with them, leaving the poor sentinel, who must not leave his beat, weaponless to discharge his duty and meet the relief guard. It is a quick way of teaching them a part of their work. Daily an officer, called "officer of the day," is appointed to have supervision of the camp. Among his duties, he visits all the sentinels at midnight. He is saluted by each sentinel as "Grand Rounds." A few evenings ago (the night was very dark) this officer was making his midnight tour, and came across an Irish sentry, who understood little about "Grand Rounds," but much about the pleasure of being relieved from duty. The sentry hailed him, "Who goes there?" to which the officer responded, "Grand Rounds!" Pat broke out, "To —— with your *Grand Rounds!* I thought it was the relafe guard." We have had many a hearty laugh at this little incident. The guard-posts are placed about ten rods apart, and, if *necessity* requires the men to leave, they summon the corporal of the guard to take their place by crying out, "Corporal of the Guard, post 6," according to their number; and, if their case be urgent, add, "double quick." Living as we do, mainly in the open air and under different dietetic rules, the post of "corporal of the guard" is not entirely one of honor ; not a mere sinecure. Working by day, or resting by night, these summonses enable us to form some idea of the health of the regiment.

For two Sabbaths I have been on guard, and I enjoyed it, especially at night. A man has so few chances

to be alone while in camp that I could but hail with
pleasure my night-watches. After the bustle of the
day, there was something very soothing in the quietness. To be in the midst of a thousand sleeping men,
hearing nothing save the measured tread of your fellow-
sentries, is like the solemnity of a large city in the
small wee hours of the night, or that silence which at
times falls on a crowd. It is a capital place for reflecting on what we are leaving, what we are leaving for,
what future we are marching into. Sentinels, not only
over a camp, but over a nation's life! Enduring hardness for a night, that a brilliant morning may dawn to
all our land! Treading the measured path of duty,
that a country may grow strong to step up to the right
and the just! Accepting a subordinate's life, that
equality may be the birthright of all!

After guard-mount, the detailed cooks go to their
work; the police force attend to the cleaning and puri-
fication of the camp; the orderlies make their report
to the adjutant, and he to the commandant, while the
soldiers lounge around, spending the time as they see
fit till about ten o'clock, when those who were not
on guard the preceding day drill for an hour or an hour
and a half. About noon we dine; then, at two o'clock,
comes another season of drilling; and, at five, "Dress
Parade." This is the grand event of the day. In two
ranks deep the whole regiment is drawn up, and go
through motions to resemble the manual of arms, so
that we may be more handy when we receive our arms.
Here the first sergeants report the presence or account
for the absence of the men of their respective companies; then the adjutant reads the orders and an-
nounces the details of officers for the following day.

"Dress Parade" implies that every man should have

on his best *uniform*. On fatigue duty, carelessness and comfort are the rules, but woe to that unlucky wight who manifests a greater love of ease and comfort than harmonizes with the commandant's idea of military propriety and carriage ! A sharp rebuke, an extra term of guard duty, or an appropriation of the lock-up to his special use convinces him that, in becoming a soldier for the common benefit, he has resigned many of the common rights and conveniences of life. Our boys look more like Falstaff's soldiers than the pride of Berkshire. Uncle Sam having furnished us no uniforms, and we, having a regard to economy, appear not only in garbs of every color, shape, and fashion, but of every quality from indifferent to shabby. If "dress" has reference to beauty and harmony with the occasion, ours is hardly a "dress" parade ; but if that word implies an infinite *variety*, we can challenge the nation to produce our superior. Dress parade is followed by supper, and after that we fill up these lovely September twilights and evenings as we see fit, with singing circles, negro melodies, dances, and occasionally a prayer-meeting, till the drums beat for evening roll-call, which is soon followed by "taps," when lights disappear from all save officers' tents, and quiet rules over the camp.

The citizens of the different towns are remembering the officers by presenting them more or less of their outfit. Last Saturday evening, Captain Weller was presented with a sword, belt, and sash, the gift of many friends. The employés of the Pittsfield Woollen Mills have made a similar present to Lieutenant Clark, of the same company, while the inhabitants of Sternsville, not to be behind, have, as a token of respect, presented Lieutenant Francis with a handsome sword, belt, sash, and revolver. The presentation speech was made

by Rev. Dr. Porter, and handsomely responded to by
the gratified recipient. The services closed with prayer
and singing, "My country! 'tis of thee'; sweet land
of Liberty." O! as the land of *Liberty*, 'tis noble,
'tis grand to draw the sword for her ; for her it is even
swee to die. I hope these swords may aid in cutting
a path for Freedom.

Report is beginning to nominate our field and staff
officers. The former—colonel, lieutenant-colonel, and
major—are chosen by the line officers ; the latter—
adjutant, quartermaster, surgeon, and assistant-sur-
geon—are appointed by the colonel, while the chaplain
is appointed by the colonel on the vote of the commanders of companies. Captain Thomas is spoken of
by some as colonel. I doubt if our Berkshire officers
would vote for *him*. He did not favorably impress us.
He has had to do with that class of soldiers who enlisted before this war commenced. Some of *them* were
pretty rough. While here he seemed to forget that
this contest has called out a higher class, many of
whom, in their own estimation, and in that of others,
are every whit *his* equal. Graham H. Root, Esq.,
our very popular high sheriff, could doubtless have
the post, but he says he is not a military man, and
don't want it. We all wish it might be our lot to serve
under him, for we would then have a colonel to whom
obedience would be a pleasure. Captain Sumner is
spoken of as major, lieutenant-colonel, or colonel; and
from all I hear, he can have his choice, but he thinks
the prosperity of the regiment will be better promoted
by choosing a commander from outside. He is more
than half right there. L. H. Gamwell, Esq., of Pittsfield, is mentioned in the same connection. If he has
the requisite military qualifications, Berkshire would

feel safe in intrusting her sons to his care.   After all,
the material for a colonel may be found in our own
camp.   Two legs are very valuable, but great battles
have been won by those who could boast of but one.

LETTER VI.

CAMP BRIGGS, MASS., September 29, 1862.

MY DEAR L.:

We are here yet, and no talk about our leaving. We are waiting to fill up the regiment. The eighth company (Π) came into camp Monday, September 22, from the southern part of the county, and has in it men of sterling worth, some of the best of their respective towns. Its roll shows ninety-one men, averaging in age twenty-three years, ten months, and five days; and in height five feet, seven and one-sixth inches.

The captain is A. V. Shannon, of Lee, aged twenty-six years. His profession is that of teacher. He is a gentleman of many accomplishments, and has had the benefit of some experience in the *rebel* service. The beginning of the rebellion found him teaching music in Texas. That business failing him, he obtained a position as clerk on board of a vessel afterward engaged in the rebel blockade. Fortunately for him, it was captured by one of *our* blockading squadron, and with the crew brought to New York, where, establishing his loyalty to our flag, he was set free. Active, energetic, resolute, I think he will make an excellent officer.

The first lieutenant is Burton D. Deming, of Sandisfield. He is one of our most reliable farmers, aged thirty-one years. He is a quiet, unobtrusive man, but of the firmest principles. As a matter of Christian duty he leaves wife and home for the toils and dangers of the army. An early death may be his; but let it come when it may, by disease or bullet, I feel sure that it will be the death of a true soldier of Freedom. He is of the stuff that enters not into the making of shirkers and cowards.

Dr. Witt S. Smith, of Lee, is the second lieutenant. He is an active, intelligent young man of twenty-two years of age, a book-keeper at home, and will make a good officer.

Joseph B. Wolcott, of Sandisfield, is the orderly of the company. He is a young man, twenty-four years old, of unblemished character. The intimate friend of Lieutenant Deming, he is of the same type of character, and we can confidently predict for him an honorable career.

The papers of the past week inform us that the President has again refused to receive negro soldiers, though pressed on his acceptance by the conservative Governor Sprague, of Rhode Island, and that he has issued a proclamation, dated September 22d, 1862, declaring freedom to all slaves of rebel masters who shall live in districts that do not, as an evidence of their loyalty, send representatives to Congress by the first of January, 1863. Well, old Abe *is* a strange man. Offering a bribe for the return of rebels to their allegiance may make the refusal of negro soldiers necessary, and I think the President, in his heart, says, "Look here! rebels! I give you one more chance to repent. I dislike slavery, but I dislike disunion and war more. Now, I have offered to buy your slaves, so that you might come back to your loyalty full-handed. I have refused to increase your causeless irritation by enlisting the negroes; but, mark me, if you are not in the Union by the first of next January, I am done with offers of mercy, and I will not only declare your slaves free, but

I will put arms into the hands of every one willing to use them, be he white, red, black, or cream-colored, free or bond." If this be his meaning, I am willing to wait and trust him. Notwithstanding the anomalousness of the whole proceeding, I am far from looking at it as a mere *brutum fulmen*. It is the President's lingering farewell to the conservatives, and his "All hail radicals!" If he be sustained in the coming elections, all right; but if he be not sustained, and the rebels do not return to their allegiance by the first of January (and of course they will not if the elections show a *divided* North), what then? His word is pledged —will he recant? Has he *ever* forfeited that word? *ever* taken any backward steps? *Never!* and I try to believe that he will be faithful in this grand hour. If Mr Lincoln *should* violate his promise, Europe would see as much, if not more, hope for the slave in the success of the South than in *our* success, and a speedy recognition of the Confederacy would be the result. Recant! and the South can readily enlist, by sympathy and by arms, the services of the negroes. Emancipation *must* come. Certainly, the first of January will see no representatives of rebeldom in our congressional halls. The President has taken the decisive step; every bridge is burned behind him. Truly, his war-cry *must* be "Liberty or Death!" Our pilot is stepping up to the great principles involved in this struggle, and we will find that God will clothe us with more earnestness as each man puts to himself this question :

> If *Heaven* should *lose*, and *Hell* should *win*,
> On whom shall lie the mortal sin?"

Ah! *that* is the question. Give us men who feel, to the very core of their natures, that the issue is between heaven losing and hell winning, and not Cromwell's Ironsides will equal us. It *is* an issue between Right and Wrong, between Good and Evil, God and Satan. The *moral* power is what we want. Then our hardships will be sweet, and our death-beds, though on the gory sod, be more enviable, more precious, than *ever* vouchsafed to warriors. Through shameful blunders, through seas of wasted blood, God will *yet* bring the nation, to whom He has showed such long-suffering, where the breezes of Freedom refresh every soul. Then, we may look back to the dreary days of 1862, to the grave-crowded Peninsula, and thank Him for deferring success till success meant not only the preservation of the Union, but of the divine Spirit living in and animating that Union. In view of this, I greet our martyred dead, counting not their seemingly wasted lives a loss, or too great a price for the assurance that *Freedom is always safe in the Union.* To make this an *eternal* verity, *I* am full willing to swell the number of the slaughtered dead. In "hopes nursed in tears," I sing:

> "Sail on! O Union, strong and great!
> *Humanity*, with all its fears,
> With all the hopes of future years,
> Is hanging breathless on *thy* fate.
> In spite of rock and tempest's roar,
> In spite of false lights on the shore,
> Sail on, nor fear to breast the sea:
> Our hearts, our hopes, our prayers, our tears,
> Our faith triumphant o'er our fears,
> Are all with thee, are *all with thee.*"

To return. Mr. Peter Springstein, of the United States Hotel, will go with us as sutler. It may be a lucrative position, but not a pleasant one. In order to make it pay, he must sell his goods at a large profit.

An inroad of the enemy, a capture of a sutler's vessel, may swallow up the profits of months. Men forget the risks, the losses, and only remember the big holes sutlers' goods at sutlers' prices make in their thirteen dollars a month. Mr. Springstein is a gentlemanly and generous man, and I wish him success as sutler to the Forty-ninth.

Dr. J. H. Manning, of Pittsfield, is acting as regimental surgeon. Perchance he may go with us. He is a kind man, and would sympathize with the sick. Sometimes sympathy is worth more than drugs. Dr. R. C. Stiles has the general medical superintendence of the post. He is my beau ideal of an army surgeon.

Well, we have now a quartermaster's department. G. E. Howard, of Lanesboro, is acting quartermaster sergeant. He is a sergeant in Co. A, and a very fine penman. Finding there was no military aptitude in me, I have entered this department as commissary sergeant. H. H. Northup, of Cheshire, a corporal in Co. C, one of the soldiers of Wilson's Creek, Missouri; G. E. Callender, Co. E, a faithful boy of nineteen, and D. C. Patterson, also of Co. E, our butcher, a *sui generis*, make up the number, who, under Lieutenant Francis, run this machine.

Army blankets, coarse, gray, and, we hope, woolen, have been given to the men. They are not entirely guiltless of shoddy, and if they last us nine months we will speak better of them then than we do now. If you lie down on them your clothes look as if you had been sleeping with a dozen cats.

We now receive our subsistence directly from the United States and cook it ourselves. Each company has a cook and an assistant cook, who are relieved from all other duties. The are generally assisted by a daily detail of two men. In addition to these, there is one styled the commissary of the company. It is his duty to see that the company gets its prescribed rations, to sell what they do not use, placing the proceeds in the hands of the captain as treasurer of the company's fund. He is relieved from guard-duty and from all other duties which would embarrass him in his work as commissary. Massachusetts *gives* each man a tin plate, cup, spoon, and a knife and fork. In the regular service, and from most other States, the soldiers have to furnish themselves with these necessaries. Some companies serve out the cooked rations to each man separately, while others place them on tables for common use. Each soldier keeps his own eating utensils clean, or by a small monthly gratuity to the cook relieves himself of that unpleasant task. We live well. Government gives us plenty of food, and some of our cooks are real experts. Come and dine at Hotel B or D or E, and you will get a meal that needs not the novelty of camp life to make it relish. It is wonderful how much the boys eat. Living out doors sharpens the appetite. Butter, pies, cakes, pickles, and many other luxuries not furnished by our kind Uncle Sam, grace our tables. Our friends bring or send so many home comforts that we must needs get away from Berkshire before we can learn any of the privations of soldiers' life. Companies D and E are the most favored in that respect. Beef, fresh or corned, and fine beef it is, furnished by D. and W. Sprague, is dealt out five days in the week. The other two days we fall back on the soldiers' friend —salt pork. Mr. H. B. Brewster brings each man daily a loaf of fresh bread.

The government ration is as follows : Bear in mind a ration is one day's food for one man. One and a quarter pounds of fresh or salt beef, or three-quarters of a pound of pork, twenty-two ounces of soft bread or flour, or sixteen ounces of hard bread, or one and a quarter pounds corn meal, eight quarts of beans to one hundred men, ten pounds of rice, eight pounds of roasted coffee or a pound and a half of tea, fifteen pounds of sugar, one and one-fourth pounds of adamantine candles, four pounds of soap, two quarts of salt, three pecks of potatoes, and a quart of molasses. Suppose a family of four men feeding at this rate, and they would use in a year eighteen hundred and twenty pounds of beef or one thousand and ninety-six pounds of pork, three bushels and twenty quarts of beans, one hundred and fifty-five pounds of rice, one hundred and seventeen pounds of coffee or twenty-two pounds of tea, two hundred and nineteen pounds of sugar, fourteen and a half pounds of adamantine candles, fifty-eight pounds of soap, twenty-nine quarts of salt, ten and a half bushels of potatoes, four gallons of molasses, besides two thousand and seven pounds (over ten barrels) of bread or flour. Can the men eat all their rations? Used as they would be at home, No; as they are in our camp, No; as they are in active service, Yes. Soldiers can not save as soldiers' wives could. Waste, there will be. The government provides for that waste. The rations a company does not see fit to draw are credited to them, and they receive money in lieu thereof. I know of companies that have added one hundred dollars a month by these savings to their company fund. Do they really get these rations? If they do not, it is the fault of their commissaries. Any intelligent man can, without scales, soon learn the amount due his company. When before the enemy, I do not suppose they get half this variety, but, by proper management, they can get money in lieu of the deficiency.

Who shall be our colonel is a question much discussed among officers and men. If Captain Bartlett can be weaned from his old regiment (I understand he can have the command of *that* if he desires it), he will be our colonel. Report says he is Captain Sumner's choice, and, as he has virtually declined a nomination to that office, *his* choice will be apt to be the choice of all. I learn that Captain Bartlett has no idea of abandoning the profession of arms, but will return to the field as soon as he is able to use an artificial leg. The following article, written by one prominent in civil and military life, as originally published in the *Boston Courier*, is now read by us with great interest :

"In the month of April, 1861, soon after Fort Sumter had fallen, and Colonel Jones's regiment had been attacked in the streets of Baltimore, the Fourth Battalion of Infantry was called upon to garrison Fort Independence in Boston harbor. On Thursday, the 25th of April, the battalion left their armory, and marched through crowded streets, and under countless flags, to the boat which was to take them to the fort. In the ranks marched a young man named Bartlett, a member of the Junior class in Harvard College. During the month passed by the battalion at the fort, his rapid progress in learning, and his promptness and fidelity in practicing the duties of a soldier, his carriage under arms, and the manly character he displayed attracted the attention of the officers. A few weeks after the battalion had returned from the fort, Massachusetts was answering the call of the General Government for volunteers, and the command of a regiment was offered to Colonel Wm. Raymond Lee. He accepted the office, and was permitted to nominate officers to raise two companies to complete his regiment. Such was the impression that Bartlett—the young Cambridge student, the private in the ranks of the Fourth Battalion— had produced that Colonel Lee was advised to nominate him for one of the two vacant captaincies. He did so, and the nomination was approved, and Captain Bartlett, with the assistance of Lieutenant, now Captain, Macy, and Lieutenant Abbott, raised a company. The regiment, since known as the Twentieth, marched into camp at Readville on the 10th of July, and there remained till the 4th of September, when it started for the seat of war. The officers' commissions were dated on the same day, and shortly before leaving Readville their regimental rank was assigned by Colonel Lee, after consultation with his field and staff officers. Their estimate of the merits of Captain Bartlett was shown by the fact that he was named senior captain, and his company, therefore, took the right flank of the regiment.

"For six weeks after the regiment reached the seat of war there was little of interest in its history. One day was much like another. Captain Bartlett's discharge of all the duties of his position was thorough; his care of his men was scrupulous and devoted. Neither he nor any other officer of the regiment had any opportunity to distinguish himself.

"On the 21st of October he commanded his company in the affair of Ball's Bluff. There are plenty of witnesses to the gallantry and coolness with which he led his men on that trying day. There are many who know that when the field seemed lost beyond redemption, when few of our troops were left on the field, and none in order, Captain Bartlett, hoping against hope. rallied men enough for one more effort, and charged with them upon the enemy's line, till, in the twilight of smoke and the shadow of trees, they could see the color of the clothes of their opponents, and were driven back by the blasting fire of those well-ordered troops.

"When the twilight was deepening, and the fire of the enemy from the heights and the dread of the rushing river were combined to drive to despair the beaten few who were collected on the shore, Captain Bartlett and Captain Tremlett, and Lieutenant Whittier and Lieutenant Abbott, all of the Twentieth, collected about eighty men, only twenty of whom belonged to their own regiment, and led them up the river and along its banks. At about a mile from the battle ground, in the race of a flour mill, they found a crazy sunken boat. They caused this to be bailed out, and found it would hold five. Captain Tremlett and one lieutenant put the men into an old barn near by, and kept them quiet there. Captain Bartlett sent the other lieutenant across with the first load, to take charge of the men as they arrived, and stood alone upon the bank to superintend the tedious transportation. The rapid current delayed the clumsy, heavy boat, the darkness of the night increased the difficulty of bringing it back to the point from which it started. Not less than sixteen trips were made before those gallant officers crossed themselves in the last trip it made. Let it be remembered that these officers, wearied by the sleepless night of Sunday, the alternate suspense and fighting of Monday, distressed by defeat and the belief that their friends and comrades were dead or prisoners, waited, within sound of the enemy's musketry, expecting every moment the swoop of cavalry, waited for hours till a boat that was little better than waterlogged and oarless had made many trips and they had saved eighty men, of whom three-quarters were utter strangers to them and to their regiment.

"Colonel Lee and Major Revere were taken prisoners on the evening of that day. When Captain Bartlett awoke the next morning, he found himself in command of the camp, his only superior officer having been ordered across the river, with all his disposable effective force, by General Lander. He remained in command during the whole of the 22d and 23d and part of the 24th, when he was relieved by the return of the lieutenant-colonel of the regiment. His action during this interval was wise and salutary. It showed thoughtfulness beyond his years. Besides the many wounded who were brought in, unhurt officers and men arrived by ones, twos, and threes, and two whole companies returned which had not been engaged. By a partial resumption of the usual routine of the camp, with a just allowance for the mental and physical fatigue of the men, and judicious employment of the band, Captain Bartlett changed in a measure the current of the thoughts of the men ; he broke up any tendency to depression of spirits, and introduced a cheerful tone, of which he himself set a signal example.

"The assistance rendered by Captain Bartlett to the commanding officer from that time was of the very highest value, and was recognized as such by him and by the regiment. He possessed a singular natural aptitude for the profession of arms, and the fidelity with which he applied himself made him rapidly master of all the knowledge that was necessary in his position, and of much for which there would have been occasion in a much higher one. His power of imparting knowledge was equal to his power of acquiring it, and he was alike remarkable for his accuracy in details, and for the ease with which he grasped general principles and the readiness with which he applied them. His services to the 20th regiment, as an instructor and as an example, are such as it is impossible to estimate too highly.

"On Thursday, April 24th, 1862, one year from the day when the 4th battalion went to Fort Independence, the 20th Massachusetts Volunteers relieved another regiment in guarding a portion of the lines before York-town. While visiting the advanced posts, Captain Bartlett was shot in the left knee, and the knee-joint and a portion of the bone of the lower leg was shattered and destroyed. His leg was presently amputated, and he was sent northward to be under the care of his friends.

"One year from the day when this gallant soldier first bore arms saw his military career suddenly checked. With the attachment and admiration that are felt for him in his regiment the public has little to do ; nor need we dwell upon the peculiar sadness of such a misfortune to one who was so conspicuous for the beauty of the tall, straight figure, which was gaining strength and fullness every day. It is his comrades who miss the glance of the clear blue eye, the sweet smile, the erect carriage, the voice, cheery in talk, powerful and full of dignity in giving the word of command. But it is right that the public should know that the officer who, with the rank of captain, not in battle, not even in a skirmish, has been maimed for life in the siege of Yorktown, was a soldier of the most brilliant promise— a man who, before his classmates had taken their degrees at Cambridge, has served his country nearly a year ; has led men gallantly and saved men nobly on the darkest day the war has brought ; and who, in all the time of his bearing arms, and in a regiment that has suffered more than any other in the Army of the

Potomac, has set to every one around him a shining example of every soldierly excellence.''

Perchance some of the above should be ascribed to the blindness of affection, and some to the tenderness that is always felt for a great affliction. Grant that, and yet there remains much for a foundation of our confidence in Captain Bartlett. Fresh from Harvard University, entering the service as a private, raised in Boston where he has influential friends — these may have led to his appointment as captain in the Twentieth Massachusetts Volunteers; but a wise man like Colonel Wm. Raymond Lee, having command of a crack regiment and a military reputation to establish, would not have selected and appointed him *senior* captain unless convinced that he was worthy of the position. That alone would warrant his election to the colonelcy of the Forty-ninth. That he has a natural aptitude for military life every *observer* would declare. As few men, he *looks* the soldier. Though quiet, there is an air of command about him that would make obedience to his orders almost involuntary. His college associates say that he surpassed them all in military studies. True, he is young, only twenty-two years of age; but age is not always wisdom, nor youth always folly. We have made up our minds to follow our leader, whomsoever he may be; wise in us, seeing that we can not do otherwise; but *Colonel* Bartlett we could follow with an enthusiastic pride.

We are all happy in camp. Our duties are so novel that they are performed with pleasure, and the magnificent weather, the presence of our friends and of hosts of visitors, conspire to make the days glide away as a pleasant dream. O! how yearningly will we recall these days when meeting the sufferings and dangers of real war.

LETTER VII.

CAMP BRIGGS, MASS., *October 6, 1862.*

MY DEAR L.:

Yesterday the gifted Major W. D. Sedgwick, of Lenox, was buried. He fell in the ruinous victory of Antietam. Amid the surges of battle, with his dying strength, he wrote in his memorandum book, "I have tried to do my duty." The army has lost a brave and skillful soldier, the nation an *earnest* patriot, and the Forty-ninth an excellent colonel; for, had he lived, there is no doubt that he would have been chosen to fill that position. Co. A acted as the guard of honor at the burial, while Captains Sumner, Weller, Garlick, Plunkett, and Lieutenants Francis, Kniffin, Wells, Tucker, Smith, officiated as pall-bearers. They buried him at close of day. The sun was setting and the moon just rising. It was a solemn scene, one long to be remembered. There was the dead hero, and there the Forty-ninth going forth as he had gone, *some* of them perchance to be brought back like him.

We have now a chapel of our own. It is half chapel, half guard-house. As the guard is required to be about the guard-house the whole of their respective twenty-four hours not spent on their beats, it has added much to their comfort, but proved a comparative failure for devotional purposes. I have heard of religious services in prisons and theatres; this is our prison (in one end there is a lock-up) and theatre; and surely *here* those services are not impressive. Scarce a month of camp-life has rolled away, and I fancy I can see some signs of moral deterioration. Prudery is not a camp vice: things are called by their plainest names, and the giving up of that delicacy and refinement of speech, observed more or less by all at home, is preparing the way for obscenity and profanity.

The past week has been enlivened by a number of presentations to officers. On the evening of September 30th there was quite a gathering at the office of Colt and Pingree, when Mr. Pingree, in behalf of the donors, presented to Captain Garlick a handsome sword, sash, belt, revolver, and a pair of richly gilded shoulder-straps, on receiving which the captain made an appropriate speech. At the instance of Messrs. Rathbun, Lieutenant Wells, of Co. C, was presented with sword, sash, belt, and pistol. Messrs. L. H. Gamwell and W. R. Plunkett spoke at the presentation. The people of Stockbridge showed their appreciation of Lieutenant Dresser, of Co. F, by similar presents, as also did the good people of Egremont and Mill River to Lieutenants Sherman and Sissons, of Co. E.

We have a *theory* that soldier life implies hardship and privation. To have more than a theory Captain Bartlett will have to exclude the numerous crinolined sutlers that throng the camp, invade our tents, and who ask no recompense but a hearty devouring of the home delicacies they bring. Lift up certain boards in our tent floors, and you will find that we are quite independent of the recognized sutler, and of our bountiful friend, Uncle Sam. We can not say much of the order reigning in our pantries, for superabundance renders that impracticable; but from their depths we bring pies, cake, cheese, butter, milk, pickles, preserves, and other comforts that make soldiering in this delightful weather one of the brightest episodes in our lives. At breakfast and supper, milkpeddlers visit us, and if it be true that "that man can not be wholly evil who is fond of milk," we show our primitive innocence and purity by sending the peddlers home with empty cans and full purses. One of our officers, to all these things, says: "Away! I'll have none of them. I'll harden myself against the day of hardness." And we say, "let him harden." "Sufficient to the day is the evil thereof." I never knew a man better prepared for abstinence at dinner by rejecting his breakfast. Success to him, but I fear his converts will be few until we bid a long adieu to mothers and sisters and sweethearts, and to the lowing kine of Berkshire.

Though Lieutenant Francis is the acting quartermaster of the regiment, yet much of the work is done by Mr. Henry B. Brewster, of Pittsfield, who expects to accompany the regiment in that capacity. I hope he may, for he is reputed a good business man and honest. It will be pleasant for our friends at home to know we have a quartermaster who will not enrich himself at the expense of our health and comfort.

We are getting our hospital in running order, though fortunately we have but little need of it. The surgeons buy, for the use of the sick, all the delicacies they need. The quartermaster credits them with a ration for each man in hospital, and charges them with what food they actually draw. The value of the remainder forms a hospital fund for the purchasing of articles of food not furnished by the government. Properly managed, there is always a sufficiency of funds to insure the sick whatever they may need or crave. The deficiency, if any, will be in preparing the food. In active service the sick may suffer from the impossibility of purchasing needed luxuries. Every man who has not had the small-pox, or been vaccinated, is being vaccinated. We are providing for our safety.

LETTER VIII.

CAMP BRIGGS, MASS., *October* 8, 1862.

MY DEAR L.:

The ninth company, I, came into camp on Wednesday, October 8th, making it pretty nearly certain that the Forth-ninth will not be consolidated with some other nucleus of a regiment, but will have an individual existence and a separate history. Its roll shows eighty-eight men, average twenty-seven years of age, and five feet eight and one-half inches in height.

Zenas C. Rennie, of Pittsfield, is captain. His age is twenty-six years. If he shows as much energy and perseverance in commanding as he has in raising his company he will be one of our very best officers.

Le Roy S. Kellogg, farmer, of Lee, aged thirty-one years, and William Nichols, car-maker, of Williamstown, aged twenty-four years, are respectively first and second lieutenant. As I have never met either of these officers, I am unable to introduce them to you. Its orderly is James McKenna, of Pittsfield.

On Tuesday, the fourteenth instant, Co. K filed into the tenth street. Captains Rennie and Weston have not only saved the Forty-ninth from being smothered in the birth, but they have also saved the county the unpleasantness and dishonor of a draft. We welcome this tenth company, insuring, as it does, our regimental life, with more joy than any other company. It is worthy of it. Born out of due time, raised from what seemed a thoroughly gleaned county in twelve days, it is not, as one might suppose, the refuse, but rather the cream, of the county. For size, general appearance, intelligence, and character, it is not surpassed by any company in the regiment. Need I, *can* I, say more? It is composed of ninety-one men, averaging twenty-seven years, five months, and twenty-five days in age, and in height five feet eight and one-fourth inches.

Byron Weston, aged thirty-one years, is captain. He occupied a prominent position in the paper-house of Platner and Smith, Lee, and is very much of a gentleman, so quiet and easy in his manners as to lead one to suppose that his forte lies outside the military life, but the great energy he manifested in raising his company, with no help from the selectmen of the different towns, shows that there is in him the real grit of the soldier.

Roscoe C. Taft, aged twenty-six years, merchant, of Sheffield, is the first lieutenant. He is a pleasant, active officer, and the large number of recruits raised for his company from Sheffield, which had sent so many before, attests his energy and popularity.

The second lieutenant is Isaac E. Judd, clerk, from Egremont. He is but twenty-two years of age, but the first glance convinces you he is a born soldier. Some men never seem at home in their regimentals; the "hay seeds stick to their collars." Not so Lieutenant Judd. He wears uniform and sword as if he were born with them. Though the prince of good fellows and full of animal spirits, yet on duty, without swaggering, he maintains the dignity of his office. He was a very popular teacher in one of the schools at Barrington, and is a superior penman and accountant. He entered the regiment as a sergeant in Co. E.

Company K is also fortunate in the selection of Sanford B. Gleason for orderly or first sergeant. He is a printer from Vermont, shrewd and active, and will look out well for his company and for himself. Thus officered and thus composed, Co. K starts well. Their mechanical ingenuity was brought into play at once in the erection of barracks, for we could obtain no tents for them. And comfortable barracks they are. As the northwesters sweep down on us these frosty nights, we would willingly exchange our tents for Co. K's barracks.

Well, we are no longer a pie-bald set, each one wearing his own uniform, but we are clothed in United States garments. We are allowed three and one-half dollars per month for clothing in addition to our regular pay. We can furnish our own clothing if we choose (of course it must be uniform with that provided by the Government), and be credited with what we do not *draw*. If we draw more than the regulated allowance, the excess is deducted from our pay. With the exception of our overcoats, we are well clothed, each one having overcoat, dress-coat, and blouse, hat [great high-crowned felt hat] and cap, two pairs of flannel shirts, drawers and stockings, one pair of shoes, one pair of trousers, and a rubber blanket. It is an amusing and perplexing business, that of fitting the boys. We give to each captain so many of each article of clothing, and he distributes them according to the men's sizes and the marks on the clothes. It not unfrequently happens that "ones" are marked "four," and fours "one." To exchange with the quartermaster is their fancied relief. Sometimes a little fellow will come with dress-coat too large for an overcoat for him and with pantaloons so long one way as to render a vest unnecessary and the other way presenting a double thickness almost to his knees. Again, some giant clothed in Lilliputian raiment will make *his* appearance, the sleeves of his coat near his elbows, while his pantaloons look as if the defunct short-clothes of our fathers had had a resurrection. Motion with him is scarce possible, while the manual of arms or the " double-quick " would be sure to result in an extravagant expenditure of Uncle Sam's toggery. The dwarf and the giant exchange clothes to their mutual comfort and improvement.

Instead of light-blue pants, we are furnished with dark-blues; so, with our black overcoats and big black hats, we look on " Dress-parade " as prepared for the solemnities of an execution or a funeral. Cromwell's Ironsides did not present a more demure appearance. If some one had but started a hymn of Dr. Watts in the true Yankee *nasal* tone, the illusion would have been complete. We are charged for dress-coats six dollars and seventy-one cents; for flannel shirts, eighty-eight cents; for drawers, fifty cents; for pants, three dollars and three cents. As the materials are good, and contractors will make money, God pity the poor who have made them. Truly, "it is not linen we're wearing out; it is human creatures' lives." How much we need to get slavery out of the way, that we may grapple with the great questions of Social Reform. *Its* aggressions and the nation's consequent danger have absorbed all our thoughts and energies. Evil itself, it prevents us attacking other and greater evils. To remove it, the land may well " sweat blood and vomit flame."

The citizens of North Adams have presented Captain Parker with sword, sash, belt, and pistol, and the people of Williamstown have done a similar favor to

Lieutenant Harvie, lacking only the pistol, which lack was supplied by the members of his company (G), through Sergeant Nordaby. Lieutenant Lyon's real merit has not been unappreciated. His former associates in Phillip's Woolen Mill, South Adams, and other friends have bestowed on him a handsome sword, sash, belt, pistol, shoulder-straps, and *steel vest*. Thus, you see, they have had an eye not only to his adornment and effectiveness, but to his safe return.

LETTER IX.

CAMP BRIGGS, MASS., *October 30, 1862.*

MY DEAR L.:

On Tuesday, the 28th instant, companies H, I and K were duly mustered into the United States service. I had not a single man rejected. A final caucus was held on Monday evening for the nomination of field officers. Though it was an informal election, it is understood to be binding, and that the formal election will but ratify the informal. This is proper ; for not knowing how soon we may leave, the newly chosen field officers should have an opportunity to equip themselves as the law directs. Captain Bartlett, and it is now declared he will accept, was chosen colonel ; Captain Sumner, lieutenant-colonel ; and Captain Morey, major. I am glad that Captain Plunkett does not leave Co. C. That company can illy spare him. He devotes himself to study and is making rapid progress. Take him away, and much of the incentive to study would be lost, for the positions of lieutenant-colonel and major are mere sinecures when the colonel is present. Remove him from Co. C, and another election would be necessary. Be assured that election, result as it may, will only weaken and demoralize the company. Captain Plunkett's own merit, his social position, his family standing all tend to make a united company of that which, remove him, will be the least united of any in the regiment. Major Morey owes his success to his creditable manner of handling the regiment at a recent battalion drill. He is a fine officer and has done much for Co. F. We, in the quartermaster's department, know that no other officer watches so closely over the interests of his men. No other has had his experience. Firm and seemingly stern, but kind, he will make an excellent major. I believe that when the men come to know him he will have an influence over them second only to Colonel Bartlett. Lieutenant-Colonel Sumner has never been deemed devoid of ambition ; so, his refusal of the Colonelcy shows that ambition in him coexists with patriotism, modesty, and good sense, otherwise he would sacrifice the welfare of the regiment to his own interest. Say what you will, a lieutenant-colonel is doomed to an inferior part, unless the colonel is absent or removed ; then *he* is virtually commander. For my part, I would prefer to be at the *head* of a company. Rank is rank, I know, but it seems to me that an ambitious man would rather fill a subordinate position with which there is an exercise of *power* than to have merely a higher rank, with almost *no* power. Of course, these remarks apply equally to the position of major.

Not only are the men drilled daily, and are improving rapidly, but the officers also show the benefits of *their* daily drilling by Captain Bartlett. It is a treat to see that man go through the manual of arms. He puts such a finish, such a *rim* to every motion. For two hours at a time he will stand on that remaining leg, till half of us believe he never had any need of the one buried at Yorktown, but it was only a superfluous member or mere ornament. Sometimes we try to see how long *we* can stand on one leg ; a few short minutes, and we require the use of both, or find ourselves reeling about like decapitated hens. If the colonel (I will call him such) needs rest, he takes it as a part of the exercise, so we can not tell which is manual of arms and which rest. The cords of that right leg must stand out like great whip lashes. There is *will* about all this. It is this quiet, intense determination, this fixedness of will, that makes us desire Colonel Bartlett, with but one leg, for our commander, over any other man with the full complement of limbs. Somehow or other, we can not tell why, we believe that he will not be the mere buffet of circumstances, but will ride over, and lead us over all difficulties. Every man salutes him, and he *always* salutes in return. In saluting, the back of the right hand is brought up to the visor of the cap, then the arm is fully extended, and brought down to the side. You can see it is no easy thing to be done *walking* on two crutches, but the Colonel does it, not halting to do it, but while walking on and in the most approved military manner. This may seem to you a small matter, but to us it indicates the *born* soldier, the man who *will* do the duties he has assumed. The other day, while riding in his carriage, he put the regiment through battalion drill. What a noble voice he has, a deep bass, yet as clear and distinct as any tenor. It is full of command. He don't have to put in any expletives to insure attention and prompt obedience. They are all in the mere voice. Over, or rather under all noise, with apparently no effort, that voice carries his orders to the remotest soldier. Take him all in all, I have yet to meet one who so fully embodies my conceptions of a commander as Colonel Bartlett. I know but little of him as a man, yet one thing laid the foundation of trust and respect. It is necessary for the commandant of the post to examine and sign many of our returns. The formula is:

"I certify, on honor, that I have carefully examined the above return, and find it to be correct." I expected that the signing of it would be a rapid and formal matter, but not so. Colonel Bartlett pledges his honor to the accuracy of the paper, and so he does "carefully examine it."

Last Tuesday, Co. D and some of Co. E visited Barrington. A sumptuous dinner awaited them, after which swords, sashes, belts were presented to the officers of Co. D, by the citizens, through Rev. H. Winslow. Each of the favored responded in a suitable speech, making the day one often to be pleasantly remembered amid sterner scenes. I believe Mr. Parley A. Russell was the main mover in getting up the presented articles. John H. Coffing, Esq., placed one hundred dollars in the hands of Lieutenant Tucker as a fund for the benefit of the sick of Co. D. Such tender exhibitions of patriotism strengthen soldiers in their determination to do their duty. Many a weary one may yet thank the considerate heart of Mr. Coffing. The citizens of West Stockbridge have presented Lieutenant Knifflin with an outfit. He merits it, being one of the most worthy and popular of all our officers. Lieutenant Noble, of Co. B, received sword, sash, and belt from the members of that company, a delicate appreciation of his merit and services. Co. K has also been the recipient of similar favors. H. C. and M. Hulbert, of New York, presented them with a silken flag, while their captain received a brace of revolvers, one from his friends in Lee, the other from Major F. Weston, of Dalton. The exercises took place at camp, speeches being made by Messrs. Branning and G. H. Phelps, of Lee, followed by the enthusiastic cheers of the company. Some unknown one of Pittsfield sent

them a drum, while the members of the company presented Captain Weston with sword and trimmings.
Lieutenants Judd and Taft each received a sword, sash,
and belt from their friends.

Our days pass pleasantly on, but with nothing of
marked interest. Fully clothed, the regiment has several times marched into town, creating quite a sensation. Now that they are uniformed, their remarkable
physique attracts much attention. They are certainly
a noble looking body of men. War is based on the
physical, and while uniform hides individuality, it
brings the physical into bold relief. I doubt if Massachusetts ever before gathered so fine a looking regiment.

On last Sunday afternoon Dr. Todd presented us
with neat pocket editions of the New Testament, in
behalf of the Berkshire County Bible Society. His
remarks were pertinent, characterized by that practical
good sense forming so large and valuable a part of his
mental nature. The Testaments were gratefully received, and will, I believe, be generally preserved and
read. Destitute of reading matter, having much unemployed time on our hands, very *ennui* will lead us to
peruse them. It will be handling a sharp, two-edged
sword, that may unwittingly wound us to our eternal
cure. I got some tracts, papers, magazines, which I
distributed among the boys. They were eagerly seized,
tracts included. A reading regiment, how much mental
stagnation is before us if we can judge the future by
the few past weeks. Much is being done to relieve this
stagnation, much more will be done, but after all, it
will be impossible to keep our army fully supplied.
That would require a large library, the transportation
of which would very often be impossible.

We are allowed to go in squads, under the charge of

officers or sergeants, to churches, lectures, concerts. A large number of us took the opportunity to hear Charles Sumner speak and the Hutchinsons sing. Did you ever hear them sing the John Brown song? As *they* sing it, it is wondrously inspiriting. While listening to them, I almost loathed General McClellan. When they went to the Army of the Potomac, singing to the soldiers without charge *he* ejected them from his lines. Why? Simply because they sang the songs of freedom. Nothing that he ever did made me believe that his heart was rotten with love for the South so much as that. Depriving his soldiers, wearied with the inactivity of camp-life, of *such* a treat—why? God only knows. Is *freedom* to him a *hated* word? Was he fearful that the glad cheers of his men would tell the foe that the old key-note had been struck ; that they were rising, in defiance of General McClellan, to a true appreciation of the issues involved ; that they were receiving an inspiration which would lead them to downright victory, a victory that would leave of slavery nothing but its scars and shame and putrid corpse?

LETTER X.

CAMP BRIGGS, MASS., *November 6, 1862.*

MY DEAR L. .

We have received orders to report at Worcester. Full time to leave these tents, through which the winds sweep bleak and cold. We expected to get off to-day, but did not, of course. How we will get through the night, I know not, for most of our bedding has been forwarded, with our stores, to Worcester. The officers are in the same fix.

On the thirteenth, Governor Andrew reviewed our regiment. He is a short, pursy man, and looks as if he enjoyed being governor. His eye, light gray or blue, is really any eye eloquent, capable of expressing tenderness, scorn, anger, all the emotions. Though corpulent, he shows that he has an *intense* soul. Massachusetts was fortunate in having her gubernatorial chair filled by such a man as John A. Andrew. He was equal to the crisis! He walked in front and rear of the regiment, closely scanning the men and their apparel, and then briefly addressed the officers. All I heard was, "Gentlemen, by a good fortune and the votes of your men, you are now officers. Be firm, but kind. Remember that each one of those soldiers is a man and a Massachusetts citizen." God bless him, the large-minded, warm-hearted, patriot ruler, and the soldier's untiring friend.

Captain Rennie was presented with a sword, sash and belt by the family of the Hon. Z. M. Crane (whose name he bears), of Dalton. Hon. James B. Crane made the presentation speech, and added his own token of respect, in the shape of a handsome Smith and Wesson's revolver. H. B. Brewster, of whose appointment as quartemaster there is now no doubt, received sword and equipments from the Housatonic engine company, of which he has been an active member. At the mess-table to-day, Lieutenant Tucker presented Lieutenant Deming, Co. H. a handsome sword, sash and belt, in behalf of his confiding friends of Sandisfield.

On Saturday evening, John Mason, Company I, stabbed Henry Harmon, a respectable farmer of Coltsville, causing his death. It was an unprovoked assault. It seems he is a deserter from an Albany regiment. So much for the bounty system. In large cities, where rowdies are so numerous, this system sweeps them into the ranks. Bounty and then desertion is their creed. Death to every such deserter should be the unvarying sentence. Talk about the *tyranny* of the government —it has not reached wholesome *severity* yet. The death-penalty is the only proper punishment and remedy for desertion. It should be applied to all captured deserters, whether they desert here, immediately after receiving the bounty, or when before the enemy. A small appropriation of powder and ball would check the growing disease.

Well, we are about to leave Camp Briggs, which some gentlemen have purchased for a *pleasure park.* While life is spared us, Camp Briggs will be a pleasant remembrance. In the sultry South, perchance in crowded fever wards, we will think of its surrounding mountains, its bracing air, and deliriously seek its pure, abundant water. We leave it to practice the lessons there learned against rebellion, to use our acquired powers for the destruction of our rebelling brothers. As the time of our departure is at hand, the camp is crowded with visitors. Partings are spoken that may be forever. Eyes meet eyes that meet no more till "every eye shall see *Him*," the pierced one, battles all over, and enduring crowns given to life's victors. How many of us, soldiers of the Forty-Ninth, will then find that we have truly "fought a good fight?"

LETTER XI.

CAMP WOOL, WORCESTER, MASS., *November* 14, 1862.

MY DEAR L.:

Here we are at our new home. My last letter left you at Camp Briggs, with the regiment under marching orders. Well, they almost mutinied that night, and no wonder. Blankets gone, wood gone, coffee gone, nearly every comfort gone, they were not in an enviable plight. Fences suffered, an old soap-house came down, all for fuel. Mr. Brewster bought them some candles and coffee, but most of the ranges and cooking utensils were on their way to Worcester. The cold night was followed by a chilly morning. They got off from Pittsfield about 9 A. M., and reached Worcester Junction about 4½ P. M. They were saluted at Dalton and Becket, and at Springfield found coffee for some and cannon for all. From Worcester Junction to the camp, a mile, the boys walked through a snow storm that would have done credit to January. A colder, fiercer storm I never experienced. We began to think leaving Berkshire meant an introduction to hardships. Hot coffee, the soldier's panacea, bread, beef, and good barracks renewed our comfort and cheerfulness. Alas! for the poor guards, who had to brave that night with no protection but those flimsy, shoddy overcoats.

The morning came, bringing a bracing air and a clear sky, and we were all out early surveying the premises. Albeit we missed the cheerful appearance of white tents, and the unpainted barracks looked gloomy and forbid-

ding, our survey impressed us that the removal was for
our good.

As you see by the heading of this letter, our home is
named " Camp Wool." Colonel G. H. Ward is commandant of the post, now consisting of the Forth-ninth
and Fifty-first Massachusetts Volunteers. Like our
own colonel, he has given a piece of one leg to the service, but Palmer has supplied him with so good a
substitute that you might think him slightly troubled
with the rheumatism, but would hardly suppose he was
the possessor of a cork leg. The Fifty-first occupies
for barracks an old pistol factory, while, more fortunate,
we take posession of barracks that *are* barracks, a separate one for each company. Here the men can stand
erect and walk about under a roof or sit by a cosy fire.
The berths are admirably arranged, each accommodat-
ng two persons, and are two or three feet from the
floor, obviating the necessity of making our bed-clothes
by night shoe-rugs by day. The barracks are new ;
some of them have never been occupied. Two frame
buildings serve for the line officers' quarters, while in
rear of them are headquarters, the present home of the
field and staff. Back of the barracks we have a fine
parade ground.

On Monday, the tenth instant, there was a formal
election of field officers. For colonel, Captain Bartlett
received all the votes cast ; for lieutenant-colonel, Captain Sumner received twenty-seven votes and Captain
Plunkett three ; for major, Captain Plunkett got thirteen and Captain Morey twelve votes. So Co. C loses
its captain, and Captain Morey loses the majorship.
A feeling prevailed in the regiment that he was too severe a disciplinarian, and hence his defeat. There was
no wire-pulling, no chicanery, on the part of Major

Plunkett. All was manly and above board. H. B. Brewster is quartermaster, with the rank of first lieutenant. B. C. Mifflin, of Boston, is adjutant. He also ranks as first lieutenant. He is a personal friend and college associate of Colonel Bartlett. He is quite young, only twenty-two years of age, and fresh from Harvard. Though a member of the Boston Rifles, he has not had much military experience. The colonel told the officers before election that, if elected, he would select his adjutant from out of Berkshire. Lieutenant Noble goes back to Co. B. He made a capital adjutant. His successor will need to be wide awake if he prove himself his superior. Dr. F. Winsor, from Rainsford Island Hospital, is our surgeon. He is a quiet, reserved man, very much of a gentleman and highly spoken of. His rank and pay are that of a major. The assistant surgeon is Dr. A. R. Rice, of Springfield. He went out with the First Massachusetts in the same capacity. He is young, but twenty-two years of age, and young in his ways, but is regarded, as I believe truly, judging phrenologically, as a very superior disciple of Esculapius. With rare modesty, he refused the position of chief surgeon. He ranks as first lieutenant. The surgeons are appointed by the governor on recommendation of the surgeon-general.

The non-commisioned staff are and rank as follows: Hospital steward, A. J. Morey, of Co. F (son of Captain Morey); sergeant major, H. J. Wylie, of Co. A; quartermaster sergeant, G. E. Howard, of Co. A; commissary sergeant, H. H. Northup, of Co. C; drum major, E. N. Merry, of the same company; while A. M. Brainerd, of Co. D, and myself respectively fill the post of adjutant and quartermaster's clerks.

We brought from Camp Briggs nine hundred and

sixty-two men. Our average height is five feet eight inches : our average age twenty-five years, four months, and eighteen days. The men enlisted are credited to the following towns :

Town		Town	
Pittsfield	140	West Stockbridge	22
Barrington	82	Savoy	18
Sheffield	75	Windsor	17
Adams	74	Tyringham	16
Lee	55	Washington	15
New Marlboro	41	Dalton	14
Sandisfield	40	Florida	12
Lenox	37	Richmond	12
Stockbridge	34	Hancock	10
Cheshire	32	Clarksburgh	9
Lanesboro	31	Mount Washington	9
Egremont	29	Alford	8
Williamstown	27	Peru	6
Hinsdale	25	New Ashford	4
Becket	24	Chicopee	2
Otis	23	Worcester	1
Monterey	23		

The average bounty paid by the towns is one hundred dollars. In our ranks we have four hundred and seventy-three farmers.

LETTER XII.

CAMP WOOL, WORCESTER, MASS. (*Thanksgiving Day*), }
November 28, 1862. }

MY DEAR L.:

It seems decided now that we join Banks's expedition, wherefor we know not. *That* is one war secret that has been kept. We Massachusetts men are glad to go with Massachusetts' favorite, willing to " go it blind " with him above any other general. People smiled when the call for seventy-five thousand men was made in April, 1861, because Banks declared it should have been for half a million. While governor of this State he foresaw this rebellion, and prepared Massachusetts to meet it by reorganizing its militia system. So far-seeing a man will lead us safely on to victory. Last Tuesday guns and equipments came. They are Enfield rifle-muskets, fresh from England, having never been inspected since their arrival. Since thus armed, the men enjoy drilling more, and also find a great addition to their labor, for it is no light task to keep a gun in perfect order. Proudly we carry them now, and proudly we hope ever to carry them ; but often, O ! how wearily.

Our shoddy black overcoats have given place to substantial light blues, in which the ladies of Worcester are putting pockets, thus adding to our comfort, and enlivening us by their presence. The people of Worcester do all they can to make us feel at home. The Messrs. Goddard, with the pecuniary help of some of our field officers, furnished us with chickens, turkeys, and other appendages of a Thanksgiving dinner, to many of us a well-timed kindness and one appreciated even by those whose thoughtful friends at home had anticipated their wants.

The field and staff were duly mustered in on the 19th instant, and there is some talk of mustering *us* as a regiment to serve nine months from the date of *their* muster. I hope not, for difficulty will surely spring from it. Some declare they will not leave the State until paid off.

The colonel has returned from Boston with a fiery little horse and a wooden leg, on which (the leg I mean) he walks rather unsteadily. His appearance before the troops on horseback, seemingly a whole man, drew forth hearty, spontaneous cheers, not ungrateful to any man who knows that the confidence of his men is a sure guaranty of success. The lieutenant-colonel and our tall major, on appearing in their handsome uniforms, were also received with cheers. We have now, not only a "tall major," *the* major, and Major Winsor, the surgeon, and a sergeant-major, and a drum-major, but we have also a "little major." A boy about seven years of age, friendless and homeless, came into camp, and has been adopted by Co. A as "the child of the regiment."

In consequence of the promotion of Captain Sumner, another election was held on the 17th for officers of Co. D. Second Lieutenant Chaffee received forty-seven votes, and First Lieutenant Tucker thirty-two. This result making a vacancy in the post of second lieutenant, H. C. Morey was elected to fill that vacancy, he receiving forty-seven votes, Sergeant Siggins twenty-eight, and R. More six. Lieutenant Morey is active, young, and popular; but, until men have been in

service, they will elect the most popular rather than the
most efficient.   C. Hebner, Esq., of Lee, has given
Lieutenant Smith, Co. H, one hundred dollars in trust
for the benefit of the members of that company.   This
unostentatious act is its own reward.

Last Sunday night we had an evidence that there is
a mixture of fiendishness in our regiment.   J. D.
Snooks, of Co. G, who was blessed, or cursed, as it
seemed, with a five dollar note, visited "the grove,"
and while there, hearing approaching footsteps, turned
round only to be knocked down with a heavy stick,
which was followed by a stab, penetrating to his breast-
bone evidently intended to be a deathly blow to prevent
detection.   When the poor fellow, maimed and bleeding, returned to his barrack, he found that he had been
robbed of his money in the unconsciousness following
the assault.   The same note was later in the evening
offered to the sutler to be changed, yet we have not
been able to discover the villain.

We have an addition to *our* mess.   A. N. Cowles, of
Co. E, who is to have charge of Ordnance and Ordnance
stores.   The addition is an improvement, for a rare,
quaint, shrewd, intelligent, laughter-provoking fellow
is he.   The members of his company have presented
their orderly, M. H. Tuttle, with a sword and sash,
thus showing their intelligent appreciation of merit.

This, I suppose, is our last day in Masachusetts for
a season, perchance for ever.   We will not all come
back.   Some will never leave.   Death has commenced
his inroads.   Allen H. Wheeler, of Co. B, from West
Stockbridge, died at home of fever, on the 15th instant.
Taken sick at Camp Briggs, his military career was
short.   Cut down in early manhood, being only twenty-
three years of age, the farmer boy has closed the battle-

life and gained, I hope, the victor's crown. I knew him not, but he is spoken of as a nice, steady man. Yesterday, Wells B. Morgan, also of Co. B, from Richmond, died of fever. His wife came here to minister to him, and he was privileged to die at home, surrounded by wife and children. He was a farmer, thirty-five years of age, and being a good soldier, we can illy spare him ; but the Lord of Hosts has signed his discharge, and we must submit. On the same day, at his home in Lenox, died John Godson, of Co. D. Consumption cut him down in his twenty-second year, leaving a young widow to mourn him, without the solace of that glory that gathers round the dead who fall on victorious battle-fields. His Irish life was offered for his adopted land, but the greedy monster, Death, too impatient to wait for the hour of conflict, laid him low before he had an opportunity to prove on the well-fought field his right to the proud appellation of American citizen. So, in the graves they fraternize, and we now go forth, armed and equipped, not knowing what awaiteth us, but convinced, alas ! too well, that the recurring Thanksgiving will show many a desolate home in Berkshire.

LETTER XIII.

FRANKLIN STREET BARRACKS, NEW YORK,
December 4, 1862.

MY DEAR L.:

Here we are in the Western Babylon. On Friday, about 2 P. M. we left Worcester for New York, *via* railroad to Norwich, Conn., and steamer Commodore to this city which we reached on Saturday, 4 A. M., having spent the night on the boat. All along the road from Worcester to Norwich, the people greeted us enthusiastically, making us feel we were indeed of some importance to them. We marched up to the Park, where we relieved ourselves of our traps, and under the guidance of Colonel Frank Howe, proceeded to partake of a comfortable breakfast. Now, that I can compare our boys with those of other regiments, I am proud of them. Physically, so Colonel Howe says, we have never been surpassed by any regiment he had seen, and never equailed save by a regiment from Maine. Until I got into the work of comparison, I was not aware that there were so very many fine faces among us. In all our thousand, you can see few evidences of dissipation, and none of real rowdyism. Never, never can we be grateful enough to soldiers. Here are men loving homes, wives and children, going forth to do what? If need be, *to die* for a country's weal, for a world's hope. They go to meet privation, sickness, suffering, mutilation, death, as our representatives, bearing in their own bodies wounds that must otherwise fall on us and our nation's life ; making their breasts a barrier to the wave of fire that threatens to sweep over the whole land, a wave that will ingulf many of them, winning for them nameless graves and places among the "unnamed demi-gods" of earth.   War ! battle ! how grand they are !   How they ring sonorously through the chambers of the soul, mingling with the symphony of angels, for it is only through wars men are made angels ; and though guns are in our hands and bayonets at our sides, we can yet say, "the weapons of our warfare are *not* carnal, but spiritual, mighty through God to the pulling down of the strongholds of iniquity."   No longer does brute force fight ; this is a war of ideas, in which carnal weapons only impress or obliterate great moral truths, the noble battling for which makes men heroes and sinners angels.

Our colonel, on his new black horse, with crutch at his back, is, of course, an object of great interest.   I send you an article written by one who has ever manifested an affectionate concern for our regiment.

CORRESPONDENCE OF THE SUN.

' NEW YORK, *November* 29, 1862.

"*To the Editor of the Pittsfield Sun:*

"At an early hour this morning I heard that the last of our Berkshire regiments, the Forty-ninth, had just arrived from Worcester, and were waiting in the City Hall Park till their quarters should be assigned to them. Hurrying thither, I soon found the familiar faces which I had so often greeted at Camp Briggs, and in all of whom I had learned to feel a personal interest.   Our attention was first arrested by a crowd of persons gathered round a carriage, which, on approaching it more nearly, we found to contain, as its centre of attraction, the youthful form and face of Colonel Bartlett. Anon a deep-toned voice rang out clear and sonorous above the din of Broadway, giving the word of command for the regiment to march, and almost like magic the line was formed, and the measured tread of nearly a thousand men kept time as they proceeded to their temporary quarters at the Franklin Street Barracks. We kept our station till the last of the blue coats had marched by us, and an ambulance with a few sick men had gone to the hospital near by, where woman's hand and woman's tact would care tenderly for them while such care should be needed. As we passed out of the Park after the regiment, we heard many a word of compliment given, with great apparent sincerity and warmth, for the healthy and cheerful looking men, for the officers generally, and for the 'tall Major' in particular. One only of the regiment deserved no compliment, and would have heeded little, if he had received one. Stretched in a somewhat dilapidated hired carriage, and its only occupant, but so spread out as to take up all its room, was the one drunken man amongst the soldiers.

"We followed the troops up Broadway, till they halted at the corner of Franklin street, and a portion of them turned down it, and began to enter the building prepared for their reception—a large warehouse capable of accommodating fifteen hundred to two thousand men. Drawing up in our carriage at the curb, till they had all safely passed, I could not but feel proud of the bearing of the men ; though the rain was now falling heavily, and had done so for an hour or more, there were no sullen or discontented faces amongst them, but jokes and laughter passed from one

to another on every side.   Brave I know these men to
be—I know it after having watched and read their faces,
and seen the determination and sincerity written there ;
and while these elements remain, who shall dare to doubt
the final issue of this conflict, in spite of blunders and
mismanagement in high places?

"It is not yet known how long the regiment will remain in New York, but their departure will not probably be delayed beyond next week, and then farewell to
the last of our Berkshire regiments till we hear of
them again amid the din of battle—and where and
when will that be?

"So pass ye on, brave and gallant Forty-ninth, strong
reapers for the harvest-field of war.   So pass ye to your
work.   And oh ! may God speed the return to your triumphant harvest home ; but ere that time shall come,
how many of your number, now gone forth in the flush
of youth and strength, shall themselves be gathered into
the already overflowing granaries of Death ?   Who shall
tell ?   In the mystery of the future let it rest.   In faith
ye have gone forth—in faith we wait your return.

"S. A. M."

Our "tall major" attracts much attention.   Some
of the papers grow merry over his size, and ludicrously
detail his proportions, while the *Express*, true to its nature, makes game of our colonel's loss.   More patriotism lies in that grave near Yorktown where rests that
shattered leg, than ever was felt by the whole editorial
corps of the *Express*.   The crutch of our colonel is
mightier than the eloquence of a whole regiment of
Brookses.   Lieutenant Tucker, of Co. D, leaves us to
take a position on General Andrew's staff.

Our barracks are roomy and gloomy and our food

scarce equal to our desires, but we are tolerably well
contented, expecting to stay here but a few days ere
leaving for Dixie.   In squads, under the charge of officers, we wander round the city, attend churches, and
visit places of amusements.   A great treat this to many
who were never before in this heart of the western
world, a treat rather provoking, considering that the
non-arrival of the paymaster puts it out of the power
of many to treat themselves.   It seems almost like
starving before a full table to see the appetizing delicacies of New York, and yet be compelled to dine in that
dark cellar on army rations.   Bad for us, we may think,
but good for our families, we all say.   Empty pockets
enable us to be proof against all the snares of Sodom.
Having often said the Lord's Prayer, we now find it answered in that, He "gives us our daily bread ; leads us
not in temptation, and delivers us from evil."

The other afternoon, rich in all their arms and in
full dress, our regiment marched up Broadway.   "Eyes
front," requiring each man to look neither to the right
nor to the left, we recognized then as a "custom more
honored in the breach than in the observance."   We
certainly presented a creditable appearance.   Wealth
was all around us, but how trifling it seemed in comparison with the wealth of sinews and of patriotic
hopes embodied in that small portion of a nation's
guard.   I send you an extract from the *Home Journal*
as a part of our history :

"A COLONEL ARMED WITH A CRUTCH.

"The 'sight' of the afternoon, for the youthful
'Fashion,' beau and belle, who were in promenade,
was a Massachusetts regiment, which, in its transit
through the city, on its way to the war, had taken oc-

casion to make a parade march through the expanding
length of this our Avenue of wealth. Our own chief
object of interest, however, was the colonel in command, armed, as we above mentioned with the very un-
accustomed weapon of a crutch!

"The colonel (whose name was FRANK BARTLETT,
if we were rightly informed) was mounted on a Vermont horse with shaggy brown mane and fetlocks, an
animal that looked as sensible in the face as he was
lithe of limb—a most capital friend for a soldier to
take with him to the wars. The equipments, as well
as the limbs of the rider, were *apparently* all complete,
each long boot with its spur riding gracefully in its
stirrup. Pistols and sword were in their places. At
the horseman's back, however, poised like the long
spear at the back of the lancer, swung the strange im-
plement which told the story—a long crutch with vel-
vet handle, betraying the wooden leg for which it stood
ready to do service. The limb was lost (we were told)
at the battle of Bull Run; and, with the wounds of
his amputation healed, the heroic soldier was now returning to active duty, leading his regiment to the
field with an alacrity that was little like a cripple! He
rode up and down the line, in fact, with the confidence
and ease of a fine horseman—the wooden leg having,
at any rate, no limp in its equitation!

"We were pleased with the physiognomy of the
wounded colonel. His head was well set upon an unusually slight frame, and his features were of the most
intellectual cast, pale and thin. He had the sandy
hair and blue eye of New England, and, under the
slouched hat of the cavalry officer, he was a picturesque
type of the *intelligent energy* which the sculptor would
strive to express in modeling 'the Yankee.' To him

and his brother officers (an uncommonly fine-looking set of fellows !) we would insure a bright welcome, if they should come this way in 'returning from the war.'

"On the regiment itself, as they stood in long line, with their winter accoutrement of blue great-coat and slouched hat, knapsack, and weapon—on their Massachusetts faces, that is to say—we looked with great interest ! We saw the qualities of which we knew well the depth and mettle. They looked hardy and honest, quiet and cool. For endurance in the campaign of hardship that is before them—for the weariness and deprivation, as well as for the fighting, when it comes —they are the stuff ! We gave them, with a moist eye, the 'God bless you !' of a brother countryman as they went from us to their 'forward march.' "

LETTER XIV

CAMP BANKS, LONG ISLAND, N. Y., *December 22, 1862.*

MY DEAR L.:

Instead of turning up amid the orange groves of Louisiana, as expected, we find ourselves encamped on an old race-course, and a precious, long-to-be-remembered time we have had of it. On the fourth instant we marched round Broadway to Peck Slip, there crossed East River, and on foot wended our way, ten miles in all, through the mud to this delectable place. Cold and hungry, we reached here at nightfall and fell to work building our little village, which accomplished, we adjourned to a celebrated New York restaurant for supper. Ye gods! such a supper for hungry men! The gentlemanly proprietors promised our kind Uncle Samuel that they would take care of each man for the munificent sum of twenty-one cents per day, providing all known and unknown luxuries, waiters, cooks, &c., &c. Fresh from the comforts of home and in the very heart of plenty, we bore it awhile, but finding being kept at twenty-one cents a day meant a mere keeping from starvation, some grumbling arose, and as the cold and discomfort increased, the grumbling began to sound like threats and curses, and no one could well tell what would have happened had not the contractors promised us a good hash and boiled breakfast for Sunday morning. Hope carried us through the Saturday night, when, waking early at the bidding of Jack Frost, not waiting for Baker, of Co. II, our chief bugler, to sound the reveille, with cup, plate, and knife in hand, we repaired to the cook shop. There was some delay there; but, knowing an extra meal was in preparation, we waited patiently till the welcome signal came. Into the half-dark shop we went. There was the smoking hash, the savory vegetables, and the steaming coffee, a pleasing prospect for cold and hungry patriots. Rapidly the hash disappeared, the boiled vegetables followed, till some one, sooner satiated than the rest, began to analyze the sumptuous feast. As the light increased, others joined in the analysis. " What's the matter, Jim?" " What's the matter? look here!" and lo! a turnip and then a potato each having a hole in it, showing how contractors make candle-sticks. "Eugh! let me out; I can't stand this," and Frank, not being able to get out, made a speedy deposit of the rich food on the floor and surroundings. " Frank, what in thunder ails you?" " Rats!" was the faint ejaculation, as Frank gave up, rather ungratefully, the remainder of his breakfast. And rats it was, or, rather, had been, for our hash-tub had been uncovered over night, and the rats had left unmistakable evidences that they had eaten more than they could conveniently carry away, and so *dropped* a little to season what remained. Well, there was an uproar that seemed to postpone the observance of the Sabbath to " a more convenient season." Still, hungry men came rushing in from other regiments, who, on hearing of their breakfast, fell to demolishing everything that could be demolished, seeking for the contractors to demolish *them*. Fortunately, they saved *their* hash. Lynch law is but the primitive administration of justice, or the grappling with an emergency or atrocity not within the ken of the statute. Ministers of vengeance we are by the call of our country, *then* we only anticipated our time. Ye dear, stay-at-home patriots, rising from warm beds to partake of healthy inviting food, don't make any long prayers to stay the fearful spread of army-demoralization if we did "gut the cook shop." Bastile, when taken, was destroyed, and the world applauded ; so applaud ye that your sons will not endure shameful oppression, whether in New York or Louisiana. The fire started, it did not burn out without extending its ravages. Sleeping in shelter tents, tents five feet long, four high, and without ends, the Fifty-third were rife for fun or riot, and fancying that their sutler had aggrieved them, they made short work with his shanty and appropriated his goods without stopping to inquire their respective prices. In connection with others, they then visited the shop of our sutler, who had *not* aggrieved them, and injured him to the tune of a thousand dollars, more or less. This was not righteous indignation, but robbery. A building containing a large quantity of powder was partially destroyed and the boards carried off for fuel. I don't blame them for *that*. Put soldiers, half starved, among loyal citizens, in canvas tents, give them each one shoddy blanket, add a fierce wind, with the mercury near zero, and you have all the ingredients of a riot. Such was our condition on Saturday and Sunday, the sixth and seventh of December, 1862. I contend we had a right to run the Government in debt for all the loose boards we could find. That it was a wild, high, warming frolic, instead of a riot, proclaims the praise of Massachusetts soldiers. General Andrew sent an officer down to our camp that Sunday morning, but could find few of our officers about, and, though it may have shown a laxity in discipline, Major Plunkett, who was in command, acted as a man of humanity in giving furloughs to nearly all till sundown that we might care for ourselves. *We* were no better off, having taken up our quarters in a deserted horse-shed, and, because there were eight tons of powder in the adjoining shed, we were not allowed to have a fire. Making up our minds that it were pleasanter to be blown up than to freeze, fire we had, in defiance of orders to the contrary. In the horse-sheds we are still existing, while the boys still endure their tents. As *we* now subsist them, they do not complain of their food, and, having erected large cook-houses, they can occasionally get warmed through. Why we were ever removed from Worcester to this hole we know not. Governor Andrew did all he could to keep us in the State till we should start South.

One of our men was murdered since I last wrote you. His name was William Stelfax, of Co. C, from Pittsfield. He was an Englishman by birth, twenty-five years of age, and leaves a family. Though wild, he was a good soldier and added much to our amusement. On that bitterly cold Sunday, December 7th, he went to one of the camps near East New York, and on his return stopped at a saloon kept by a German named Schellein. On leaving, Stelfax bought and paid for a pint of whisky, which, on being put into his canteen, he asserted was only half a pint. Schellein gave him the lie and knocked him down. Several Germans were in the shop, who sided with the landlord, and who with slung shots again knocked Stelfax down and also his comrade, McDonald, of Co. C. They left, but Stelfax returned and kicked the door, when four muskets were fired, one discharge entering Stelfax's back, causing his death in a few minutes. When this murder became known at the surrounding camps, the soldiers came, sacked the house, placed a rope to a tree, intending to hang Schellein if they found him; but not finding him, set the building on fire, burning it to the ground. I am happy to say that the Forty-ninth had no part in *burning* either the cook-shops or this house. Major Plunkett was there and searched the house for the murderer, and finding he could not prevent its destruction, ordered his men to leave, and they did so, though, if human, they did not look on the fire with much disapprobation. On that same Sunday John Mallally, of Co. C, lost a leg by being run over by the cars.

Near two hundred of our regiment, with many officers, are doing provost duty in New York, or, in other words, arresting deserters. In doing this work they meet interest and danger, and having good quarters, they prefer it to the discomforts and monotony of camp. Lieutenant Kniffin, of Co. B, is assistant provost-marshal. Of course he does well in that position. Doing well with *him* is the rule, not the exception. On the 6th instant Co. C held an election, and Lieutenant Foster was chosen captain, and Second Lieutenant Wells first lieutenant, and Fourth Sergeant George R. Lingenfelter second lieutenant.

There must have been nearly thirty thousand troops here on Long Island when we came here. Measles are making sad work with the Maine boys, and we have forty-seven on our sick list, but no dangerous cases. Colonel Bartlett is now commandant of the post. Our official title is "Banks's remainder expedition." Expedition to where, we can only guess at. Texas, we all say, and hope. Some of our neighbors have already sailed with Banks, and we would be glad to follow them to-morrow. General Wool expresses his determination

to keep us here as provost-guards, saying he can rely on
us. If so, here will mean Troy, Albany, all over his
department. While this is complimentary to us, we
hope General Andrew will come off conquerer, and take
us with him to Dixie as his body-guard, as he says he
will do. So, the two generals must fight it out.

Quite a number of us have been to hear Beecher. **Of**
course we were interested. He is greater in the pulpit
than on the platform. Perchance, because in the former
he is less cramped by notes. He is a provoking character. You have to call him an orator, though he violates
nearly all the rules of oratory. His gesticulations are
wild, and scarcely ever in harmony with his subject.
Something there must be defective in his oratory. A
truly eloquent man will not always make ineloquent
gestures. The fact is, Beecher is *not* eloquent. There
is much vehemence about him, and but little intensity;
much fine word-painting, much arousing speech, but
little awakening the passions of the human heart. He
is singularly devoid of pathos. He can move his audience to tears of exultation or indignation, but he
rarely touches the deeper emotions of their souls. I say
he is greater in the pulpit than on the platform ; but in
the former he is not the great *preacher,* only the greater,
because less restrained, *lecturer.* He is more esthetic
than emotional. He defends the right, however un-
popular, because it *is* right; and his nature is so healthy,
that he detects wrong with a fine instinct, and is so
enamored of moral beauty, that he sees its opposite only
to shrink from it. Though he believes in the grand
doctrines of Christianity, he appears to me more the
moral than the *Christian* reformer. He does not rush
into the arena dealing his heavy blows against sin,
shouting, "The love of Christ constraineth me," but

leaves the impression that he is champion of Humanitarianism rather than of Christianity. A great, benevolent, useful man, I imagine his inner life would show a strange conflict between orthodoxy and heterodoxy; a holding to Christ as a beautiful, lovable character, an introducer of men into the purer activities of heaven, rather than as, primarily, the Saviour of sinners from the damnation of hell. A bold man is Beecher, but he lacks the courage to tell the world that because slavery and intemperance are peopling the pit of woe, he throws himself against them. I did not intend an analysis of the foremost preacher in the land, but let it go. Hearing him was quite an event in our war life, and has furnished us with something to talk over. Crowds of soldiers were there, and if you want to appreciate in some degree the honor of a soldier's position, just put on an army overcoat and cap, and go to Plymouth Church. You will be treated as one of the defenders. of a free gospel. At the close of the evening service, Mr. Beecher married an officer of a Maine regiment to the lady of his choice. His remarks were very appropriate; and to us soldiers, the whole affair was very solemn and impressive. She has, at least, secured, if not a husband's care, a right to bear his name and to mourn for him; and, if sorrow too great for concealment should visit her, the privileges of a respected grief.

Companies used to range in alphabetical order, but now they stand according to the rank of their respective commanders. Captain Weller holds the right, the post of honor, as senior captain. Captain Garlick the left, as second in honor, and Captain Train the centre, as third in rank. His is the color company. Rank and honor seem to go according to priority of commissions. Commencing at the right, we thus stand: A, H, F, D,

E, I, G, C, K, B, the *number* of the company corresponding with its position in the battalion, while the
number of the *captain* accords with the date of his commission.

Perchance you would like to know the grades of pay
as well as the grades of rank; the following table will
give you all needed information. It may be well to
advise you, that while the Government supplies "enlisted men" with food, clothing, and medical attendance in addition to their pay, the officers are obliged to
feed, clothe, and equip themselves. If sick, they have a
right to the attendance of the surgeon, but not to a place
in the hospital without pay. They are usually charged
seventy-five cents per day, but, I apprehend, charging
is the exception, not the rule. Considering that the
Government allows each of them one dollar and twenty
cents per day for subsistence, this is not a hard rule.

Captains or commanders of companies are allowed
$10 per month each for the responsibility of clothing,
arms, and accoutrements.

It is presumed, that where officers have no servants
or horses, they do not draw pay for them. Facts show
this to be a very violent presumption.

OFFICERS OF INFANTRY	Per month.	Number of rations per day.	Monthly commutation value.	Number of horses allowed	Monthly commutation value.	Number of servants allowed.	Monthly commutation value.	Total monthly pay.
	$ cts.		$ cts.		$ cts.		$ cts	$ cts.
Colonel..	95 00	6	54 00	3	24 00	2	49 00	222 00
Lieutenant-Colonel	80 00	5	45 00	3	24 00	2	49 00	198 00
Major.	70 00	4	36 00	3	24 00	2	49 00	179 00
Surgeon....................................	80 00	4	36 00	3	24 00	2	49 00	189 00
Captain......................................	60 00	4	36 00	....	....	1	24 50	120 50
First Lieutenant	50 00	4	36 00	....	....	1	24 50	110 50
Second Lieutenant........... ...	45 00	4	36 00	....	....	1	24 50	05 50
Adjutant, in addition to pay, etc., of Lieutenant............	10 00	....	....	1	8 00	1	24 50	13 00
Quartermaster, in addition to pay, etc., of Lieutenant..	10 00	....	....	2	16 00	1	24 50	26 00
Assistant Surgeon...................	53 33	4	36 00	1	8 00	1	24 50	121 83
Hospital Steward....................	30 00	....	....	....	....	....	....	....
Sergeant Major.......................	21 00	....	....	....	....	....	....	....
Quartermaster Sergeant	21 00	....	....	....	....	....	....	....
Commissary Sergeant............	21 00	....	....	....	....	....	....	....
First Sergeant........................	20 00	....	....	....	....	....	....	....
Sergeant.................................	17 00	....	....	....	....	....	....	....
Corporal..................................	13 00	....	....	....	....	....	....	....
Private....................................	13 00	....	....	....	....	....	....	....
Principal Musician...............	21 00	....	....	....	....	....	....	....
Musician..................................	13 00	....	....	....	....	....	....	....

LETTER XV.

Long Island, N. Y., *January 6, 1863.*

MY DEAR L.:

Here we are at Snedeker's barracks, which are nothing more than stables and barns fitted up for soldiers. They are a decided improvement on the canvas tents in which we shivered from December 4th to 23d. True, we have but about two hundred feet square we can call our own, which, in this rainy weather, is a mud puddle, and our bed-rooms are stalls, and fires are not allowed, yet we are quite cosy. We can keep warm, for our stables are tight and we have plenty of good straw, and if vermin visit us, why the extra scratching will render flesh-brushes superfluous. The barracks were cleansed before we took possession, but our predecessors, thinking they could find a new stock on ship-board, left that which we could have dispensed with, having some of our own on hand—lice. Fine combs, frequent washings and unguentum preserve to us a doubtful victory. Our victories might be permanent had we not some comrades who never raise the cry of extermination. Thicker cuticles or the force of old habits prevent *them* seeing that "cleanliness is next to godliness." *This* is one of the drawbacks to the pleasure of soldiering. Hunting rebels and traitors through forests and swamps, *killing* them for the sake of humanity, has something poetic and inspiring about it, but hunting seams and hems of garments for "crummies" and showing *them* no quarter is an occupation that the concentrated genius of all the poets from Homer down to Tennyson can not invest with the beautiful. Some say, all animal life will have a renewed and glorified existence in Heaven. If so, "I pray thee have *me* excused." Our boys generally keep clean, but there are enough lovers of dirt among us to secure us an unbroken succession of vermin. You know how brief are your ablutions in a cold *room*, and washing in winter time at the out-door pump is not apt to result in perfect cleanliness. Did you ever wash a woolen shirt in cold water while standing in the cold? If so, enough's said; you can understand why some soldiers do not change their underclothes more than once a month. Do not imagine that filthiness is one of our vices. Far from it. Though not as clean as we would be at home, yet, as a regiment, we are "Excelsior." Dr. Winsor is active and conscientious in the discharge of his duties, and sees to it that we keep ourselves in passable order, and every man must appear at dress-parade neat and clean: yet after all, there will be some who, keeping the outside of the platter clean, leave the inside corrupt and defiled. Compared with sickness, wounds, death, this familiarity with dirt is a small thing, but judge ye (and there are many men in this regiment who have been nurtured more delicately than yourself) by it some of the minor sacrifices of a soldier's life. And that life is full of such minor sacrifices, rendered bearable only by considering them as necessary to a nation's preservation. We must go to bed and rise at stated hours; we may not know the luxury of a stool, to say nothing of an arm chair, with the accompaniments of a pipe, a book, a blazing fire, a shaded lamp, and a congenial companion, whose silence is more eloquent and sympathetic than the words of many men. To live "cribbed, cab-

ined, confined," not able to leave our pen without so-
liciting permission from a temporary superior: to eat
food poorly cooked, with beans, meat, rice, molasses,
potatoes, all on the same plate, making us half believe
our friends at home have sent us here as a punishment
for the over particularness of the past; to obey unan-
sweringly men, some of whom we know are our inferiors
in everything but rank: to hear, with no chance of escape, profanity and obscenity: to lie on straw in a close,
unventilated stall (soldiers are sworn enemies to ven-
tilation, especially those from the country); to find to-
day's duties so similar to those of yesterday that it is
difficult to recall the day of the week: to realize that
you are mentally stagnating, with scarce a book to stir
up the pool of thought; to find ambition and energy
dying before monotony and *ennui;* these and a hundred
other things are the unknown, unappreciated sacrifices
every intelligent *soldier* is called on to make. More
strictly do these remarks apply to troops in winter
quarters. Save a short morning drill and dress-parade
we have no exercise. Is it any wonder that our muscles
become flabby, and with appetites unnaturally keen,
our digestion is impaired, so that the soldier's foe, Diarrhœa, even now visits us? Our mental natures being in abeyance, the physical becomes more arrogant,
so that even *our* meals are the great episodes of the day.
You would be surprised at our appetites, and seeing us
drink from two to three quarts of coffee or tea daily,
would wonder that we were not all on the sick list.
Do not think we complain. No, we receive these things
as a necessary prelude to the sacred duties of battle,
yet wish it otherwise, believing that the prelude weak-
ens us. Troops would learn the tactics of war sooner,
would carry with them more enthusiasm, could they

go at once from their rendezvous into active service.
Two weeks of drilling near an enemy would have advanced us as much as we have advanced in all these months, and added greatly to our enthusiasm. We are mental, if machines, and the dry routine of barrack-life is using the machines without any oil.

A friend of J. E., Sergeant of Co. F, has presented us with an army library of one hundred volumes. The books are such as are published by the American Tract Society, Boston, the reading of which will tend to keep fresh the solemn earnestness that moved many of us to enlist. I used to denounce card playing, not as a sin *per se*, but as a foolish wasting of time, and as leading to many vices. I do not denounce it *now*, and can only wish it was never more abused than by our boys. Give a man friends, books, to make pleasant and profitable his leisure hours, and card playing is only less silly than dancing. What shall our poor fellows do? Almost nothing to do or to read, how shall they spend their time? If John Wesley was right in declaring it not expedient to converse on *religious* subjects more than an hour at a time, how can we expect a crowd of men, many of whom are irreligious, to spend *their* hours profitably in conversation? Soldiers are really overgrown children, and need playthings, amusements. Certes, I have never had the heart to deny them the pleasure, the mental excitement of cards. Very seldom do you see any card playing on Sundays, though in the absence of religious services, and of the usual drill, it is the longest day of the week. Colonel Bartlett has occasionally read in our presence the Episcopal service, but as he has been for some time engaged in New York as acting Brigadier-General, those occasions have been very rare. I am pained to confess that prefanity is increasing among us. It does not seem to result from increased wickedness so much as from forgetfulness of God. I have asked some of the most recklessly profane if they were in the habit of swearing at home. Most of them said they were not. It is a fungus of camp soil. The colonel has endeavored to put a stop to it, and had the army regulations relative to it read on dress-parade. For each oath an officer is fined one dollar, and cashiering is the threatened penalty of continued profanity : while one-sixth of a dollar is forfeited by a private for each offense, and some kind of corporeal punishment for a continuation of the habit. We were all sworn *into* the service, and if these penalties should be enforced, a good many would swear themselves *out*, and go home penniless. I am glad that the army regulations read as they do—it is something to be right, though in naught but books— but how to enforce them is the question. A profane officer will not bring charges, and an unenviable life that private would have who should assume to be the Mentor of the regiment. Certainly, he would require to be put on detached and extra duty too, and if he should receive a moiety of the fines, would find his position the most lucrative in the service. Hiring men to play the spy, the informer, will not rectify this evil. Nothing but religious truth pressed upon the heart, backed by the example of officers, will remove this fearful, vengeance-inviting reproach. If you imagine that profanity is the general rule, you will wrong both officers and men. Many have not yet forgotten the teachings of earlier days. Quite a party of us were talking on this subject the other evening, and we counted up the officers who were not known to be profane. Quite a respectable majority appeared on the side of morality. The colonel was the recipient of some oaths at Worcester. After "taps" he was making his nightly perambulation, and on hearing some noise in one of the barracks, he opened the door thereof and commanded quiet. Not recognizing his voice, but recognizing the gust of cold air, they ordered him to shut the door, and begone, in language stronger than contemplated in the army regulations. When they found out who the intruder was, there was a noiseless creeping to bunks, and a great calm, only broken by the loud snoring of those who had so suddenly abandoned the practice of swearing. Like a sensible man, as he is, the colonel went on his way, if not rejoicing, at least amused.

Though, since his election, we have seen comparatively but little of him, that little has only increased our confidence. Daily, he draws the reins of discipline tighter, but with such judgment, that we are learning subordination without complaining. *He* would have to draw them very tight indeed before we would rear or kick. Singular, what command he has over men. He is a *born* commander. Quiet, reserved, yet there is not a man or officer in the regiment who does not feel that obedience to him is half involuntary. While no one more than himself is a stickler for military etiquette and for a proper respect paid to superior rank, yet no one is less assuming or dictatorial. Emphatically, he treats a private as well as an officer. I have known when he has, as he afterwards ascertained, wrongly rebuked a common soldier, send for him and frankly apologize. You can imagine nothing that would so strongly bind to him the hearts of a proud soldiery, who, but yesterday, were the peers if not superiors of many of their officers. He might visit the men in their quarters, or in the hospital, and speak jocular or sympathetic words, and they would call him a jolly or fine fellow : he might buy them holiday luxuries and institute games for their amusement, and they would praise him, but all that would not awaken such reverence for and confidence in him as that simple apology, recognizing, as it does, that each soldier is a man, and presuming he has the feelings of a gentleman, which even a colonel is bound to respect. To awaken affection by the arts of the demagogue is not in *him*. He could not do so if he were to try. Naturally he is the exclusive, the aristocrat. The adjutant, his former college mate, lives with him as a brother. I know not how great is his intimacy with the field officers, but he is *not* intimate with the line officers (captains and lieutenants are called line officers, the others are called field and staff officers). A recognition of the distinction of rank may have something to do with this, but natural reserve, and perchance some diffidence, underlies it all. Our democratic love of equality was somewhat startled by the reading of an order on dress-parade to this effect : that soldiers will not sit down in officers' tents unless invited, and on entering them will remove their hats. We were unnecessarily startled, for it was merely stating that an officer's tent is his private dwelling, and in it we should observe the proprieties due from one gentleman to another. Some of us, with foolish pride, find it hard to cheerfully recognize superiority of rank. Saluting a superior does not imply any inherent inferiority in us : we salute the rank, not the man, *always*. Prouder, really, are we who salute than they who receive and return it, for by the very act we evidence a more sacrificing patriotism. Though Captain Chaffee told the colonel

that there were men in his company (D) who would
grace the saddle (field officers, you know, are allowed
horses), and so there are, yet he and all were not unwilling to have their tents secured to themselves. I
have seen many an officer's tent crowded with loungers.
That order has made those same tents so much more
commodious, that I shrewdly suspect that the colonel
was only its *adopted* father. No order has ever been
necessary to secure to *him* the same respect he claimed
for his brother officers. We have a noble set of officers. They "bear their blushing honors meekly."
You scarcely ever see any of them presuming on their
rank. They know, that by the free choice of their
men, they are what they are, and act as become those
who will, if spared, soon resume their former equality.
In the necessary exercise of discipline they must needs
offend. It may anger us *now ;* we will see it in a truer
light hereafter. The army is a good school in which
to learn subordination, yet I would not fancy being too
long a student therein. I see how military despots are
created. Get in the habit of rendering unquestioned
obedience to another for a few years, and you almost
lose your capacity of resisting his will. Though older
than most of our officers, it will be some time after our
return to private life before I can be as familiar with
them as if I had never been their military inferior.

We have had a change in our roster. Lieutenant
Clark, Co. A, has been honorably discharged. Sickness
prevented his being with us save a few weeks at Camp
Briggs. Second Lieutenant Francis was unanimously
elected to be his successor, and Orderly Sergeant George
Reed unanimously elected second lieutenant. This
places A. Howe in the position of Orderly. As his pre-
decessor, he was one of the three months' men, and is

worthy of a similar promotion. Co. A is a happy company, none being more united, as witness the above *unanimous* elections. Freer with their officers, perchance, than are the men of any other company, yet no other company is under better control. They are worthy of the right, the post of honor.

On the same day, December 31st, 1862, Orderly John Doolittle, merchant, of Monterey, was unanimously chosen second lieutenant, Co. F, to supply the vacancy arising from the resignation of Lieutenant Sweet, who is prevented from going with us by severe and continued illness. If health be spared him, Lieutenant Doolittle will creditably fulfill the duties of his position. The promotion of a first sergeant by the *unanimous* votes of his company is a good guaranty of popularity.

On the twenty-third instant we had another election in Co. C, the governor having refused to commission Lieutenant Foster, who was previously elected to that position. Fourth Sergeant George R. Lingenfelter, of Pittsfield, was duly chosen, having received nearly all the votes polled. He is a blacksmith, twenty-eight years of age, and in his six feet one and a half inches looks a proper successor of the "tall major." Though belonging to that company, I am but little acquainted with him, but as he was a good fireman at home, is well drilled, and has always faithfully discharged his duties, I hope the squabbles of Co. C are ended in the election of a good commander.

On going into the yard or camp the other morning I saw a man standing on a barrel. A gag was in his mouth, his hands were tied behind him, and on his breast was a card on which was written, "A Liar." His captain had placed him there because he denied knowing the whereabouts of his brother, who had absented

himself without leave. A crowd gathered round, and
of course sympathized with the victim. Some one pro-
posed three groans for the captain, and if he had not
speedily released the man there would have been a small
mutiny. I don't know when I felt more indignation.
Guilty or not guilty, no officer has a right to punish
unless a court-martial condemns the accused ; yet this
is not unfrequently done. The punishment of flogging
is abolished in the army, and every commander has to
devise some substitutes. It is a pity that men can not
be punished without degrading them, without crushing
their self-respect. It is well all have not as wild blood in
them as I felt in me while gazing on that poor man. It
seemed then to me that, unless I was full of grace, such
an indignity would awaken "vengeance blood alone
could quell." Certainly I am not alone in such feelings.
If so, such punishments, drying up self-respect and substituting a vengeful malice, are not consistent with an
officer's future safety. Such a withering insult to pride
would make fiends of many. Some form of punishment
is necessary—what shall it be? Fining the sinner will
not do, for frequent offenses would consume all his
wages, and, if married, beggar his family. Confine-
ment on bread and water, standing on barrels before
headquarters (now near the public road), carrying ball
or log and chain attached to the ankle, *standing* with a
heavily-loaded knapsack, increased guard-duty, are the
usual penalties of disobedience. The offenses are not
of a flagrant nature ; simply running guard, staying
beyond the allotted time, and occasionally intemperance
and theft. The other evening, while the regiment was
drawn up for dress-parade, we witnessed an amusing
scene. One of the boys had imbibed too much of the
ardent, and, feeling valorous, made a charge on some

poultry. The enemy fled, save an ancient goose, which was made prisoner. The conquering hero was bearing away his trophy, when he discovered that the foe had received a re-enforcement in the shape of a stalwart Dutch (they are nearly all Dutch here) dame. Knowing that "hell hath no fury like a woman scorned," he concluded that the "double-quick" was the best way to keep his blood warm and to save his Christmas dinner. So, off he ran, and the dame after him. The ardent played havoc with the "double-quick," which *then* had more "time" and "motions" than are laid down in Hardee. The dame drew nearer, and just as he reached the road where the regiment was drawn up she grasped him, and secured the coveted property. Perchance the cackling of geese saved old Rome, but it did not save our hero from condign punishment. The night's rest sobered him, and when morning came he took his stand upon a barrel where he could overlook the scene of his discomfiture. A crowd gathered round him, and, pointing to the letters "U. S." on his belt, he wanted to know what they stood for. Some said "United States," and some "Uncle Sam," and others "Union Savers." "No! no! they stand for *Unfortunate Soldier*." Pretty good that; wasn't it? Standing on a barrel from reveille to taps, that is from 7 A. M. to 9 P. M., searched by a northwester, perchance for three consecutive days, is no light punishment. Enduring it, I have known men's legs to swell so that the surgeon demanded their removal. Truly, this is a mortifying fact, and more so because the punished have really deserved *some* punishment.

There is a company here belonging to the Third New York Merchants' Brigade. We call them "mackerels." They are a disgrace to the merchants of the metropolis, for they seem to be the refuse of Five Points. Many of them are not fifteen years old. They are wretchedly clothed and fed, and under the charge of a sergeant-major who knows no more about governing than a Hottentot about preaching. They are now under Colonel Bartlett's care. Reckless and abused, punishment is their general rule. If these are a specimen of New York soldiers, no wonder that the New Yorkers looked upon *us* as prodigies of strength, neatness and propriety. Go into their yard, and you will see the "mackerels" standing on barrels, or with barrels on their heads, or lugging about a ball and chain, or bucked. Say you, what is "bucking?" The hands are tied together in front of the knees, beneath which a stick is put, resting on the inside of the elbows, thus cramping the poor victim so that he has the sharpest angle imaginable to sit on, and if he does not sit still, over he rolls as helpless as a log. It may not be very painful, but it is certainly unpleasant, degrading, and wondrously amusing to—spectators. S. H. Rossiter, of Company B, was corporal of the guard over the mackerels. He is a Christian gentleman, educated and refined, than whom no cause or country ever boasted a purer soldier. He was ordered to "buck" them. Half amused, half indignant, he hesitated; then went to his captain and asked him if it was his *duty* to do *that*. On being told that it was, he calmly did the disagreeable work. There was the true Puritan soldier. "Though *duty* be ever so unpleasant, so apparently revolting, I'll do it." I watched him, and felt assured *there* was a man who would never flinch, no matter how fierce the conflict. We have many such. O sacred indeed should be the cause claiming the sacrifice of *such* lives.

The cause *is* sacred indeed, worthy of myriad of hecatombs of the best and purest. We hoped so always: we *know* it now. The Proclamation of Emancipation, dated January 1st, 1863, sweeps from our minds all doubts. The country claims our all. We offer it freely. Lincoln was *not* unfaithful. The words have gone forth to be sounded in every slave cabin through the South. "I, Abraham Lincoln, solemnly declare near three millions of slaves free, and will maintain that freedom with all the power of the Government." Grand! never to be forgotten words! words that will grow grander through all the ages; words that will lift up the name of Abraham Lincoln above common names; aye, above the name of *Washington*. Lincoln has had more need of moral courage than had Washington. When the latter lived, Freedom was, to all, a sacred word. Lincoln's Proclamation finds it almost a tabooed word, fit for fanatics, but hardly consistent with the respectability and conservatism of the gentleman. Washington stood up for a liberty that had primary reference to a noble, *white*, Anglo-Saxon race; Lincoln links his name with the choicest earthly hopes of the degraded *blacks*. An *already* prepared nation vindicated Washington. Lincoln's freedom finds degenerate sons of liberty-loving s'res ready to crush it under their scorn. Brave words! brave President! In the White House he holds the same views that he rang out on the prairies of the West. Among other things for which I devoutly thank God is Abraham Lincoln. I recall many of my words. His leisure is faster than my haste; his folly is wiser than my wisdom. Like a child feeling for a father's hand in the night, so have I put out my hand, hoping to lay hold of something that would sustain me. I find that hand inclosed in the warm grasp of the President; his kind eyes are upon me, and he

says: "I send you forth to do battle for God and Freedom—Go!" and I go, blessing God that I have strength
to go: not counting my life dear unto myself, that I
may do something, however little, to bring permanent
victory to the banner of Liberty. Now, I can imagine
a man going into the valley of hell, when earth and
air are crowded with death-dealing missiles, with a
sweeter, wilder joy than into the marriage chamber;
wedded to death for Freedom's sake, clasping Liberty
in a dying embrace, breathing out his life on her lips,
shouting:

> " Whether on the gallows high,
>   Or in the battle's van,
> The noblest place for man to die,
>   Is where he dies for man."

I thank God I live; I see the sun of Freedom rising
full-orbed; and as it flashes on the old flag, the *dear*
old flag, stripes seem all hidden with stars that reflect
the glory of God. The jubilant hours of April, 1861,
have returned, save that their animating *hopes* are now
fruition. If it were necessary to clamber up to the
height of this day, that the Peninsula should grow rank
with Northern blood, I hail the martyred dead as having
gloriously died. I can now unreservedly give myself,
all of myself, body, brains, heart, to my country. Her
cause is now God's cause. Humanity is on our side.
What though that Proclamation is to be indorsed with
the blood of tens of thousands !

> " Life is thought, not breaths; deeds, not years;
>   And he lives longest who best fulfills life's great ends."

" It is not *all* of life to *live*." In one single hour, in
some forlorn hope, a man may throw his life against a

giant wrong, and in that hour win for truth high vantage ground, and do more for the best interests of the race than by a whole century of peaceful existence.

The words have gone forth. To *all* our Flag now means *Freedom*. Those words can *never* be recalled. The die is cast. We recognize that our nation's life is to be saved by justice and righteousness. Intervention dies as those truly *American* words fall on the hearts of Europe's millions. There is no despot, however powerful, however much he may desire the abandonment of our principles, and the death of our institutions, but knows that any crusade against American *Liberty* will be at the peril of his crown and life. If never before, Christendom will read "equal rights for all" on our flag. Reading it, their expanding souls will loosen their shackles, and our land will hasten to fulfill its mission: the civil and religious enfranchisement of the world.

Ere long, men made free by this Proclamation will have the privilege of *fighting* to sustain it. Six months will not roll away before we have many a corps de Afrique Let them come; with their own red right-hands let them carve out for themselves honor, freedom, and nationality. Radicals and conservatives may struggle on. The nation's heart can *now* rest. Under God our future is safe. *Now*, we will have *victories* in deed as well as in name. Murfreesboro strikes the key-note of the war. The pride of the South then went down before the power of the Free West. *Dark* hands will see to it that that pride shall no more vaunt itself against the "flag of the free." Rivers of blood are yet to be shed, but, looking into the future over countless graves, I forget present sorrow, and exultingly press on, crying, "This war pays, this war pays." As nothing but some unforeseen providence shall confine me to my safe position in the quartermaster's department when comes the call to arms; having fully resolved to share all dangers as well as glory; and so knowing that I may never again visit home and loved ones; yet, I say, "This war pays! The victory *now* sure to come will be worth vastly more than all it will cost!" We are recovering our Union, completing our liberty. We are obtaining security that the precious blood of our slain shall not have been shed in vain.

I am sometimes awed as I recognize the wonderful dealings of God with this nation. Suppose Breckinridge had been elected President in 1860, what would have been our condition?—or Douglas? Secession and war would have followed, and as death had already been fastened upon him, Johnson, of Georgia, now in the rebel service, would be our pilot. Had the war commenced ten years sooner, how illy we would have been prepared for it, materially and morally. Says the eloquent Bishop Simpson, "God has been preparing us for the conflict during many years. He has raised up among us the genius of invention. The railway has been laid down, the harbors of the ocean crowded, the sickle displaced by machinery, in order that men might be spared to fight in this war. So, too, when perfidious England sent out her war-ships to prey on our commerce, the American people were prepared to send them bread. The sewing-machine had been rendered subservient in like manner to the wants of the soldier, and God sent the invention in readiness for the struggle. The conversion of the soldiers was prepared for, too, by that wonderful outpouring of prayer which visited the Christian world a year or two since. God was on our side, and would yet give us the generals and ability to close up the war."

The holidays are over, and, though we missed the luxuries and friends of home, we kept up some of the festivities of the season. The ladies of Sternsville sent Co. A. freight paid, a box of comforts and luxuries, weighing six hundred pounds. Co. E was also generously remembered. Pontoosuc and Hancock did not forget their soldiers. Many individuals received tokens of home affection, so we became quite familiar with the sight of express-wagons. Mr. Brewster supplied the members of his department with a Christmas dinner, equal to what we were wont to have at that season at home. Captain Garlick and Lieutenant Dresser treated their respective companies; and on the afternoon of New Year's Day Colonel Sumner drew up the regiment in line, and, amid the cheers of the men, distributed a liberal supply of crackers, cheese, apples and ale, the gift of Mrs. J. R. Morewood, of Pittsfield, who also favored us at Christmas with a liberal supply of cake. And so passed pleasantly away our holidays at camp.

We will not carry all who were "mustered in" with us to Dixie. The surgeon has been weeding out the incompetent. How some passed the first surgeon's examination is a mystery. With many of the discharged the spirit may have been willing, but the flesh was certainly too weak. Better send them home than freight our hospitals, only to be relieved by their early burials. As we are going to the most unhealthy part of the South, the grave-yard of the Southwest, where many of us will find graves even if we never see an armed rebel, it is well to carry no already superannuates with us. Since I wrote you we have lost Henry W. Cain (K), a farmer from Adams, who died at home of consumption, on the twenty-second of December. He was a good man, but his strength was not equal to his patriotism. As camp

exposure hastened his death, we record him among our
"fallen brave."

Four months have passed away and no pay. This
delay works out real suffering to soldiers' families, especially in those States that do not provide State aid to
the families of volunteers. Bless Old Massachusetts!
Her provident legislation assures us that *our* families
are not entirely destitute. We need money, if for
nothing else, to buy tobacco. You may preach anti-
tobacco with some hope of gaining a few converts any-
where save in camps. Give a man very many unemployed hours, and tobacco, if not a necessity, is a wonderful solace. The pipe, the fine-cut, makes up the
deficiency in quantity or quality of food, and is a positive, indescribable luxury. The sutler trusts each soldier to goods amounting to two dollars per month, but,
as most of them have exhausted that credit, the prospect of going South without money is anything but
pleasant.

LETTER XVI.

LONG ISLAND, NEW YORK, *January* 23, 1863.

MY DEAR L.:

I sit down to write you my last letter from this camp, as we have orders to report on ship-board. Though anxious to face the realities of soldier life, we leave Snedeker's barn-yard with a good deal of regret. Our stay here has, on the whole, been pleasant to all. A great many of the soldiers' wives have visited us this month, putting us in mind of the bright days of Camp Briggs.

We have had fine quarters here. The officers of Co. F and Sergeant-Major Wylie have barracked with us, and many a jolly, cheery hour have we spent together. Getting the right side of the butcher and baker, we have been supplied with *army* luxuries, and, given to hospitality, have often feted officers and their ladies. We will not soon forget the old barn-yard, with its festive scenes, its mock court-martials, and its joyous associations. In sundering partnership with Co. F, we retain in our department as wagon-master and as a *souvenir* of those happy days, Orrin Hulet, one of those men whom you can always count on and implicitly trust; an old soldier and consistent Christian, who only needs the absence of his employer to do nearly double the work that that employer would have required at his hands.

On a recent visit to Pittsfield, his fellow-members of Housatonic Engine Company presented Captain Lingenfelter with a sword and trimmings, through T. Clapp, Esq.

The high honor of bearing the colors falls on Thomas Bach, sergeant in company F. He is a noble looking fellow, and a soldier of the Florida war. H. R. Fowler, corporal (D), carries the white flag of Massachusetts, while Corporals T. Biety (A), E. W. Pierce (B), E. E. Ensign (E), a college-mate of the colonel, and an educated gentleman, A. J. French (F), H. A. Glazier (G), E. W. Bliss (H), and T. Carey (K), form the color-guard. Their main duty is to defend the flag. Proud and dangerous post! Battles have been lost and won by the "color-guard." You know not what an inspiration the "colors" bear with them. Let them be but advanced, and a shrinking regiment grows proud and strong. Invocations to them, though trite, will always find an answering response in the hearts of true soldiers. Misses A. and S. Learned, of Pittsfield, presented us with two small but handsome silk flags, on which are marked name of regiment. E. Ende and J. Bryce (A) bear these flags, and are called markers. D. Dalzell (K) remains behind as orderly to General Wool. T. M. Judd (F) and A. A. Loop (D) are detached as clerks at headquarters, positions the importance of which can not be estimated merely by the extra pay of forty cents per day. There are no pleasanter posts in the army. They can live like gentlemen, and have access to many important secrets. They are both well worthy of their promotion. H. D. Adams (E) is ward-master; we all say, "the right man in the right place." E. W. Steadman (F), noted for his proficiency in that part of drumming called "rolling," is now drum-major.

We have been very busy lately in getting our writing

done up. You have no idea what a vast amount of writing is necessary to keep a regiment in proper order. The fifth sergeant of each company acts as captain's clerk, and you may depend on it his office is no sinecure. Most of them are superior business men, who could command large salaries at home, yet for seventeen dollars per month they leave all at duty's call.

Who will look after deserters in New York since the provost-guards of the Forty-ninth have been ordered to join their regiment? Our boys gained for their regiment an enviable name while discharging their delicate and often dangerous duties. From ten to two at night they would search grog-shops, dance-houses, and dens of prostitution for deserters. While thus employed they arrested and returned to their regiments twelve hundred. Sergeant E. II. Murray, of Company D, won for himself much credit for prudence and courage while in command of his provost-squad of twenty-two men. Several times his life was in almost as great peril as it would be in battle, but unflinchingly he did his work. Men that can be bribed with liquor or seduced by dissolute women would make but poor provost-guards. Few things proclaim more loudly the praise and merit of our regiment than General Wool's persistent effort to keep us in the provost work. Strange hiding places deserters sometimes found. On more than one occasion Sergeant Murray found a frail sister *standing* in the corner of a room to receive him with greater respect, but, as a married man, and so supposed to be a judge of crinoline, he could not but fancy she was possessed of a wonderful amplitude. Perchance desirous of the honor of introducing a new fashion to the consideration of his lady friends on his return to Berkshire, he ventured to make some observations, and so tried to view the marvel on all sides, when, to his surprise, he discovered that the lady wore high-top boots and suspicious pantalettes. Curiosity being stronger than gallantry, he led the blushing damsel aside, and lo! the crinoline was delivered of a full-grown man— a deserter. What will not woman do when she loves "not wisely, but too well?"

Adieu to New York, to the North.

On leaving, I send you

WAR SONG,

WRITTEN FOR THE FORTY-NINTH REGIMENT MASSACHUSETTS VOLUNTEERS.

Air.—"Columbia, the Gem of the Ocean."

Old Berkshire, from hill and from valley,
  Her pride and her glory sends forth ;
Her brave sons unitedly rally,
  With the legions that pour from the North,
With firm will and manly endeavor,
  The Star-spangled Flag to uphold ;
Oh, give us old Berkshire forever,
  And her own Forty-Ninth, brave and bold !
(Chorus) And her own Forty-Ninth, brave and bold,
      And her own Forty-Ninth, brave and bold,
      Oh, give us old Berkshire forever,
      And her own Forty-Ninth, brave and bold.

We leave home and friends far behind us,
  And the scenes we have cherished so dear,
The ties that no longer must bind us,
  We sunder them all with a tear.
Ourselves from our kindred we sever,
  Till war and its perils are past ;
For the Flag of our Union forever,
  We swear to defend to the last !
(Chorus) We swear to defend to the last, &c.

By our Colonel, well skilled in commanding.
   Into battle we wait to be led;
On a single sound leg he is standing,
   But he's sound in his heart and his head.
At his bidding we're going to follow
   O'er the fields of the South far awa',
And we'll vanquish the rebels all hollow,
   Three cheers for our Colonel! Hurra!
(Chorus) Three cheers, &c.

Our Lieutenant-Colonel and Major—
   We know they are faithful and true,
And victory's certain presager
   We hail in their ardor to do.
At their lead, in right soldierly manner,
   The base rebel foe we'll pursue;
And we'll tear down the secession banner,
   And fling out the red, white, and blue!
(Chorus) And fling out, &c.

Our Captains are prompt to their duty,
   Lieutenants alert to each call;
Our Staff boasts of valor and beauty,
   And in fact we are fine fellows all.
In Pittsfield, where we came together,
   In Worcester's generous town,
And even in Long Island weather,
   The old FORTY-NINTH takes 'em down!
(Chorus) The old Forty-Ninth, &c.

Farewell to the homes we are leaving;
   Farewell to the friends whom we know;
Farewell to the lasses now grieving;
   We'll think of them all as we go.
For all these our bosoms are yearning,
   While duty is beck'ning afar;
And we'll give, till God speeds our returning,
   Three cheers for "sweet home;" Hip! Hurra!
(Chorus) Three cheers for sweet home; Hip! Hurra!
      Three cheers for sweet home; Hip! Hurra!
      And we'll give, till God speeds our returning,
      Three cheers for sweet home; Hip! Hurra!

LETTER XVII.

STEAMSHIP NEW BRUNSWICK, before New Orleans, }
February 7, 1863

MY DEAR L.:

As I may have an opportunity to mail you a letter soon, I will get one in readiness. On Friday, the 23d ult., the regiment embarked. By some mismanagement, the sick who were to go with us spent the night at Brooklyn in a cold car. We leave some of our number to recruit in the New York hospitals before going South. Our ocean camp, the steamship Illinois, was comfortable, being a staunch California steamer, but we were unduly crowded, having on board our own regiment, some companies of the Twenty-first Maine, and representatives of several other regiments, in all thirteen hundred men. The berths were so arranged as to be well ventilated.

The dock where our good ship lay presented a busy scene. Very many were there to bid us farewell. Fathers, mothers, wives, and scores of Massachusetts men made up the crowd. Sad hearts were hid by cheerful faces, but, alas! the sigh followed the smile. Men afraid of playing the woman assumed an unnatural levity, and friends parted as if they were sure to meet with the returning morn. The colonel's parents were there. Pride in him could not make them forget that dire day before Yorktown. Might not the future, though still more glorious, be yet more dire? Who could tell? Who but the great Searcher of Hearts knew

the struggles of that hour?   All the " brave go not to
the field."   There is more than *poetry* in these lines:

THE BRAVE AT HOME.

BY T. BUCHANAN READ.

The maid who binds the warrior's sash,
 With smile that well her pain dissembles,
The while, beneath her drooping lash,
 One starry tear-drop hangs and trembles,
Though Heaven alone records the tear,
 And fame shall never know her story,
Her heart has shed a drop as dear
 As ever dewed the field of glory.

The wife who grinds her husband's sword,
 'Mid little ones who weep and wonder,
And bravely speaks the cheering word,
 What though her heart be rent asunder—
Doomed nightly in her dreams to hear
 The bolts of war around him rattle—
Has shed as sacred blood as e'er
 Was poured upon the plain of battle.

The mother who conceals her grief,
 While to her breast her son she presses,
Then breathes a few brave words and brief,
 Kissing the patriot now she blesses,
With no one but her secret God
 To know the pain that weighs upon her,
Sheds holy blood as e'er the sod
 Received on Freedom's field of honor.

I need not dwell on the parting scene. 'Tis too fresh,
too much a matter of vivid feeling for expression.
Some kind friends cheered our hearts and the hearts of
the peddlers by scattering around cigars, apples, and
oranges.   What cared we for those favors?   Little, but
much; very much for them *as* tender expressions of
woman's appreciation of our sacrifices.   Those earnest-

eyed women of the dear old Commonwealth looked on us as *their* defenders.

The hours passed on, when about noon General Andrew and staff arrived, and the increased bustle betokened that the time of our departure was at hand. General Andrew's first act was to eject our sutler and his stores from the ship. Liking Mr. Springstein as we do, and seeing no necessity for such a step, our introduction to the brigadier was not calculated to prepossess us in his favor.

At noon of January 24th we swung loose from the wharf, amid responsive cheers, and very soon were hidden from the last lingering look of those who mournfully sang:

> "Now blow, gentle gales, o'er the dark blue sea,
>   Bid the storm-king stay his hand,
> And bring my soldier back to me,
>   To his own dear native land."

We had two brigadiers on board, with their respective staffs. General Andrew has seen service, having been with Banks in upper Virginia, where he was severely wounded. General Dwight is a little, pompous, kid-gloved man, but as brave as a lion. He is one of five brothers in the army, and served with honor and wounds on the Peninsula. The members of their staffs were generally very young, boyish and exclusive: if I should say *puppyish*, most of the boys would think I had hit the nail on the head for once. I never saw such a snobbish set. Those whose sensitiveness had been wounded by submission to superiors were comforted. Before the awful dignity of staff officers a captain or a lieutenant was nothing, and noticed by them less than we are noticed by our officers. We never knew how to appreciate *our* officers before. There is nothing snobbish about *them*. In my verdancy, I expected that the various officers would be mutually introduced, and that there would be a pleasant fraternization, a union of hearts, that would produce union and enthusiasm in the field. But not a bit of it. Those little dandy lieutenants on the staffs strutted about in their fine clothes like peacocks, and scarcely noticed even our colonel, while hardly a word passed between them and the inferior officers. They chilled the air, and one was sorely tempted to accidentally (?) trip them up as they passed along. I suppose they have Boston pluck, and that is all that you can say in their favor. These men are fools. Don't they know that the aversion they awaken in us will weaken them on the day of battle? They have to lead where personal influence and respect may turn the scale of victory. For them we feel nothing of that kind. Colonel Bartlett could do more with one of our companies than these exclusives with the whole regiment. Well, let them pass; they may redeem themselves, and in gazing on their valor we will forget their follies.

Companies A and E were down in the lower part of the hold, anything but comfortably situated. There were three tiers (or stories) of bunks for the accommodation of the men. The Maine boys took it rough and tumble on deck, and surely rough and tumble it was, especially when it blew great guns off Cape Hatteras. There were two cabins, the lower of which was occupied by generals, colonels, majors, and captains, and the upper by lieutenants and us small fry. The officers found board at the hands of the steward for a dollar and fifty cents per day, a price at which the steward did not get poor, considering that most of his guests were more than satisfied by the mere smelling of food. The well ones do say that it required considerable ingenuity to get enough to satisfy their appetites.

The regiment fared badly. For a day or two we had fresh beef, but that was soon consumed, and we were confined to " salt horse." Barrels thereof, already cooked, stood near the cook-house, but were not much patronized. We had no water save sea-water distilled by being used in the boilers, and of that a very insufficient supply. You can judge then, why *salt* beef went a-begging. The horses of *our* officers were not taken on board, but we were troubled with fifteen staff horses, who used more of the meagre supply of water than we liked. Consumed with thirst, you can imagine how happy we felt when we heard one of the exclusives say, " I don't care a —— whether the men get water or not, but my horse shall have it." O what an inexpressible joy to follow *such* men into battle ! Toward the latter part of the trip we got short of coal, which lessened the quantity of steam, and also our supply of drinking water. Fed on salt food, deprived of coffee, put on half rations of water, it was a wonder that we did not mutiny and push the thirsty horses into the ocean. They had no right to crowd so many on board. To cook for thirteen hundred men we had two steam-boilers and a space of four by five feet. *We* cooked there, the Maine boys did *their* cooking there, as did also the detached men of some other regiments. Cooking day and night would not prepare a sufficiency of food. All the rations due could be had, but they could not be prepared. Coffee is the soldier's staff of life, and when for days, chilly days, too, scarcity of water prevented us having any coffee, we were pretty well down in the mouth. Pretty good fellows we are, or we would have stormed the cook-

house and compelled officers and horses to a *pro rata*
distribution of water. Provoking enough it was to see
hot steaks and biscuits and pies go to the cabin tables,
but that we were willing to bear, for it was in the programme, but " no coffee " was something we never imagined. Given a cup of coffee and then a little tobacco,
and a soldier will be pretty reasonable.

Of course we have nearly all been sea-sick. Sea-sickness never kills, but it makes many wish it would. It
is all I ever dreamed or thought or feared of the nasty.
Provoke a sea-sick man, and he would almost strike his
mother, if he had strength enough. Show me a man
who is gentlemanly while thus tormented, and I will
show you the highest type of the *genus homo*. A sea-
sick man don't swear ; he is beyond that ; literally he
don't care a —— for any thing. Old Neptune is a
nasty, miserable tyrant and cheat. When you are first
taken, you vomit freely and think you are all right, and
wonder why people make so much fuss about a little
nausea, but by and by, when you have given the old
sea-dog all your food, and think you have a receipt in
full, the heaving of the ship stirs up bile and gall, too,
and you begin—to vomit? No, you don't—you wish
you could ; you would give one of your babies for a good
vomiting spell—but you begin to *retch*. Do you know
the meaning of that word? Go to sea in foul weather,
and we had scarcely anything else, and you will loath-
ingly remember its meaning all your life. Lie down
on the flat of your back, and you are then only less than
deathly sick, but once roll over and away you start,
perchance at night, tripping over sleepers (how can they,
how *dare* they sleep?) for the side of the ship. *Now*,
certainly you can vomit—yes, a little froth, and nothing
else. Retching there for an hour and no relief, you go

back to your bunk and lie on your back till your bones
ache, and you *must* move, and, moving, you must get
up and run, for certainly *now* you will find the relief
which can alone make life endurable. Pale, blue-gilled,
on you go: the boys see you: "Hallo! Johns, how are
you? there he goes!" and you hang over the railing for
an hour, looking more like a sick calf than anything
else, till your legs ache and you are wet with the cold
spray, and then down you get on your haunches. The
old ship makes a plunge, and over you go on the deck
in a pool of filth to which the foulest spittoon is abso-
lute sweetness and cleanness. Some fellow, not man
enough to share your sickness, comes along. "Well,
Johns, how are you this morning?" You look up and
see in the tormenting eyes a twinkle, saying, "What a
fool you are to give up to it." You don't knock him
down, for you have not strength or energy enough for
that; you don't swear at him, for *that* requires an effort;
and, as you are quite sure you will die if not relieved
soon, your conscience protests against misusing your
waning power in that way; but you do inwardly pray
that he may soon be as sick as yourself, and malevolence
can no farther go. Some one tells you that lemon juice
will work a speedy cure. With awakened hope you
stagger after a lemon. Now, you see nearly every man
sucking at one, and you get yours at last. You squeeze
it, and as the acid descends you feel something rising;
you choke it down, determined to give the lemon a fair
chance, but all in vain; so you pitch it in the sea, and
once more hang over the dirty, slippery rail. "Johns,
poor fellow, I pity you; go and drink some sea-water
and you will find relief." "That's so," and with a
queer sort of thanks, you rush to the pump, crowd your
way in, and gulp down the worse than castor oil. Sure

enough, you vomit freely, hurrah!—Eugh! it is only
the sea-water you throw up, and then you are sicker
than ever. Reckless, you get down on your back again,
lie there till *necessity* urges you up, and then some one
tells you that you can soon overcome it by resolutely
walking. Well, you try it. The plaguey old ship is
drunk : why can't it be still? Saying nothing, holding
hard your breath, up and down you stagger just as long
as your legs will carry you, and then stop, and then—
retch and retch your life away. Perchance there is a
calm, the craft is sober again, and you begin to think
you may possibly see something worth living for. True,
your head is a vast bee-hive, but once more you crave
food. O luxury of luxuries then, a boiled potato and
a little salt ! If the calm continues, coffee is the nectar
of the gods, but hard-tack and salt-horse scarcely their
ambrosia. Now, you think the time may come in the
far distant future when you can hear, without shuddering, your sweetheart or wife sing, "A life on the
ocean wave, a home on the *rolling* deep." You look at
the big ditch, and dimly perceive some beauty and
grandeur, and have enlarged views of the Infinite, and
awful conceptions of Eternity, and see the sun rise and
set in mid ocean with awe and solemnity, but at the
same time have an idea that that bank of clouds in the
west is something more than the hangings of the sea-
god's regal couch. More than half convinced that the
dwellers on the ocean are not all fools, and that Neptune has some royal and redeeming qualities, you go to
your sound sleep. Ere morning you hear great giant
thunderings at the sides of your vessel, and find your
bed on rockers, and wake up in the darkness to discover that you have been a fool to trust in the deceptive
promises of monarchs. Then all your bitter experience,

intensified, is renewed, and you have to go through with
the after pangs of the sea-birth. *Then* you solemnly
register your vows that once get out of *this* scrape, neither
man nor devil nor Uncle Sam will ever get you into it
again. "Ah! my dear fellow, I wish I could be sea-
sick ; you will stand the Southern climate so much better for this purging." Bah! I wish he *could* be sea-
sick, and as for Southern climate, I would swallow it,
malaria, ague, yellow fever, black tongue and all, only
to be once again on terra firma, no matter though it
were a desert and a solitude.

Well, none of us died, though nearly all were sick.
For awhile the officers' table was far from crowded, and
the ringing of the dinner-bell awakened no hurry nor
interest. Old Nep. was no respecter of persons. Stars
and eagles and straps all bowed before him as master.
O ye dignified ones! how unstarched you looked when
you relinquished your dinners with so much more
rapidity than grace, assuming positions the most careful study of Hardee never taught you. These new
motions first became fashionable about mid-afternoon
of the day we left New York. The freshened air had
invigorated our appetites, and just as *we* had discussed
the merits of our rations, and while the, to us, unknown luxuries of the cabin were lingering on the
palates of the officers, and as they, full of food and of
high hopes, were parading the quarter-deck, they began
to find that the "Narrows" was the sea-monarch's
custom-house, and tribute in the current coin of his
realm was demanded. *Nolens volens*, they paid it. So
generous was one of them that he gave up, not only
his dinner, but his teeth also. Sure he was, at that
time, he would never need teeth again. While those
who sat at the first table were thus strangely digesting

their repast, some of their successors exhibited an aversion to their food, and, without waiting to return thanks, hurriedly sprang on deck. Privates are not allowed on the quarter-deck, but there was plenty of room for them there *that* evening. When the hour comes that comes to nearly all, there is no time to rush up three flights of stairs, and so you can imagine the highly scented condition of the hold. Imagine still farther, delicately reared men doing police duty there the next morning. So we continued : well when the ocean was calm, and sick when it was rough, which was nearly all the time. As for myself I was about the sickest of the sick, and have signed away all right and interest in that treacherous thing called the sea. To endure that for nine months, and I guess I would say, "perish my country, and all its hopes forever !" I'll stand by the bond, and deliver my native land from all its enemies, but in the name of my stomach, of all that is *in* me, or *ought* to be in me, I protest against fighting an enemy who never has the manliness to meet you face to face. Well, it is over, and as we sail up the Mississippi we are determined to open it before our time of service shall have expired. When comes the fierce conflict and we waver before the foe, "Rally, Forty-ninth, or you must return by the way of the *ocean*," will endue us with a courage that no rebels can resist. The following lines by Colonel Sumner are very suggestive. *He was there.*

EXPERIENCES AFLOAT.

O gentle muse! O gracious muse!
  Bestow thy smile on me,
While I describe the wondrous sights
  I see upon the sea.

Old Ocean is a "heavy swell,"
  A deep old salt, for that;
You'll find your error, if at first
  You take him for a flat.

No rower can withstand his roar,
  For blows he's ever ready;
And whoso keeps his company,
  Is apt to get unsteady.

He brags what flags wave o'er his waves,
  He boasts his ships are whalers;
With gales regales us just to show
  How he assails the sailors.

Ah me! I'm six days out from shore,
  A cleaned out, luckless rover;
Another six days' cruise ahead,
  And so, I'm half-seas over.

I feel so "cabined, cribbed, confined,"
  I scarce can draw my breath;
There's no more comfort in my berth,
  Than if it were my death.

I go upon the upper deck,
  They call "the hurricane;"
I spy a seat hard by, I strive
  With all my might to gain.

The passage thither seems up hill,
  I'm just a'going to soar;
When lo! there comes a sudden lurch—
  I'm sprawling on the floor!

With stern resolve I seek the stern,
  The ship's in mad carouse;
The masts, as to their master nod,
  The bow is making bows.

The smoke-stack is exceeding sick,
  It vomits forth a cloud;

A deathly pallor seems to sit
  On every sail and shroud.

I look down in the engine-room,
  The struggle there is fine ;
The old ship's stomach seems disturbed
  Almost as bad as mine.

An after-thought conducts me aft,
  How very queer I feel ;
The things go dancing round me so,
  My brain begins to reel.

Then comes the strange sensation on,
  The like you never knew ;
There's nothing for it but to run
  Eugh ! E-ugh !!   E-e-u-g-h !!!

O grim old Neptune ! once release
  Your precious hold on me,
And you may play your pranks at will ;
  I'll never go to sea.

STEAMSHIP ILLINOIS, AT SEA,   }
OFF COAST OF FLORIDA, Jan. 30, 1863. }

We had rough weather nearly all the way from New York to Florida. Howard and Hulet were the only men in our department fit for duty. We might feel pretty well, but get down into the hold where our stores were kept, and the old nausea would send us up stairs on a "double-quick." On Monday, January 26th, about 10 A. M., we reached Fortress Monroe, where General Andrew went on shore for orders, and whence we mailed a good many letters. Fortress Monroe, with its quiet bay, its various crafts, its monitors, and warlike surroundings, was an interesting sight to us landsmen, many of whom never before saw a fort or a war-ship.

General Andrew having returned, we again headed
south about 2½ P. M. Having gone a little way we were
startled by the cry, "man overboard!" A poor fireman, maddened by liquor and the heat of the furnace,
rushed on deck, and thence into the ocean. As soon
as possible, the ship was stopped, a boat lowered, and
vigorous arms bore it on toward the struggling wretch.
In the white track of the ship we could see an atom
which we knew was a drowning man. The water had
cooled his fever, and brought back the desire for life,
for which he fought hard. The boat neared him; he
sank and rose again and again, and sank to rise no
more. Neptune had received a tribute he must restore
to *his* Master. Was it because we ourselves were going
on an errand of death that this startling episode failed
to startle us? As the waves closed over the dead,
leaving no trace behind, so did the waves of our lives,
every day becoming more serious, close over this scene,
leaving scarce a ripple.

Between Fortress Monroe and the coast of Florida
we had what *we* called stormy weather, bringing chill
to every bone and sickness and discomfort to nearly all.
We were disappointed in the height of the billows.
Waves running *mountain* high is poetical, but not true.
Forty feet, their highest elevation, make a poor show
of a mountain to men who have been cradled by Mount
Greylock and Everett. If mountain relates to discomfort, they were high as Mount Blanc. One night they
dashed over the ship, rushing down the hold, putting
out the lights, and rousing the boys with the conviction
that Nep. was coming a little too near for safety. I
don't know how many prayed, but I do know some
swore as if fight rather than fear was uppermost. Hearing the profanity, and remembering the prayers that

had cradled many of them, one almost expected that the God of the Ocean was coming to visit us in vengeance : but mercy prevailed, and we lived till Friday evening to see land again. That sunset scene, sun sinking in splendor to its ocean bed, gilding the evergreens of Florida, the treacherous sea as calm and almost as lovely as a sleeping babe, the air balmy as spring, all gave us a fuller idea of the meaning of "Sunny South" than we ever had before. Saturday and Sunday, the last of January and the first of February, were days long to be remembered. Then we wound round into the Gulf of Mexico. The sun was a little too warm and coats became oppressive. A delicious languor crept into your system and mere existence was a pleasure. I don't blame the Southerner for being lazy. Life seemed to be made there merely for eating a little and basking and dreaming in the sun. We have grand, *glorious* sunsets in the North, where everything is clearly cut and as brilliantly distinct and vivid as if elaborated by the most skillful artist ; but we have no such sunsets as closed that first day of February. A great bank of clouds rose in the west, looking so much like huge cliffs that you momentarily expected to hear the orders, "Port your helm," to avoid a collision. There is nothing distinct about a tropical sunset. All things are blended together as sweetly as a pleasant dream. You don't *see* poetry in the clouds; you *feel* it. Enjoyment, not analysis, is your duty. Though Sunday, and a chaplain was on board, we had no public religious services, but I fancy there were few who were not benefited by the sermon then preached by Nature. Tempted by the softness of the air, I slept two nights on deck. I slept well. To wake up and see the chaste moon smiling on you ; to hear the soft ripplings of the waves, and look out on the vast ocean, was enough to make one forever forswear the effeminacy of feathers and roofed chambers. So I thought till on that Sunday night I was awakened by the falling rain, the howling wind, and the rolling deep. Then came a storm, and I wrote myself down as a fool to put any faith in old ocean. Only the last evening I was ready to swear eternal love and fealty; and now, when that beauty yet thrilled me and that love made me happy, a sudden nausea drove me to the ship's side, where I believe I offered up my last tribute to Neptune, and with that tribute forever closed my heart against his seductions. We never saw any loveliness in the ocean after that. Monday morning we rolled in the trough of the sea, fearing the breaking of the shaft and the consequent engulfing of us all. The afternoon found us at the mouth of the Mississippi, where a pilot came on board. As soon as he sprang on the stairs he cried out. " Port your helm!" but too late, for in a few minutes we were fast on the bar, and there we lay despite the puffings and groanings of the vast engine. As the owners of the boat received fifteen hundred dollars per day for the use thereof when in motion and twelve hundred when at rest, they were better satisfied with the grounding than were we, notwithstanding our time was going on just the same.

On the following evening we were greeted with a tropical thunderstorm; none of the sharp, loud claps of thunder we were familiar with at home, nor any of the vivid flashes of lightning, but all was blended noise and fire. Each clap of thunder would roll and reverberate till followed by another clap, keeping up one continuous, melancholy, angry din, while the whole atmosphere was so charged with electricity that you could scarcely tell when one flash of lightning ended and the next began. It was almost unbroken flame. O! it was grand. In the midst of the night we drifted out to sea, where we found ourselves rocking next morning, and shivering before a cold wind not unworthy of March at home, and infinitely more penetrating. We got back again to the bar, and lay there till Friday afternoon, when the New Brunswick, a small ocean steamer, came down from New Orleans, and took the soldiers and some of the stores on board. We left the Illinois cheering her kind captain, half cursing her crabbed cooks, glad to bid farewell to the staff and to the ocean, remembering the latter with kindness only for the delicious sea-bathing, and the two days that heaven lent us to show how attractive a home we may ultimately reach. It is a matter of doubt whether the Illinois can get over the bar at this season of the year. Strange that the bar is more of a bar in high water than at low water. The rushing tide of the Mississippi, now full five miles an hour, brings down so much more mud than when low that the bar rises in height more rapidly in proportion than the water. Of course, the river is muddy, but then the water is sweet, so we have plenty of drink, and though our coffee has an indescribable color, yet it *is* coffee, and we are satisfied. We are pretty well over sea-sickness. It does not leave you weak, but with powers of digestion equal to the consumption of more hard-tack than you can masticate. On board this boat there is no table for officers, and so they are dependent on our humanity for coffee, hard bread, and salt beef, those staples of a soldier's larder. Relieved of the incubus of the frigid staff, a right jolly good time have we had in coming up the river. The colonels, majors, and a few captains filled

up the few state-rooms. so the lieutenants and some of
the captains were bedless, save the floor. Not liking
that, they tried to make a night of it, and to keep all
awake. Till about 2 A. M. they succeeded pretty well,
but at last succumbed, finding sleep more of a necessity than frolic.

Early dawn found us on deck, gazing at Secessia.
Now, green fields, orange groves, palatial mansions,
and slave cabins fully occupy our attention. Budding
trees, variegated with groves, in which we can see rich,
luscious, mouth-watering oranges, make it hard to realize that this is only the seventh day of February.
The contrast between the homes of the planters and of
their laborers is suggestive of the fact that, in the ever-
during struggle between the "privileges of the few and
the rights of the many," victory *had* here crowned
the wrong. And as I gazed on the river, ten feet
higher than the foundations of the houses, kept back
only by the levee, I could but think that the time was
fast coming when the rushing, swelling Mississippi of
a Christianized public sentiment would sweep away the
levee that avarice, interest, and indifference had thrown
around slavery, and swallow up the distinctions based
on the wrongs of centuries. In low, malarious places
we see many camps, from which come cheers of welcome. 'Twas good to see houses and green fields, but
better still to see the Old Flag and its blue-coated defenders. On we sail up the river, to open which, that
the produce of the West may again find an unob-
structed pathway to the markets of the world, is our
mission. We believe it will be the scene of our *triumphs*, probably of our *graves*. Be it so ; this morally
barren soil needs precious blood to purify and enrich it.

LETTER XVIII.

STEAMSHIP NEW BRUNSWICK, *February 18, 1863.*

MY DEAR L.:

My last letter to you found us drawing near to New Orleans. T. W. Judd, who carried the mail to the office and cheered our hearts by bringing us letters from home, was the only one favored to see the city. We saw deserted, rotting levees, frowned on by numerous gunboats, everything to denote war. and its destructiveness, nothing to convince us that we were before the great metropolis of the Southwest. Divers pieces of calico and a few carriages pleasantly reminded us of the friends and comforts of the North. Peddlers brought us pies, apples, and oranges ; of the latter you could get three as large as pound apples for ten cents. You had better believe that those who had any money left rapidly invested it in that inviting stock. We tasted *oranges* for once. Some, who had put their faith in Uncle Sam's promise of early payment and come away penniless, looked on at the feast with looks that did not say much about *re-enlisting.* We have been served shabbily. Many of us are not able to buy tobacco ; and those who have a little of that needful on hand are compelled to chew in secret or squander their stock or stultify their past generosity by refusing a comrade's appeal.

About 2 P. M. of February 7th we started up the river and reached Carrollton, a town of three thousand inhabitants, seven miles above New Orleans, with which it is connected by railroad. We were somewhat disappointed in the Father of Rivers. He rolls along in muddy majesty (above the mouth of the Missouri he is as clear as the Hudson) and at a tremendous pace, but he is smaller, narrower than we expected, in no place more than two-thirds of a mile wide. He is a capricious fellow, rising above his ordinary level in the spring, at New Orleans thirteen feet and at Cairo sixty feet, digging out huge tracks on one side and yielding up a part of his domain on the other. He spawns a species of fiddlers, a crab-like fish, who, by honey-combing the levees, get up a dance of mad waters far from agreeable to men who live ten feet below the surface thereof.

On reaching Carrollton we were met by quite a number of the Thirty-first Massachusetts. It was a truly pleasant reunion. I then took my first trip in Secessia—Northup and I made for an oyster-saloon. For a stew we were each charged forty cents. Everything salable is on the same scale. They have no pennies here—nothing less than "picayunes," which formerly meant six and one-quarter cents each, but are now reduced to five cents. Perchance this little custom is the basis of the reputation Southerners have for generosity. They are *not* generous with their money, only reckless. Yearly that little town of Boston contributes more to charitable and religious purposes than the whole South. I find the negroes are alike reckless as their masters, charging the most exorbitant prices for all they do or sell and squandering their money with a perfect looseness. Being compelled to buy five cents' worth or nothing leads to this careless improvidence.

Many of us have prepared ourselves for this warm clime by having our heads sheared, so we look ugly enough to scare the long-haired Southrons. The residents here are mainly Germans. Occasionally you meet a native, who, with his fierce eyes, long hair, light-sleeved, short-tailed coat, closely-fitting pants and shining black-silk hat, looks as if he belonged to another race. Some of these natives have a low, mean scowl on their faces, and would be dangerous if their courage were equal to their fierceness. They are generally taller and larger-boned than we are. Men, women, and children are sallow. Any careful observer would see that, for real grit, manly defiance, persevering valor, we are almost infinitely superior. There *may* be Southern *gentlemen*. I have as yet seen no one that had a right to answer to that call. I have seen men of wealth, but they looked like a cross between the Spanish brigand and the overseer. Gazing at them is apt to make you doubt whether it is possible or desirable to live in peace with them. I suppose the chivalry are all in the army. Everybody here looks lazy.

Of course, I strolled around among the darkeys, talking with nearly every one I met about slavery and freedom and trying to find him who preferred the former to the latter. I have not yet succeeded. I shall continue my search. There are a good many genuine Africans here. I learn that *they* came down from up the river. The resident negroes are nearly all mulattoes and quadroons, some of whom are handsome. The women seem proud of their almost white children, holding the fruit of their adultery as an evidence of their charms. Judging by the extreme hideousness of some of these mothers, I was led to conclude that Southern passion was superior to Southern taste. No wonder that the poor wenches blush not. They have never been taught the sacredness of woman's virtue.

If they bring a free child into the world, they may be cursed for increasing a hated and feared class; if they bring forth a slave child, they are praised; but in neither case taught that God has said, "Thou shalt not commit adultery." The Southern code strikes out the "not" and emphasizes the "shalt." Men and women alike testify to the brutal lust of the whites, it being no uncommon thing for the master or overseer to drive the husband from his bed and take his place, or for women to be fearfully scarred who, through caprice or principle, refuse their adulterous embrace. *Enceinte* women are often whipped. They are laid with their faces to the ground, which is so excavated as not to endanger the life of the child. Slavery alone could present such an instance of hellish ferocity and avarice. I wish that it could be said that amalgamation is confined to the Southerners. I fear it is not so. I saw an old woman of seventy on the levee who had come down from up the river. On inquiring how she supported herself in freedom, she said she had been a midwife at one of the camps. "Midwife at camp! what on earth do soldiers in camp need midwives for?" "Oh!" said she, "the darkey women will fall in love with the Yankee soldiers, and I have to take care of the little mules." Alas! for human nature. With others, I have always considered the negro as peculiarly sensual. If so, phrenology is a lie. The heads of the men are very deficient in animal force, the major part being *above* and in *front* of the ears. Singular, but true, the heads of the women indicate great animal passions. Difference in toil and exposure will hardly account for this difference.

While at Carrollton a whole colony of contrabands were moved there. I saw a girl of seventeen going through all the antics of a monkey or a boy of six years.

That is the only specimen of the rollicking, joyous, devil-may-care African I have seen. I had no doubt that the negroes, if not a happy race, were at least careless and light-hearted. Observation begins to compel me to rewrite my former theories and to set down their joyousness and happiness as a plantation lie. I have been with them a great deal, and never before saw so much of gloom, despondency, and listlessness. I saw no banjo, heard none but solemn songs. In church or on the street they impress me with a great sadness. They are a sombre, *not* a happy, race. I attended one of their class and prayer meetings at Carrollton, and, in speaking to them, incidentally said: "The first gun fired at Fort Sumter cracked the chain of every slave in the land." I was surprised at the response. "Glory! Hallelujah!" sounded from all parts of the house. Old men cried, clapped their hands, and all gathered round me as if I were an angel of good tidings. With no gentle pressure, they shook my hand, almost hugged me, and called down all manner of benedictions on my head. Yet they do not appreciate or care for freedom! In every prayer, blessings were invoked for our officers and soldiers, and especially for our sick. We left Carrollton about 1 A. M., the 17th inst. Getting on the boat at that late hour, Captain Chaffee, a thorough anti-slavery soldier, heard a plaintive voice singing, "Am I a soldier of the cross?" and "Don't forget to pray." He followed the voice, and was led to an old negro woman. She told him she came there to pray for our success and that God would make us soldiers of the cross. Poor old woman! freedom would benefit *her* but little, but in the thick darkness she was praying for it and seeing in *us* God's agents to usher in the wished-for day; she was also praying that we might be morally prepared to share in its triumphs. Yet the negro does not desire freedom! On our way up from Carrollton, one got the woodpile between him and the whites, and then vigorously waved his hat in welcome. It was our only welcome. Tears, half of anger, half of joy, filled my eyes; and, if there were another half, half of intense determination to do something to give that negro the right to greet the old flag before all the world, with none to molest or make him afraid. Talk about a race having such intense, *unsatisfied* longings as a happy race! Absurd! Thank God, the old flag now means freedom to all under its folds.

"*Fremont* is music. For that or for some other reason every negro remembers the name. They may know nothing about Lincoln or his proclamation, but they know something about Fremont. That glorious campaign, in which he was standard-bearer, a campaign of principles, a campaign when Seward was radical, and Lincoln was stepping up to the height of January 1st, 1863, stirred up alike every fear of the master, and every hope of the slave. Fremont was the North star brought down to the Gulf, their first and enduring love. O, to see *him* range the South! Then the end were at hand.

"Do not think I have the negrophobia. Remember this is my first letter from the land of Slavery. Subsequent letters will be less *dark* than this, but in nearly all the inevitable negro will appear. Sambo was the occasion of this war. Sambo is in the fence. Sambo will not down, and poor correspondent would I be if I ignored Sambo. *He* will wind up the war. For the present, farewell to Sambo."

On Sunday, the 8th instant, Colonel Sumner led the regiment through the streets of Carrollton. Fifteen days on shipboard made the march very pleasant. Save the negroes going to church, you would not imagine that it were Sunday. Sunday here means business, frolic, and holiday. The days are divided into mornings, evenings, and nights; afternoon is an unmeaning word.

On Monday, the 9th, at five P. M., we encamped about half a mile from the river, on ground as flat as a board. Scarce of tents, the boys piled in seven or eight thick, involving the necessity of sleeping two deep. We got our tents up, when orders came for us to start at once up the river. Some of our goods being on the Illinois, secured us a respite. Flies (in February) and spiders as large as walnuts are a part of our reminiscences of Carrollton. Being at the closing up of the rainy season, we had half a dozen showers daily. The smallest cloud baptized us, and we obtained a deeper insight into mud than ever before. Strong must be your soles if you did not leave them. Dig down eighteen inches, and you reached water. The air was so warm that many abandoned their underclothes, a hazardous experiment where the ground is very damp and fogs so heavy that the sun does not rise till near noon. Though again favored to eat soft bread, we had no cook-houses, few cooking-utensils, and our drink was Mississippi water, of the consistence of thin mud and the color of strong lemonade. Diarrhœa seized nearly all of us, and fever followed hard after—as not even at Camp Briggs were our streets kept clean, being not merely a matter of pride and taste, but of health, of life.

Last Sunday we had a rain. Thunder and lightning accompanied it. We never witnessed such before. The wind strained every tent-cord, and overturned the sutler's tent. Round every field there was a ditch and a bank three or four feet high. The rain filled up the ditch, and began to reach our tent-floors. Co. A, occupying the lowest part of the ground, had a strange experience. As the rain increased, they would raise their floors till they could raise them no higher, and then perch themselves on cracker-boxes, with feet on high, a position that had one advantage. They were willing to rise early next morning. The water filled up the whole camp, being on an average two to three feet deep. Next morning we found no traces of the storm save wet blankets, damp soldiers, and some surface mud. Where that water went to we never could imagine. It could not have been absorbed ; for, before the rain, digging eighteen inches would bring you to the water. Some say that all the ditches slope towards Lake Ponchartrain, where there is a powerful engine to throw the water over the levee. Powerful indeed must be that engine.

On the 13th, we witnessed the burial of a soldier from New Hampshire. The first we had seen, it impressed us solemnly. First, went the brass band, playing a solemn dirge ; then the hearse or ambulance (a two-wheeled cart with a linen cover, used for conveying sick, wounded, and dead, looking like a baker's cart), and then twelve soldiers with reversed guns. They marched very slowly to the grave, where they buried their comrade : and having fired three volleys over his grave, returned to the lively music of the band. The solemnity was so oppressive that I could see great propriety in banishing the gloom by stirring, cheerful music. I went to the soldiers' cemetery. The graves are less than two feet deep, of which six inches are water, rendering it necessary to bore holes or put stones in the coffin to sink it. Each grave is marked by a headboard, on which the name, company, and regiment of the dead are marked. An officer keeps a record of the cemetery, to enable those who may wish to exhume the remains of their friends to ascertain their respective graves. Among the wooden headboards was a marble stone, a token of a brother's affection. On many of these were inscriptions. I copied this one:

> " Weep not for me, my wife and infants dear ·
> For I am not dead, but sleeping here ;
> So after me no sorrow take,
> But love my infants for my sake."

Poor, dear fellow ! he was not much of a poet, but the rude lines were touching. They told where his dying thoughts were turned, and how the patriot was lost in the husband, the father. Many New England homes are linked to that graveyard with chains of sadness. Each grave has its own unwritten history of hopes and joys offered up for a nation's life and purity. That cemetery is fast being filled up, and it is only a small one of hundreds. So let it be, if God's truth can only thus be maintained. Gloomy are our recollections of Carrollton. It is truly a fever-spot. This country is not fit for the residence of men. Leave it for a decade of centuries, and geological changes may render it habitable. At present it is well termed the ''graveyard of the Southwest.'' One of *our* dead lies in the cemetery at Carrollton, William W. Rossiter (B), Richmond. He was a farmer-boy of eighteen years of age. He died on the morning of the seventeenth, of typhoid fever. Fortunately, his brothers were allowed to be with him in his dying hours. Thus went down to the grave the Benjamin of the flock. He was a nice, good, moral boy, full of life, and liked by all.

Another New England home to be darkened. We left some of our sick behind us—sick, we fear, unto death. We left them among strangers. William Deming (II) died on board the Illinois, the eighth instant. His disease was of the nature of an abscess in the head. He was a young farmer from Sandisfield, aged twenty-four years. A fine man, a much-esteemed citizen, a soldier always willing to do his best, he died not alone, for some of his comrades remained on the ship and ministered to him. He was buried on one of the islands at the mouth of the Mississippi. We expect that that mighty river will mark our triumphs, but we did not expect it so soon to mark our burials.

On last Sunday Colonel Bartlett read to the regiment the church service. His rich voice was in unison with the richness and majesty of that liturgy, producing so good an effect that we the more earnestly desired to have the labors of a good chaplain. That we are without a chaplain is not the fault of Governor Andrew, for, on the representation to him of our lack in that respect, he requested our colonel to appoint one, or to give him authority to do so. The following extract from Colonel Bartlett's letter in reply shows his position relative to this important matter:

" The position of chaplain I consider one of the most difficult to fill, and I have seen such evils follow from the presence of inefficient or unworthy chaplains (not in Massachusetts regiments), that I have hesitated to nominate anyone for that position, unless I found some one who was qualified, both in character and ability. Such a one has not offered yet. Your correspondent is misinformed as to the observance of the Sabbath in this regiment. There are the regular duties of the day, such as 'guard-mounting,' 'Sunday morning inspection,' and 'dress-parade,' which are never omitted, but besides these it is a day of rest.

"I have always afforded every opportunity for the men to attend divine worship on that day. I have also read the services myself on that day to all who desired to attend, it being one of the duties of the *commanding officer* in the absence of a chaplain."

I don't wonder that the colonel hesitates in this matter. Before the weeding-out process many of the chaplains were a disgrace to the service, and productive of evil only. Better no chaplain than one who is immoral, lazy, or indifferent. Men have filled that position who, at home, could never get or keep a charge, or whose reputations stood in great need of repairs. I know a chaplain of fourteen months' standing who has never preached a sermon to, or held a prayer-meeting in, his regiment. One bright Sunday morning I attended services at a neighboring camp, and there were not forty of that chaplain's men present. No duties prevented their attendance. Be assured *he* neglected his duty. Let a chaplain do his work well, and he will bind the hearts of the men to him, and save souls from death. We want earnest, brave men, men who will carry the gospel to the battle-field, men like that monk who attended Marmion on Flodden field—

> "A pious man whom duty brought
> To dubious verge of battle fought,
> To shrive the dying, bless the dead."

Well, if not fated to be ministered to as we desire, we may thank our colonel that no unworthy representative of the Master shall make us distrust the sacred profes-

sion, and sow seeds of infidelity in our hearts. If not
blessed with one who might be to us a " saviour of life
unto life," we are not to be cursed with him who would
be a " saviour of death unto death."

On Monday, at 4 P. M., we got orders to go up the
river, and it was Tuesday 4 A. M. before the troops were
on board. Twelve hours in the mud is military, but
not pleasant. Leaving Carrollton, we left no regrets,
save that we had to bid farewell to our cooking-ranges,
and to find out what luxury there is in food of which
smoke is a large ingredient. Where we are going we
know not: perchance to battle. Already some have
shown symptoms of bullet-fever, a fever which really
prostrates a man. Rallying from that he may be the
bravest of the brave. Imagination presenting danger
in every form, he will find the reality so much less than
he feared that he will not be nearly so apt to be panic-
stricken as he who meets that experience for the first
time in the presence of the foe. This is the fiery baptism of battle. Dealing out cartridges somewhat
strengthens the impression that we are nearing the
hour when men's souls and *reputations* will be tried.
Our trip up the river has been very pleasant, though all
hands have been reduced to planks for beds, and for
food to the primitive hard-tack, salt beef, and coffee.
Many of the mansions lining the river are all we have
imagined of Southern wealth and luxury. The white-
washed slave-cabins looked comfortable.

On Tuesday evening we anchored off Donaldsonville,
a small, war-wrecked village. The fog was so great
that we feared traveling in the dark would result in our
running into a bar or snag, and a probable visit from
guerillas. So we rested under the guns of Fort Butler,

a neat, trim-looking citadel, and heard the sunset gun. and saw the descending flag. all of which was to us novel and warlike. Quite a number of gunboats are wending their way up the river ; so perchance before another mail-day rolls round we may have struck a blow for God and our native land.

LETTER XIX.

CAMP BANKS, BATON ROUGE, LA., *February* 21, 1863.

MY DEAR L.:

To date a letter from "Camp Banks" again brings to mind our life on Long Island, but here we are with balmy air, budding trees, and opening gardens. We reached this city, the capital of Louisiana, about Wednesday noon. The high bluff on which the city is built is an agreeable contrast to the fever level of Carrollton. Our camp is about one and a half miles east of the river, from which we draw our water. Poor as it is, it is more wholesome than well-water. The citizens generally use cistern-water. Our camping-ground was once occupied by the rebels for a similar purpose. A battle was fought here last August, and the trees show the effect of shot and shell, while bones of animals and of *men* testify that we gained no *bloodless* victory. The boys have brought several unexploded shells into camp, one weighing one hundred and thirty-seven pounds ; a substantial reason for the rebels' fear of gunboats. We have the best ground for a camp in the neighborhood, sloping so as to remove all fears of being again drowned out. Near it is our parade-ground, a vast field of several hundred acres. Here we have brigade drills, the regiment being now merged into the brigade. We belong to the First Brigade, First Division, which consists of the Hundred and Sixteenth New York, Forty-eighth, Forty-ninth Massachusetts, and the Twenty-first Maine. Colonel Chapin, of the

Hundred and Sixteenth New York, is our acting brigadier. He had experience and wounds on the Potomac.
and is considered reliable and worthy. Our major-
general is C. C. Augur. an old West Pointer. and reputed to be one of our best generals. Banks has gathered around him men of fine military ability. Augur.
Grover. Emory, Sherman. Weitzel. Arnold, form a
brilliant constellation. In a recent division review we
saw none superior to our own Forty-ninth. I have not
yet seen its *physical* equal.

Now we are living a military life. Guards no longer
slouch along with unloaded guns or run to their tents
when off their beats or are careless as to who pass or re-
pass. All that is altered. Within a few miles is the
enemy, so sentinels feel that in their watchfulness the
safety of many lives depends. You will seldom hear
that it is such an hour of the day. but it is just before
or after reveille, or guard-mount, or dress-parade, or
roll-call, or taps. Watches are almost superfluous.
To our other duties is now superadded that of picket.
A certain number of each regiment are detailed daily
for this important work. The picket-lines extend from
river to river, forming a semi-circle of five or six miles.
The pickets carry all their traps with them, so as to be
ready to join in march, attack, or retreat at a moment's
notice. Three occupy a post. In daytime one stands
guard and the others rest ; but at night only one rests
at a time. In case of an attack. they fire two signal-
guns to prepare their camps for action, and then fall
back on the reserve pickets. If practicable, resistance
is here made to the advancing enemy : if not practicable, they retreat to the camp, firing their guns. Our
nearest pickets are but half a mile from us, too near
to give us time to "fall in" if they were beat back by

a superior force : but there are cavalry pickets or scouts much farther in advance, so we sleep securely, though the sudden firing of two guns in quick succession the other night rather startled us. Picket-work has some charms about it, and also many inconveniences and dangers. Occasionally they are fired into by guerillas. There is some romantic and patriotic politeness about army-life. While the pickets file past the "field-officer of the day" on their way to their respective posts, he remains uncovered, as if to say, "Guardians of an army's safety, you go *nearest* the foe to watch over and protect us and, through us, the nation ; yours is the post of danger and of honor : with uncovered head I salute you." While sentinels around the camp are called "quarter-guards," these are known as *"grand guards."* No one is allowed to pass the pickets without a permit from headquarters. Not infrequently some proud dame, who has stayed beyond her allotted time, presents herself to the officer of the picket, and is consequently escorted by a gallant blue-coat to the provost marshal. Judging by her sullen demeanor, she does not appreciate the gallantry. More amusing is it to see one of our boys chaperone some greasy African wench to the same officer. All along the road he will be met with sallies of humor that keep his blushing damsel on the broad grin. Our sense of the ludicrous is apt to make us forget the deference due to woman, no matter what her color. "Twould argue a higher self-respect did the damsel meet the humor with anger rather than with mirth. It is hard to have *self*-respect when you have never enjoyed the respect of others.

Baton Rouge is quite a pretty place of some four thousand inhabitants, mainly situated on a bluff, about forty feet above high-water level. The streets are broad, regular, shaded, and *now* clean. Save the penitentiary, it has but two large buildings, one of them now in ruins: yet, even in ruins, the State-House is beautiful, especially to Northern eyes, for the yard is as green as are ours in June. It is a grand and beautiful wreck. Here was fought the battle of Louisiana Secession, and treason triumphed. Then came the battle of last August, and treason was vanquished, and the old flag once more waved over the pride of Louisiana. Soldiers, Union and rebel, were stationed there when the building was fired. How or by whom, no one knows. Each side accuses the other of the deed. The magnificent library, the fine furniture, the treasures of art, were all consumed. Only Powers' statue of Washington was rescued from the flames. Naught now remains but the massive and beautiful frame. Lower down the river stands the Deaf and Dumb Asylum, a long white building, with large wings. It is four stories high, and round the entire building run two deep verandas, which, with the spacious rooms, admirably adapt it for a hospital. Like the State-House, the yard is enclosed with a fine iron fence and filled with all kinds of flowers and shrubbery. The dwelling-houses are mostly one story in height, with an attic, destitute of cellars, which cause the buildings to rot, and nearly every one boasts a deep piazza, the best-patronized part of the house. As the doors are generally open in the middle of the day, we can see how Southern houses are furnished, which is in a style very inferior to corresponding houses in the North. Carpets are few in number, and the walls are seldom papered. It is not unusual to see pianos in rooms thus destitute. Coolness and cleanliness are, at least, secured. Green *shutters* are attached to doors and windows to keep out the heat. The beauty of their gardens is shut in from the view of outsiders by high fences, which, with the howlings of dogs inside, indirectly refer to the peculiar institution. The bed is the great feature of the room, being of the high, solid posters and heavy top-pieces of the eighteenth century. They are often eight feet long by six feet wide. The neighboring woods supply them with moss, which, when dried, makes the best of mattresses. The rods and rings for curtains point to probable mosquitoes, of which, they say, they have *some*, but aver they are not as bad here as elsewhere. I have heard that same remark in latitudes where I could scarcely discern the color of my horse for the pestiferous hordes, so I draw less comfort from their statement than do others. The city boasts four churches, one of which, the Methodist, is a handsome and commodious edifice. There are occasional services in the Episcopal and regular services in the Catholic church ; otherwise you must worship in the Methodist church, now under the care of the negroes. Judging from the number of stores, this was once quite a business place. Most of those now occupied are in the hands of Northern men, who keep a poor stock, but are not deficient in their charges. Take away the trees and shrubbery, and you can not find what you would term a handsome place in town. Few who can afford plantations live in cities, save doctors, lawyers, ministers, and merchants. The wealth is in the country, to which towns are the merest adjuncts ; land-owning, and consequent slave-owning, is the criterion of respectability. Who own the land will be the rulers. Hence the home-power of Southerners, hence their opposition to homestead-bills. Even in England, an extensive land-owner, though a *parvenu*, has more local influence than an acreless *lord*, though in his veins **runs** the blood of all **the How-**ards. The North knows little or nothing of the power of leaders. **We** thank **our** free schools for it; we ought also to thank that Providence which has divided the soil among many owners. Perchance the latter flows from the former blessing. Feudal South can only be republicanized by impoverishing the great landlords. The war will do, is doing, that. Then democracy will gravitate to the country and the aristocracy to towns and cities.

The north part of the city is ornamented by the arsenal buildings and grounds. They are pleasantly situated and quite spacious. Thanks to the loyalty of Secretary Floyd, they **were** well filled with arms and munitions of **war. Of** course, the rebels seized all. Around the arsenal a series **of** earthworks are being thrown up, and near by is Fort Williams, which, when finished, will enable us to hold this place with comparatively few men. Butler, Banks, or somebody else has been and gone and done it. Negro regiments are actually being gathered together at the arsenal. If they are free, why not let them *fight* to preserve that freedom? We are beginning to laugh at ourselves that we ever hesitated in this matter.

Saving the lack of boards for tent-flooring, we are pretty comfortable. Lumber is hard to get at it here, and many have found a better quality than that usually furnished by the Government, though some dismantled houses may bear testimony to the violation of orders. Mahogany is a tropical product, and we find it makes good tables, shelves, and floors. For a day or two we could get no bread, and the quartermaster had to receive some fervent blessings. Get soldiers away from the refinements of life and doom them to camp inactivity, and they present to view many evidences of self-ishness. Some are born grumblers; and some who never fed themselves at home so well as Uncle Sam now feeds them make it a rule to snarl at the quantity and quality of their food; while those who left homes of luxury take to army fare as if they had been born to it. Save fresh beef, which finds its way only to soldiers in the hospital, we are as well fed as at Camp Briggs. Recently dried peaches were issued in lieu of rice. Some greedily devouring all they could get thereof, would go round complaining that it was not so bulky and nutritious as rice. We used to worry ourselves; now we let them complain. True, we at times have pork and salt beef belonging to the order of "animated nature," and it is amusing to see how differently different persons receive it. Some will cry out, "Look here, cook, it's no use of *carrying* that to the cook-house; put it down and give me a whip, and I will drive it for you;" while others will curse as thieves all connected with the Government. I used to set down the whole race of quartermasters and commissaries as vampires on the soldiers, and give unlimited credit to all the complaining letters from the army. That day is past, for I know that some of our well-fed regiments are not chary of their censures. Having nothing to read, often nothing to do, their god is their belly, "and what we shall eat and what we shall drink" the great questions of their lives. We need active war to drive back this murmuring devil, and to evoke our manliness and heroism. A regimental quartermaster has but lit-tle chance to defraud. A shrewd company commissary knows how much his company is entitled to, and is present at the delivery of the rations; so that cheating *him* is no easy work. After a regiment is brigaded, the

medical department draws for the sick, so that *that* main
chance of stealing is not open to the quartermaster.
When you rise above a regiment, quartermaster and
commissary are distinct officers, the latter having charge
of eatables, and the former of nearly every other kind
of Government property. Here there is a field for pec-
ulation : and when you rise higher, to division and post-
quartermasters and commissaries, you get into a region
where fortunes spring up almost as rapidly as Jonah's
gourd, especially if provost-marshals form a part of the
iniquitous firm. The assertion that this war would
have been closed ere this had officials had no opportunity to trade in sugar, molasses, and cotton is not
entirely without foundation. As yet, General Banks
has kept himself from suspicion, and Butler was too
shrewd to do anything that his enemies could get hold
of ; but certainly his brother owes him a large debt of
gratitude for orders that *accidentally* made *him* a mill-
ionaire. Witness this : On reaching New Orleans, Butler prohibited the circulation of the notes of various
banks. 'Tis said that the brother bought up millions
of these notes for a mere song. Soon after, an order
was issued requiring the notes of these same banks to be
received as legal tender, stating that, as the people had
received them in good faith, it was no more than right
that the banks should redeem them to the extent of the
gold in their vaults and the responsibilities of the stock-
holders. You see the point.

LETTER XX

Camp Banks, Baton Rouge, La., *March 2, 1863.*

My Dear L.:

How we pity you poor chilled Northerners, who can see nothing but snow, and hear naught but the rude blasts of Boreas, while *we* gaze on green grass, soft skies, budding trees, and hear the cooings of birds and the ripplings of rivulets! "Ripplings of rivulets!" I must take *that* back, for I don't want my imagination to be so developed under a Southern sun as to produce a result which you, in the unromantic North, would call "lying." There are no "rivulets" here, and of course the ripplings were not in my eye; but somehow there is such a charm about *our* life, such an actual luxury in mere living, that what you have not in reality you have in imagination. Rivulets, indeed! nothing like them, except muddy bayous, which are so still and sluggish that I take much credit to myself for having even *imagined* "rivulets." It takes hills and stones for "rippling rivulets." As for hills, we have nothing but river cliffs, and stones—I have yet to see the first stone in Louisiana. But it is glorious living here in March. Throw yourself down, half in shade and half in sun, and forget your pores are drinking in fever, and you are almost ready to perpetually divorce you from the rigid North. We have had a few "right smart" cool days, and one or two marked with a chill damp, that enables you to understand why the half-clothed African thinks that even *this* is too far North for his race, and you no longer wonder at the many dropsical specimens you meet, the result of cold : but generally speaking, we have had weather that only needs permanence to make life a physical paradise. It is worth a few *hours*— mark, I don't say *days*—of sea-sickness, to spend one of our mornings in these grand woods. Wood here must be unusually tough, for great oak-branches shoot out from the trunk from sixty to eighty feet, almost *horizontally*. Pendent from every branch, for eight or ten feet, is the thick, rich moss, or tillandsia, which gives to the forests such a weird, antique look. Get in deep enough to shut out sights and sounds of men, and you can fancy yourself an inhabitant of the antediluvian world. Imagine these branches, with their parasites on either side of a stream, down which you are gently gliding, and you will agree with Epicurus that living means simply enjoying. Some of these woodland views awaken in you a protest against all activity; and when, imbued with the delicious torpor, you return to meet cool-eyed, firm-nerved Northerners, you know that *they* must master the denizens of such scenes.

We make use of this fine weather to do up our wash- ing. I have been washing some flannel, and wringing out the same. I don't think I will ever complain of the quantity or quality of another wash-day dinner ; and, as soon as I get home, my women folks must have a clothes-wringer. Cook and wash and mend for your- self a few months, and you will never again think wo- man's work is easy, and that you could do the same in half the time she takes. If our washing does not result in whitening our clothes, it, at least, purifies them, and stays the development of a peculiar class of rebels, who have already been sufficiently troublesome.

If the paymaster should visit us, we could for a while vary our diet, and only for "a while," with steak at fifty, butter at sixty, cheese at forty cents per pound; eggs at a dollar a dozen, and other edibles in proportion. Speaking of these things reminds me of a clean, cool, spacious market-house, which I thought was no longer used, for I never saw a speck of food in it. They do their marketing here between daybreak and sunrise. They commence by drinking drip-coffee from cups about the size of those we once used when soldiering was only playing, for which they pay the *reasonable* sum of ten cents each. Vegetables are not weighed or measured, but sold by the plateful, while beef-steak does not refer to any particular parts of the defunct animal, but rather to the whole carcass, finding it as they do, from the neck to the tail, and selling it for from twenty-five to fifty cents per pound. Men who have graduated on hard bread may attack these steaks with some hope of ultimate success, but I could hardly recommend the business to those who have not cut their eye-teeth. Captain Morey has been to New Orleans and brought back with him our ranges. He has been very kind to his men, but I doubt if he ever did *so* kind a deed before. Instead of all bread, we draw part flour, and visions of slap-jacks and sirup once more rise before us.

"Drill" means work now. The company-drill in the morning and the brigade-drill in the afternoon fill up nearly six hours of the day, and the boys wilt under it. They have been in the habit of having their systems locked up with the cold till May; and this early thawing out produces "spring fever," accompanied with much of diarrhœa and some symptoms of typhoid. We report one hundred and fifteen sick, few of them seriously ill, while the great majority are well enough to stay in their "quarters." Poison lurks in the smile of beauty. Throw yourself down on the ground, though in full glare of the sun, keep up this habit, and you do not contract a cold, as in the North, but a fever. The ground damp is our enemy. It is hard to convince the tired soldier that there is danger, aye, death, in lying down on that sun-heated, dry ground. He believes it when he finds his last farewell to loved ones was final. Bad air, bad water kills many, but the earth-damp is the one great scourge. Breathe poison, eat poison, and the lungs, the stomach, with the aid of open pores, will soon throw it off; but *absorb* poison through the pores, and a visit to the hospital is almost inevitable. We left Nelson Webster, of Co. E, at Carrollton, prostrate with typhoid fever. He died there on the 20th of February, aged twenty-one years. He was, perchance, the stoutest man in the regiment, but of his company he is the first to die, and of the regiment the seventh. These stalwart ones *break*, they can not *bend*. He has two brothers in the army. A nice man, a good soldier, a young husband, has gone. Aged parents, a lonely wife, will mourn for him, and learn as *we* but faintly can, the terrible expensiveness of war. Happy, if they can so scan the glory of the blood-bought future as to say, "This war pays."

We are anxiously waiting for a mail from Berkshire. "Waiting for letters" has a world of meaning now. When the first mail comes we will seem nearer home. Now, there are the two thousand *unbridged* miles between us and loved ones. As many of us are moneyless, and as stamps can not be had for love or money, we can appreciate the kindly wisdom of Congress in allowing staff-officers to frank our letters, leaving the recipients to pay the postage. Newsboys bring us New York papers, for which they only charge twenty-five cents. With so little to read, paying a quarter for a paper ensures such a reading as newspapers seldom get.

I attended religious services at the camp of the Forty-eighth Massachusetts last Sunday. Few were present, and on the parade-ground a battery was firing. Strange thundering of God's truth and cannon! Not so strange if we keep in mind that the "truth" is the parent of the "cannons." Those cannon would have remained in the ore-bed had men been willing to bury truth. Now, Truth seeks to send her message by cannon where she can not send it without.

We have established a Masonic Lodge, so as to make Louisiana seem as much like home as possible. Captain Morey is W. M.; Lieutenant Kniffin, S. W.; Captain Train, J. W.; Lieutenant Tucker, Secretary; Major Plunkett, Treasurer; Colonel Sumner, S. D.; and Quartermaster Brewster, J. D. It is called "Berkshire Camp Army Lodge." We meet in the Masonic Hall, where we hope to have many pleasant "communications" and properly induct candidates into those mysteries which have never made any worse, but have benefited many. Once get into a Lodge, and you have the best style of equality. The major-general enters without noticing you, and perchance does not notice you after you leave the hall; but while *in* the hall all distinctions are merged in the common title "Brother," and his excellency may find the private his masonic superior and respectfully salute him as such. Masonry says:

> "The rank is but the guinea's stamp,
> A man's a man for a' that."

The hegira of females has placed the negroes in comfortable, well-furnished houses. As confiscated property, who has a better right to it than they? They certainly hugely enjoy it. They occupy the houses with the consent of the provost-marshal. Many of the men are in the government employ; some keep restaurants, while the women board officers for ten dollars a week, and wash clothes for a dollar per dozen. The heavens drop fatness on *them*.

Last Sunday I attended the Methodist church. The negroes fitted up the basement for their own use, but, now, in the absence of the whites, they worship in the body of the church. The pastor of the church is somewhere within the rebel lines. I went into the Sunday-school. A touching scene it was, to see those who could barely spell teaching those who know not the merest rudiments of learning. I saw in it a race, a nation, struggling up to intelligence and nationality. The gate of education, so long ruthlessly closed against them, was gradually being opened. Once open, they step into that temple whose inspiration is freedom. Happy for them, they enter it through the Gospel gate, that the light which will show them their wrongs will also show them the Great Sufferer, who exclaimed, "Father! *forgive* them, they know not what they do." Well for the slaves, well for the nation, well indeed for the oppressors, that the enlightening of the bond is in the hands of *Christian* teachers! We need never fear a repetition of the horrors of St. Domingo, unless the slaveocracy shall madly attempt the re-enslavement of the enfranchised.

Seeing an intelligent mulatto woman, I asked her if certain white children were really negroes. She said they were, and then freely spoke of the intercourse between the whites and blacks. "You can see," said she, "by my color, that my mother was not a true woman, but she warned me, and by God's grace I have been preserved from the horrors of prostitution." Trained up in the family of a pious Northern Presbyterian minister, who obtained his slaves by marriage, yet treated them like immortal beings, she had many advantages, and saw but the bright side of the curse, if a curse can have a bright side. Yet, her statements but increased its heinousness. Often women who were members of the church had to be expelled for adultery. The ladies of the South were well aware of their husbands' unfaithfulness, and it was no uncommon thing for these mothers to be whipped to satisfy the rage and jealousy of their mistresses. She also stated that, until a few years past, the negroes were denied religious instruction. I guess she spoke truly, for I have heard them again and again, in prayers and testimonies, thank God that *now* they were privileged to worship him with none to molest or to make them afraid. Instead of spiritual training and plantation churches, they were whipped for holding prayer-meetings in their cabins, and compelled to pray in secret. Thus fades away another "plantation lie."

Wild and emotional as are the negroes in their religious meetings, they forget not that politeness which forms so prominent a part of their nature. If they leave a prayer-meeting before its close, they will shake hands with the preachers and then bow alternately to the men and women, bowing to their own sex last. Say that they chafe not at their fetters! When living in the South I often noticed they met the whites moodily, but those of their own color with a politeness bordering on the extravagant. No Frenchman can excel the darkey beau in grimaces and politeness, but in nine cases out of ten that same beau would pass you with indifference or a sullen courtesy.

They are not as quiet in church as you might desire. If they want to leave or enter, they do so at any time during services, save the service of prayer, in which they all kneel. If the preacher gets up the "rousements," they think the sermon will do ; but the prayer-meeting, with its singing and praying, is their ideal of worship. Here they give full vent to their mingled excitement and devotion by shouting, clapping of hands, and jumping. Solemn and grotesque is the scene. In the regular services the preacher reads two lines of the hymn, which, when sung, is followed by reading two more, and so on till that service is ended. Unable to read, and few having hymn-books, this plan secures congregational singing, but makes sad havoc with the music. I never like the singing of negroes. They rarely rise above a minor, and that slow and full of sadness. In their prayer-meetings, any one can start a hymn of his own choosing ; and, though they frequently grow wild and excited in singing it, or some *impromptu* hymn, it is more a loud wail than a burst of joyous melody. Rely on it, there is a conscious burden on their hearts. They are gifted in prayer. Passages of the truest eloquence could be culled therefrom. Often the whole audience is moved with a seeming joy as they praise God for his mercies, but that joy does not spring from thanking him for home, wife, children, but because he has delivered them from temptations and enabled them to endure sorrows. It is a *mournful* joy. When praying about their enslaved condition, or for the dying, or for the salvation of poor sinners, they unitedly break out into the most plaintive chorus imaginable. I can't describe it, but to my dying hour I shall remember it. It seemed like the *incarnation of sadness*. I could think of nothing but a mother in heaven wailing for her *lost* son. Sometimes it would come from the lips of one or two, or, as all were united in sympathy, it would spring spontaneously from all in complete harmony, making rolling billows of oppressive sadness. "Billows of sadness" seems like a very foolish expression, but it did appear to me as if every heart was a pool of grief, and that some thought, too deep for tears, had merged those pools into an agitated stream. Almost like a nightmare it clings to me, ever presenting depths of sadness and resignation beyond my conception.

Negroes are dressy, and some dress in good taste. The men are attired as poor men generally are, yet all look clean, and some aped the dandy; while the negro guards, clothed in their new uniforms, with bright bayonets at their side, seemed too proud and happy to be dangerous. Most of the women wear turbans of Madras handkerchiefs, and wonderfully becoming they are. I saw one (woman I mean, not turban) who might have sat for an African queen. Many of the mongrels are very beautiful, with their fine hair, straight or wavy, and their blue or dark eyes, always soft and lustrous and half concealed by the long lashes. They look more like voluptuous Italians than negroes. A Southern gentleman told me that they are more docile and affectionate than the unmixed negro and less hardy. Mulattoes in the North are generally scrofulous; not so here, but they are prone to consumption. He said they were generally unchaste. Query: *If true*, is that the result of their *physique*, or of the temptations their

good looks invite? I think the latter, for he did not
include the men in his assertion.

Speaking of dress; it puzzled me to keep from laughing right out in meeting when some jet-black negress
would appear surmounted by a white bonnet, and
clothed in white, with low neck, half revealing *dim*
charms, and bare arms finished out with white kid
gloves. A promenade on Broadway would not amuse
our Yankee gals half so much as to attend church here.
They would have to be *saturated* with piety and propriety if they kept on their go-to-meeting faces. A
strange race, a *tropical* race, they surely are. Get accustomed to the exuberant, grotesque forms of beauty
Southern nature presents, and you begin to believe that
the negroes dress properly and poetically.

Lieutenant Francis and I remained after the services
were closed, and freely talked with several men of mature age, one of whom was the lame colored preacher,
who gave five thousand dollars for himself and family.
He earned it as a carter. Another one paid his master
eighteen dollars a month for twenty-four years to privilege him to live with his family. Talking about the
negro's inability to support himself was a broad joke to
them. Francis told them *they* would have to finish the
war. "That's so," was their emphatic response. They
realized that the time was near for them to come out actively on our side, but they said they wanted to be sure
we could protect them; for those who had favored the
Yankees on their first arrival fared badly when the
rebels returned. "Make us sure the rebels won't come
back, and we be left alone, and we'll do our part." I
thought that was cute enough for a prudent *white* man.
When the lieutenant read to them of the bravery of
Colonel Higginson's negro soldiers, they were glad, but

not surprised : but they *were* surprised when he assured them that in Massachusetts the negro had equal rights with the white man, and was as eligible to any office. While talking with them it seemed like profaning God's workmanship to doubt the ability of their race to properly enjoy freedom.   Carlyle asserts the divine right of man to any position he can possibly fill.   This war latently asserts this of the African.

We have two negro regiments here, and Colonel Sumner, no negrophobist, says they can beat the Forty-ninth drilling.   We have not seen our superior in this department, so that is praise enough.   I saw them on parade. Great lusty fellows with breasts like women's ; they take us down as far as brute strength is concerned. When I contrasted their elastic, vigorous steps with our wan looks and increasing debility I felt that they had not been recruited any too soon.   Dressed in full uniform they made a fine appearance and marched as one man.   In mere drill they must beat the whites ; for "time," which is so important an item in drilling, is a universal gift to them.   Their docility, their habits of unquestioning obedience, pre-eminently fit them for soldiers.   To a negro an order means obedience in spirit as well as letter.   In marching "eyes front," keeping the eyes fixed so as to strike the ground about fifteen paces straight ahead ensuring head and shoulders carried square is the direction.   Watch white soldiers when marching through the streets, and you will find many disobeying that order.   These negroes could hardly have told you that there were any sidewalks. Properly officered, and they will make the *best* soldiers in America.   As an intelligent Southerner said, " Your boys do not know what they are fighting for ; some are afraid they are fighting for the darkey, and some are afraid they are *not* fighting for him. The Constitution and the Union as a rallying cry is weak for it is not understood. *Our* boys have hate, at least, to nerve them. Yours have not even that strength, and I have always contended that interference on the part of England or France would hurt more than help the South, for it would give you an earnestness, a vindictiveness that you now lack." These remarks are pertinent, but they do not apply to the negroes. *They* know what they are fighting for. They know they are bursting from slavery into freedom ; and if freedom be but dimly understood their fears teach them the full meaning of *slavery*—teach them now as never before. Give them officers who will call out their latent manliness, who will work on their religious sensibilities, rallying them to their hopes of freedom, and you can carry them nearer the gates of hell than any regiment of whites. They certainly need *white* officers for a while, and the best of officers, too, for they will, like children, lean much on their superiors. Till they learn to respect their own race more than they do, colored officers will be a failure. Government is removing the few who have been appointed. Negroes have *dash* about them ; more than *we* have. "*Best* soldiers in America :" I mean it. Take Northern soldiers, the equals, perchance the superiors of their officers at home, and they see those officers living and treated as gentlemen, while they, perchance, are cleaning *their* sinks, and doing other menial duties. Duties, *necessary* duties they are, but it requires a constant summoning of self-respect, a constant recollection of the dignity of the cause to keep them from underrating themselves, and from believing that assertion so often used by the ignorant, "A private is no better than a dog." Make such men corporals and sergeants, and while they gladly take the positions to secure a little less of toil and exposure, they are insulted if you think that such petty offices dignify *them*. Not so with the negro. Put a United States uniform on his back, and the *chattel* is a *man*. At one bound he springs higher than if one of our privates should be made a captain, and it is a bound to manly self-respect. You can see it in his look. Between the toiling slave and the soldier is a gulf that nothing but a god could lift him over. He feels it, his looks show it. See him on guard. He is erect, not slouching; he seems to say, "I am guarding my freedom and my manhood." Make a reasonable excuse, and when no enemy is near the white sentinel may pass you, but the negro is deaf to all. He obeys his orders literally. The whole machinery of the camp, if controlled by proper officers, is to *him* a self-respect developer. Would you really bring out more of his manhood give him a little power, make him corporal or sergeant, and he may strut like a peacock, but he is nevertheless more of a man. If self-respect, *increasing* self-respect, is a source of strength, of soldierly excellence, then the negro soldier will surpass the white soldier. On the field, where *dash* may be required, he will have no superior; but when call is made for unflinching courage where there is no excitement to sustain, nothing but the firm will, he will show that he belongs to an inferior race. That does not degrade him; it is only putting him by the side of the French, the Italian, the Spanish, who, tested by this, must yield the palm to the American, the English, the German; and tested by this, all must yield to the sons of New England.

Negro soldiery is an experiment, I grant, but I think an experiment full of promise. I am glad that Massachusetts is raising a regiment of free negroes. They need elevation more than their slave-brothers, for, save a greater knowledge of the vices of civilization, they are their inferiors. Social caste has degraded them more than slavery has degraded the bond.

I tell you, my friend, this war means *Negro equality*. Don't be startled, and conjure up a mulatto nation as the result of general amalgamation. *That* is not "negro equality." If any man wants a black wife, let him have one : it is only a matter of taste. "Negro equality" is not *social* equality, for there *is* no such thing, even among whites. There are, and always will be, classes in society. It is not *political* equality. Minors, women, many foreigners, do not vote, and it would be unwise to allow the negroes to vote until they are more enlightened. Negro equality is simply the right to make the most of himself, the right to secure any position he can fill. It means making a man of him and letting him alone. Give him free access to schools, churches, cars, lectures, ultimately the polls and offices, and to whatever society he can find access. I know I always revolt at shaking hands with a darkey or sitting by him. but it is a prejudice that should shame me. Southerners don't feel it, Europeans don't feel it : strange that it should be confined to Northerners. If a negro can find admittance into Upper Tendom ; if he can secure a college professorship ; if the people want him to be Governor or President, why *my* "negro equality" is to simply say "Amen!" If, with all my start, he outruns me and secures earth's honors, I say let him do so. His superiority will not make me really inferior. Negro equality exists in Europe. The law of popular tyranny there does not discriminate between him and a white man. So let it be the world over. So it will be ere long in America. When they have learned to respect their own race we will have in the army negro officers. Now, if they should signally honor and benefit the country it will not do to drive *them* out of halls, churches, or from public tables ; neither will it do to send such men down into the servants' quarters if they should happen to enter your dining-room while you are eating. Make them *free* and you have got to grant them equality. There is no help for it, and the sooner we get rid of our foolish prejudices the better for us. In me those prejudices are very strong. I can fight for this race more easily than I can eat with them. Their mouths are generally cleaner and purer than ours, for they have better teeth, yet it was a hard dose for me to drink from the same glass with them at one of their love feasts. Southern children grow up, play, and eat and sleep with them, and kiss them, and those children, when men, may give up the playing and eating part, but not the rest. If so many thousands can conquer their prejudices by their lust, certainly principle will enable *us* to at least tolerate them.

I have no fears about the manner in which God will settle this matter. Physically negroes are of an inferior or weaker race. Like the Indians, they will disappear from before us. Outside of slavery they do not increase near so rapidly as the whites. Inside of that dark province they increase wonderfully, because they are stimulated to add to their number as fast as possible. When free each would ask, " Can I afford to marry and to take charge of a family?" Many would answer, " No," and refrain from marriage. As slaves they say, " Master must take care of us and of our children," and children they freely beget. In the competition of life only the strong, the healthy, will secure wages sufficient to support families. You see how this will operate to lessen their ratio of increase. It has done so in the North. Free negroes there increase less rapidly than free negroes in the South. For many years they will add greatly to their number in the Southern States, but their ratio of increase will grow less in proportion to the migration of white workingmen, with whom they will have to compete. They will fade from before us : and if white men capable of laboring in Africa should settle there, as foreigners have settled here, the same results would be produced. The strong must rule. They need not *oppress*.

In the mean time, while elevating themselves to the condition of freemen and being prepared as missionaries to the inhabitants of tropical climes, they should have our sympathy. We all admit that they are human: if we deny them all the *virtues* of humanity we attribute to them all its *vices*. It is the merest balderdash to say that they are too lazy to support themselves. I know they are lazy. The example of the whites and the climate make them so. For nine months in the year men living in this section must be lazy. Every action will demand an effort. I am sure *we*, placed in their position, would make as few efforts as possible. Hunger will be stronger than indolence. Give them the pecuniary, social, and mental stimulants that have made us what we are and they will follow closely on our heels. In strong intellectual powers they will never equal the Anglo-Saxon and Teutonic races. Who do? Do the Irish, Spanish, Italian, Portuguese? In the sensuous— and I use that in its highest meaning—they will surpass us. In music, oratory, painting, fine arts, they will lead most of the nations of the earth. Had we been crushed for centuries as they have been we might have made greater resistance, but, ceasing to resist, we would have sunk lower than they have done. There is a national *elasticity* about them. Soon adapting themselves to slavery, they will be easily adapted to freedom. We have ceased looking on them as fools, and give them credit for much smartness, mingled with a good deal of low cunning. A great work is before them—carving out a nationality. Remember *they* have no storehouse of historic recollections. They can find nothing in the history of their last fifteen hundred years to inspire them. We have Plymouth Rock, Bunker Hill; we have Washington and a host of worthies, each an inspiration to noble deeds. Take all these away and substitute slavery and we would gather no strength from our past but vengeance. Were they a ferocious race, *that* strength would ere this have opened rivers of blood. Let this speak: "Every man presenting himself to be recruited strips to the skin, to be surveyed by the surgeon. Not one in fifteen is free from the marks of severe lashing. More than half are rejected because of disability arising from lashing with whips and the biting of dogs on their calves and thighs. It is frightful. Hundreds of them have welts on their backs as large as one of your largest fingers." Women's persons would show marks of the same brutality. The war did not come any too soon. The concentrated agony of a million bleeding hearts is Freedom's ransom price. She was fettered in the house of her friends. As she goes forth on her glad mission, out of the agony comes a voice, "It is finished."

LETTER XXI.

Camp Banks, Baton Rouge, La.,
March 13, 1863, 9 p. m.

My Dear L.:

Here we are all ready to march on Port Hudson at a moment's notice. Last Monday morning about 1 o'clock we were warned to prepare for a march. Our wedge tents, with all dress-coats and superfluous baggage, have been stored in the arsenal buildings, and so we are learning how much comfort can be found in two pieces of cotton-cloth, about five by six feet, buttoned together over a ridge-pole, without any ends, called shelter-tents. True, our six-footers have to double up their knees, otherwise their pedal extremities will be unsheltered, but we find much more comfort in them than you would suppose. Two occupy one of these tents, and in marching each man carries half a tent. It rained hard on Tuesday night, yet, with rubber blankets to piece out with, we kept dry, but I fear this frosty night will try our patience and make us vote *shelter* tents a lie. Frosty nights, foggy mornings, and hot days put us in mind of a Berkshire September.

This has been a pleasurably exciting week. We are going to meet the foe, and that brings out our manhood. Waiting five days is very tedious work, but we have had reviews, by General Banks, of almost all the brigades and divisions in the army to relieve the tedium. I know little about tactics, but I do know no regiment appeared to better advantage on review than the Forty-ninth. Banks *looks* the soldier. He is a splendid horseman. The reviewing general remains uncovered as the colors are borne by, which are lowered or dipped in his honor. Now there's some poetry about *that*.

Some of the brigades are off. We shall march about twenty thousand strong. The Forty-ninth will send seven hundred and thirty-three men : one hundred and thirty-one sick, of whom fifty-one are on light duty, will be left behind to aid in garrisoning the arsenal. Rumor has it that General Foster, from North Carolina, with thirty thousand men, is coming up the river. I fear that it is too good to be true. As most of the boys have turned in for the night, I presume we will not start before morning ; and as the contingencies of battle may prevent me writing you again, I will now post you as to matters and events up to date.

On Saturday, the 7th, we expected to hear the first gun of our campaign. Seventy wagons, two pieces of artillery, and some cavalry came along, and we fell into line. We knew we were after forage, and understood there was a strong probability of meeting the foe. Through the thick Louisiana mud, which is mud, indeed, we pressed our way onward. So early in March, yet the heat was so great that some fell out of the ranks. We reached an extensive sugar establishment and halted. The teams began to load up with *wood ;* Dr. Lacock, the owner thereof, rode back with our colonel to his house, and we knew that he professed to be Union, because of the thousands of hogsheads of sugar and molasses we were forbidden to enjoy any part. The boys were mad ; they believed the darkeys, who said that Dr. Lacock was a good Union man *when there were no rebels about,* and they could not well see how a good Union man could live five miles beyond our lines, guerrillas all around him, in a place where *we* could not come unless armed to the teeth, and yet his fine house and stock and crops all unmolested. It was a great humbug. The negroes said there had been some rebels near that morning, and when we reached the sugar-house we drew up in a military style to guard against a probable attack from the adjoining thick woods. Finding that attack a mere myth, some deemed it advisable to look into the secrets of sugar-making. Strange how curious Yankees are. I suppose that secret was in the centre of a great hogshead of very nice sugar, for I found a great many soldiers carefully exploring there, and, fearing they would not have time sufficient, many threw away their rations and filled their haversacks, hoping to analyze their spoils in the quiet of camp and be rewarded in the discovery of the arcana. Of course, this must have been their intention, for they certainly would not have violated orders. Some, doubtless, thought that the secret was in the molasses barrel, judging by the way canteens were filled with that saccharine fluid; and as I looked upon beards, mahogany stained and powdered with a rich yellow powder, I concluded *some* thought the surest way of getting at it was to try the sense of taste. Thus *sweetly* engaged, we were oblivious to all care of the rebels, when some dignitary of the quartermaster department accosted us in language more forcible than polite, and so we concluded to abandon our search, and fell into the ranks looking so innocent that no one would have thought we had confiscated the sugar and molasses of a "good Union man." Over the road, which had become almost dusty, we wended our way to camp, voting all *such* foraging expeditions a bore and bewailing the waste of money spent for that wood as if it were from our own pockets. *Now*, we begin to see why *wood* and not *sugar* was sought after. It was to enable the gunboats to operate against Port Hudson. Capture that stronghold and we can settle the mooted question of Dr. Lacock's loyalty and perchance transfer his delectable stores to our commissary department.

Though not fully acquainted with the strength of the enemy's works at Port Hudson, we know enough to convince us that there is serious work before us, or, to use camp slang, that "we are going to have a dusty hunt." In that work some of us will fall. Ere another week shall have passed away we will have veterans' experience, and perchance the Forty-ninth may be allied to the pride of Berkshire by many a bloody grave. Without any exaggeration, we are eager for the fray. We came to do the work of soldiers. It is hard to think that fighting is not a part of that work. Young hearts find it easier to "do" than to "suffer." "Learn to labor and to wait" is no easy task. While some eagerness to meet the foe is manifested, there is no bravado. We go to a stern duty, and, though martial pride duly influences us, yet the thought, "it is our duty," is our main source of strength. Our faces are not blanched, but I doubt not there are many timid hearts among us. Timidity, fear, is not cowardice. Said Wellington, as he saw a man pale as a corpse marching steadily on in a forlorn hope: "There goes a brave man: he knows his danger and faces it." Cowardice is the shrinking from duty through fear. The strong *will* makes the brave man, and when that will is stiffened by a manly pride and, above all, by a sense of duty, the brave is elevated to the hero.

"The brave man is not he who feels no fear,
  For that were stupid and irrational,
  But he whose noble soul its fear subdues,
  And bravely dares the danger nature shrinks from."

Danger faces us. We know nothing about the land defences of Port Hudson, save that there are series of earthworks defended by over twenty thousand men. They ought to repel three times their number. Certainly we have not nearly enough men. I doubt that Banks has forty regiments in his whole department. They will not average seven hundred and fifty men. Many of these are cooks, teamsters, &c., who do not count in the field. If the fleet fail we are incompetent to do the work alone. As a river defence Port Hudson is more formidable than Vicksburg, for the river there makes a right angle, exposing any passing ship to the uninterrupted range of seven batteries for five miles.

While waiting for the "forward march," we are beginning to get hardened. All the spare blankets and other peculiar comforts connected with our department have been sent to the arsenal, and we find using one and the same blanket to lie on and to cover us is not quite the thing. Your hips will work through before morning, and you are glad to hear the morning drum beat. Officers have prepared themselves for the march by confiscating horses and mules, by the valuable help of contrabands or servants. Mounted on these nags, we would create no little sensation in Berkshire. Johnny Merry (A) was fortunate enough to "draw" a charger, but unfortunately for him, the charger made a charge with his hind leg on his ankle, and sent him to the hospital. Brewster "drew" a horse, and Howard, who is very fond of riding, rode him into town, and— walked back, carrying bridle and saddle. A colored matron laid claim to him (to the horse, not to Howard), and satisfied the provost-marshal of the genuineness of her claim : so the quartermaster drew a blank that time.

Speaking of the darkeys, reminds me that I have often read of the joyous labors of the sugar season : how they anticipated it with pleasure, and grew fat while working up the sweet cane. I was rather taken back when an old colored man told me that the masters used to try to frighten the negroes away from us, saying that we would sell them to Cuba, where they had two sugar seasons yearly. Why they should be frightened at the prospects of doubling their joy, I could not see, but it lies here ; the sugar season is one of exhausting, *killing* labor. The mills, once started, know no rest, and all the sleep the hands get is from midnight to two hours before day. I remember Mr. Clay stated in the Senate that sugar hands did not average seven years of life ; that, as the planters needed twice as many hands during the season as they could work the rest of the year, they found it cheaper to keep only as many as they could profitably employ in the comparatively idle season, and to put *them* on double labor when hurried. True, this killed off many, and involved the necessity of buying more slaves ; but the murdering plan was the cheapest, and therefore adopted. Sugar season, a joyous, fattening time ! Alas ! for another slavery lie.

A Southern gentleman told me, " we must have slavery or abandon the cultivation of sugar, for though slaves did less than free laborers would, their labor was *certain;* you could rely on *so much* being done." If this be true, then I say abandon the sugar crops of Louisiana. We get about one-third of our sugar from

this State, and to protect that unnatural crop from
competing with West India sugar, we put a tariff of
two cents a pound on the latter. This is protective
tariff with a vengeance, or rather protection to slavery.
The South should not attempt to raise sugar, for it is
a forced crop. If it can not be raised without forced
or slave labor, God never intended it to be raised at all.
Small farmers will yet raise it by free labor. There is
no need of every cane grower owning an expensive mill.
One mill would answer for a dozen sugar "farms"
(the negroes rarely ever say "plantation"). The colored people look upon our preparations for leaving with
great interest and solemnity. They fear the return of
the rebels. Let the army retire and hundreds must
suffer, for on us they live. We will miss their *neat* restaurants. Neatness seems to be a negro virtue. T.
Back (F), our color sergeant, has been recommended
for a lieutenantcy in one of the negro regiments, on the
ground of experience as a soldier in the Florida war,
and as an *overseer*. He should fail because he has been
an overseer. No man should command negroes, unless
he would give bonds never to spell negro with two "g's."
Observers say free negroes won't work under their old
overseers. Negro troops will prove an expensive failure,
if having been an overseer recommends a man for their
command.

Lieutenant Noble (B) is Adjutant and Assistant
Quartermaster in the Ambulance corps. It is a responsible post. He will do well therein. A. N. Cowles (E)
having been promoted to the post of Ordnance Sergeant
of our brigade, our happy family loses him, and adopts

R. K. Bliss (B) his successor, as Armorer. He is a skillful mechanic and a pleasant companion.

As we may not return to Baton Rouge, but, conquering Port Hudson, press on to Vicksburg! thence to East Tennessee! thence to Charleston! and through Richmond! home, I would like to give you some idea how wealthy Southerners live. Not having been there myself, and prowling guerrillas make the visit a dangerous one, I am indebted to the observing eyes of F. K. Arnold, one of the most intelligent and reliable of Co. E, for this description. "The Perkins place is situated on the Perkins road, about three miles southeast from Baton Rouge. The mansion is beautifully situated on a rise of ground. Access from the road is by a drive half a mile in length, lined on either side with trees. Near the house are China trees reaching above the roof, and being in full bloom, load the air with a delicious perfume. In the yard and garden are roses, cactuses, pinks, verbenas, and many plants unknown to us, and also a hot-house. The mansion is of brick, seventy feet front and thirty deep. On one end and in front is a tasty two-story veranda with cast-iron front. This, as well as the various rooms, is lighted with gas made on the premises. A broad hall divides the house into two equal parts. On the ground floor are twelve spacious rooms, each having a fire-place with marble mantel and hearth and fine chandelier. The doors are of imitation oak. A broad brick walk runs in front of the house, the step into which is made of alternate blocks of black and white marble. Two artificial ponds, once the homes of sunny fishes but now of disgusting water-snakes, are near the house. The whole place shines through its neglect as having once been the residence of taste and culture, aided by all the appliances of wealth. There was also a very large brick sugar-house, with two large stationary engines. The evidences of vandalism are everywhere apparent; windows and blinds smashed, gas fixtures broken, doors torn from their hinges, immovable furniture broken, new billiard table all ripped up, iron safe stove in, picture frames with the canvas cut out, walnut writing desks, dressing bureans, wardrobes, &c., more or less defaced." Several estimated the original value of the furniture of this mansion at fifty thousand dollars. And here *we* are with cold coffee in our canteens, hard bread and salt beef in our haversacks, shivering under thin blankets, only waiting for orders to strike a blow that will prostrate that whole institution which builds for a few oppressors *such* mansions, while it dooms the entire peasantry of the land, black and white, to hopeless poverty and wretchedness.

LETTER XXII.

Camp Banks, Baton Rouge, La., *March 21, 1863.*

My Dear L.:

I don't know whether I quote this doggerel correctly or not :

> "The King of France with thirty thousand men,
> Marched up the hill, and then marched down again."

Well, that is our experience. Here we are back again, next to our old camp. We did not lose a man in our assault on Port Hudson. We did not see an armed rebel. The whole thing was a "feint." Successful, I suppose, for Banks has officially informed us that "the object of the expedition is accomplished." Well, we come back in no very pleasant humor. After screwing our courage to the sticking point and writing solemn, patriotic letters home, preparing them to mourn over us proudly, it is really provoking to be alive and well, not even having learned whether our guns would go off or not. Glory! I fear thou art not for the Forty-ninth.

On Saturday, the 14th, at 5 A. M., we started. We carried no baggage, save overcoats and blankets. Instead of going by the woods road, we lengthened out our march near two miles by going through the city, which was *military*. Emory and Grover led the way; our division (Augur's) brought up the rear. The baggage-wagons and artillery were sandwiched between the different brigades. The morning was cool, the road was in fine order—trees just budding out and festooned with vines and moss were on either hand; so for five miles marching was a luxury. We reached the Bayou Montecino without any incident save the breaking down of a wagon, which led to a generous hospitality in the matter of bread and butter and cheese. The butter was excellent. I learned (whether before or after eating it, deponent saith not) it was some of the veritable butter that disappeared during the raid on the sutler's tent on Long Island. The negroes were in advance of the advance, having laid down an India-rubber pontoon bridge in the place of the fine country bridge destroyed by the rebels, and also a wooden one. "Our army swore terribly in Flanders." Had good Uncle Toby sat by me on the far side of the bayou and heard the drivers as they got their mules over the stream and up the hill, he would have concluded that the army kept up the old practice. Mules, carts, and harness are all spoils of war. The carts are nearly twice as large and heavy as our carts. They put a mule in the shafts and then one on either side, and away they go over the *un-railed* bridge. Each outside mule being afraid of the water, presses from it, and if they are equal in strength they get over safely, but if one pushes harder than the other, there is danger of cart and all going into the stream. I would rather charge a rebel battery than drive a mule team over that bridge. When over, fifty men, more or less, help the mules by pushing, striking, kicking,, and swearing to get up the hill. With the green stagnant water we filled our canteens, and pressed on. We had passed the shade, and now we were to try the effects of the Louisiana sun. In the whole march but seven of our regiment fell out. A few miles beyond the bayou, and we came to a burning house, said to have been fired because an officer was shot from there. We stopped to kill a cow for our dinner, and taking half in our wagon, reached our stopping place about noon. The boys stood their march of fifteen miles well. Marching is our *work*: everything else is play in comparison. Carry a bureau, alias knapsack, on your back, though it may have nothing in it but an overcoat and two blankets, and a ten-pound gun with sixty rounds of cartridges, and haversack filled with food, and canteen holding a quart of water, and you have a load that will bow you over, make you round-shouldered, and give shoulders, chest, and back many an unpleasant twinge If the roads are muddy and the weather hot, and especially if you are in the rear of a column, necessitating a number of "double-quicks" to keep up, you have a job that is more like hard work than to mow an acre of grass, or to cut two cords of wood in a day.

That afternoon we encamped in two large fields—one occupied by our horses, wagons, and artillery ; the other by the infantry. Like magic, our little white houses arose. The fences furnished us with flooring, that saved us from contact with the damp ground. After you know how, you can make quite a cosy bed of two rails, separating them a little to let the hips down. The Southerners, with a commendable foresight, put up rail fences about ten feet high, and often ten or twelve rails in one panel. Since Uncle Sam has ceased paying eight dollars a cord for our wood, we have been dependent on our own axes for this essential, and often shut up to the exclusive use of green wood. No one can complain of the quantity or quality of this *fence* wood. Soon the blessed coffee was smoking before us, and on our rations we dined. Ere long, some wanderers would come in with sweet potatoes, or a leg of mut-

ton, or a quarter of beef, or a hog, and a little conversation with them would result in the mysterious
disappearance of a squad from each company. Our
officers were all blind that day, and when they were invited to partake of a broiled chop, or a little tender-
loin, or perchance a piece of fried chicken, with some
fine sweet potatoes, they did so as a matter of course,
perchance, in their innocence, thinking that the enter-
prising Adams Express Company had just arrived with
some delayed luxuries from home. Successful foraging
cheered the boys, and made them forget lame shoulders,
galled feet, and general fatigue. If health requires
that meat should cool some time before cooking, I am
afraid that, on that Saturday afternoon, we laid up
materials for much future sickness. An unlucky hog
or frightened sheep would run on the points of our
bayonets, and we, that there should be no waste, would
soon have him in the kettle. Sometimes a stray bristle
would tickle our throats, teaching that many hands
make *haste*, if not waste. We did not institute very
lengthy inquiries as to the loyalty or disloyalty of the
coveted property. All about there were so steeped in
treason that we never could be fully satisfied of their
loyalty till we knew if they were eatable or not. Judging by that standard, the loyalty of many was above all
suspicion. Too late came the knowledge, and we tried
to comfort ourselves with the reflection that, even in
death, they served their native land—thus proving us
lineal descendants of them who threw suspected witches
into the river to test their connection with the devil.
If they swam, they were to be burned as guilty; if they
sank, mourned as innocent martyrs. Though we never
stopped to ascertain if the cock and his mate crowed
for Abe Lincoln or Jeff. Davis, yet we became fully

convinced that they all belonged to a race of *tough* rebels. Teeth sharpened on hard tack, jaws made strong by exercising on commissary beef, were compelled to own that the old Chanticleer was too much for them. Happy were those who did not go after water. Our fountain was a hollow filled up by the overflow of the Mississippi. Dip your dish in, make rapid circles to scatter the scum and dirt, and you could, after casting out the stagnant particles, have a pail of water that a Berkshire farmer would give to his hogs—only when all the springs had failed. There is no accounting for taste, yet it did seem to me as if the water would have been purer if that good fellow *above* me had postponed washing his shirt and body till after I had filled my pail, but he did not see it in that light, and I went back to make and drink my coffee, at times imagining something scraping my throat, as if rebels had got within the citadel. When we have to use such water, we should strain it before boiling, and a towel that has not been used too long, or an old shirt, answers very well for that purpose. We think we have already exceeded our allowance of dirt, and that each one is well into his *half bushel*.

We had a sleeping chamber that night that was certainly *unique*, and a serenade that I shall never forget. Imagine yourself under a cart, with a pair of mules tied to the wheel on either side, pulling said cart first to the one side and then to the other, accompanying their efforts with braying—that most discordant of all sounds—which would be taken up by one after another, till such a concert as pandemonium alone can get up would banish all sleep, and you have the *status* of *our* department on the night of the 14th of March, 1863. About 11 o'clock a deep bass was added to the concert. It was the cannon's opening roar. Till near morning it was continuous, shaking the ground we laid on, which was only about eight miles from Port Hudson. We listened to the sullen firing, and with a soldier's joy awaited the coming dawn. It came with rapid, heavy firing and much confused harnessing of teams and artillery. Men spoke in whispers, and we faintly caught the word "retreat." Nearer sounded the guns, and lo! our whole division marched swiftly on *from* Port Hudson. Then came rapid, heavy firing, then a lurid glare mingling with the opening light, then a noise and shock that made the solid ground tremble, and then stillness and darkness. Fast we walked, and awe and half-panic seized many hearts. The sun arose, and no enemy followed us. On we went, dispirited, angry, fully believing we had suffered a severe defeat, and wondering why our division had been idle. Gradually we learned the facts. We doubted them long, and when it was officially declared that "the object of the expedition is accomplished," we esteemed it only an official lie to cover up a defeat that the unemployed troops might have converted into a victory. This is the history of the whole affair: Banks wanted to get past Port Hudson to cut off rebel supplies from up the river. In this he succeeded, as the Hartford and Albatross passed the batteries and landed some troops north of the stronghold. The land move was only a feint to aid the passage of the fleet. *How* we aided we can't see. The near firing, the light, the shock, were the death throes of the Mississippi. She had reached the upper part of the enemy's works and was almost out of danger, when, in the smoke and darkness, she grounded. While trying to get off she kept the enemy from their guns by firing *two hundred and fifty shots* in thirty-five minutes. Her crew were taken on board the iron-clad Essex, and she was then fired. The fire lightening her, she swung round by the force of the current and headed down stream. The guns of her port battery, which had not been fired, becoming heated, the venerable old frigate paid a parting salute to the rebels at the same time that she fired the minute guns over her own grave. Had she floated down stream stern foremost it is impossible to conjecture what would have been the result, inasmuch as her guns would have been discharged on her own crew, on the neighboring bank. Fragments drifted past Baton Rouge, causing the loyal to fear and traitors to hope.

The wagon trains and most of the brigades stopped at the Bayou Montecino, but our brigade marched into Baton Rouge and then immediately back again. While few or none fell out of the ranks in coming to the bayou, fearing the enemy might be behind, yet they returned from the city like scattered sheep, mad at themselves, mad at their generals, and mad at the colonel's horse, which kept on a mad pace, requiring the boys to trot to keep up. They did not keep up, but came in singly or in squads—hot, footsore, and tired. We encamped in an old cornfield, and it rained as it can rain only in Louisiana. It was a wet, gloomy night for us. Our shelter-tents proved a failure. Hulet and I slept, or tried to sleep, on a bed of cracker boxes only three feet wide. You may judge of the comfort of the regiment when I tell you our bed was almost Excelsior. Many of the officers took refuge in a dirty, but dry cabin, and looked forward to a good rest, but soon an order came that no man must sleep without the limits of the camp, and their hopes of comfort died out as they accommodated themselves to beds of rail, beneath which scorpions and lizards rested, and on which the generous rain descended. Our brigadier general was not much better off. He made his headquarters in a negro hut, so as not to disturb the ladies who occupied the mansion house of Mr. Pike. Co. C was sent out as pickets. Traveling through the mud for two miles they reached their posts, when they were informed that they were sent out in mistake, and through the now heavy rain they gladly returned, and on arriving at camp there learned that the order *calling them in* was a mistake, and they must return. In the mud and rain and dark they went back again. Glad they were that they had caught a mule, on which they lashed their tents and blankets. They were not so glad when the mule vamoosed, leaving them tentless and blanketless. Coming from Puritan land, their religion may have been rather *blue*. Certain it is that some *swore* till the very air was blue ; but they had to grin and bear it, comforted with the reflection, "'Tis sweet for our country to be *ducked*." Finding that his sweet potatoes were fast disappearing, Mr. Pike made a virtue of necessity and opened the holes for public use. These, with a few stray hogs and sheep and the inevitable coffee, the soldier's *elixir vitæ*, kept up our courage by keeping our stomachs filled. That Sunday passed, the only one in my life in which I could find no trace of the Sabbath, prick up imagination never so much.

We stayed at Bayou Montecino till yesterday afternoon. The weather was fine, so fine that nearly every one abandoned his woolen underclothes. Nothing of note happened. One morning we hoped to have a brush. A brigade went out toward the Clinton road, on a double quick. Alas! for our dreams of glory, it was a false alarm. Some nice vases, goblets, and articles of *certa* found their way to our camp from abandoned houses. A fancy upholsterer stored his stock in a remote cotton-gin house, safe, as he thought, from the touch of the vandals. That stock grew "small by degrees and beautifully less." What is pilfering? Is taking property lying about loose, having none to claim ownership, pilfering? If so, silence is discreet. War makes sad havoc with our ideas of *meum* and *tuum*. Strictly honest men, yet haters of rebels, might find that some of their Southern habits have a proclivity toward free quarters at Lenox. "I must live," said a man to Dr. Johnson, trying to excuse some defalcation. The grand old hater of wrong responded, " Sir, I don't admit that necessity." So, perchance, rebels and *quasi*-Unionists might have said as they saw us thinning out their stock to keep our lives comfortable. Certainly, though our consciences are not as tough as their beef, *that* larceny never troubles us. Last Monday we made a raid on the sugar-house of a Mr. Williams. Save the half idiotic wife of the overseer, the whites had fled. The negroes, glad to see us, piloted us to the luxuries. Half of the brigade must have joined in that raid. Men forgot their sore feet and lame backs. Sugar, molasses, and sweet potatoes were before them. Canteens were filled with molasses; haversacks, rubber blankets, even shirts bursted with sugar. For once the Government ration was enough. Next morning the order came to march. What to do with the sugar, fifteen pounds to a man—and the molasses, a quart each—was the question. Stowing away what they could stagger under they gave the rest to the negroes and the quartermaster. After this distribution they learned that marching orders had been countermanded. Then there was quite a rush on us for their sugar. some claiming twice as much as they had deposited. We gave it out *ad libitum*, heartily glad to get rid of it. Most of that Tuesday morning was occupied in making and eating molasses candy. Each man with his stick in hand gathered round his company fire and took his share of the goodies. The Lieutenant-Colonel's beard gave evidence that he had not outgrown his early tastes; the "tall-major" bowed in reverence to the boiling sweet, and brandished his candy stick with as much gusto as any subaltern; all the officers practically acknowledged, "a fellow feeling makes all equal," save the Colonel and Adjutant. I hope the reserve of headquarters was penetrated by a dish of army candy.

Rough experience brings its blessing in the form of a ration of whisky. The lovers of that article would have been better pleased if they had been allowed to take their whisky and *quinine* separately. As it is now served, vacillating Sons of Temperance resolve to abide by cold water. All but the cold. I used to be an ultra-temperance man, but since driven to decide between going without fluid or drinking something called water, obtained from the nearest bayou, *below* where horses and mules drink, and wash, at least, I am led into sympathy with Paul's advice to "take a little wine for thy stomach's sake and thine often infirmities." Levity aside! our drinking water is horrid and obtained from the dirtiest places with the most filthy surroundings. We have never yet pushed away dead mules to fill our canteens, but we have drunk water that your farmers would hardly wash their hogs in. Here in the city the water is cleaner, but very unwholesome. The Colonel will not allow us to drink it, so all our drinking water is carted from the river. While that is muddy it is

sweet. Throw a little alum into it and you clear it.
Of course, this is not practicable, so we must drink it
as it is. The fine sediment in it is absorbed by the
kidneys, and produces gravel, stone, and other diseases
of the kidneys. The water being so poor and warm,
having no snap to it, we use coffee to excess; hence
diarrhœa. Generally we issue half coffee and half tea,
but the former, seemingly more of a stimulant, is the
more acceptable. O! for one glass of Berkshire water.
I long for nothing so much. How often our fevered
sick yearn for the old springs by their mountain homes.
Alas! many will never again quaff from those springs.
Sickness is increasing rapidly among us. In some hospitals claret-wine is given to the patients. An iced-
claret punch is considered the *summum bonum* of all
drinks. To me claret seems a cross between sour cider
and poor port wine. You can buy it for fifty cents a
bottle in New Orleans; here we pay $1.50 for it. It
can not fairly be called an intoxicating beverage.

We returned to Baton Rouge, and be assured that
the "feint" has made us faint indeed. We settle
down, believing that there is nothing for us but camp
monotony and fighting the unseen enemies that lurk
in the air and water of Louisiana. Now, the ill effects
of enlisting men for so short a period are being manifested. "When is our time out? When will we go
home?" are the great questions of interest. The
strong ask them—for they see a dull future; the weak
ask them—for *they* see a short future bounded by the
grave. They only hope to expand their horizon of life
by an early move on Berkshire. The once prostrate
here rarely rally till the cool weather comes. Alas!
death comes more rapidly. Some hope that we will be
mustered out in Massachusetts, May 15th, being nine

months from date of draft, which our volunteering prevented. Some put it as late as June 10th, and some think we will not leave *here* before June 19th, when the term of service of seven companies will expire. If the Government wants us to re-enlist it will do well to send us home as early as possible, even straining a point in our favor. Give us a few months of Berkshire air, and we could return even to this grave-yard, and not have one-third as many on the sick list as we now have.

The soldiers generally like the enrolment act. No felons in the army; that is right. Make the cause too sacred for *felonious* hands to handle. Putting the minimum age at twenty years is a mistake. The statistics of the British army show fifty per cent. more of sickness in troops of twenty years and upward than under that age. Men of forty-five can stand more than boys of eighteen, but once prostrate they rally more slowly. Youths have a wonderful recuperative power. Our boys, under twenty, stand it better than any other class. Years have not robbed them of their elasticity. They rarely think of fatigue until they are exhausted. The increased prudence of maturer years does not count as much as youthful energy.

LETTER XXIII.

Camp Banks, Baton Rouge, La., *April 13, 1863.*

My Dear L.:

After quite a long interval, I take up the thread of narrative of the doings and surroundings of the Forty-ninth. On the 4th instant we moved to our present camp, which is on a rolling, shadeless spot on the borders of the city. The field and staff are in contiguity to a majestic oak, making their quarters as pleasant as can well be imagined for this vicinity. The soldiers are being massed together, the trees near our old camp cut down so as to give unbroken range for cannon, the fort and fortifications strengthened and finished; these things, in connection with Banks's movement on the west side of the river, do not teach that we shall always be holiday soldiers. If any movement be made on Port Hudson, troops and supplies from Texas through the Teche country must be cut off. Otherwise we might take that Gibraltar by storm, but would fail in reducing it by siege or starvation. Many of the troops in this department are nine months' men. If anything be done, it must be done by us, for Banks has not enough without us to reduce Port Hudson. It admits of serious doubt if, *with us*, he can add the surrender of that place to his laurels. I think he is preparing to starve out his foe, if storming should fail. To the east of us we have thrown up a series of rifle-pits between us and where the enemy will probably come, if he come at all. Do you know what a rifle-pit is? Well, it is a pit two or more feet deep and about three feet wide.

The dirt taken from it is thrown up on the side whence the attack is expected. The defenders of the pit stand therein while firing on the foe. Their heads are about the only parts of their bodies exposed, while they have full range of their assailants. The soldierly neatness of our colonel is apparent in the superiority of our rifle-pits over those thrown up by other regiments. *Our* pits are as finished as if they were parts of a permanent fortification. With spade in hand, he showed us how the work should be done. A nice house, with fine shade trees, stands right in the way of our fire. It will soon come down. *We* enjoy the prospect of its fall more than do its secession occupants.

"The children of this world are wiser in their generation than the children of light." Traitors take more pains to instil treason into their little ones than we do to imbue ours with loyalty. The children of this house, ranging from eight to twelve, seem quite well posted in the garbled statements that have cheated the Southern people. Many times have they half amused and provoked us. I saw a little toddler of three years of age, and asking her to kiss me, in remembrance of my own babe, I received the answer: "I won't tiss a Yankee." I laughed, so her mother thought she would reveal still more of her child's treasonable precocity, and put her through the rebel catechism. I send you three questions, with their answers, as specimens:

"Who are you, my child?"

"A rebel, by the grace of God."

"Who are the chief enemies of our happiness?"

"Lincoln and Seward."

"Is it wrong to kill a Yankee?"

"No; on the contrary, it is an act meriting the favor of God."

I have scarcely met a rebel, old or young, that was not quite well posted in the fancied wrongs of the South. I fear our people are not so well conversant with the *rights* we are defending. I heard the national song of the Confederacy, "The Bonnie Blue Flag." In poetry and music it is as much inferior to the "Star Spangled Banner" as the Confederacy is to the Union.

Speaking of our colonel's neatness reminds me that we are unquestionably the banner regiment of the first division in that respect. Soldiers copy after their officers. Neatness is a prominent characteristic of our commander. Who ever saw him looking slovenly? Who ever saw the lieutenant-colonel, or major, or adjutant, or surgeon dress unbefitting their rank? None. Go through our streets, you will say " neat": see our boys on parade—is there a musket unbrightened, a button or a brass unpolished, a sloven among them all? Not one. If one there should be, he had better keep close behind his file leader, for if the watchful eyes of the colonel (the boys say he can see out of the back of his head) should fall on him, he would have an opportunity to learn how nearly united are cleanliness and godliness, while standing guard under the weight of a loaded knapsack. The boys grumble at the time and toil this cleanness demands, but are well satisfied when they compare themselves with some of their neighbors, whose officers are careless in their attire. Berkshire never saw us in all our wealth of white gloves and glittering brasses. Many a future household will thank the Forty-ninth for lessons and habits of neatness. Company G are now acting as provost guards. They have a comfortable, gas-lighted house to live in and many of the appliances of civilization. Their duties are of a character to attract attention, and I think the *neatness* of the regiment led to one of its constituent companies receiving this compliment. This neatness reacts on our self-respect. A man with a clean body and clean clothes is not so ready to do a mean action as when body and clothes are dirty. A dirty Christian! did you ever see one? I never did. This attractiveness costs labor. A gun is a hard thing to keep clean and unrusted in a humid climate like this. Exposure on guard and picket duty makes it yet harder. Our white gloves were not purchased by the men without some dissatisfaction. The right of the colonel to compel them to buy articles of clothing not specified in the regulations or furnished by the Government is questionable. He did not *compel* any to purchase, but I understand he sent for one of the malcontents and *gave* him a pair of gloves. I have heard of no trouble since.

We live in our wedge tents, and our shelter tents furnish us with awnings that do much to break the fierce rays of the sun. Guards no longer walk their beats, but sit down under protecting awnings. Oh, it *is* hot here! Our tents are like ovens. Driven by the suffocating heat within, we go out only to meet the intolerable rays of a Southern sun. The nights bring no coolness, only the dank moisture. The winds blow high here. Often you can see the leaves rustling in the breeze, and pant in vain for a share thereof. Generally, there is some fresh air stirring on the river. Fortunately our main hospital is on its banks. By keeping their houses closely shut up during the day, the residents manage to be comfortable, but they say that in July and August keeping cool is an impossibility, but that the perspiration will roll from you while doing nothing and in the coolest places. We can readily believe them, for now, in April, our bodies are always moist. See us in our thick woolen garments, and you would suppose we would dissolve in perspiration, but this is the only climate in which a man can wear flannel next to his skin with pleasure. The constant perspiring destroys the itching, burning sensation so familiar to flannel wearers in the North. Speaking of itching reminds me that nearly every one is more or less troubled with the "ground itch," supposed to be caused by lying on or near the damp ground. White pimples, filled with humor, appear on the body. The itching is intolerable, and the only relief is wholesale scratching. until the blood runs. This produces scabs, which in some cases cover the whole person. This itch is a kind of outlet to fever. Drive it in and fever is almost sure to follow. Perchance bathing would mollify our torment. Until the snows of the Northern streams, that feed the Father of Rivers, are melted, the river is too cold for bathing.

Already we have flies in legions, and hordes of mosquitoes innumerable. Add to these, lizards (Howard felt something crawling up his back : on examination, a venomous, green, snaky lizard presented itself). spiders larger than walnuts, insects vaster and more numerous than ever entered our minds to conceive, and you can form some idea of the delights of a soldier's life in the "Department of the Gulf." The Government has furnished us with mosquito bars, so we rest in some degree of peace, lulled to sleep by the threatenings of myriad foes, turned into a doubtful music by the judicious arrangement of a little netting. Holland (A) came in from picket, and on his face you could not put a pinhead without covering the mark of a mosquito. He said they bit through his rubber blanket. Whether that was fact or joke. I know not; but we are prepared to swallow nearly any mosquito story, however large. I shall never think of a tropical climate without recalling the tropical prolificness of all pests.

C. Markman has resigned his post as cook of Co. B, and *we* have been fortunate enough to secure his services: so we are living as to make going home a matter of comparative indifference as far as the table is concerned. If we could only secure the destruction of the multitudinous ants, and had an extra hand to keep the flies out of our mouths while eating, and if it did not require so much dexterity to use a knife in lieu of a spoon in conveying butter from the dish to our plates, we could get along quite well. In some of my rambles outside the lines I secured several gallons of dewberries (remember, it is only April), many of which were twice as large as walnuts, and if you could have tasted our pies, you would have thought the lines had fallen to us in pleasant places.

Report has it that we to go to the "Army of the Potomac," and that our places are to be filled by three-years' regiments. Nine months' men should never have been sent so far away, but as that class are mainly from New England, and this is a "New England Expedition," we were sent here. I hope this report is true, for we would like to get out of this grave-yard. Going home is the great topic with us. Start any theme, and it will get around to that before the conversation ends. We have all kinds of rumors on that subject. The time of seven companies really ends the 19th of June, and no sophistry can extend it longer. We were mustered in as *companies* for nine months, and if discharging us at that time is inconvenient and embarrassing, the fault is not ours. Any attempt to keep

us longer will awaken bad blood, causing demoraliza-
tion, if not mutiny. Had we sworn to remain nine
months from the date of regimental organization, we
would keep our bond, but now we claim the letter of
the law. We will submit to our fate, however unjust.
We are in the eagle's grasp, and squirming will not
avail us. Mutiny, and how will we be fed, how get
home? These are questions more easily asked than
answered. This solicitude about a speedy return to
Massachusetts dishonors our patriotism, say you. If
assured that our country's welfare demanded our prolonged stay, we might be willing to stay, but now we
see only the wilting of our sick and the burial of our
dead. Put us before the enemy, and we would see the
19th of June pass by, and grumble, but our latent patriotism would be evoked, and we would not disgrace
our native State. *Nous verrons.*

Colonel Bartlett says we do not drill as well as we
did six weeks ago. That is true; we have not the snap
and vigor we had then. We are worked overmuch.
To-day there is company drill of near two hours in the
morning, in the afternoon brigade drill and dress parade, occupying near four hours. To-morrow you go
on picket or on guard. If on picket, you do nothing
the day of your return but appear at dress parade.
The next day you take your turn in the regular duties.
If on guard, the following day finds you doing police
duty and engaging in brigade drill. As sickness has
so reduced our numbers, picket and guard duties come
unpleasantly near each other. I do not know that the
colonel is responsible for this overworking. Were we
healthy and in the North, our labors would be just
enough to keep us fresh and vigorous. As it is, they
exhaust us. Though a cold snap reduced our sick from

168 to 116, yet we are mere shadows of our former selves. On leaving New York we averaged fifteen pounds per man more than when we enlisted. Now we average at least fifteen pounds *less* than when we entered the service. It is difficult to find a man who is not afflicted with diarrhœa. Men, disturbed by the operations of that disease half a dozen times in the day, would be called *sick* at *home; here* they are on the *well* list, and do full duty. This insidious disease is rarely overcome while living on camp fare. If not speedily overcome, it becomes chronic, and then farewell comfort, energy, life itself.

Our diet is as good as soldiers can expect in such a climate. If the meat and coffee ration were reduced one-half and the deficiency made up in vegetables, it would be better for us. There is much difficulty in obtaining a full supply of vegetables, even of potatoes, many of which are uneatable. Mixed vegetables, and desiccated potatoes, have been served out, but they don't take. With beef soup they might answer. Our salt beef is generally good, but this climate is too warm for pork. It becomes soft, oily, and maggoty. I can not see why salt fish can not be issued instead of meat. Herrings, mackerel, &c., would do much to render the rest of our food palatable. Of soft bread, we have enough and to spare. The excess enables us to get our washing done by negro women. Some luxuries find their way to the camp by the sale of meat not consumed.

Good cooking would do much to make our food healthful, but how can that be secured with one stove for a hundred men, more or less? Beans were prohibited for awhile, but finding we could get nothing in lieu thereof, we have returned to them. Cooked right, and we have no food so popular and wholesome ; but poorly cooked, and they are more fatal than rebel bullets. The officers enjoy better health than the privates. This is mainly owing to their better style of living. Though the law provides for the payment of rations not drawn, it is almost impossible to secure that payment. Who is to blame, I know not. Hard crackers toasted in hog grease is a favorite dish. Nothing can be more unwholesome, and the prohibition of the surgeon fails to stop the evil. Oh, for pay-day! Then the boys could get something to gratify their palates, and their diarrhœa would be checked. With some, that disease is the result of insufficient food. In its incipient stages, I have known it to be cured by an *abundance* of good food. This long delay of pay-day has much cramped our sutler, rendering him unable to obtain goods so as to trust us. This has been bad for us, and worse for him. I do not think he will make a fortune out of his position. Mr. Springstein is not fitted to be a sutler. He is a generous gentleman. I know few men who will do more to oblige another, and from what I can see, a *successful* sutler must be a compound of energy, extortion and closeness. A desire to go with the regiment, to spend the winter in the South, more than to make money, led him to accompany us. Captain Morey recently distributed a case of claret wine among his men. Among his many acts of kindness to his men, none has been more acceptable. He and Captain Weston have done much in this way to add to the comfort of their men, as have also many of the other officers. As a body they have shown much anxiety for our welfare.

The *morale* of the regiment does not deteriorate. Sundays are inspection days and holidays, but they are dull. Religious services are few and far between; no books or tracts to read, few things, save less drilling

and less card playing, to indicate the presence of the
Sabbath.   A member of the Christian Commission
preached for us last Sunday evening.   Drawn up on
the three sides of a hollow square, in the moonlight, we
listened to the grand old truths, the foundation of all
duties, and thought of Sunday evening meetings in
Berkshire.   God bless that Christian Commission.
The members of it work gratuitously for our temporal
and eternal welfare, and are doing much to raise up a
Christian soldiery.   God is measureably baptizing the
army.   I doubt not more, proportionably, are converted
in the camp than at home.   Soldiers will not return
corrupted.   On the whole, they improve.   They may
be divided into three classes.   First, Christians; these
knowing that peculiar temptations surround them,
that the unconverted are watching them, and that death,
by disease or bullet, may soon visit them, are led to increased watchfulness, and therefore grow in grace.
Second, moral men: moral by the power of education,
association and absence of temptation, whose morality
is not fastened to faith in Christ: these deteriorate.
Third, the dissolute, the rough: men who have had no
religious education, nor learned subordination at home.
These are benefited by their military experience.   If
liquor is as scarce and hard to be obtained in other departments as it is in this, the army is as good as a temperance society.   Officers can purchase liquor: enlisted
men can not.   The drunkenness of the Army of the
Potomac lies with the former.   Why should they have
the right to buy rather than privates?   Is a drunken
officer less prejudicial to the service than a drunken
private?   Do shoulder-straps render a man less liable
to temptation, or more impervious thereto?   I have
seen but two drunken officers in this whole department;

and but little reflections can be cast on their chastity. If licentiousness exists, it shuns the gaze of day. Sunday, when we came here, was kept as it is in France, but now all business is suspended, and we have the quiet of a New England Sabbath, though quite recently the theatre was open on a Sunday night. This mockery of a theatre is quite well patronized by officers and negroes: our empty pockets would keep us away, had we any desire to go. One of our general's staff officers demeaned himself by serving as stage-manager and actor. Whether it is because we are better than we were formerly or not, I know not, but punishment has become obsolete among us. We are an orderly set, as an army. A secessionist remarked that he did not know how our men were kept so quiet; you would not know, if you did not see them, that there were any soldiers about; that one company of their troops would make more noise than our whole army.

Frequent mails keep us in pleasant communication with Berkshire. The *Republican* and *Eagle* are almost as welcome as letters. The latter, especially, posts us in local matters and in many little items our friends do not write about, for getting *every* thing done or said at home has a charm for us now. Letters on both sides fail in details. Brevity is not now the soul of wit. Mail day is a great day with us. The lucky ones show by their cheerful looks that they have "heard from home," while to the sick letters are more invigorating than all the remedies of the surgeon. Unhappy they for whom mail after mail brings no token from absent friends. "Are you sure there is nothing for me?" "Quite sure!" and the hungry o..e clings to the hope that it may have been miscarried to some other regiment, and will soon find its way to him. When that hope dies out, home-sickness takes hold of him, and if he be otherwise sick, hastens him to the hospital or the grave. This is a *real* sickness. We have much leisure time, we know not how to fill it up, and so dwell often and long on the friends at home, till a desire for them is an unsatisfied soul-yearning that really prostrates. *Then*, a word of sympathy is as the voice of an angel. *Yearning* for this unattainable has shortened many a soldier's career. "Died of home-sickness" should be written on many a grave. The victims of this disease are not babes or cowards, but the finest spirits of the army. Alone in a crowd, craving sympathy and fearing the sneer, they wilt and die. How little our relatives understand what comfort and strength their letters inspire. If they did, they would always keep letters on the stocks, noting down what Harry said, or that sister has a new frock, or that the baby is beginning to walk, or that Mr. Smith is to be married to Miss Brown: all these things that go to make up their daily lives.

We have given up all hopes of a supply of reading matter. We hunger for something to read. Books are borrowed weeks in advance. Even Reynolds's trashy novels are read *through*, and that, too, by educated men. "Nothing to read," is the deep-toned complaint everywhere. The people at home do not know what sacrifice means. This mental hunger is fearful. Roam through our large hospitals and see what freedom costs. Till quite recently there were no *beds*. The sick lay on their one blanket till putrid, running sores were the result. No one stood near to brush away the flies and insects. Now all have beds, and mosquito bars enable them to rest in peace. Perchance all is done that can be done for their comfort; our hospitals are airy, sweet, and clean, and what delicacies can be obtained the sick receive, or at least the Government provides and pays for; but, oh! how unlike the ministrations of home. *Villains* find their way into the hospitals. Money and articles of value sometimes mysteriously disappear, to say nothing of luxuries sent to or bought for the sick. There *must* be a hell for *such* villains.

We hear favorable news from Banks, who is now in the Teche country. He is sending cotton, sugar, and molasses into New Orleans in quantities sufficient to meet a large share of the expense of this expedition. The rebels have cut the levee above us, on the west bank of the river, in hopes of flooding us out.

Adjutant General Thomas is now engaged in raising negro troops. How public opinion has changed! He used to be a bitter pro-slavery man. Many unwilling negroes are conscripted into the ranks. I do not object to that, but I do object to paying the negro soldiers less than whites. They do as much or more work, are exposed to the same hardships and to greater dangers, for their capture will be followed by their death, and they therefore should be paid the same. Paying a negro less for the same services than a white man is one of the remaining chains of slavery. Between the enlisting and the plantation scheme we hope that they may be cared for, and the fearful mortality that has cut off thousands be lessened. The next winter will be a dreary one for many of them, and no doubt selfish men on Government plantations will greatly abuse them, so that it may even seem that "abolishing slavery means abolishing the slave." The transition state will be accompanied by much distress and a sad mortality, but order will ultimately come out of chaos, and, having endured the pangs of freedom's birth, they will secure its blessings.

Death has been busy among us. The soul-eating monotony has often been broken by the funeral procession. We are learning too well the funeral call, with its mournful music, its measured tread, the reversed arms, the closing volleys, and the lively air played on returning from the grave to banish a sadness that will not be thus exorcised. Seth R. Webster (K) died of fever at the General Hospital in this place on the 15th of March. He was a married man, from New Marlboro', aged thirty-seven years, and is spoken of as a very nice man. His battle was fought in the hospital, where so many soldiers close their career of patriotic self-sacrifice.

On March 20th death made its first inroad into Co. A by striking down with the hand of fever William Taylor, formerly a finisher in Taconia Mills, Pittsfield. He died in the General Hospital at New Orleans, and leaves a wife and child to look for his return in vain. He was sick several weeks. As a soldier he was steady, faithful, and reliable. For once mirthful Captain Weller was sobered. He felt, indeed, that his family circle was broken. His sadness did him honor.

Morton Olds (F) died here March 21st. Fever was his foe. He was a steady, even-tempered farmer boy, of eighteen years of age, from Sandisfield.

Fever also struck low in death, March 22d, Eugene W. Pierce, Sergeant (B), of Windsor. He died, I believe, as he was returning to this place, but was buried at New Orleans. His father came on to visit him, but death had finished his work ere his arrival. He was one of our reliable farmer boys, aged twenty-one years, with bright eye, denoting no ordinary intelligence. He

was a good soldier and was one of the "color guard."
The common foe gave him no chance to guard those
colors amid the smoke of battle. His wish doubtless
was, *while so doing*, to give his soul out to God.

Allen M. Dewey, corporal in Co. C, died at New Orleans on March 23d. He was taken sick just as we left
Carrollton, and lingered with fever for six weeks. His
sufferings were borne with gentle patience. I saw him
lying on his one blanket emaciated, the bones working
through the skin, which was raw and marked with putrid
sores, gasping for breath, yet seemingly resigned. When
we made a feint on Port Hudson many of the sick were
removed to New Orleans. He was one of that number.
I fear it hastened his death. One of his comrades says
he died with all the calmness of him whose peace with
God was made. He was from Pittsfield, aged thirty-
five years, a melodeon maker by trade. He was a faithful soldier and a genial companion. We shall miss his
pleasant smile and that rich voice which so often cheered
us with its melodious song. Heaven's choir has received him, and his war has terminated in a hallowed
peace.

On the same day typhoid fever cut down Lyman
Lindsay (E) at this place. He was one of our Sheffield
farmers, aged twenty-two years, and his officers speak
of him as a *good*, nice boy.

Alexander Smith (C), of Lenox, died here March
28th. He was a shoemaker by trade, and only nineteen
years of age.

Nelson B. Stetson, Corporal (K), died at the General
Hospital, on the 1st instant, of fever. He leaves a wife
and child. He was one of Windsor's best soldiers, a
farmer, aged twenty-eight years. He was faithful and
reliable in all the positions of life, and, from all I can

learn, met death as one who had learned that "the sting of death is sin, but thanks be to God, who giveth us the victory through our Lord Jesus Christ." I attended his funeral. We went to the hospital, where hundreds far away from home are learning the hardest lesson a soldier or any one can learn, "to suffer and be strong." Roses in full bloom perfumed the fresh air blowing from the river, but very many were wrapped up in the insensibility or delirium of fever, inhaling, perchance, the fragrance of flowers that grow around the old homestead and cooling their fevered brows with breezes from their native hills. We went into the "dead-room." There were several corpses there, each one marked with the name, company, and regiment of the deceased. Discarding the coarse coffins furnished by Government, we tenderly placed all that remained of our comrade in a neat coffin, provided by the thoughtfulness of Orderly Gleason, and bore him without the lines. At the foot of a tree just bursting into bloom, on the shore of the Mississippi, we buried him. 'Twas sad, and tears from manly eyes attested how near home it came to each of us. Many have looked forward to an early return to Massachusetts, perchance Nelson among them; many loved ones there have counted the few intervening days, and as that quiet grave buries the hopes that gathered round him, so other graves will receive some of our number and the affections clinging to us. Friends will look for *our* return in vain and realize something of the price paid for a perfected liberty.

Near this grave Charles Bartholomew, of the same company, is buried. He was a boy of eighteen, from Sheffield. Fever closed his career yesterday. In the army, burial follows death speedily. Neat headboards are placed at each grave, on which names and regiments are painted. For a few years those boards will tell who for their country did die ; then they will disappear, and nothing but the heaped mounds will eloquently speak of that class, who, martyrs at a bleeding nation's call, were yet denied the proud privilege of dying on the field of strife. The authorities are preparing a cemetery to receive our dead, but these scattered graves seem more eloquent to me than any well-ordered grave-yard.

LETTER XXIV.

CAMP BANKS, BATON ROUGE, LA., *May* 10, 1863.

MY DEAR L. :

The long-desired paymaster has been here. Major Brodhead paid A, B, E, and F on the 23d ult., and then, the money giving out, the payment of the rest was deferred till the 30th ult. We were paid up to March 1st. When we contrasted our little piles with those of the officers, we were almost willing to bear their superior *burdens* for the superior pay. I do not think they are paid too much. A *real* officer is worth more to the service than a private. If increased pay would increase their efficiency, I would be in favor of that increase. Their expenses are greater than ours. They have to pay for the food they do not buy at cost of the Brigade Commissary three times as much as for the same kind of food at home. I have seen them where money could not secure food, and they were dependent on our generosity. The members of Co. D and E received on an average eight dollars more than the rest of us, yet only received pay from date of enlistment. By an error in pay-rolls, eight companies drew pay only from time of going into camp. Though sickness is alarmingly on the increase, yet pay-day has advanced the health of some, and would of more could delicacies be secured here. Pies and cakes are poison, for they are generally shortened with grease obtained from pork sold by the soldiers, some of which was diseased. Vegetables are scarce, and in this land of plenty

I have seen no edibles equal to the products of Northern gardens save dewberries. Provisions are so high that we can purchase but few good meals without curtailing the comforts of expectant friends at home. Large quantities of greenbacks have been sent to those friends. God bless the dear boys, needing money and its comforts so much, yet to be so mindful of the claims of parents, wives, and children. *Such* men will fight. For the first time for months have our sutlers (Springstein and Langdon) been in funds, but pay-day came too late for their success. They can not send North for supplies, and so have to purchase their goods at Louisiana prices. Of course, we pay very highly for everything we buy, and then blame them unjustly. Two dollars per pound for tobacco makes a big hole in our pockets. Pay-day brought liquor and intoxication to light, so it became necessary to close the saloons. For the sins of the few the many were punished.

The great event of the week has been the arrival of the Sixth and Seventh Illinois Cavalry, under Colonel Grierson. For eight hundred miles from La Grange, Tenn., to this place they rode on their errand of destruction. This raid injured the rebels millions of dollars. Near Bayou Montecino they met some Louisiana cavalry, by whom they were cheered, but they changed their tune, when they found out their mistake, on being led prisoners to this place. The Illinois boys are now our lions. Dusty, dirty, and worn they look, but manifest a good deal of that pride which one of their number expressed : "I would not give up my share of the honor of this raid for a farm in Illinois." Many of them exchanged their worn-out horses for the blooded nags of aristocratic stables, and not a few sported watches and various articles of jewelry. It was a grand raid, and has given Banks what he much needs, a body of cavalry.

> "Who has not heard of Grierson's raid.
> And the feats of valor therein displayed ?
> 'Twas a brave, bold dash through the hostile land
> That scattered terror on every hand,
> Making the rebel heart afraid
> At the daring valor of Grierson's raid.
>
> Through their cities and over their streams
> The flag of the Union once more gleams ;
> There's a curse on the air, but in under breath,
> As the troopers go on their work of death ·
> Like lightning flashes each loyal blade,
> To light the path of Grierson's raid.
>
> Onward, yet onward, the blazing roof
> Echoes in flame to the cavalry hoof;
> And fleeing forms in the midnight air,
> Revealed by the war-pyre's ruddy glare,
> Tell the story in fear displayed
> Of the woful, terrible Grierson's raid.
>
> Onward, yet onward, upholden the rein,
> Till the Union lines are compassed again,
> Where a meed of grateful honors is due
> For the troopers bold, and tried, and true ;
> And history never has deed portrayed
> That brighter shines than Grierson's raid."

The prisoners. one hundred in number, were visited in the prisons by many of the citizens of the place, and supplied with luxuries and bouquets. Most of them were large, fine looking, but poorly dressed. Some of Co. G's men escorted them to New Orleans, where, I suppose, they will be paroled, and set loose to fight us at Port Hudson.

Humanity and prudence triumph, and we are worked much less than before. We have dress parade at 8 A.

M., then have nothing to do till 4 P. M., when we go
out to battalion drill. The morning drills had become
a farce. The considerate officers would take their men
out as ordered, and then drill them in sitting and
lounging exercises. So reduced were we that it was
rare to see twenty men in a company at those drills,
and the boys say that one company presented itself at
dress parade numbering one officer and one private.

L. Hedger (E) won the brigade prize of $5 for the
best shot in the brigade. W. J. Campbell and F. Kill-
redge (C) were the next best shots. We think that is
pretty well for a regiment, many of whom never fired
a gun before entering the army.

On the 20th ult., Companies A, D, and K, under
Colonel Sumner, visited Du Planche's plantation, nine
miles below this place, to obtain corn. The men dined
as usual, while the officers enjoyed Du Planche's hospitality, which was extended to the rebels only two days
before, when near twenty of our men were killed and
wounded. A Mr. Conrad, brother of C. M. Conrad,
former Secretary of War, *contributed* some forty hogsheads of sugar to our commissary department. Various books, bearing the name of Miss Conrad, now en-
liven our monotony. My hands are *almost* clean of
plunder : almost, for at the deserted plantation of a
tyrant, Mr. Hatton, I "drew" six law books. The
books were odd volumes, scattered about on the floor,
doing no one any good. War *may* obdurate the conscience, but I read them with great tranquility and
peace.

On the 15th of April, Sergeant Brooks (C), Sergeant
Siggins (D), and Orderly Gleason (K) were appointed
by the colonel as second lieutenants in their respective
companies. How Governor Andrew will think these

appointments tally with the law requiring the *election* of the officers of militia regiments I know not. The two last are of that class from which officers should come; intelligent, prompt, reliable. The above were appointed to fill the vacancies occasioned by the resignation of Lieutenant Wells (C) (he never joined us after we left New York), Morey (D), and Taft (K), the latter of whom was prostrated with sickness. Lieutenant Gleason was presented with sword and sash by his associate officers of Company K. Colonel Sumner has been engaged for months as president of a general court-martial. Very many cases have been tried before that court. Talented, discriminating, firm, humane, his superior for that post could not be found in this department. Lieutenant Judd has been appointed Regimental Treasurer, for which his uncommonly fine business habits peculiarly adapt him.

Porter has passed Vicksburg with a part of his fleet, and now Banks can hold communication with Grant. A signal station has been located on the topmast of Farragut's flag-ship, which runs up near Port Hudson, and signals to those stationed on a mast of one of Porter's vessels. This is rather provoking to the rebels, but they can't help themselves. Nightly we hear heavy firing up the river, and hope the "forward march" will soon call the Forty-ninth into line.

Alas! how changed are we from the men who marched in that celebrated "feint" on Port Hudson. Then, we were worthy of any foeman's steel. Now, we are but spectres. Our sick list stands seven officers and two hundred and ninety-five "enlisted men." Remember, these are only they who are "excused from duty." We do full duty as long as possible. Many of the "well" properly belong to the sick list, and some in that list are shirkers. Mortifying it is, but true, that well men are found to play sick and to endure many of its penalties. The result is, the surgeon becomes suspicious, and not being infallible, remands some of the really sick to duty, and doing it, they die. A surgeon's task is no pleasant one. It is hard to decide who of reduced men are fit for duty, yet that duty must be done. The proud-spirited ones magnify their ailings that they may not be charged with attempting to "shirk" their duties. Dr. Rice tells of one man in his old regiment who cheated all the surgeons and got his discharge. When he left the harbor on his way home, he threw away his bandages and crutches and cursed them all for fools. If the surgeon could become personally acquainted with all the men, the characters of not a few would shield them from suspicion and undue labor. Dr. Winsor is a gentleman, and conscientiously performs all his duties. Naturally of a reserved temperament, he does not receive credit for the sympathy he really feels. We generally attribute to Dr. Rice superior medical abilities, and though with some peculiarities, a larger sympathy. Young Morey makes an excellent hospital steward. I do not think our Northern physicians understand the proper treatment of the zymotic diseases of the South. It seems strange to give quinine to men while fever is on them.

Every morning the sick call on the surgeons, who examine and prescribe for them. I have seen hundreds join in that procession. A mournful procession it is, one that would agonize many a Berkshire heart. I see it often, but never without sadness. Ask many of them what ails them and they can not tell. An unseen foe has consumed their strength. Yet their fever-lighted eyes, their emaciated forms, their shuffling walk and drawling speech tell too plainly that sickness with *them* is not shirking from duty. They return from the surgeon "excused from duty." How now to pass the weary day before starting for home is the question, for few expect a return of strength till they reach home. Alas! death is preparing for them a final home. The water they drink, everything they force into their unwilling stomachs produces or increases a strange feverishness. No cool spot invites them to rest. Their tents are like ovens, yet they must choose between them and the unbroken rays of a Southern sun. Hordes of flies by day and insects by night prevent repose. Few gentle breezes fan them by day, and the night brings no coolness save the dampness recking with malaria, a dampness so great that our easy boots are hard to draw on in the morning. Thus day and night pass. Each morning finds them weaker; nothing to do, nothing to read, sources of conversation almost dried up, they pass their weary hours as best they can, sadly enlivened at times by letters from loved ones they fear they may never again see. Often the consuming monotony is gloomily broken by the funeral drum announcing that with another and yet another comrade the weary struggle with its longings for home is ended. At last they are borne to the dreaded and crowded hospitals. There, though they have better care and diet, unless they have much of energy, they rapidly fail. Sick and sickness are all around them, the gossip of the comp (an unconscious tonic) hushed, the mind has naught but to prey on itself. Then comes from many a heroic soul: "Is *this* to be my end? Was it for *this* that I left parents, wife, children, all? Is *this* being an encumbrance to the army, the realization of my hopes of serving my country? Am I *here* to die, where no glory can gild the final scene, and where none of the tenderness of home can alleviate my then anguish? Oh, for one hour's strength! then the rush of battle and the soldier's grave; that around that grave those who love me may mourn, not with *pity*, but with a proud sorrow, saying 'he died as he listed with his face to the foe.'" No glory can gather round the final scene! Despairing hero! he erred: a halo of Christian and national glory has gathered round many such final scenes. The uproar of battle is marked by no grander victories than won by the uncomplaining heroes of the hospital. It is easy work to meet death when a world is watching every blow, ready to bind the victor's crown alike upon the brow of the living and the dead. But, to fight a long, slow battle with unconquerable disease, while our brothers are meeting the foe on the ensanguined field, whence our spirits fly, calls for a loftier courage than that which places the banner of the "forlorn hope" on the citadel of the enemy. *Then*, one all-comprehensive thought of home and loved ones, one grand rush and *victory or death*. Not so, him who sees Death an already crowned victor, walking the wards of the hospital to *his* cot. *He* has time for the anguish of parting. *He* mourns at what seems to him an almost inglorious death. *He* saddens as he thinks how his aged parents will weep to hear their only boy in death is lying low, or else forgetting he is dead, will sit and listening wait for his step upon the garden walk, his hand upon the gate. He knows that a sister's eye would flash could she but hear that he had nobly fought and bravely died; that pride would mingle with a wife's sorrows to learn that in the thickest of the strife he *fighting* fell, and for the honor of the dear old flag he yielded up his life. He thinks of his boy and imagines that in life's battle he would fight the better and the braver to know his father's soul went out to God upon the field of strife. War has no sadder chapter than that which records the struggles of the true soldier, when he finds that God has ordained the hospital, not the field, as his place of martyrdom. It is *this* that lends bitterness to death, and hard the struggle before the sinking soul can exclaim, "Thy will be done."

Soon we may add to our "fallen brave" those who die as soldiers crave to die. I would inscribe an humble "In Memoriam" to the heroes of the hospital. Death, tired of waiting for the hour of carnage, has reaped many into the lonely graves that deck the shores of the Mississippi since I last wrote to you. I wish I were better acquainted with their lives, that I might do them justice.

William J. Glead (B), a farmer boy from Otis, aged nineteen, died here of fever April 14. He was a stranger to me. I only know him as a good soldier.

Caleb C. Hinman, of the same company, died of fever April 16. His age was twenty-two years. He was a farmer from Becket. He was unmarried.

Isaac V. Wilcox (D) was cut down by fever April 18. I attended his funeral. We buried him near Stetson (K), sad to bury him in his early prime (he was but twenty years old), trebly sad to know that he was the third one of our number who was borne that same day to burial. We fired the volleys over his grave, and thought of a home in Barrington over which a great darkness was settling, and returned realizing that one who though weak in body was ever ready and faithful as a soldier would no more greet us. Beloved in life by all he was. We love him no less now. A mother gave two of her boys to the service. God has seen fit to make the gift of one an eternal gift. Happy the parent who turns away from this bereavement with a deeper, purer love of country.

In Sheldon E. Gibbs's death by fever April 21st, Co. F lost a quiet, fine soldier and Stockbridge a good citizen. He was twenty-eight years of age, and a daguerrian by occupation.

George Kolby (D), of Barrington, died April 21st, at this place. His age was twenty-seven years. He was a German, the stoutest man in his company, one who all prophesied was most likely to endure the wear and tear of a soldier's life. Death met *him*, as he meets so many in this climate, in the form of diarrhœa. He leaves a wife and two children to mourn his early death.

James A. Jourdan (B) died of fever April 22. He was a farmer from New Ashford, and though thirty-six years of age leaves no family. He was a good soldier.

On the same day, of diarrhœa, Co. B lost a good, moral man and an excellent soldier, in the person of Isaac Denslow, farmer, of Becket. His age was thirty-nine years. He leaves a family to remember the Forty-ninth with sadness. He was a nurse in one of our hospitals. Death met him, and wife and children were far away, strangers nursed him, and comrades buried him.

Ebenezer Hinman, farmer, of Sheffield, aged fifty-nine, died of diarrhœa in our camp hospital April 24. He was the oldest man in the regiment, and while he had health could do and endure as much as any other, but like old men, and especially in this climate, he had but little reserved strength to fall back on in the time of sickness. He came with us because the members of Co. E wanted his advice and care. Though garrulous, Captain (he was once a militia officer and quite well posted) Hinman was a nice old man, of excellent principles, and died with so pleasant a smile on his face that we thought he must have "laid down to pleasant dreams."

Nelson M. Case (F), of Sandisfield, aged twenty-two years, died of fever in the hospital at this place April 25. T. M. Judd, his brother-in-law, was hastening to see him, but death traveled more rapidly, and Nelson died without a brother's presence. He was a good soldier. That is a matter of course, for he was a *Christian* soldier. Early had he dedicated himself to God, and he entered the army as a matter of duty. An only son, his parents could illy spare him, and by pecuniary arguments tried to convince him that duty and interest pointed to his remaining at home. He felt his country claimed his services, and they were cheerfully rendered. He was pleasant in his life, and though sorrowing parents in their loneliness may find it hard to see that his early death conduced to a nation's welfare, yet his grave eloquently teaches lessons of patriotism. His brother-in-law has had his remains exhumed, that the soil that gave him birth may also give him a final burial.

Sandisfield has lost another of her citizens. Milton Smith (H), aged forty-four years, died April 28th. He was cook for his company. I believe he leaves a family. He was sustained in death by a trust in Christ. He so lived amid the temptations of camp that all unite in saying, "a *good* man has gone to his eternal rest."

Waldo R. Fargo (F), of Monterey, died here May 2. He was one of our fifers. He was but twenty years of age. He left a good home to share the privations of his soldier comrades. He was an excellent penman and accountant; one of those bright young men whose loss causes us to feel that this war may be a blessing, but a blessing bought with the most precious part of our wealth. At home and abroad was Waldo esteemed. With him I close the sad list. It may be a *glorious* list, but so covered with blasted hopes that many years will roll away before weeping eyes can fully discern the glory. They sleep in their quiet graves, a small portion of the host of New England's dead.

"Oh! chant a requiem for the brave, the brave who are no
    more,
New England's dead! in honored rest they sleep on hill and
    shore;
From where the Mississippi now in freedom proudly rolls,
To waves that sigh on Georgia's isles, a death hymn for their
    souls.

But not *alone* for those who die a soldier's death of glory;
Full many a brave, heroic soul has sighed its mournful story,
Down in the sultry wards and cots, where *fever's* subtle breath
Has drained the life-blood from their hearts and laid them
    low in death.

As proud a memory *yours*, oh! ye who murmured no com-
    plaint,
Who saw Hope's vision, day by day, grow indistinct and faint;
Who, far from home and loving hearts, from all yet held most
    dear,
Have died! Oh! noble, cherished dead, *ye* have a record here.

New England! on thy spotless shield, inscribe *these* honored
    dead.
Oh! keep their memory fresh and green, when turf blooms
    o'er their head;
Oh! deck with fadeless bays their names, who've won the martyr's
    crown."

LETTER XXV.

CAMP BANKS, BATON ROUGE, LA., *May* 19, 10 P. M., 1863.

MY DEAR L.:

The long expected "forward march" has come. We are directed to be in line in light marching order to-morrow morning at 5 o'clock. We feel *this* is no false alarm, no feint. We are to go home a tried regiment. We shall soon show if we merit the proud appellation, "Massachusetts Soldiers!"

Last Wednesday we marched sixteen miles as guard to a supply train; thought the whole regiment was going, but when we found the colors were left behind we knew there was little chance to win honors. The major was in command. All we did was to carry food to Dudley and return home.

Lieutenant Tucker (D) takes a position on Colonel Chapin's staff. It was urged on him. I hope our loss will prove his gain. R. D. More leaves us to aid the Brigade Quartermaster. C. French is in the office of the Medical Director. They are both from Company D, and are detailed to do work requiring much business talent and clerkly skill. More of the members of Company D have been detailed to fill such posts than of any other company in the regiment.

As we are on the verge of solemn events this *grave* poetry, as copied from the tombstone of a cemetery in this place, may be pertinent:

" Here lies buried in the tomb,
A constant sufferer from salt rheum,
Which finally, in truth, did pass
To spotted erysipelas."

And again. " Here lies the body of David Jones ; his last words were, ' I die a Democrat and a Christian.'" Poor fellow ; he got party first and Christ last. In the closing hour when men are apt to see truth most clearly he may have seen the *incongruity* of his two professions, and desired to establish their *congruity* by a death-bed testimony. If he had reference to *modern* Democracy it needed that the testimony be made as solemnly as possibly.

I heard a soldier pray at one of the negro meetings that God would hear the prayers of fathers, mothers, wives, and "the lispings of our little ones." Oh, the power of those little ones ! There was scarcely a dry eye in the house. Plainly we saw our "little ones" kneeling in prayer for us, for there are few soldiers' children that have not been taught thus to pray. I hope that God *will* hear those " lispings." We are nearing the hour in which prayer will mean more than it ever meant before.

We will march about four hundred and fifty strong— all of the thousand who left Berkshire deemed fit for duty, and many of them are *not* fit. The convalescents will stay to aid in defending this place. As our brigade has been alone for some time, we have manned the entire picket line. We leave behind us among the sick some of our most reliable men. Our marching against the foe without them will be one of their heavy trials. The trial is greater when they reflect that even their absence from the field is not likely to lengthen their lives to the day of reunion with the loved ones of earth.

My next. if my own obituary shall not prevent it. may tell of battles fought and won with the blood of my comrades ; so I will prepare against that sad contingency by recording our deaths up to this date.

William D. Leonard (K) died here May 12th, of fever. He was from Savoy, a married man. aged thirty-two years. He is spoken of as a very nice man, one who attended to all his duties.

Samuel C. Bells (D), farmer, of Barrington, died of typhoid fever May 14th, aged twenty years. The regiment loses in him a good soldier, and his company a fine associate.

Seth R. Jones (A), a Savoy farmer, aged twenty-two years, died of chronic diarrhœa in this place. May 16th. A few days before his death he came from the hospital to the camp, and his looks caused us to hope that he would soon return to duty. The next news was that he was dead. His captain speaks of him as a tip-top soldier. He was steady, much respected, and sincerely mourned.

On the 15th inst., Francis Joray (I) died of fever, at the age of thirty-eight. He was from Stockbridge, and leaves a family to mourn the loss of their provider. He was a good soldier. Though France gave him birth, he died in defense of American principles.

Sandisfield and Company H lost a steady, fine man and reliable soldier (one of my best, says his captain) of diarrhœa, on the 16th inst., Frederick P. Seymour, aged nineteen. He was a fine-looking man, and his character corresponded with his appearance. He was a farmer.

James J. Smith, aged thirty-nine years, surveyor, of Sandisfield, died here on the same day, May 16th. He leaves a family to cherish his name. He was a good-

hearted man and respected by his comrades. Sandisfield has lost many of those she offered for the nation's
weal. May their memories be cherished by her citizens
and their examples imitated. We feel that death has
been greedy ; alas! these are merely the first-fruits,
and I close this record to go forth to his *harvest*. There
is life in death. *Our* death may be necessary to the
life of Freedom. If so, amen!

LETTER XXVI.

Before Port Hudson, La., *May* 26, 7 a. m., 1863.

My Dear L.:

Precisely at 5 a. m., May 20th, Col. Sumner (Col. Bartlett being sick) led us from camp, and without any noteworthy incident we reached Merrick's plantation, about sixteen miles from Baton Rouge, where we encamped for the night. For the first five miles the road was shaded with trees, and the boys got along comfortably. If a man has any vitality left, a march through a Southern forest is a matter of great pleasure. Everything is prolific, and in many places the underbrush and vines make an inpenetrable jungle. The trees are gigantic; from their branches hangs the melancholy moss, and often grape-vines descend and take root and send up other vines, till you have before you miniature Banian-trees. Vines of various kinds form grottoes that are wonderfully beautiful, and, twining round stunted trees, present pyramids of beauty that would make *our* lawns, could they be transplanted, the cynosures of all eyes. Conspicuous, pre-eminent is the magnolia. From a bed, first of very dark leaves, then of bright yellow ones, springs a large whitish flower, "a thing of beauty and a joy forever."

The ravages of war had marked the houses on the road since first we marched over it. The road itself was torn up or obstructed in places. With the usual amount of swearing, our trains safely passed the Bayou Montecino, and we followed to meet the fierce rays of the sun. Then the debilitated condition of the men was apparent. Not seven alone fell out, as in our first march ; their name was scores. Many of them were unfit for the work before them. In defiance of the advice of their comrades, almost in defiance of the commands of their officers, some joined us. Honorably excused by others, they could not excuse themselves. From afar they scented the battle, and their convictions of duty were so strong that they could not stay behind. Perchance some have a dim presentiment that Death is on their track and that the monotony and loneliness of camp would but hasten the ravages of sickness, and they have come, hoping that activity, excitement, and change of scene may strengthen them, or that they may strike one blow for their country and find soldiers' graves. Hope and will carried them over weary miles, till failing nature caused them to succumb. We loaded our wagons with them, and thus riding a while and resting a while, their comrades—in some cases, officers —carrying their guns, they kept up or came staggering on behind. In all their weakness, they remembered that the enemy was in front and that their country needed every fragment of a man who could fire a gun at the foe. The buoyancy and cheerfulness that characterized our first march towards Port Hudson had disappeared, but in its stead was a determination, a fixedness of purpose, that boded no good to rebels. Many of these men were fresh from the hospitals; others could have remained in camp, where were some who needed nothing but courage to be effective men. Impending battle tries the stuff men are made of.

We had marched near twelve miles, when orders came for Co. G to return to Baton Rouge. That company is not *exclusively* composed of Christians, and as they re-

traced their steps, they showered on the author of that
order a volley of expletives not to be found even in
Webster's Unabridged. Their return was a matter of
regret to us all, for they numbered nearly twice as many
as any other company—their duties as provost guards
having secured them from exposure and consequent
sickness and death. I regretted it for Capt. Parker's
sake. He was too unwell to command his company, so
rode with us, hoping to be counted in the day of battle.
They may find consolation in the enlargement of their
sphere of duties at Baton Rouge, and if the rebels learn
the weakness of our force there, they may have an opportunity of exhibiting their prowess in battle.

The colonel rode to the ground in a carriage. We
greeted him with cheers. We did not mistrust the
lieutenant-colonel and major, but they were untried.
In the colonel we have implicit confidence. His voice
alone keeps a regiment steady, it is so clear, so indicative of self-possession. I never heard a voice fuller of
command.

"One blast upon _that_ bugle-horn was worth a thousand men."

Save the firing on the river, the night of the 20th
was uneventful. We killed a mammoth ox to serve
out in the morning. You can judge of its condition :
Some of us secured the liver, and searched the animal
in vain for a quarter of a pound of fat to fry it in.

The morning of the 21st found us early in line,
and _beefless_, we hastily breakfasted, and continued our
march. We had marched but a few miles when the
battle of Plain's Store commenced. Grover had encountered a masked battery. I met a pioneer carrying
a gun in addition to his axe and shovel, and relieving
him of his gun, took my place in the ranks of Co. D.

I was but little acquainted with the officers or men of
my own company (C), and between Capt. Chaffee and
myself there was much sympathy in relation to the
great principles for which we were to fight, and quite
an intimate acquaintanceship, so I ranged myself under
his command. Slowly we pressed our way. Soon
wounded men and bleeding horses were brought to the
rear. Shells shrieked and bursted. Our first battle
had begun. A strange sickness came over me. I
doubted if it were right for *me* to fight, and was tempted
to retreat to the safety of the quartermaster's department. But *that* was no time to reconsider a grave
question, so I fell back upon the conclusions I had
reached in quieter times, though, in the fear and excitement of the hour, I could not recall the arguments
that led to those conclusions, and determined I would
walk in the path of duty, though it led to the jaws of
death. I felt no more fear that day, for *will* triumphed.
We pressed on to the music of shells—a music shrieking, wailing, infernal. They tore through the woods,
in which Co. A was ordered to skirmish. Then the
49th was advanced beyond the 48th Mass., and the
firing lulled for several hours. Facing new dangers,
we ate but little dinner, and endured the suffocating
heat as best we could, till again called into line. We
reached a large field, stacked our arms, and expected
there to bivouac for the night, but before leaving the
ranks our ears were greeted with discharges of artillery.
Just ahead of us another masked battery had been discovered. The firing was so rapid that the roar was
continuous. Oh, it was grand! I never heard anything half so inspiring. It made the wild blood leap
through the veins, and stiffened every muscle. I had
heard of the "joy of battle." I understood it then.

"Fall in, Forty-ninth;" and we wheeled round, bringing the left of the regiment (B), instead of the right (A), in front. We marched into a dense wood. The roar of artillery was mingled with the continuous volley of musketry. The genius of treason could have selected no more appropriate place for a masked battery. B, K, and C pressed on till they crossed a main road, and fired three volleys at the enemy. The road through the woods was so narrow that we could see but little in advance of us. Then came, "About face! double-quick!" We thought it was an order, and one-half the regiment turned *from* the foe. I heard it plainly, though I did not "about face." I saw that a large number did not wheel round, and so I went forward to see and do what I could. There was no panic, though the broken 48th was tearing through our ranks. As soon as we discovered our mistake, we wheeled and pressed forward. We reached the main road. A caisson with a pair of horses tore past us. We could hear wild shouts, and drew up in line of battle to greet the advancing foe. He did not come. The colonel ordered us to charge bayonets. Following him, we entered a tangled thicket. Finding that neither man nor beast could get through there, we came back and "changed front"—always a nice piece of tactics—thus bringing us into our accustomed positions, and marched back, hoping still to flank the rebels. Just ahead of us was the gallant 116th New York. As we came up, they charged with a wild cheer across the road and through the woods. We passed by the slain and wounded, half averting our gaze, fearing the sight of the first dead might unman us. Then we met Gen. Augur, who said, with all the coolness and suavity of the drawing-room, "This way, colonel, if you please, with your

regiment." The colonel bowed in response, and we
marched into an open space. Here the enemy had us
in full range, and the shells shrieked and bursted over
our heads as if a legion of fiends had been let loose.
The colonel and adjutant alone remained mounted.
We kept on in good order till we reached a fence, on
either side of which we marched to the edge of the
woods. I could see the splinters fly from the rails, assuring me that the valley of death was indeed before
us. Though not quailing, it was quite a relief to hear,
right on the verge of the fiery forest, the order, "Lie
down." We obeyed. Shot and shell plunged past us,
which seemed not half so fearful as the unbroken roar of
musketry. While lying there, what seemed a new battery, and very near us, opened its treasures of death.
The colonel directed Capt. Weller to ascertain its position. Alone, he stepped into the dark woods. A cannon-
ball almost grazed him, but he safely returned, unable
to give the needed information. The firing lulled and
ceased. Right there the colonel put us through some
tactics, so as to increase our self-possession. About
that time a corporal of Co. I came straggling from the
rear. The colonel wanted to know what he meant by
being away from his company. He hesitated, and the
major was ordered to cut off his chevrons, or corporal's
stripes, which punishment was speedily inflicted.

Soon after we had silenced the enemy before us, the
battle reopened in the rear, near our hospital, endan-
gering the wounded and causing our quartermaster and
his staff to run a gauntlet of fire. For three-quarters
of an hour that fight was kept up, and then the enemy
retreated. So closed a day's fighting, which had lasted,
with an occasional lull, for nine hours. The rebels were
whipped at every point. Their dead and wounded left

on the field greatly exceeded ours in number. Our troops bivouaced for the night on the battle-field. At midnight General Gardner sent in a flag of truce, and received permission to bury his dead the next day. Our loss is nineteen killed and eighty wounded, and a few missing. Some of the missing were found making excellent time towards Baton Rouge. The casualties in our regiment are as follows: R. A. Green (A), ankle slightly; J. B. Scace (A), bullet passed through fleshy part of his leg—he is doing well; S. Kettles (I), hand slightly; Lieutenant J. Tucker (D), right leg. The brigade flag made a conspicuous mark and drew many shells, one of which exploded near Colonel Chapin and his staff, partially stunning the colonel and shattering Lieutenant Tucker's knee, so that his leg had to be amputated. He bore it well, and his fine physical health will carry him safely through it. As soon as the colonel heard of Lieutenant Tucker's loss, he sent a message to him to be sure and have his leg cut high enough. His own was cut too low down and often he suffers much. He receives our hearty sympathy, for he is a valuable officer and a genial companion. Deprived of one limb, yet his appreciation of the sacredness of the cause is such that he will feel vastly richer than those who, by staying at home, have preserved all their members and sullied their honor.

In describing the battles in which we may be engaged I purpose to describe to you only the part our regiment takes and so much of the engagement in general as may be necessary to enable you to understand *our* history. A *soldier* actively engaged sees a good deal of smoke, a good many men fighting, and can tell you but little save what transpired in his immediate vicinity. We traveled nearly north from Baton Rouge on the road to Bayou

Sara. Plain's Store is situated where that road crosses the Clinton and Port Hudson road. It is, or was, simply a drug-store and postoffice on the lower and a Masonic lodge on the upper floor. North of this store, on the Bayou Sara road, a masked battery opened on us, commencing the afternoon's fight or the battle proper. General Augur had sent a section of artillery down the Port Hudson road, with the Forty-eighth Massachusetts as a support. You are aware infantry troops always accompany artillery, otherwise a small force of the enemy could spike or capture our guns. Suddenly, and but fifty feet from the Forty-eighth Massachusetts, Miles's Legion, comprising near a thousand men, opened fire. The Forty-eighth ran down on us, just as part of our left had emerged from the wood-path across the Port Hudson road. Two of our artillery horses were killed, so that the gun could not be brought off; it fell into the hands of the foe, but was afterward recaptured. Our left stood steady and checked their advance. Seeing but a few men across the road, the rebels came on through the woods to flank us and were met by the One Hundred and Sixteenth New York, who were behind us. Had we been able to penetrate the thicket when ordered to charge bayonets, we would have hemmed them in between us and that regiment and bagged them all, thus lessening the number of future foes and giving us much of that honor which now properly belongs to the gallant One Hundred and Sixteenth. That regiment made a grand charge through the woods, and when the enemy rallied near a grave-yard, repelled it and victoriously closed the day.

Our boys acted well. It is strange that they were not panic-stricken. *Veterans* might have been when ordered to "About face! double quick!" (we thought it was an order) amid the heavy firing of concealed foes, while one of their own broken regiments was tearing through their ranks. One or two disgracefully fled, but the rest were obedient to the orders they understood. The field officers were in front, where the danger was, and when they came to the middle and rear of the long column (we could only march through the woods four abreast), and we knew what to do, we coolly did it. Sergeant-Major Wylie was knocked over and stunned by the wind of a shell, and several of the officers narrowly missed the fatal blow. R. H. Wilcox (C) had a bullet pass through his cap-box, belt, blouse, and which was finally stopped by his pocket Testament at Luke xxi, 31. For once, at least, he *felt* the power of the Word. His life-preserver was presented, through Dr. Todd, by the Berkshire Bible Society. If spared to return he ought to be a *life* contributor to that society. Captain Garlick captured a rebel in the woods alone. Our adjutant acted nobly, riding his little sorrel into the thickest of the fire, and showing himself heir of the old Boston pluck. We like him now better than ever before. Before he appeared to us only as an adjunct to the colonel. Not intimate with the officers, not remarkably well drilled, not devoid of a little of Boston self-complacency (though always the gentleman), and especially not being a Berkshire boy, he had small hold on our confidence or affections; but we *adopt* him now. If he is not as cool as the colonel (who is?), he is his brother in courage. How soldiers love the brave! When we were lying down on the ground and saw him quietly sitting on his horse we concluded, "He'll do;" and though he was quite emphatic in his remarks and not very flattering when we "about face," we like him none the less. When they were stepping back after that false order (we only re-

treated a few steps), Captain Halstead came dashing
through the woods shouting, "Don't be d—d cowards."
I could not help replying (Massachusetts' pride was
up): "We are not d—d cowards; only tell us what to
do." Chaffee brought his company (D) around, and
the rest followed suit, and all was well again. It was
amusing to see Sergeant Murray (D) take a bewildered
fellow by the shoulder, wheel him about, saying, "The
rebs are this way;" and when he *so* understood it, *that*
was the way he wanted to go. Before attempting to
charge through the thicket we drew up in a diagonal
line across the Port Hudson road, ready to fire. Every
second we expected to see the foe. Strange thoughts
flashed athwart our minds, the prominent one being,
Will I get a chance to fire before I am hit?

The next day dispatches were read before every regiment that Grover had joined Banks near Bayou Sara,
and that Grant had so invested Vicksburg that General
Pemberton could not use his siege-guns. We cheered
with an energy that thrilled like electricity. Oh, to
have made a bayonet charge *then!* Soldiers, machines!
Far from it. The *individual* may be; the *collective* is
the most excitable, easily influenced object you can
imagine. General Sherman has come up the river road,
and hems in the rebels on the south, our left; Grover
and Emory on the north, our right; and we on the
centre. Beat us or surrender they must, *escape* appears
impossible. We have a large park of artillery, which
is being added to by heavy siege-guns from the fleet.
The vessels above and below Port Hudson may give us
some help, but they can not attack it in front, for the
river, still falling, has fallen so much that the channel
is too narrow for naval manœuvres. By assault or siege
the land forces must do the work. We are in high

spirits. We have met the foe, and have not been found wanting. The monotony and inactivity of camp life are over, and we begin to understand why soldiers are healthier on the march than while in camp. Our rations taste more like food. We have something to look forward to, and the prospect of a larger battle experience calls out our pride and our ambition, and awakens the determination to be worthy of Massachusetts and of the cause, and, I may say, of Berkshire. There is a charm to us in that word. "Rally, Berkshire!" would inspire the Forty-ninth more than any other war-cry. "Rally, Massachusetts!" is too large; the individual is lost in it; but each one realizes he is a part of Berkshire, and is well content so to demean himself that *Berkshire* may say, "Well done!"

I visited Plain's Store. It showed the marks of war. One of our solid shots passed through the lower story, disemboweling one man, while in the woods was found another man torn in pieces by a shell. Another shot burst open the door of the Masonic Hall, and entered, not regarding the Tiler nor waiting the permission of the Worshipful Master. It was the novel initiation of a candidate, who gave ocular proof of his ability to "work" well. A ball struck a piano in the adjoining dwelling, playing "Hail Columbia," with variations. Solid trees were cut down, whole panels of fence broken and scattered, and on the ground were bushels of grape and canister.

Sunday morning we marched nearer Port Hudson. A hot march it was. We progressed slowly, sending out skirmishers to clear the way and prevent us falling into an ambuscade. While on the road Gen. Banks passed by and was greeted with hearty cheers. His looks inspired confidence, and the manner of controlling his

fiery horse bespoke nerve. He pleasantly remarked:
"I see straw hats are all the fashion." Of course we
had to laugh. He was dressed plainly and wore a
slouched hat. The pictures of battles representing all
in imposing attire are far from the truth. If the truth
must be spoken, soldiers on a march look slovenly, and
the officers appear but little better. Traveling in dust
ankle-deep destroys all distinctions in dress. When
marching you must not suppose the order of the parade
ground is observed. So we keep together it little matters how we step or how we carry our guns. We slouch
along, talking, smoking, laughing. I want to tell you
once for all that a "line of battle" is the whole regiment in line two ranks deep. Mass men as they are
when parading through streets, and scores would be
uselessly slain. Formed in line, a regiment, brigade,
or division sweeps on, and if followed by another, there
is generally quite a space between them. The front
rank fires and then wheels to the rear of their respective
companies and reloads while the rear rank is firing.
This is the rule, but often the practice is fire how and
when you can, only fire and that low, for it is easy
when shooting at an enemy five hundred yards distant
to send your bullets over their heads. We had marched
about two miles when a masked battery opened. Fortunately it was directed away from us. Had it been
directed up the road hundreds of us would have fallen.
To obviate this one of our batteries made a *detour*
through the woods, and we looked on at the artillery
duel in comparative safety. The rebel shells mostly
fell short, disturbing nothing but some young corn.
Ours must have been better aimed, for in an hour they
withdrew their battery. While the duel lasted it was
very earnest and inspiring. Through all that Sabbath

day batteries contended with each other, and at night we encamped in the woods within a mile and a half of Port Hudson, rocked to sleep by a music which is becoming quite familiar to us.

We are yet in the woods ; officers and all roughing it alike. Our only complaint is with reference to the water, which grows scarcer and meaner the further we advance. You may judge of quantity and quality by this incident. On that Sunday I was so desirous of a drink that I went over to where the Indiana battery was engaged, a mile and a half off, hearing that near there water could be obtained. Disregarding, in my thirst, the heat, the distance, the exploding shells, I went to the spot designated. I smelt the fluid, turned from it with nausea, and then swallowed one mouthful, which proved a more speedy emetic than the "ipecac" of the surgeon. For cooking we cart water from the neighboring wells, meagre in quantity and poor in quality. A tablespoonful serves for a man's toilet. Our main occupation yesterday was the discovery and destruction of wood-ticks, a small, speckled bug with numerous legs, to each of which is attached a claw. He or she (it is venomous enough to be a "she" rebel) burrows under the skin, rapidly causing a small boil, and when you try to pull him off you pull a piece of the flesh with him, and an irritating sore remains to add another pest to your fond recollections of the Sunny South.

Dr. Rice has reached us, having traveled over the road from Baton Rouge alone and at night. A battle would be preferable to that night road. Running his horse saved him from the attentions of some strangers, who requested him to halt. Dr. Reynolds has been added to our medical strength. This filling up the complement of surgeons suggests some unpleasant features of the future. Colonel Sumner narrowly escaped capture on Sunday by riding too near the rebel pickets. We could illy spare him. We got some fresh beef to vary our diet. One of the boys had such a hankering after his mother's milk-house that he thought it was a shame that the milk of a dying cow should be wasted, so he filled his cup with that desirable fluid while she was kicking off the mortal coil. Day and night the men are required to keep on their equipments, a burden that has to be borne to be appreciated. We nearly lost a part of our Wagonmaster Hulet; a piece of a shell passed right under his foot as he lifted it up. Mr. Brewster saw it and wondered why he did not drop. His hour had not come, for which *we* are very thankful.

Accompanying us is a Catholic priest in a carriage. He is amply prepared to act the good Samaritan to the wounded as well as "shrive the dying and to bless the dead." All honor to the nameless Christian. In contrast is a Mr. Kelty, a brother-in-law of Lieut. Siggins. One of his sons was killed in battle, and one murdered in cold blood by a rebel officer, now at Port Hudson. He comes on a message of vengeance. Such are life's contrasts.

Last night will long be remembered by us. We thought it probable the enemy would try to break through our lines. Gen. Augur prepared to receive him. Opposite the woods where we are encamped is an immense field, bordered all round by a high fence and a thick blackberry hedge. At right angles to the Port Hudson road is a lane. Part of our brigade was placed in the main road and part in the lane. Gaps were made in the fence for our artillery. An open half mile was before us. Hid, as we were, they could not see us. Had they come they would have rushed into such a

slaughter-pen that I shivered as I thought of it, and
examined the priming of my gun. We lay down in
the moonlight and gazed across the field so intently that
we fancied we saw them approaching. The Colonel
rode along our line, saying: "Be steady! don't fire till
I give the command; wait till you can smell their
breaths, and then cut them down. If I see any man
skulking to the rear I will kill him just as I would a
rebel." We waited for hours, but no enemy came,
though heavy firing on the right kept us in constant
expectation of their presence. In the hush of night,
hearing nothing but the suppressed breathing of our
comrades, waiting the moment of slaughter, the quiet
moon gazing down on us as if teaching that our warfare disturbed not the serenity of Heaven, yet furnishing us with an approving light, we grasped our guns
and gazed o'er the field, peopling it with the advancing
foes of God and humanity. It was a weird and never-
to-be-forgotten scene. At last we were allowed to sleep
on our arms, a few keeping watch; and so passed the
night quietly away, though an occasional gun would
cause us to grasp more tightly our weapons and to
sleepily open our eyes to see nothing but the quiet moon
keeping sacred watch above us. As the morning
dawned we rose from the ground and from fence corners, and wended our way back to camp and coffee.
There are rumors afloat that this is to be an eventful
day, so I will bring this letter to a close. No doubts
about being in the line of duty now trouble me, so I
trustingly await coming events, determined to live or
die, as a higher power may decide, in furtherance of
the cause of righteousness and justice.

LETTER XXVII.

BEFORE PORT HUDSON, LA., *May* 27, 9 A. M., 1863.

MY DEAR L.:

Yesterday morning we were aroused to the solemnity of a soldier's life. Volunteers to constitute a "forlorn hope" were called for. One field officer, four captains, eight lieutenants, and two hundred men were desired from each brigade. We were expected to furnish five from each company. As nearly as we could learn, a part were expected to run from the woods and bridge the ditch in front of the enemy's parapet or breastworks with fascines and then return; the other part to cross the bridge thus made and assault the enemy at the point of the bayonet. How great the distance to run under fire none knew, nor anything of the nature of the ground, nor the width and depth of the ditch. Of the latter, rumor says it is fifteen feet wide and twelve feet deep. We judge by the ditch before our fortifications at Baton Rouge. Calmly the officers of the different companies presented the matter to their men. There were no attempts to awaken excitement, no appeals to patriotism. The order calling for volunteers stated that their names would form a "roll of honor," to be filed at headquarters, from which to choose subjects for promotion. I think that had no influence with *us.* If more than the requisite number volunteered, five from the volunteers of each company would be drawn by lot. Quietly and rapidly did they come forward, as follows: Major C.

T. Plunkett, Lieutenant T. Siggins (D), Lieutenant R.
T. Sherman (E).

Company A—A. C. Howe, C. P. Adams, D. Greber,
J. Malcolm, A. Wiesse, W. L. Burkett, E. A. Landon,
L. Merion—8.

Company B—S. H. Bennett, M. Goodell, A. V.
Barnes, W. Merchant, I. Nourse, G. M. Wood, G. Fitzgerald, E. Brown—8.

Company C—J. N. Strong, F. E. Warren, E. King,
L. J. Newton, J. Noble, G. W. Fields, S. W. Tifft, O.
Murray, N. Cummings, J. N. Knight, T. A. Scott, R.
H. Wilcox, H. T. Johns—13.

Company D—W. S. Gilbert, T. Hensey, D. Heacox,
M. S. Reynolds, E. N. Hubbard, F. N. Deland, C. W.
Shutts—8.

Company E—M. H. Tuttle, W. Amstead, F. K. Arnold, G. E. Callender, W. J. Clark, L. Hedger, H. S.
Hewins, A. Loomis, J. B. Loring, W. L. Wilbar—10.

Company F—A. P. Silva, H. S. May, J. Crosby, G.
B. Potter—4.

Company H—E. Ingersoll—1.

Company I—Z. Barnum, W. Wilson, D. Winchell,
A. Smith, A. Farnum, A. S. Farnum, H. Vosburgh,
R. Groat—8.

Company K—J. Curtis, P. Culver, J. J. Wolfinger,
S. W. Carley—4.

It was hoped that the volunteers would all be unmarried men, and five of such will be selected from the
volunteers of each company where it is possible. Callender, of our department, came up on Saturday, and
you will find his name in the above "roll of honor."
Though I feared his friends might think I influenced
him to take that step, I could not feel free to urge him
not to. I knew nothing to prevent him, yet I believe I

feel more anxiety about him than about myself. Hulet wanted much to go and fill up the complement of his company (F), but it would not do to so deplete our department. We left Captain Rennie sick at Baton Rouge, and though far from well, he has followed us, but will not be apt to go into the field, as F and I have been ordered to guard the rear.

The volunteers secured sixty-two instead of forty-five (remember that G is at Baton Rouge); the fascines were prepared by binding branches and twigs together with grape vines, thus making bundles about eight feet long, one foot in diameter, and weighing from fifteen to thirty pounds. I fear they are too heavy. If lighter, they could be carried as shields if the ground be smooth, which is quite unlikely ; now they must be shouldered, leaving the vitals all exposed to the fire of the foe.

I would not have you think *all* our brave men volunteered. Many a man of family, who will demean himself to-day as a Christian soldier, left the superior danger to those less trammeled, though some felt that duty called *them* to the advance. I know not why I volunteered ; it seemed so much a matter of course, as it was the duty lying nearest to me. I thought it was but right that *I*, who had urged so many to enlist, contending that Freedom was at issue, should not bring a reproach on that cause by any seeming unwillingness to risk my life in its defense. We expect momentarily to be called into line, and "the five" have been selected from no company but Co. C. I volunteered as one of D, and therefore am still in doubt as to whether I am of the elect or not. Amid the tumult and activity of the hour it is quite probable that no selections will be made, but that all who have volunteered will go with the "forlorn hope" save the representatives of F and I.

Major Plunkett was really disappointed in the selection of Lieutenant-Colonel O'Brien, of the Forty-eighth Massachusetts, as leader instead of himself. Two thousand volunteers were called for to represent forty regiments of infantry. Judging by the "Forty-ninth," the "forlorn hope" will number nearly 3,000—one-half to carry fascines, the other half to storm the works. Lieutenant Siggins (D) commands the fascine detachment of our brigade. As Lieutenant Sherman (E) is sick, I do not know who will command our stormers. If we have forty regiments before Port Hudson, we are less than twenty thousand strong, for each regiment will not average five hundred fighting men. We have cause to doubt the result of this day's work.

Yesterday, after the volunteering and making of fascines were over, you could find many penning messages to the loved ones at home. On boards, on knapsacks, in secluded places, they were writing, and if some cheeks were white, and tears rolled down manly faces, I think you will credit them to some other cause than fear. Having joined them in those farewell epistles, I know something of their emotions. Perchance, the struggle between love of home and friends and the love of country and duty was harder to pass through than the fiery baptism before us. Some may not have made their wills (for we have but little to will save Government claims), but many willed their souls to God, or set their last seals to earlier consecrations. In such hours thought is very active. Happy they whose thoughts are fastened on the atoning sacrifice, so they can meet man's wrath, well assured that they die, if die they must, battling for a cause only less sacred than that that hallowed Gethsemane and Calvary. I will not say "*less* sacred," for here, with the booming of cannon in my ear. I can hear the great sufferer saying, " Follow *me*." It is a part of the same cause—it is *our* Gethsemane, *our* Calvary. This morning was ushered in with the thunder of artillery. Hastily we breakfasted, and are now sitting in the woods, waiting the "forward march." Serious and cheerful all seem. There is no swaggering, but a quiet falling back on the fixed will. More than one face is pale, but the firm, set lips speak of a power that can hold shrinking nerves steady, though in the face of death. L——, I may not live to see the close of this delightful day, but this morning finds my soul more exalted than ever before. The terrific cannonading summons up all my manhood, and at times I feel the sublimity of our mission and the success sure to crown our sacrifices, that I am almost ready to shout, "Glory to God in the highest, peace on earth and good will to men!" Through war we are pressing on to a peace that will be a precursor of that time when men "shall beat their swords into ploughshares and their spears into pruning-hooks, and learn war no more." *This*, even *this*, is more really peace than we had three years ago. We are now "working together with *God*." Those monster guns seem to shriek out, "Lord, open Thou our lips, and our mouths shall show forth *Thy* praise;" and over all, under all the thunder, sounds the grand old diapason, "God and Freedom." I am glad I am right here. I would not, for much wealth, miss the grandeur of this hour. I can form some idea how much a soul can live in a short time. Here scribbling, perchance, my last lines, my heart goes out in thankfulness to God for controlling events so as to lead to the Proclamation of Emancipation. Graves are opening before me; wounded, dying men are being carried to the rear ; yet, I see how much better all the slain of our battle-fields, all the martyrs of our hospitals, all the agony, loneliness, and desolation of ten thousand darkened homes, than a continuation of our national curse, that crushed the many and peopled the abode of the damned. You may think I use strong language; but I feel strongly, hope strongly, and, with God's blessing, will fight strongly. I know *now* full well that my courage will not fail me. Help has been given me, so that, though my whole system be unmanned, *will*, stiffened by a sense of duty, will carry me through. Never less did I feel vindictiveness; but the foe is in the way of this nation doing God's work, and I shall willingly fire no random shots. I am glad to know that on our right and on our left are massed *negro* regiments, who, this day, are to show if the inspiration of Freedom will lift the serf to the level of the man. Whoever else may flinch, I trust *they* will stand firm and baptize their hopes in the mingled blood of master and slave. Then we will give them a share in *our* nationality, if God has no separate nationality in store for them. "Fall in, Forty-ninth!" is sounded. Farewell!

LETTER XXVIII.

Before Port Hudson, *May 30, 1863.*

My Dear L.:

Having passed safely through the bloody scenes of the 27th, I sit down to give you an account thereof. When ordered to march, we went down the road for about a quarter of a mile and there filed into a corn-field on the east side of a wood, where we remained for half an hour. I suppose this move was to take us out of the range of the shells, which we could see bursting around us. Our pickets, under the command of Capt. Chaffee (D), had a place only less dangerous than the open field. They formed part of the support of Holcomb's (2d Vermont) Battery, which kept up a fierce fire on the enemy, which was fiercely returned. One shot struck a gun-carriage, smashing it to pieces without injuring any of the men surrounding it. Shells bursting in the air, sending down an iron rain, wounding several, made picket work one of no ordinary interest. While lying by the wood, as I was taking a few notes, and the major had just observed, "This will make history for you," an order came that led me to the writing of history with something besides my pen. We were commanded to return to our camping ground and bring the fascines. Some of the volunteers went, and some who had not volunteered were *detailed* to go. *They* expected merely to carry the fascines to the members of the "forlorn hope," and then rejoin their companies. We started

for them, and after stacking our guns, shouldered them.
Callender got hold of a very heavy one. I gave him
my light one, and with the help of Mr. Kelty, of whom
I spoke in a previous letter, carried his. When we
reached the place where we left our regiment, we found
it was not there; so, almost fainting with the heat (it
was then noon), we bore our loads onward. On the
north edge of the last wood, between us and the enemy,
we saw our regiment. Call was made for additional
volunteers to join the storming party. Some responded.
I bore my fascine till General Augur met me and told
me to throw it down, as no one man could carry it. I
told him perchance *two* of us could; but he said, "No;
go back to your regiment." I started to obey him,
when I met the storming party advancing. Fortunately
I did not stack my gun with the rest, but strapped it on
my back, so if I lost my fascine I need not be idle.
Thus I was prepared to join our stormers and went with
them the rest of the day. You can now see why some
who volunteered did not go in the forlorn hope, and
why some who did *not* volunteer went. It was one of
those mistakes no one is responsible for. Those who
did not volunteer, yet went, bore themselves as bravely
as the original volunteers. Capt. Halstead, of Gen.
Augur's staff, seeing Geo. A. Holland (A), a small,
brave fellow, with a fascine nearly as large as himself,
expressed his doubts as to his ability to carry his load,
but Holland said he would like to try it, which so
pleased the major that he told him if he came out safely
to report to him; he would be happy to see him. I
send you a list of those of our regiment who actually
went in the "forlorn hope:"

Lieut. T. Siggins† (D).

† Wounded.

Company A—D. Greber, C. P. Adams, J. Malcolm, L. Merion, G. Holland, H. Grewe—6.

Company B—S. H. Bennett, M. Goodell, W. Merchant, I. Nourse, A. V. Barnes, E. Brown—6.

Company C—J. N. Strong, F. E. Warren, E. King,† I. J. Newton, G. W. Fields, H. T. Johns—6.

Company D—W. S. Gilbert, T. Hensey,* D. Heacox,† E. N. Hubbard, H. G. Mansir, F. N. Deland, C. W. Shutts—8.

Company E—M. H. Tuttle,† J. H. Wood, G. E. Callender,† W. Amstead, L. Hedger, W. L. Wilbur,† W. J. Clarke, A. Loomis, C. O. Dewey—9.

Company H—E. Ingersoll,* C. Wright, M. T. O'Donnell, W. F. Fuller—4.

Company K—J. Curtis, P. Culver, J. J. Wolfinger, S. W. Carley,* B. Devine, J. Decker—6.

Though unwell, Lieut. Sherman went with his company, and acted bravely till he fell, severely, we fear fatally, wounded in the head and breast. Capt. Lingenfelter (C), was sun-struck before going into the field, so the command of his company devolved on Lieut. Brooks, Lieut. Foster being at Baton Rouge, sick. As Capt. Chaffee was on picket, and Lieut. Tucker (who was on Chapin's staff) wounded, and Lieut. Siggins in the "forlorn hope," Lieut. Smith (H) was put in command of Company D, and led them bravely and well.

The volunteers of our brigade (to which had been added the Second Louisiana, Col. Paine commanding) collected in the woods. In the meantime Holcomb's battery had been advanced to the front and opened a fire more rapid than ever we had before heard. It was one unbroken roar, stirring up fighting blood as no martial music could do. We could feel the ground

* Killed.　† Wounded.

tremble. The wind from his guns shook our clothes as leaves shaken by the breeze. While lying there a shell came crashing, bursting over our heads. As was natural, we bowed, seeing which, Col. Chapin remarked, "It is only a good-morning to you, boys." A piece of the shell slightly wounded H. A. Bristol (D) in the leg. Soon after our whole brigade filed into the woods. We lay there an hour waiting the signal of attack. In the lull of the cannonading we could hear heavy musketry firing on our right, telling us that our brothers were already engaged in the fierce strife. I had just carved "49th M." on a tree, when some one, foolishly I thought, cried out, "In fifteen minutes we start." A mortal fear came over me, and a deathly sickness. It seemed as if I had taken all the emetics and purgatives known to *materia medica*. I felt I *could* not go. I was unmanned, and amid all my mind was preternaturally active, bringing up home, friends, things past, and things to come. This was my "bullet fever," my baptism of fire. Summoning up what will had not been submerged, I gradually became myself again, resolving to go on till strength should entirely leave me. Not *there*, not *there* to faint and fall was my prayer. Let nature not fail till I saw the foe. That baptism over, for the rest of the day I was as free from fear as I am now. I can truly say I felt not the slightest resemblance to fear, and was never cooler in my office than on the battle-field. As we were entering the woods Dr. Rice gave each man half a gill of whiskey. It was well done, for tremulously excited as we were, it was almost impossible to swallow hard bread and salt beef.

At last we were ordered to fall in. The fascine-bearers were in advance. General Augur said : "Now, boys, charge, and reserve your fire till you get into the fort ;

give them cold steel, and as you charge, cheer! Give them New England! A Connecticut regiment is inside, but they have exhausted their ammunition. In fifteen minutes you will be there. Press on, no matter who may fall. If ten men get over the walls the place is ours." We answered only by grasping tighter our guns. Lieut.-Col. O'Brien appeared in a state of intense excitement: "Come on, boys; we'll wash in the Mississippi to-night." We emerged from the woods, turning to the right up a main road. A small belt of timber to our left hid us from the foe. The artillery had ceased firing; all was quiet till we passed that small belt and came in full view of the rebels. Then bullets, grape, and canister hurtled through the air, and men began to fall, some crying, "I am hit!" and one, "Oh, God, I'm killed!" Advancing a few yards, we wheeled by the right flank and started across the fatal field. Then we could see our work. Full two-thirds of a mile distant we saw the parapet lined with rebels, and great volumes and little jets of smoke, as muskets and cannon bade us defiance. For a few yards the field was smooth, but difficulties soon presented themselves. A deep ditch or ravine was passed, and we came to trees that had been felled in every direction. Over, under, around them we went. It was impossible to keep in line. The spaces between the trees were filled with twigs and branches, in many places knee-high. Foolishness to talk about cheering or the "double-quick." We had no strength for the former, aye, and no heart either. We had gone but a few rods ere our Yankee common sense assured us we must fail. You could not go faster than a slow walk. Get your feet into the brush and it was impossible to force them through, you had to stop and pull them back and start again. As best we could we pressed on : shells shrieked past or bursted in our midst, tearing ground and human bodies alike : grape and canister mowed down the branches, tore the leaves, or lodged in trees and living men. Solid shot sinking into the stumps with a thumping sound or thinning our ranks, minie balls "zipping" past us or *into* us, made our progress slow indeed. As the storming party was less heavily loaded than the fascine-bearers, we would get ahead of them and had then to tarry until *they* got in advance. They were our bridge. If *they* failed or fell, *we* were helpless. With anxiety and despairing sorrow we saw them fall, some from bullets and some from sheer exhaustion. Seeing Callender down. I said : "For God sake, up. my boy ! *We* can do nothing without you." He cried, "Go on ! go on ! I'm wounded." Turning my eyes I saw Lieut. Siggins drop his sword and put his hands to his mouth, from which the blood was gushing in torrents. It was no time to help him, so on we pressed. Soon a bullet came tearing through the left sleeve of my blouse. I thought but little of it. My one thought was, will enough of the fascine-bearers be spared to bridge the ditch ? Again we had got in advance of them. They looked more like loaded mules than men. Nearly all of them were behind. They *could* not keep up. As I watched I could see one after another drop, and round me voices moaned out, "O, God ! O, God !" and bleeding men dragged themselves to the safe side of the felled trees. Some, too badly wounded, lay where they fell, all exposed to the deadly rain. I saw no more of the fascine-bearers, but, the white flag of Massachusetts passing by, I followed. It was the State colors of the Forty-eighth Massachusetts. Soon the standard-bearer was killed ; an officer grasped the colors and waved

them aloft.   In less than half a minute his blood had
dyed the white silk of the banner.   We had then got
within forty rods of the parapet.   Save a few scattered
soldiers, we were alone.   Officers we saw none, so down
we lay.   Five of us were together, and were congratulating each other on our safety.   One poor fellow had
just put down his canteen, from which he had been
drinking, when a bullet passed through it into his leg.
He sought the protection of the nearest log.   In less
than five minutes I was the only unwounded one of
the party, and a bullet had rent my blouse right over
the heart.   Having no protection but a few thin
branches, I fell back a few rods where the branches
were thicker.   By this time I was nearly exhausted, so
I threw down my gun and rested awhile.   Campion (D)
and a 116th boy were to my left, and soon Curtis (K),
one of the fascine-bearers, joined us.   Finding it was
useless to carry his burden any longer, he had thrown
it aside and was seeking a gun and cartridges.   A
wounded man gave him his.   While resting the 116th
soldier felt worried that I did not fire.   I asked him,
"What's the use?"   "It will show your good-will any-
how," was the brave fellow's answer.   Rather amused
at having my "good-will" impeached, and having got
breath again, I went to work, firing about twenty rounds
in the direction of the big gun, which I could only
guess at by the smoke.   My gun got so hot and foul
that I dared fire it no more.   At one time I thought a
bullet grazed and burned me.   It was my hand coming
in contact with the brass of my cartridge-box.   The
sun had made it so hot that I could not touch it.   Heat
and smoke and powder produce an intense thirst.   Gun-
shot wounds at first are not very painful, only numb-
ing, but they are followed with feverish thirst.   Th

cries of the wounded for water were heart-rending. I brought a lemon to soothe me in case of accident. I tried to keep it, thinking I would need it, but the wailing of the wounded was too touching, so I comforted one of the bleeding ones with it. God bless the dear boys! They did not complain nor lose their interest in the fight. Hearing that we were short of cartridges, they would roll over and painfully take off their cartridge-boxes and throw them to us. One good fellow, who was wounded in the leg, threw himself on his back and fired as rapidly as he could load his piece. We had been there nearly an hour, and as the fire slackened, Col. O'Brien came springing across the logs, waving his sword, shouting, "Charge! boys, charge!" I put my bayonet on and rose up to "charge." Seeing less than a dozen men ready to obey the order, I laid down again, knowing that obedience thereto was only a reckless casting away of life. In half a minute, just ahead of me, he fell dead.

As we entered the field we veered to the left, and the regiment to the right. I stood up, hoping to see our boys. It was not prudent to stand very long, but I saw a body of men, their flags waving in advance of all, and thought I could distinguish the dark blue pants of the Forty-ninth. I was right, for I afterwards learned that the men I saw were the Forty-ninth and Second Louisiana. Oh, how grand and beautiful did that old flag look amid the smoke of battle! How majestic compared with the sinister stars and bars that floated defiantly on the parapet before us! Toward the close of the engagement we were exposed to much danger by shots from our rear. Some men, too cowardly to come up, were firing from the woods half a mile distant. All over the front of the field you could hear the cry,

"Fire higher." I know not if any were hurt, but some narrowly escaped wounds and death at the hands of these cowardly comrades. By this time the whole brigade had sought shelter, and was pouring into the enemy a stream of lead that kept them from the parapet and from working their guns. Had another "forlorn hope" with another brigade then attacked the fort under the protection of our fire, Port Hudson would now be ours. Yet, perchance their cessation from firing may have been the result of massing their forces against Sherman on the left, for *he* did not attack till near two hours after we did. I took advantage of the comparative quiet, and it was only comparative, to find Lieutenant Siggins, Callender, and some others of our wounded. I found poor Siggins unable to speak ; a ball had entered his mouth, passed out of his throat, and then struck his arm. He wrote to me for drink. I got him some coffee, but he could not swallow it. He wanted me to take him off the field, but that was impracticable, and would only have endangered several lives. I consulted with some officers, who told me it would be in vain to go for medical help. Our surgeons and assistants placed themselves in quite as much danger as they had a right to do. Siggins pointed to the regiment, and gathered up sufficient strength to say, "Go." Hunting the regiment on such a field and under fire was an unnecessary exposure, and could result in no service, so I did not go, but, finding a sheltered place, threw myself down and slept. By that you can judge of my exhaustion. I had hoped the battle hour would bring so much excitement that I would be strong, but my experience was like that of others—exhaustion absorbed excitement. A man on such occasions uses up a great deal of his vital energy. How long I slept I know not, but when I awoke some were stealthily carrying off the wounded on rubber blankets, of which we obtained a few from the dead. For a while we would creep along with our bleeding burdens, almost on all-fours, expecting every moment to be greeted with a shower of grape. That shower coming not, we became bolder and walked erect, and soon bearing away the wounded, occupied all. Why the enemy did not fire on us as we were retreating we can not imagine. According to the laws of war it is honorable to do all you can to cripple a retreating foe. Firing was going on on the right, but they allowed *us* to retire unmolested. It is said that some of our men on the right getting into a ditch and no chance of escape presenting itself, hung out a flag of truce, and escaped under that flag, and therefore the consequent cessation of hostilities. I know not how that was, but certainly we breathed more freely when we reached the shelter of the woods. There we met a surgeon, who gave us some kind of liquor. What kind I know not, but I never tasted anything half so good. The nectar of the gods was nothing in comparison.

Leaving the field we found the road lined with ambulances and squads of men carrying the wounded on stretchers and blankets to the hospital, which was only an open place in the woods above our camp. All kinds of rumors met us. The Colonel was mortally wounded, the Lieutenant-Colonel killed, the Major missing or dead, and Capt. Weller had fallen at the head of his company. A sad, gloomy time it was. At last I obtained these particulars. The regiment pressed its way onward farther than any other, save the Second Louisiana. The Colonel was on horseback, the only mounted man in the field. He had to go that way or stay behind. With his regiment he *would* go. How he got through the ditches and over all the obstructions I can not conceive. His little horse leaped obstacles that seemed insurmountable to any horseflesh. Struck with his daring, it is said that the rebel officers commanded their men not to fire on *him*, but deadly missiles flew thick and fast in that valley of death, into which duty led him ; and having gone about fifty rods, a bullet slightly wounded him in the heel of his good leg and another shattered his left wrist. Attempting to grasp the reins with his right hand, he fell over the head of the horse, which ran to the rear. It is said that when some one came to help him he asked them : " Did you see Billy ? he jumped like a rabbit." I think that is true, for doubtless his main fear was that he could not go with his regiment ; and, though wounded, he felt a soldier's joy that he had been enabled to do his duty until he met a soldier's fate. It was a consolation to him that the absence of one of his legs was not the reason why he did not go farther, but rather one of those casualties to which every one was exposed. Our left went up right opposite to the enemy's great gun, charged with grape and canister. Their loss was fearful. Captains Garlick and Weston especially had an opportunity to show what stuff they are made of. They kept the left in that torrent of fire steady and firm. There were no braver men on that hero-crowded field. When they sought shelter, Sergeant Rising loaded the guns and Captain Weston fired near a hundred rounds. I knew that Rising would not fail. He is a Christian soldier. Stern duty alone led him from a luxurious home. Such men *never* fail. Some shirked, but on the Christian soldiers no reproach can be fixed. Rev. J. H. Wood (E) convinced his company that grace and courage went hand in hand. Sermons proving the reality of religion, its power to strengthen and comfort, were preached on that field with an unction that silenced scoffing and crushed infidelity. Rumor has it that a craven fear of life dishonored some of our own regiment, but among them were none whose banner-cry was "God and Freedom." The bloody record of that day shows the immense value of a noble idea, compared with the success of which life is but the merest dust in the balance. It becomes those who profess a religion that teaches a swallowing up of the fear of death to quit themselves valiantly. They did so, and that reeking field, with some of its slain and wounded, will convince a whole generation that "religion is not a cunningly devised fable, but the power of God unto salvation (from unmanly fear) to them that believe."

Quite early in the engagement Colonel Sumner was disabled by a wound in the shoulder, and the command devolved on Major Plunkett, who did well and came off safely. I could speak in the highest terms of officers and men, but as well-doing was the general rule and shirking but the exception, I refrain, for I might inadvertently fail to mention all. It is not my mission to reflect on any, neither do I credit all the charges of cowardice that come to my ears. Cowards in self-justification may accuse others, especially when they have some real or fancied wrong to avenge. *I* saw no man shirk. In the "forlorn hope" none did less than his whole duty. One man with the regiment sought shelter behind a log, but the Colonel's threatening to shoot him drove him back to his company on the "double-quick." He feared the Colonel's pistol and indignation more than the grape-shot of the rebels. One fellow sought shelter by the wounded Callender, who asked him where *he* was wounded. Alas! he could not tell. General Chapin was killed by a bullet crashing through nose and brain. He threw up his hands, exclaiming, "My God! they have killed me," and died, one year from the day he was wounded on the Peninsula. He was an excellent officer, a brave and *good* man. Perchance he would have been spared had he not gone to the field in full uniform. T. Bach (F), our color-bearer, bore the flag grandly, and though a six-footer, a conspicuous mark for the foe, escaped unhurt, while every other color-sergeant in the brigade was either killed or wounded. Thrice did the colonel reprove him for going too fast. Our flag has fewer marks of the battle than almost any other. Some dodged to escape the showers of grape; *that* would cause their flags to wave to and fro, making them more liable to be torn. Bach dodged not, but walked proudly erect, as if feeling the dignity of his mission, and a strong west wind blowing, kept the banner flying back, and so presented but a small mark to the foe. If our colors are not so battle-scarred as are some others, not superior cowardice but superior courage is the explanation. All honor to him! The colors are to the soldier *almost* as was the ancient Shechinah to the Jews. *Those* dishonored, and every true man feels a share of the stigma resting on himself. High advanced, in the "fore front of the hottest battle," have they ever been. We'll follow them to victory or honorable burials.

"A fierce fight is a wonderful builder up and tearer down of reputations. Heroes vanish and the underrated step up to the confidence of their comrades. Before, you may estimate a man according to his position or pretensions; after, you know his true character and respect him accordingly. The morning of battle comes;

an untried regiment is to enter a new field, to walk through a fiery furnace, which shall try the inmost soul of each. They advance. The fire in the furnace is growing hotter and hotter. It is impossible to avoid the ordeal. What is in the men's souls will certainly be forced out. The enemy says nothing, for he has no powder to lose. You will hear from him soon. On they march—tramp, tramp, tramp—and whiz, whiz, come the leaden ounces, and rut, rut, comes the grape by the half bushel. A dozen, fifty, aye, a hundred fall. Now, where is Colonel Bluster? Sick! Go near him and he gets worse; your presence aggravates the disease. It has been coming on ever since the 'forlorn hope' was formed. Well, where is the modest Captain Tagg, one we had thought should have remained in his mill or behind his counter? Walking quietly along the length of his company, noting each absentee, and steadying all by a few kind, quiet words. Back, lying snugly behind a log, you may see Captain Blunt, whose hereditary heart disease alone prevents him from carrying out his repeated threats against the rebels. And there is Captain Dainty! the village dandy. He looks dirty enough now, but you see he has got a blazing fire in his eye and in his heart. *His* company will fight. They don't laugh at him now. So old idols are pulled down and new ones set up. The boys know why this colonel was sick, and he can never control them again. Captain Blunt will threaten rebels no more in their presence. That two hours' fight was like a sieve into which a shovelful of gravel had been thrown. The sieve was most terribly shaken; the sand fell through, and only the pebbles remained.

"It is curious to note the diseases affecting certain soldiers on receiving news of an impending battle.

Sick ones leave the hospitals and well ones seek to occupy the beds just vacated. The bully of the squad is
sick. He has a terrible pain in his right arm, his legs
feel queer, his head reels. Do you order a coffin for
him? If the surgeon is a little verdant, he will send
him to the hospital, and in a few days boast of his
ability to cure diseases. If he has been a surgeon before, he will see that he is put in the front rank on the
morrow, or give him corn-gruel by day and blue pills
at night. Then there are others who are always in their
places when the column is formed, but when the grape
comes they are to be found in the rear with a sprained
ankle, or terribly overcome by fatigue, or sunstroke, or
with a wrenched back, and are not found again till
they return shouting 'victory,' and telling of the way
they dropped big rebels, who would certainly have killed
them if they had not—shirked behind a stump. These
are they who make the loudest noise on their return
home, and as you listen to their valorous deeds you are
surprised that any rebels are left unkilled. You wonder
that they jest over the bloody scenes of a battle-field,
remembering

> ' He jests at scars who never felt a wound.' "

By and by you understand them, and though they
may not be poets, you find they have a vivid appreciation of Butler, who writes :

> " Those that fly may fight again,
>   Which he can never do that's slain ;
>   Hence timely running's no mean part
>   Of conduct in the martial art."

" Bullet-fever " is a real fever, from which few are
exempt. To feel fear is natural ; to yield to fear is

cowardice. Some never carry fear with them into the
battle-field. They leave it on the fiery margin. There
they experience the terrible baptism of battle, with its
sinking and sickening and trembling, which for the
time unmans more than mortal disease. Happy they
who overcome this before facing the foe. Then no
danger of panic reaching *them*. Having conquered
their own hearts and nerves, they may be killed, but not
subdued. It is *will* that counts in the composition of
the brave. If there be enough of pride, of moral
strength, to call up *will* you have the unflinching soldier. Weakness of will is often counteracted by strong
convictions of duty. I *will* do my *duty* has made many
a timid heart brave, aye, kept them steady before death.
though their nerves trembled at every burst of artillery,
every "zipping" of a bullet. They who experience
this baptism suddenly when in actual conflict will become panic-stricken and spread the leprosy of fear over
a whole regiment, perchance, a whole army. A man
may go through several conflicts and never be thus
tried. Constant excitement, a series of victories, may
delay the hour of his soul's trial. At Plain's Store we
were rushed into the midst of danger so unexpectedly
that activity and excitement precluded that baptism.
Not so on the 27th. For twenty-four hours we faced
the question and endured the ordeal. Strengthened,
we passed through it, and made the "Forty-ninth"
not unworthy to be ranked as Massachusetts soldiers.
I have written much about emotions and experiences.
I could not have done so the day after the battle. Then
it would have seemed profane. Now it is easy. Soldiers living on the verge of death may not become indifferent to slaughter and wounds, but they regard them
with much less concern than do you who only read of

them, and soon rise above their sadness. It is well
that it is so. A constant exercise of sympathy would
illy prepare us for our stern work. Morbidly afraid at
home of the sight of blood, it affected me none on the
field, though I nearly succumbed when I visited the
hospital on the 28th.

To return to the regiment. I give you a list of our
killed and wounded. You will see that Captain Weller
is not among the slain. but it is not his fault, for he
was conspicuous among the brave. From our own men
and from men of other regiments I hear his valor
spoken of in the highest terms. Though wild and rollicking, we never heard Weller swearing that he would
do great things, but when the time came he *did* them.
Francis nobly seconded his efforts, and together they
received the unflinching support of Co. A., than which
there is no braver company.

Colonel W. F. Bartlett, wounded ; left wrist, severely;
right foot, slightly.

Lieutenant-Colonel S. B. Sumner, wounded; left
shoulder, slightly.

Company A—Killed: L. M. Davis. Wounded: Captain Weller, leg, slightly; Lieutenant Francis, head,
slightly; J. Bryce, right arm amputated; M. H. Horton, head, slightly; C. E. Platt, leg, slightly; W. Reed,
head, slightly; H. Rucktashell, side, slightly; J. Rod-
gers, knee, slightly : W. Tuggey, neck, badly; H. L.
Root, leg, slightly.

Killed, 1 ; wounded, 10.

Company B—Killed: J. M. Gamwell, G. Fitzgerald.
Wounded: Lieutenant Kniffin, arm, slightly; A. F.
Bliss, leg, flesh wound; S. H. Rossiter, breast, seriously; W. D. Bliss, leg, flesh wound; H. R. Clark,
side, slightly; J. A. Francis, head, slightly; S. L.

Sturtevant, foot; F. Belcher. right leg amputated; C. H. Cook, chest, severely; **H. D. Wentworth.** abdomen, seriously; H. H. Davis, flesh wound, leg.

Killed, 2; wounded, 11.

Company C—Killed: A. Griswold. Wounded. Captain Lingenfelter, sunstroke; Lieutenant C. H. Brooks. **leg,** flesh wound; W. H. Cranston, abdomen; E. King. **leg.** flesh wound; J. H. Olin, head, severely; J. W. Bowles, head, severely; D. Braumwalder, thigh; J. H. Wells, sprained ankle; J. Stevens. shoulder, slightly.

Killed, 1; wounded, 9.

Company D—Killed: M. **Bracken,** T. Hensey, **M. S.** Reynolds. Wounded: Lieutenant T. **Siggins,** throat. severely; **H. A.** Bristol. leg, slightly; J. W. Evans, side, severely; D. Heacox, elbow, slightly; B. Shelley. hand; J. McGowan, leg; M. S. Beach, back, slightly.

Killed, 3; wounded, 7.

Company E—Killed: **H. S. Hewins.** Wounded: Lieutenant R. T. Sherman, side and head, severely; M. H. Tuttle, shoulder, slightly; **G.** H. Palmentier, shoulder, severely; F. K. Arnold, wrist, severely; W. Fogarty, hand, slightly; D. Foley, hand, slightly; J. E. Hinton, wrist, severely; W. Maxwell, head; W. J. Wilbur, both thighs, severely; **G. E.** Callender, hand, slightly; **A.** Brett, side, slightly.

Killed, 1; wounded, 11.

Company H—Killed: Lieutenant B. D. Deming, A. Allen, E. Ingersoll. Wounded: A. Hitchcock, arm; H. L. Beach, severely; **J.** Vincent, head, slightly; J. Northway, hand.

Killed, 3; wounded, 4.

Company K—Killed: H. E. Warner, S. W. **Carley. L. Funk,** T. C. Shaw, **S. Dowd.** Wounded: Lieutenant I. E. Judd, groin, slightly; **Lieutenant S. B. Glea-**

son, thigh, slightly: R. E. Phelps, leg amputated: H.
A. Parmlee, elbow: G. W. Allen, leg, severely; S.
Brocha, leg; J. W. Bidwell, head, seriously; S. M.
Fullerton, shoulder, slightly: G. Watler, leg; D. S.
Bliss, thigh, severely.

Killed, 5; wounded, 10.

On that fatal day sixteen were killed and sixty-four
wounded; eighty in all, of the 233 men of our regiment who went into the field. When we consider that
we were under fire less than three-quarters of an hour before ordered to seek shelter, we may well call it a fierce
conflict, for more than every third man was cut down.
This was about the average loss in the whole brigade.
Of the eighteen officers engaged, eleven were killed or
wounded. If that is a test of their valor, brave men
were bravely *led*. Considering the short time we were
actually under fire without shelter, and the history of
this war records no more fearful slaughter than met the
first brigade on the 27th of May. The old name of
the field was *Slaughter's* field. In the best blood of
New England its name has been confirmed in baptism.
Of the forty-four who went up in the "forlorn hope"
only three were killed and six wounded; or one in five.
Thus, it turned out that ours was the path of safety.
It happened in this wise: When we came in sight of
the rebels, they fired at us with every kind of weapon
in their possession. Grape and canister were mixed
with solid shot, shell, and bullet; but when they saw
the whole brigade following us closely, and then marching to the right of us in line of battle, they bestowed
their deadliest discharges on them, and from that time
we were mainly greeted with bullets; especially was this
the case after they saw that most of the fascine bearers
were disabled, rendering *us* comparatively ineffective.

With the regiment proper went up 189 men, of whom 71, or two in every five, were killed or wounded.

Sadly we returned from the unavailing sacrifice. The night was full of gloom. Nervous reaction made it still more gloomy. It seemed hard to send men after such a day's labor to stand on picket during the night, but necessity knows neither law nor mercy, and the old picket had not been relieved for forty-eight hours. To increase our gloom the battlefield took fire, and in agony we thought of our comrades, struggling with pain and thirst, on whom the billows of flame were rolling down, and none to help them, none to save them from the most fearful of deaths. We could do nothing but gaze and shudder. Humanity led some of the rebels to face the bullets of our pickets and extinguish the flames before they acquired full sway. All night long the surgeons were at work. On the operating table were the victims, whose shrieks of agony, but partially deadened by chloroform, illy prepared the wounded all around them for *their* hours of martyrdom. Lying but a few rods from the hospitals, frames unstrung after the physical and mental efforts of the day, we slept but little, and were glad when the morning came, that we could see to aid the suffering or get away from their harrowing cries. The most severely wounded bore the surgical operations with the greatest calmness. Perchance their exhausted natures soonest yielded to the influences of stupefying draughts. Too much praise can not be awarded to the medical authorities. Nearly everything wounded men could want was at hand. Ministers of the Christian Commission and others did all that loving ingenuity could devise for their comfort; but, having done all, how much was left undone that home care would have performed! Happy they who, in insensibility or fatigue, could forget the surrounding horrors. The conscious could but imagine the worst. They knew not whether they carried in themselves the sentence of disfigurement, incapacity, or death. I visited them in the morning, found most of them cheerful and doing well; but laid one side, with hands tenderly folded and faces respectfully covered, were the dead, showing that a fearful night had followed a bloody day. The surgeons continued at their work without a moment's intermission. Seeing them amputating with sleeves rolled up, splashed with blood, here a pile of booted legs, there a pile of arms, was more trying than the horrors of the battle-field. As fast as they were operated on, they were carefully conveyed to Springfield Landing, and thence to Baton Rouge, where ample provisions had been made for their comfort. Ere the evening of the 28th, nearly all had been thus removed. On the road to the landing, at Lilley's Station, a tent had been put up, where the wounded received iced-claret punch and such other luxuries as they needed or craved. Never was any military department in so high a state of excellence as is the "Department of the Gulf." Wounds, sickness, may be before us, but what mitigations our circumstances will allow will be ours. In spite of all, many of the wounded will die. In this climate, with blood already diseased, hemorrhage soon follows the slightest wound. The extremest care has to be taken to prevent the wounds from becoming maggoty. We hear that some of our most severely wounded are doing well, and that of those reported "slightly wounded," not a few are hovering on the brink of death. God prepare loving hearts in New England for soul-darkening news. Patriotic fathers, mothers, wives, children are there who will *try* to bear their sorrows proudly, but for a while nature will conquer patriotism. Sad though they will be that they were not present to receive and speak the last adieu, yet it were sadder to gaze upon fearful sufferings no love could alleviate. Certainly, not *then;* aye, not till other affections have in some measure led them from their great loss ; perchance *never* will they be able to say with the stern Roman :

> "Thanks to the gods! my boy has done his duty.
> Welcome, my son! There, set him down, my friends,
> Full in my sight; that I may view at leisure
> The bloody corpse and count the glorious wounds.
> Who would not be this youth? What pity 'tis
> That we can die but once to save our country."

Away from these mangled frames I might enter into sympathy with such sorrow ; *here* I value more even that "grief that does not speak, but whispers the o'er fraught heart and bids it break."

After we returned to the camp everything was done to render the boys comfortable. The major set the example, and was zealously followed by the officers. Late as it was, and fully engaged as were all of the medical department in caring for the wounded, he would not rest till a full ration of whisky was furnished. In our inmost hearts we thanked him. Muscular exertion drawing the blood to the muscles, mental anxiety drawing it to the brain, our stomachs loathed food, and even commissary whisky was a luxury. It allayed the fierce, burning thirst. What rest we got that night was mainly owing to the major's pertinacity in securing for us our ration of liquor.

Almost the only pleasure in returning to camp was the meeting those from whom the surges of battle had separated us. We clasped hands, and eyes were wet.

Not unfrequently did we embrace as women. Officers and privates were brothers then. They had been baptized into one family. Never will those with whom I went in that "forlorn hope," how *forlorn!* be as common friends again. There we entered the sacred *brotherhood of soldiers.*

On the morning of the 28th, we brought in our dead. The burial party saw many guns, blankets, etc., lying round, but under a flag of truce neither side can carry any thing away, and so they brought nothing but our slain. The pockets of some of these had been rifled by (we have reason to fear) members of the 2d Louisiana. One or more from each company comprised that party, so as to be able to identify all. Mutilated as many of them were, identification was difficult. They brought them to the eastern verge of the wood, where we rested just before we charged. As best they could, without coffins, they buried them. A few years and the mounds will disappear and nothing will remain to show where our Berkshire brave rest. They died well and their works do follow them. Liberty needed a fresh baptism. Their hearts, not unwillingly, yielded the sacred element. So long as Liberty lives their memories will be cherished. Names will be forgotten, but from the graves of these "unnamed demi-gods" shall go forth a living spirit that will raise up an unbroken succession of those who count duty to country a part of duty to God. To these graves every patriotic heart is united, and proudly may they slumber over whom God and humanity say "Well done!" The burial party report that the rebels have put up new guns with which to open other graves if Slaughter's field shall again be made the scene of conflict. As nearly as they could judge, the ditch is fifteen feet deep and eleven feet wide, and the parapet eight feet in height.

Gloomily we passed the day after the battle, doing nothing but writing home and resting. Towards evening the body of Lieutenant Deming was brought in, and we were preparing to have a prayer-meeting when the order came, "Fall in ! Forty-ninth !" We could hear firing to our right, and knew not but that our courage was again to be tried. Unstrung nerves and timid hearts protested, but a few steps of marching and that feeling passed away; yet we were glad to find that nothing more serious was before us than to guard the lane, to cut them off if they should try to escape. We were revengeful enough to hope they would try it. We had been in a slaughter-pen where the advantage was all on *their* side ; now we desired them to come on where positions would be reversed. Of course they came not, and we have but little reason to expect that they will come. Our repulse has doubtless encouraged them to believe they can hold their ground, but unless we are attacked by a strong force from the rear, Port Hudson will ere long be ours.

I approach the obituaries of our slain with diffidence. My materials are so limited that I can but do injustice to some with whom I was least acquainted. Of many, all we know is they went through life, quietly performing its duties, until in discharge thereof they died at the bidding of their country.

Lieutenant Barton D. Deming was in his thirty-second year when he nobly died. Before the war, he lived the life of the quiet farmer, respected by all. "Respected by all," is emphatically true of our late comrade. Comfortable in circumstances, happy in his domestic relations, retiring in his disposition, nothing but the voice of duty called him to a soldier's life. He became a soldier because he was a Christian. Making his will, and

prudently regulating his affairs, on the supposition that
he would not return, he was prepared to do all that was
required at his hands. Singularly quiet, only those
most intimate with him knew his worth. In the command of his men he was kind, ever laboring to smooth
their pathway. I roomed with him on the steamship
Illinois, and found him gentle and obliging, grateful
for every attention, and claiming little as his *right*.
None ever said "shoulder-straps" lifted him above
himself. Few wore the marks of rank, thinking less
of them. Though deficient in self-esteem, he knew full
well that the *man* was greater than the *officer*, and his
military worth consisted in throwing around the latter
the dignity of the former. The boys on picket wanted
no more considerate commander than Lieutenant Deming. Sickness gave a sombreness to his countenance
that was not in his heart. He was unwell when he came
up to this place, but sense of duty was stronger than
illness. When we were lying down on the edge of the
woods, I looked at him and thought Lieutenant Deming
had a presentiment of death, his face was so sad. He
himself seemed to think the day would be a fatal one
to him, and requested Lieutenant Smith (II) to take
charge of his money, but as Lieutenant Smith was to
meet the same danger, he refused. He was last seen
alive at the head of his men, gallantly urging them on.
His death could not have been a painful one. A ball
pierced his head, speedily ushering him from the battle
of life to the peace of Heaven. In response to his
friends in Sandisfield on receiving from them a sword,
he wrote, "Hoping you will hear a good report from me
if ever on the field of battle, I bid you all God speed."
The report will go back to his native town, and better
none need desire. Their gift was stained with his own

blood.   His pockets were rifled, and their contents, including his watch, gone.   He kept his money in a pocket in the inside of his shirt.   That Lieutenant Smith secured.   We brought him to camp and buried him in the field opposite.   Away from loved oves, he was not without sincere mourners.   Honored in life and in death, his friends may well mourn for him proudly.   We feel that death has been to him great gain.

Luther M. Davis (A) was a farmer, from Pittsfield, aged twenty-one years.   When found his body showed marks of having been burned, but the fire added nothing to his suffering.   His death, caused by a shell taking off the top of his head, must have been instantaneous.   An excellent soldier, one of the very best of his company, a steady, frugal, good man, a youthful husband, he there sank to his honored rest.

John M. Gamwell, corporal (B), was a carpenter and school-teacher from West Stockbridge.   He was a very fine, well-educated man, respected in his company.   He was wounded in the leg and arm and bled to death, at the age of thirty-seven years, leaving a family to mourn him and to remember May 27th, 1863, as the burial-day of many a fond hope.

Garrett Fitzgerald (B), aged twenty-one years, from Lanesboro, was a brave Irishman and an excellent soldier.   He was one of the original volunteers for the "forlorn hope," but, owing to circumstances I have detailed above, he did not go therein.   He leaves a wife to hope in vain for his return.

Henry D. Wentworth (B), a farmer-boy from Windsor, aged twenty years, was so fearfully wounded in the abdomen that all that could be done was to give him opiates to ease his sufferings till death should usher him to his heavenly home. He bore the reputation of a Christian soldier, and died May 29th as he was being conveyed to Springfield Landing, where he now lies buried. Of course, he was a good soldier. "He was a Christian boy," said one of his comrades. He fell in a cause worthy of a Christian's death. Having kept himself unsullied from the vices of the camp, and dying as he did, who may say "he died an *untimely* death?" Such a dead son is worth more than many living sons.

Albert Griswold, corporal (C), was a quiet, excellent soldier. He was a farmer from Dalton, aged twenty-seven years, and leaves a wife and child.

Marcus Bracken (D) was an Alford farmer, aged thirty-one years. He leaves behind him a family. Another brave Irish soldier poured out his life's blood in Freedom's cause.

Thomas Hensey (D), shoemaker, from Barrington, was yet another of the sons of Ireland who, on that sad day, gave up his life that this country might remain the hope of the world. He was a remarkably good soldier, and in his twenty-second year nobly fell in the vain attempt to bridge a way over which we might reach the heart of slavery.

Mills S. Reynolds (D) was a good soldier from Barrington. He was one of the original volunteers, and fell in his nineteenth year.

Horatio S. Hewins (E), aged twenty-three, was a fine, quiet, honest farmer, from Sheffield. A good member of a good company. His name belongs to the "roll of honor," though he did not go in the "forlorn hope," for which he volunteered.

Eugene Ingersoll (H), of Lee, aged nineteen years, represented in himself his own and a father's willing offering to a needy, bleeding country. He was a bright, smart, well-educated boy and a fine soldier. Though sick, he joined his company when we were ordered to march on the foe, but soon fell out of the ranks, and we carried him in one of our carts. Alone of Co. H he volunteered in the "forlorn hope," and doing its perilous duties he met a soldier's fate. Pride will mingle with the grief in that Berkshire home when loving parents hear that Eugene was faithful unto death.

Albert Allen (H) was another of those farmer boys Sandisfield sent to the war, and of whom, in life and in death, she may well be proud. Death has been busy with her soldiers, yet has made her rich in patriotic memories. Her dead, lying in honored graves on the shores of the Mississippi, are the most precious part of her wealth. Young Allen, only twenty-two years of age, was one of the noblest of her boys. Steady, moral, a first-rate soldier, he did honor to a mother to whom country was more than children, of whom she gave several to the army. One, an officer, was killed at Vicksburg, and now Albert lies at Port Hudson. *She* can appreciate how much the freedom of the " Father of Rivers " costs. We left him sick at Baton Rouge, but his eager soul yearned for the field of duty, and so, escaping from camp, he joined our ranks, and now proudly sleeps among the "fallen brave."

Theron C. Shaw (K) was one of those fine, pleasant farmer boys of whom Sheffield gave so many to the ranks of the Forty-ninth and to the graves of Louisiana. He was but eighteen years old when he was much torn by an exploding shell, and died.

Luther Funk (K), of Mount Washington, was a nice, clever boy of eighteen. He was shot through the bowels on the 27th, and died the next day. He fought and fell by his father's side ; fell so nobly that the soldier heart of the father must have *then* been prouder of his dying boy than ever before. Parental love could not save him, but by his grave has placed a good headboard to note the place of his burial. This done, and the lonely father turns again to meet the foe.

Solomon Dowd (K), farmer, of Monterey, aged thirty-six years, was fearfully mutilated. His leg and hip were smashed by a discharge of grape and railroad. His left hand was cut off. Returning, he said to his captain, "I couldn't bring back my gun, but it is so battered that it will be worth nothing to the rebels." He was an odd being, but died, on the 28th, a hero's death.

Stera W. Curley (K), farmer, from Monterey, aged thirty-eight years, was a Christian warrior. He was one of the "forlorn hope." Quiet and firm, he made a model soldier. He was wounded in the wrist and bound up that wound, when another bullet entered his heart and closed his noble career. He leaves a family and a name of which that family may well be proud.

Henry E. Warner, sergeant (K), aged twenty-four, farmer, from New Marlboro', was shot in the thigh before he had far advanced in the field. He wanted his captain to stop and bind up his wound, but that was impossible; and Weston, speaking a few kind, *last* words to him, led on his company to where was appointed for *them* a fearful reaping. He bled to death, and there was none to help him. Round him were the dying and the dead. Up amid the hills of Berkshire were parents, wife, child, who but little thought on so bright a day so dark a cloud was gathering over their future. They knew not that Henry, dying, was yearning for them, and that on Slaughter's field his soul was going out to God. He was a worthy man, with an education and character that would have secured him an honorable position in life, but *not* a position more truly honorable than the one hallowed with his dying blood. He fell, and a nation's brightness and glory is his mantle, Freedom's renovation his epitaph.

"*Immortal names! O, noble ones!* A nation's heart will throb
For ye who fell in manly prime for freedom and for God;
And woman's eyes grow dim with tears, and manhood bows
   its head
Before thy deeds of valor done, *New England's honored dead.*"

The Colonel has gone to Baton Rouge, and we hear that fears are entertained that he will lose his arm. To lose leg and arm, and to go thus maimed through life, would be a heavy lot. The wound in his heel is very slight and will trouble him but a little while. I suppose he is lost to us for the remainder of this campaign, and it is a loss we deeply feel. The major interests himself personally in our well-being and measures yet higher in our esteem, but we feel that ours is an irreparable loss. For months we have tested our commander, and always found him up to our expectations. I am too little acquainted with him to know whether he has the qualities of a great *general*. Admiring him as much as I do, I should doubt the propriety of substituting him for Banks, but would have no hesitation in voting him in as a brigadier. Colonel Paine (though outranked by Colonel Johnson, Twenty-first Maine), Second Louisiana, is now in command of our brigade. I suppose he was appointed because his is a three years' regiment, though when the nine months' men go home he will have only his own and the One Hundred and Sixteenth New York regiment for a brigade. Had Bartlett not been wounded, I think he would now be in his place. Confidence in him is not confined to us, but I have heard privates and officers of other regiments express regret that he could not be Chapin's successor. In that position he would be saved much exposure and many dangers, and would imbue his whole command with a confidence that would render them twice as effective as under Paine. We praise Bartlett because he emphatically treated a private as well as an officer, in some cases better, for I have known him to censure officers for tactical mistakes in no very polite words, and that, too, in presence of their own men. He erred there, for such censuring was calculated to destroy the respect of the soldiers for those officers and to awaken insubordination. I look upon it as a grave error. Mistakes in tactics were the unpardonable sins in his sight, and drew from him on one occasion language more forcible than pleasant. It was the only time that I knew him to use words that were not peculiarly appropriate to the conventicle. I have had a good deal of business intercourse with him and always found him reserved but respectful, and this is the testimony of all privates who have been thrown into his presence. I have never heard any of them say that the colonel treated them otherwise than as gentlemen. In the transaction of public business I found him scrupulously exact and honest. One of his greatest virtues as a military man is his coolness. For that he is remarkable. He has not popular manners, can not unbend and be sociable yet maintain his dignity to his inferiors, and is bashful (when we cheered him as he left his carriage and mounted his horse as the battle of Plain's Store commenced he blushed as if ashamed of his popularity), but he is a strong, faithful man, in whom a regiment may confide and in whom they may fully rely. Take him all in all, the colonel of the Forty-ninth is a marked man. We have been proud of him, and in bidding him a virtual farewell as our commander nearly every heart adds the fervent "God bless him!"

We have also lost our adjutant, and that, too, just as we were beginning to appreciate and admire him. He goes on General Dwight's staff. Colonel and adjutant gone, eighty killed and wounded, we feel almost as if the Forty-ninth was disbanded, forgetting that scattered around is quite a formidable number yet remaining. Lieutenant Francis is now acting adjutant, and a better one we could not well have. We knew he was kind, polite, a good business man, and he has proved himself a brave soldier. Fred makes a good officer. He has those qualities that the surgings of battle bring out in bold relief. He ought to make arms his profession.

It is said that our brigade is not to be put into the front again save as a matter of extreme necessity. That is right, for we are dispirited, having lost confidence in our generals. Who originated the assault of the 27th we know not. Some say that all the generals were opposed to it, but Banks insisted; and others have it that it was Chapin's project. It might have been a success had the attack been made simultaneously on the right, centre, and left; but, as it was, Weitzel on the right, where the enemy had some works *outside* their parapet, commenced at 6 A. M. and was engaged till 4 P. M.; *we* assaulted at 1:30 P. M., while Sherman did not start till 3 P. M. At 2 P. M. he received peremptory orders to charge. Then he had to mass his men and form his storming party. Being attacked at different times the enemy could mass his forces against each division, and so cut us off in detail. After we had been on the field over an hour we could see them double-quicking to the left to repel Sherman, who, from all I can hear, was drunk. When he did attack he recklessly exposed himself and was wounded in his leg, which has since been amputated. The fascines were too heavy and few. Had a thousand skirmishers crept up, as they might have done in comparative safety, they could have kept the walls clear and silenced most of the guns, so the bridges could have been laid and the stormers entered upon their bayonet work unexhausted. It was a premature assault.

Few scenes are as full of moral sublimity as that of a brigade walking right up into a valley of fire. See one man in a righteous cause facing death, and all within us is called out in admiration. How much grander the sight when a long line of a thousand meets a wave of fire that they must dash back, or allow it to submerge a nation's fondest hopes! To see them enter where earth is crowded with deadly missiles, and death is hurtling through all the air, is a spectacle never to be forgotten, the resemblance of which confirms us in our high estimate of man's inherent devotion to his convictions of duty. Humanity needs such spectacles to keep alive our hopes for the race, which in time of peace seems to be digging its own grave amid the rubbish of earth.

Under the walls of Port Hudson the mooted question was forever settled, and friend and foe admit that "the negro will fight." The First and Third Louisiana Native Guards assaulted on the right. The former regiment was composed mainly of free negroes of French extraction. Many of them were men of liberal education and wealth. They were commanded by negro officers. The latter regiment consisted of slaves or contrabands, the field officers of which were white, and the line officers black. Thus, free and bond, but negroes all, 1,080 strong, gathered together to prove to the world that valor and manhood are not the exclusive attributes of the white race. They *did* prove it, and for all time. Men who had often cowered beneath the master's lash met those masters in the death struggle, and manifested their God-given equality. All agree that none fought more nobly than the " native guards." They drove the rebels from their outer works, and against them, *behind* their formidable intrenchments, made *six* distinct charges. *Six* times they repeated *our* charge. True, they had to advance but two hundred yards under fire, while twelve hundred yards lay between us and the foe, but *six* times did they go over the ground, heaping it with their slain, and pressed into the ditch, over which a few gallantly passed, and mounted the ramparts of the foe. Short of ammunition, their negro brethren of the engineer regiment carried them cartridges, defiant of the iron hail that poured down on them. Three times beaten back, their commander, Colonel Nelson, sent to General Dwight for orders. That earnest son of Massachusetts replied: " Tell Colonel Nelson I shall consider he has done nothing unless he carries the enemy's works." Perchance, Dwight felt infallibly proving the valor of the African was worth hundreds of their lives. He was right, and they felt it, too. Hoping against hope, realizing that they were to lift up their race from the degradation of centuries, three times more did the remnant go into that valley of flame. Human bravery was ineffectual to accomplish impossibilities, and the survivors, heroes all, sadly but triumphantly returned. Nearer than any others did the "black brigade" go, and many a proud master found in death that freedom had made his slave his superior. We had expected that they would be equal to a grand rush, but did *not* expect that they would show valor where valor meant the extremest exercise of the human will. The 27th of May was not a lost day. A race of serfs stepped up to the respect of the world, and commenced a national existence. The bond everywhere will remember that charge, and woe to them who shall try to re-enslave a race which has now such a wealth of historic recollections.

" Dark as the clouds of even,
Ranked in the western heaven,
Waiting the breath that lifts
All the dread mass, and drifts
Tempest and falling brand
Over a ruined land ;
So, still and orderly,
Arm to arm, knee to knee,
Waiting the great event,
Stands the black regiment.

" Down the long, dusky line
Teeth gleam and eyeballs shine,
And the bright bayonet,
Bristling and firmly set,
Flashed with a purpose grand,
Long ere the sharp command
Of the fierce rolling drum
Told them their time had come,
Told them what work was sent
For the black regiment.

" 'Now,' the flag-sergeant cried,
' Though death and hell betide,
Let the whole nation see
If we are fit to be
Free in this land, or bound
Down, like the whining hound—

" Bound with red stripe's pain
 In our old chains again !"
Oh ! what a shout there went
 From the black regiment !

" 'Charge !' Trump and drum awoke ;
 Onward the bondmen broke ;
 Bayonet and sabre-stroke
Vainly opposed their rush.
Through the wild battle's crush,
With but one thought aflush,
Driving their lords like chaff,
In the gun's mouths they laugh ;
Or at the slippery brands
Leaping with open hands,
Down they tear, man and horse,
Down in their awful course,
Trampling with bloody heel
Over the crashing steel,
All their eyes forward bent,
Rushed the black regiment.

" 'Freedom !' their battle-cry—
'Freedom ! or leave to die !'
Ah ! and they *meant* the word :
Not as with us 'tis heard,
Not a mere party shout :
They gave their spirits out ;
Trusted the end to God,
And on the gory sod
Rolled in triumphant blood,
Glad to strike one free blow,
Whether for weal or woe :
Glad to breathe one free breath,
Though on the lips of death.
Praying—alas, in vain !—
That they might fall again,
So they could once more see
That burst to liberty !
This is what 'freedom' lent
To the black regiment.

" Hundreds on hundreds fell,
But they are resting well ;
Scourges and shackles strong
Never shall do them wrong.
Oh ! to the living few,
Soldiers, be just and true !
Hail them as comrades tried ;
Fight with them side by side :
Never, in field or tent,
Scorn the black regiment !"

I credit the assertions that the rebels barbarously refused the negroes burial until the stench of their corpses made it a matter of self-preservation, and that they inhumanly murdered their wounded and prisoners, piled them up on the parapet, and nailed them alive to the trees, where their comardes could witness their dying struggles. I credit it, because they have often declared they would show them no mercy if they fell into their hands, and because I know that nothing would so enrage them as to be compelled to measure arms with a despised race, who had always rendered them the most servile obedience.

It is now time for roll-call, and I close this long letter. Roll-calls are becoming solemn things. On the morning of the 28th eighty men were not there to answer. When the names of the dead were called, the only answer was a solemn silence, and we thanked God for our own preservation, and sadly thought of the bereaved who shall call on loved ones only to hear from their lonely graves, " Dead ! dead ! dead !"

LETTER XXIX.

BEFORE PORT HUDSON, LA., *June* 10, 1863.

MY DEAR L. :

We are yet encamped in the woods from which I
dated my last letter, and are much improved in spirits.
The depression, caused by what seemed to us a useless
sacrifice of life, is wearing off, but we are not as buoyant
and reliable as we were before the late battle. Then, we
went, fully confiding in our generals, wherever ordered,
and went cheerfully. Now, we would obey, if commanded to repeat that charge, but with so much of re-
luctance as to destroy half our efficiency.   Confidence,
once lost, is regained slowly.   Now, if Banks would but
come and utter some earnest, patriotic remarks, sympa-
thizing with our losses and our valor, it would bind us
to him and anew to the sacred cause.

Massachusetts troops are enigmas to those who know
them not. They are cold-blooded, and to hear them
talk before fighting, you might esteem them cowards.
Some men know what "battle-joy" means.   They are
generally earnest, deep-souled, nervous men, who are
never quiet save when working. Their central natures
are so strong that they do not find happiness in the
trifles of life, but give them genuine excitement and
they show what manner of men they are. The prospect
of a battle, in a cause sacred enough to enlist all their
sympathies, is joyous to them. Taking no pleasure in
slaughter, morbidly shrinking from blood, they yet

hail that hour with gladness, feeling that there is a time vouchsafed when they can practice the heroism their souls have garnered. I can dimly see that there is such a class in the world, but they are not from Massachusetts, yet, save in the matter of *dash*, this nation has no better troops. Talking as if they would like to go home and shun the coming danger, yet, at the word of command, they step to death as coolly as to dinner. Where the *dash* fails, and nothing but *will*, hardened by contact with moral education and principle, can uphold, they are pre-eminent. I saw our farmer-boys, seemingly as cold as Greylock, and about as enthusiastic, meet the wave of fire as if they had been trained from boyhood amid the veterans of Napoleon. When bullies succumbed, those quiet ones, who would so suddenly have disappeared from a bar-room fight as to be taunted with cowardice, pressed firmly on, or calmly met the death duty and pride would not allow them to shun. There is no man so fully imbued with personal pride as a son of Massachusetts. At home he will quarrel with that distribution of wealth that puts another in a place of imaginary superiority to him, and with a good deal of desire to drag others down to his level, will persistently labor to place himself at the head of the list. This democratic equality, sometimes run mad, this constant asserting, in the face of fancied superiors, "A man's a man for a' that," is not always attractive, but ally it, in a greater or lesser degree, with convictions of duty, and you have a soldier, who, in the bloodiest field, will prove his divine equality. The 27th of May gave me, who am not "to the manor born," a better insight into the pluck of Massachusetts braves than I ever had before. I know none who will meet impossibilities with more of hope and will. Though they have not the showy courage of some, yet they deserve the *foremost* rank.

We hear little now about time being nearly out. Most are indifferent about a few weeks, more or less; the great question is, Will we be spared to go home at all? There are rumors of an attack on the right to-morrow, and some brigades are preparing their fascines, and we may possibly have a part therein. Not a few think it hard to be thus pushed into danger so near the expiration of their service. Were they yet bound for over two years, they would have no such thoughts. Now crops out the evils of enlisting men for so short a period as nine months; yet I suppose men who had enlisted for ten years would feel the same way were their hour of discharge so near, but it looks worse for us, for we have done so little and seen so few dangers.

The "Sunny South" sounds nicely enough as you ride over Berkshire hills, facing a northwester, with the mercury twenty degrees below zero, but *here*, with that mercury at 95° in the shade for weeks at a time, the poetry all disappears. Get under a tree and look down the road you have to travel for a mile, and you can think of nothing but a "furnace of fire." Every mote in the air looks like a particle of flame. An hour after sunrise or an hour before sunset, and it is seemingly as hot as at noon. A heavy thunder-storm passes over, and the next day is as oppressive as the day before. For the whole twenty-four hours your body is moist or dripping with perspiration. If you are cool at night, it is nothing but the dank moisture driving fever to your vitals. Showers have been infrequent, and the dust, pulverized by the tread of thousands of men and beasts, is more than ankle deep. The trees and bushes are covered with it, and in the sunlight look like smouldering fires. We dress accordingly. A straw hat, a shirt, a pair of breeches and of shoes (sometimes stockings) complete our wardrobe. Some tried to dispense with the use of shoes, but the ground was too much like fire to allow them to continue that kind of economy. Our dark-blue pants have no successors in this department, and we are saving our new light-blue ones to appear creditably when we march through Pittsfield ; so a more ragged set can scarcely be found this side of the Five Points. Who finds a pin labors to make himself presentable; but, as our "pin-money" is about exhausted, we fear that decency will yet drive us to the original fig-leaf. This might be avoided were our blouses as long as the demands of modesty. As we brought no change of apparel, some need those blouses as substitutes for the shirts they threw away. As the Government has nearly doubled the price of shirts, a few economical ones made a search for water, and found some thin mud in the ditch of an adandoned rebel fortification. There, minus soap, they graduated as washerwomen, and quite frequently dried and ironed their wash on their backs, so as to return within the prescribed time. Truth requires me to say that they did not much improve the appearance, though they may have added to the sweetness of their garments. Whole clothes are desirable everywhere, much more in a country where bugs and insects of all kinds, from wood-ticks to lizards, are seeking places of shelter. Flies and mosquitoes have not yet followed us to camp, for which we are duly thankful.

Port Hudson, as a *hygienic* institution, is vastly superior to Baton Rouge. I see Lieutenants Foster and Reed, Orderly Jennings, and others have left the hospitals of the latter place for the post of duty and of health.

We are all in better physical condition than for months before. Considering we are in the field, we are fed well, and hugely enjoy our rations. It seems that Uncle Sam has been reserving the "best wine for the last of the feast." Our sick are improving rapidly. Though we experience somewhat of monotony, it is the monotony of excitement, by which we thrive.

Our army is constantly gaining ground. We have driven the enemy from many of his advanced earthworks into the main parapet. The way we work is this: We, that is, infantry soldiers, throw up a breastwork as a protection to artillerists, some six feet high inside and from thirty to a hundred feet long, according to the number of guns to be placed in position. Bales of cotton are rolled along, behind which we commence digging. A solid shot striking one of these bales square or a shell bursting against it makes much confusion, but that is not often done. The greatest danger is from discharges of grape and canister. The breastwork is from fifteen to twenty feet thick at the bottom, sloping up to about three at the top. The hole from which this dirt is taken makes a ditch outside the parapet. The embrasures or port-holes are lined with sand-bags. Here the artillery is posted. Now, as the gunners are few in number and most of them unarmed, it becomes necessary to protect them, otherwise the enemy might make a sudden attack and capture or spike our guns. A gun is spiked by driving a rat-tail file into the touch-hole. This can not be pulled out, and the gun is useless until redrilled. To prevent this rifle-pits are dug on each side of the battery. Here infantry troops are placed to repel any attack. This is called "supporting a battery." Batteries are thus placed all along our semi-circular front from river to river, a distance of fully ten miles. If these batteries can hold their ground others are established still farther in front, or, in military parlance, we "advance our parallels." Thus we have been advancing, constantly driving the enemy before us into closer quarters.

There is more of this kind of work going on on the right and left than on the centre. Frequently the rebels have made *sorties*, but with no success. The other day they came too near on our right, but retreated when they saw the *negro* regiment rushing on them with fixed bayonets. They acted as if *they* believed the negro would fight. They remember the 27th of May, and have no wish to try that valor, intensified by the vengeance their own barbarous treatment of negro prisoners has aroused. The foe fires but little, evidently hoarding his ammunition. Their silence is mysterious and oppressive. They quietly allow us to put up batteries right under their noses. Less than half a mile distant we have in position some guns that fire one hundred pound shells. With the naked eye they could see us at work all unsheltered, and yet not a disturbing shot, save a few random bullets. Recently an officer rode within fifty yards of the fort without molestation. What does it mean? Scarcity of ammunition or a snare to invite us on to destruction? We know not. I learn it troubles our leading officers. Port Hudson itself is nothing but a collection of a few houses, a store, and a church, but the fortifications are nearly five miles in length and two in breadth, so it is almost impossible to materially injure the garrison. If shells come too thick they retreat to their underground holes and are safe. When but few batteries are opening on them they soon learn the range of our guns and dodge the missiles. Where men lie down on the inside of the parapet, a shell has to burst just at a particular point or they will be un-scathed.   We have poured a great deal of hardware into that Sebastopol, and can see we have injured a great many trees, but rebel prisoners and deserters and our own comrades who have escaped from their clutches all unite in saying we have disabled them but little.   We fire constantly, and by day dismount many of their guns, which they replace at night.   Thus, we scatter the wealth of the nation, but secure immunity from all their guns save those that are in the rear or on the river. Entire days pass and they fire not a shot.   With the greatest secrecy we put up earthworks, and find nothing to evidence the presence of a watchful enemy.   Getting bold, we walk on the top of them or climb above the hedges to pick blackberries, which, to our comfort, are here found in great abundance, and, save an occasional bullet from some riflemen stationed in the trees, are not molested.   One of our boys in picking some berries lost a finger, to remind him that berrying here is not *quite* as safe as in Berkshire.   Our fire worries and exhausts the garrison and kills horses and mules, burying which is so dangerous that they are allowed to rot above ground.   We have so hemmed them in that they can not drive their beeves to water, therefore they die ; and their time of starvation or surrender is hastened.   Some-times at night they let horses out, which wander into our lines.   Killing them would but further taint the air, and as many of them are distempered we gain little by their loss.   We receive but little help from the gunboats. If they could assail the enemy in front we might get up such a bombardment as would lead to a capitulation ; but now, that the river is sixty feet lower than Port Hudson bluffs, they would have to elevate their guns so high that the balls and shells would go clean over the rebels into our midst. The foe can but know where we are situated, and if they are not really entirely destitute of ammunition they would shell us. Massed as we are they could do fearful execution.

By assault or starvation alone can we succeed. Assure us that no enemy will fall on our rear, and the latter is the preferable manner; but instead of being assured of that we have many reasons to believe the contrary. Several hundred (rumor says several *thousand*) rebels having been seen about Clinton, some fifteen miles distant, an expedition, under General Paine, was sent on the 5th to disperse them, in which they succeeded. It was one of our dustiest, hottest days, and in a march of ten miles no less than forty-eight fell sunstruck or exhausted. Our regiment was spared that toil. Quite likely, ere another mail goes, we may again assault this stronghold; for we hear it is decided soon to open on them with all our guns, and if that fails to bring them to terms, then an assault. To make that assault unnecessary Banks is adding to his already large park of artillery monster guns and mortars. The 11-inch guns are taken from the fleet, and worked by marines. They throw ninety-pound solid shot or a hundred and twenty-pound conical shell for four miles. As they are being placed within three-quarters of a mile of the rebels they will do much execution as projectiles as well as shells. The guns weigh upwards of nine thousand pounds each. Mortars look like the mortars druggists use to compound medicines in only on a vaster scale, being about three feet long and two feet in diameter (these are rather small ones) at the mouth. A peck of powder is used at each discharge. How anything like accuracy of range can be obtained is a puzzle to all save gunners. Colonel Hodge, of Massachusetts, has

an engineer regiment composed of stalwart negroes,
great, lusty fellows, who put our muscles to shame, on
whom the burden of preparing earth-works for batteries and the rifle-pits mostly falls.   They are some of
them who carried boxes of cartridges to their comrades
under the fire of May 27th.   Their work is replete
with danger ; but the silence of the enemy emboldens
them.   *Some* of this work falls on us.   The other night
our boys were occupied in rolling bales of cotton along
the road across which we charged in the late battle.
It was a hazardous task, but they were not molested.
I suppose Banks has nearly two hundred pieces of artillery independently of his gunboats.   There is scarcely
a foot of ground from river to river but what is covered
by our cannons.   Miles of roads are being made through
the woods, bridges span nearly every hollow, while
league on league of rifle-pits attest our industry.   We
are fed well, and we understand the order is to give the
best of the food and the heaviest of the work to the
nine months' men.   So where the three years' men get
oily pork we get good salt beef, and then a few furlongs
of rifle-pit digging is thrown in to keep us from dyspepsia.   Keen as are our appetites we would be willing
to have shorter rations and shorter work.   The law is
get what you can out of the nine-monthlings, and save
the three years' troops for subsequent labors.   Right,
I suppose, but our bones protest, and we are all becoming "nigger-worshippers."   Every day adds more or
less to the African element, and we gaze on their
splendid forms with some envy and much joy, for our
toil is in inverse proportion to their number.   Never
fear that soldiers will be found objecting to negro en-
listments.   One hour's digging in Louisiana clay under

a Louisiana sun, and we are forever pledged to do all we can to fill up our ranks with the despised and long-neglected race.

Each day prisoners are brought in. Most of them are fine-looking fellows. In their butternut clothes they look much more presentable than we do. Save a little red facing on the collars and wristbands of officers you can not tell them from privates by their dress. In this they show a wisdom all officers would do well to imitate. They report that their only hope is in Johnston compelling us to raise the siege, and that many of the officers are willing to surrender, but General Gardner is determined to hold out to the last ear of corn. He is a deserter from our army, and in his haste to join the rebels did not stop to resign his commission, so he may fear that his surrender will be followed by a deserter's death. He does us honor overmuch. I fear we have not yet reached so commendable a severity.

Before our army shut them in the rebels confiscated much of the food of the surrounding planters. Hearing that we could exchange some of our hard crackers and doubtful pork (we can't get *all* beef) for chickens and milk, Hulet and I visited a Mrs. Cage for that commendable purpose. Her husband is in the rebel army, and she is blessed with forty slaves, or to use the euphonious language of the South, "forty head of niggers," so attached to her that they will not leave her. We left our rations and got the coveted delicacies. That lady and her children ate the food we carried as greedily as our children eat pound-cake. I found that she did not fear the Yankees, but stood in mortal terror of the black troops, saying that when we leave they will murder, ravage, and ravish. If they should ravish, who taught them that power meant the right to use woman as their passions might dictate?

> "He that of old did bend the oak,
>   Dreamed not of the *rebound*."

Pilfer the negroes do, but not more than white soldiers, and strange that consciousness of power don't lead them to pilfer more. Treat them kindly, and they will quietly forgive the wrongs of centuries; but any revival of plantation manners will rouse a devil that only blood and outraged beauty will appease. The negro *is* of a docile race. In my numerous conversations with them I never heard them threaten their former masters, and hard as it may be to hear it, they behave better than the great majority of white soldiers. Punishments among them are far less frequent, and I have yet to hear of one instance of their outraging female purity. They seem to be too glad that they are free to harbor thoughts of vengeance. Slavery in Louisiana is dead, and if the masters will not attempt to revive it they can live at peace with their negroes; but any attempt to re-enslave men who have felt the inspiration of May 27th will arouse a fiend before whose ravages the horrors of St. Domingo will sink into insignificance.

We have several of their camps near us. They are neat and clean, and a visit to them pays. For the first time, I have seen some of the native joyousness of the negro cropping out, and have gazed on the first banjo. They are beginning to realize that they have paid for their freedom with their blood, and have a right to be happy. General Paine sent word to *us* that we must stop our singing of hymns; why, we could not tell; but

General Augur, who tents near the negro camp, does not disturb *them*, and so our nights are often blessed with their songs of praise, as they assemble in prayer-meetings. More fortunate than we, they have their wives with them, at least, women they *call* their wives. Generally, the negro has but dim conception of the sacredness of the marriage relation. If his wife is sold from him, he looks upon her as dead to him, and marries again. If unwilling, he is often forced into wedlock, for the Moloch of Slavery demands for his victims unbroken generations of children. In these times, when a voice is saying, "Overturn! overturn!" the original husband and wife sometimes meet; and I have heard of cases where the second marriage, not being a happy one, has been rectified by the parties mutually returning to their first loves. The distribution of the children might cause *us* trouble, but *they* have been taught that the child follows the mother and that the father is *merely* the author of their existence. At our last visit to Mrs. Cage, we found the chickens had disappeared, and the brigade commissary had levied on her cows, and, worse than all, her servants had caught the inspiration of Freedom and joined the "damned Yankees." I was rather disappointed, thinking that I had at last found a nest of them who so loved their mistress that they preferred slavery to freedom. Some assert that negroes are not human; certainly they have a strange nack of doing what human beings do when placed in similar circumstances. Liberty has a charm to the poor serf; but liberty in union with the flesh-pots of our commissaries is irresistible.

A few days since, the medical department treated us to iced claret-punch. Grumblers might have discovered that the claret was hardly in full proportion to the water, but, as it was sweet and cold, we gratefully quenched our thirst with it, and hoped they would not become weary in well doing. We have been cleaning camp and doing other work indicative of a prolonged stay. For the first time since leaving Baton Rouge, we are allowed to go about without wearing our equipments. We have been enabled to recover a good many of the guns left on the battle-field. Our artillery and sharp-shooters have kept the rebels away, and the boys bring the trophies in. Each side sends pickets out, and in that Golgotha they renew the scenes of the 27th on a miniature scale. At first the skirmishers came in at night; but now they skirmish by day and do picket-duty at night. A battle implies less exhaustion and mental anxiety than a day's skirmishing. They grad-ually creep up as near the parapet as possible. Out-side thereof come rebel skirmishers, within twenty rods of them. There they lie all day, baked in the hot sun. If they show any part of their bodies, a bullet zips by them to remind them that discretion is the bet-ter part of valor. They must load on their back or side, and fire whenever they get a chance. Sometimes they put their hats on twigs and elevate them above the protecting stump to draw the bullets of their opponents, and then, exposing themselves to fire, learn by the num-ber of balls rattling round them that they are watched by *many* pairs of fierce eyes. Strange that so few are hurt, and those are generally the victims of rebel rifle-men perched in trees! From some of the trees you can see jets of smoke, but it is almost impossible to locate the enemy. Occasionally a mass of something is seen dropping from the branches, and no more smoke springs from that place. Often they spend hours without dar-ing to move. One poor fellow was trying to reach a good shelter, when the order to open fire compelled him to drop down where he then was, behind a small stump barely sufficient to hide his head. On his face, the sun pouring down on his spine and driving the hot blood to his brain, he lay all that livelong day. He dared not move to load or fire, or to reach his canteen or haversack. The "forlorn hope" was nothing to *that*. Lieutenant Sissons, who, leaving the hospital, which was so nearly his death-chamber, is now here in command of Company E. He went out skirmishing, and on his return from his neck to his hips was one solid blister, the sun having thus scorched him through his clothes. Battles tell but a small part of the dangers and discomforts of the soldier. After such a day, a night of picket-duty closes up the work of twenty-four hours. At first our skirmishers kept up a pretty rapid fire, but, finding that only increased their danger without doing execution, they now rarely fire unless they get a good aim. Towards night the setting sun blinds our boys and gives the rebels a fine chance to damage us. Sunrise reverses the position of affairs, and now the firing is mainly confined to those two seasons. You may ask, What good results from all this? If it were not done, rebel sharpshooters would creep up and cut off our gunners. Not only is that now avoided, but we can keep them from setting up or manning their cannons. The foe put up sand-bags on the top of the parapets, leaving small spaces for the rifle and for sighting it, and, strange as it is, in some cases our men send their unerring bullets right through these apertures, and crashing into eyes that are seeking chances to destroy us.

On the 31st ult., Colonel Paine, acting brigadier, sent for Captain Rennie, who is reputed a good shot, and asked him if he could hit a man at a distance of twenty-five rods. The captain said, "Yes," and they together climbed a tree, from which the colonel showed Rennie the work he had carved out for him and a squad of sixteen picked men. It was to silence two 64-pounders on either side of the roads, guns which so galled us on the 27th. Five of the men followed the captain to within ten rods of the parapet, and kept those guns silent the rest of that day. About 3 p. m. the rebels sent a small detachment over their breast-works to flank them, when they retreated safely, despite the various leaden invitations to tarry, one of which saved the captain the trouble of carrying his cap for six feet and affectionately severed a lock of his hair as a memento of work so done as greatly to please the brigadier, who, from a tree, was watching the *modus operandi*, and, on seeing the enemy's flank movements, felt certain that there would be a fresh sprinkling of blue-breeches among the butternuts that night.

Exciting as are these scenes, they wear on the troops and deplete our small army. Battle and sickness reduced our number, between the twenty-third and thirtieth of May, 1,000 men. Up to June 4th, *we* have lost by death and wounds 80, and by sickness 75 men. By disease and sunstrokes this army loses fifty per day. War is fearfully expensive. To keep effective an army of half a million, it is necessary to recruit yearly 123,-000 men and to maintain 58,000 in hospitals. In view of these facts and of our emaciated sick, refusing the aid of the negroes was almost a crime. In this department there are twelve whites sick to one black.

Lieut. Kellogg (I) has been honorably discharged and has left us. He sent in his resignation long before we commenced this campaign. Captain Train has returned to Baton Rouge. I wonder that he remained so long, suffering as he did with erysipelas. His feet and the lower part of his legs are one solid scab. In the absence of our surgeons, he not only commands the camp, but is surgeon thereto—no ordinary compliment for a homœopathist to receive from an old-school medical director. I can but believe his system of practice would work better than that of the heroic school. The captain's sympathetic nature would add to the efficacy of his drugs. Many of the sick want sympathy above everything else. God pity them, as they gradually die, away from all held most dear! There they lie, hearing the groans or delirious cries of their comrades, only relieved by the carrying away of corpse after corpse. Quite a number of our men have lost fingers or toes by accidental discharges of their own guns. Such accidents are mortifyingly frequent. J. Smith (E) and R. Vanderburgh (J) were wounded while skirmishing.

It is said the rebels lost 280 on the 27th. That may explain the reason why they did not molest us as we carried off our wounded. M. H. Tuttle, orderly of Company E, led our storming party, and led it well and bravely. He was one of those who almost stole away from the hospital to do his part where brave men were needed. We fear that Lieutenants Sherman and Siggins will die and that the Colonel can not save his arm. Some others of our wounded are very low. Johnny Bryce (A) has had his right arm amputated. He and Ende, of the same company, were markers, whose duty it is to bear small flags, one of which is placed at each end of the column to enable the regiment more readily to form a straight line. Doing that work, amid the scenes of the 27th, belonged to the heroic, and in doing it young Bryce lost his arm. His empty sleeve will long teach lessons of patriotism more eloquent than the finest speeches of those who only scent the battle from *afar*.

> " It tells of a battle-field of gore—
> Of the sabre's clash—of the cannon's roar—
> Of the deadly charge—of the bugle's note—
> Of a gurgling sound in a foeman's throat—
> Of the whizzing grape—of the fiery shell—
> Of a scene which mimics the scenes of hell.
> Till this very hour, would you e'er believe
> What a tell-tale thing is an empty sleeve—
> What a wierd, queer thing is an empty sleeve?"

Few poems convey so good a *general* idea of a fierce conflict as these lines of Bayard Taylor :

"Then the rattling roll of the musketeers,
  And the muffled drums and the rallying cheers :
  And the rifles burn with a keen desire,
  Like the crackling whips of the hemlock fire :
  And the sighing shot and the shrieking shell,
  And the splintered fire of the shattered hell,
  And the great white breaths of the cannon-smoke,
  As the growling guns by the batteries spoke
  In syllables cropped from the thunder of God—
  The throb of the cloud where the drummer-boy trod,
  And the ragged gaps in the walls of blue,
  Where the iron surge rolls heavily through,
  That the Colonel builds with a breath again,
  As he cleaves the din with 'Close up, men !'

" And the groan torn out from the blackened lip,
  And the prayer doled slow with the crimson drip ;
  And the beamy look in the dying eye,
  As under the cloud the stars go by !
  But his soul marched on, the captain said,
  For the soldier in blue can never be dead !
  And the troops sit in their saddles all,
  As the statues carve in an ancient hall ;

" And they watch the whirl from their breathless ranks,
  And their spurs are close to the horses' flanks,
  And the fingers work, of the sabre-hand—
  Oh, to bid them live, and to make them grand !
  And the bugle sounds to the charge at last,
  And away they plunge, and the front is past ;
  And the jackets blue grow red as they ride,
  And the scabbards, too, that clank by their side ;
  And the dead soldiers deaden the strokers' iron-shod
  As they gallop right on o'er the plashy red sod—
  Right into the cloud all spectral and dim,
  Right up to the guns black-throated and grim,
  Right down on the hedges bordered with steel,
  Right through the dense columns, then ' Right about wheel !'

" Hurrah ! a new swath through the harvest again !
  Hurrah for the flag ! to the battle, amen !"

The accompanying verses, from the ready pen of
Lieutenant-Colonel Sumner, will give you an admirable
description of the part our regiment really took in the
memorable battle of the 27th of May. The high hopes
that animated us on entering the field ; the reversion of
feeling when we met, not danger and death, but obstructions that convinced us we could die, not conquer ; the gloom surrounding the fall of our leaders ;
the dauntless pressing on, though thus bereft ; the
seeking shelter only when exposure was fool-hardiness ;
the silent bearing away our comrades ; stepping over
our dead ; our mingled sadness and pride on returning
—all are here portrayed as only could be done by one
who had been an active participant therein :

THE CHARGE OF THE FORTY-NINTH

"Forward, now, the Forty-ninth !" the General's mandate came ;
"Attention, Third Battalion !" was the Colonel's prompt ex-
    claim ;
Now, you sons of Berkshire, your crowning hour has come,
Prove your fond fidelity to ancestry and home !

Straightway from the undergrowth our gallant boys upsprang ;
Rapid and sonorous the familiar accents rang :
"Right face ! Lively ! Forward, march !" Meanwhile in each
    eye
Mark the firm resolve that dareth both to do and die.

Through the tangled bushes stealthily we tread,
While the shells are bursting madly overhead ;
Now we reach the open, and, across the plain,
See the rebel cannon spouting leaden rain.

"On the right, by file in line !" rapidly we form ;
"Forward, march ! Guide centre !" Now the fiery storm,
With redoubled fury, vexes earth and sky,
As our glorious banner greets the foeman's eye.

Gallantly, before us, in the thrilling scene
March the storming party, with musket and fascine ;
See ! Their steps they hasten ! "Double-quick "—now, then,
Comes the tug of battle ; quit yourselves like men !

Ah, what rebel cunning had prepared the way !
Felled trees, logs, and branches in our pathway lay ;
Still our flag moves forward ! aye, and not alone,
For our line of battle bravely holds its own.

God of mercy, help us ! Twice the murderous balls
Strike our hero Colonel ! ah, he reels ! he falls !
Our Lieutenant-Colonel, "Onward ! Onward !" crying,
In an instant stricken, on the field is lying !

Yet our boys undaunted, with their might and main,
Strive to gain the ramparts, but, alas ! in vain.

From those fatal ramparts, looming still **afar,**
How the foe exultant hurls the bolts of **war !**

Through our ranks, where glittered bayonet-blade.
See what deadly havoc shot and shell have made !
Of that proud battalion—fresh-lipped men and brave—
Scores now groan in anguish : some have found a grave.

Strive no longer vainly, **now that hope is** past .
Let the logs and pitfalls be your shield at last ;
Down, then ! Down for safety, ye who still survive ,
Thank the god of battles, **ye are** yet alive.

Softly soon the day-king sinks unto his rest.
And the grateful twilight deepens in the west .
Hushed the din of battle ; now, with footsteps fleet,
Weary, saddened soldiers make their swift retreat.

Lo ! what scenes confront them, as they **rearward tread ;**
Here a comrade wounded, there a comrade dead !
Friends at home, and kindred, ah ! what would you **say,**
Could you see your petted Forty-ninth to-day !

This, at least, in future say, with honest pride,
" Berkshire boys right nobly fought, and bled, and died ;"
Ever let their actions be rehearsed in story,
And their names encircled with a wreath of glory

Henry Richardson (H). of Sandisfield, **aged** eighteen
years, died in the hospital at Baton Rouge, of consumption, **June 9th. He was a fine, steady boy.** long sick,
and has gone **to his rest.**

John W. Fitzgerald (D), carriage-maker, from Barrington, aged nineteen years, died of diarrhœa in the general
hospital at Baton Rouge on the 30th of May. He was
a fine Irish boy, and a steady, good soldier. The main
dependence of an aged mother, his loss will be severely
felt.

Company E and Sheffield lost in the death of our drummer-boy, *Henry L. Holmes*, an excellent soldier, and a promising lad of nineteen years. He died at Baton Rouge, June 1st. One of his officers said, "He was the finest kind of boy." When a soldier so demeans himself among soldiers as to merit such an encomium, you can imagine how great the sorrow in that blighted home that gave him to God, his country, and his lonely grave.

Henry L. Beach (II), dentist, from Lee, aged twenty-three, was wounded May 27th, and died at Baton Rouge, June 3d. He was a brave, steady, and reliable soldier, and an intelligent man. Among those who, unconscious of our experience of the past fortnight, are fondly awaiting the return of the Forty-ninth, there are hearts to whom that return will bring no joy, save pride in their patriotic dead. To that increasing number is now added the young wife and child of our buried comrade.

James Cressor (I) died of typhoid fever on the 4th inst., at Baton Rouge. He was a Canadian, and enlisted from Pittsfield. His age was eighteen years.

Charles Edward Platt (A) died at the general hospital at Baton Rouge on the 6th inst. He was wounded in the leg at the recent battle. Neither he nor any of his comrades thought his wound was serious. When they were about to remove him from the field, he requested them to leave him and attend to others who were more severely injured. He was taken to the city, and there died. Perchance his life might have been preserved, had he received proper care; but, not considering himself in a dangerous state, and being one of those who rarely complain, his wound was not dressed for some days after his entering the hospital. Mortification set in, and soon ended the career of one of our best boys.

He was a son of C. B. Platt, of Pittsfield, who was op-posed to his enlisting on the ground of his youth, being but seventeen years old. Large and stout for his age, he thought he could do the duties of a soldier, and, until that fatal day, none did them better. His officers speak of him in the highest terms. Leaving a comfort-able home, knowing nothing of hardships, privations, or dangers, he went forth, yearning to do something to maintain the honor of his country, and in every sphere measured up to the claims of duty. Untried, he yet faltered not when came the order to enter the valley of death. His young heart may have trembled, but his firm will bore him on till the bullet of the foe laid him low. Bearing up against the temptations of the camp, bold in the fiery furnace, his soldier-life was worthy of imitation; but prouder, sweeter still his death. Always moral, yet it was reserved for the gloom of the hospital to witness his union with Christ. Teachings that had often been impressed on his *mind* then sank into his *heart*, and brought forth that faith which enables the dying lips to utter "I have fought a good fight." His last words were asking a comrade to write to his parents, and say to them that he should meet them in heaven. Thus, thinking of his earthly and his heavenly home, he departed to his Maker. There will be deep sorrow in that earthly home, but some ray of glory from the heavenly will gild it. Happy those parents of whose son it can be said, "He lived well and died a Christian soldier." Human hearts, though throbbing in sorrow, will sweetly remember that—

> "The golden bells of the city of God
> Have rung his welcome in."

Godfrey Wolfinger (K) died of typhoid fever at Baton Rouge on the 8th inst. He was a farmer boy from

Stockbridge, aged eighteen years. A fine boy he was, and a good soldier. Poor, dear fellow! How he yearned to participate in the dangers of this campaign! Begging so hard, he received permission to start with us, but soon had to return. Truly, *his* zeal was greater than his strength. The brave-hearted lad fought his last battle amid the dreariness and loneliness of the hospital, and "after life's fitful fever, sleeps well." All honor to the noble soul that craved no higher boon than to fall fighting in the thickest of the strife, for the honor of the dear old flag to yield up his life. God accepted the unaccomplished heroism, and among the "fallen brave" of the Forty-ninth we write high up the name of Godfrey Wolfinger.

Frederick Belcher (B), a New Ashford farmer, was a steady man, and a brave, reliable soldier. On the 27th he was wounded in the leg, and recovering from that, was attacked with diphtheria, which caused his death, June 10th, in the twenty-first year of his age. He leaves a brother in the same company, to go home without the Benjamin of the household, and to hear one of the saddest refrains of this war: "If I am bereaved of my children, I *am* bereaved."

LETTER XXX.

Before Port Hudson, La., *June* 15, 1863.

My Dear L.:

We yet call this, our old camp, home, though the regiment is here but a small portion of the time, having for several days lived in and about rifle-pits, a life more novel than pleasant. Familiarity breeds contempt of rebels, and whereas we used to stay in the pits the greater part of the time, crouching down behind the earthwork, now we wander about as if almost unconscious that behind the parapet we can see so plainly, and within easy rifle range, there are thousands of lurking foes. Occasionally a few bullets whiz past us, and we look around to see if any one is hit : and if all are safe, seem about as unconcerned as if we were in the old Bay State. We fire but little, for the enemy rarely gives us a chance to make our shots tell, and Yankees count the cost, even where Uncle Sam foots the bill. Our food is cooked in the rear, and brought to us by cooks and by the musicians, whose occupation now being gone, thus render themselves useful. Bailey, cook of Co. D, thought he would carry out the breakfast a few mornings since, and was administering allopathic doses of strong coffee, when a spent bullet hitting P. Devanny, of that company, in the shoulder, assured him that if cooking was less heroic than soldiering, it was certainly safer. Our rifle-pits, being well shaded, are not very uncomfortable in dry weather : but as the fashion is now to have a shower nearly every evening, the foot or eighteen inches of water that collect therein make our beds resemble feathers *only* in the quality of softness.   The second night on taking possession of these pits we slept *in* them, defiant of their muddy condition.   The night before we kept awake and tried to do so that night, but sleep conquered our aversion to water and mud, and, resting our backs against one side and propping our feet against the other, we sought the balmy restorer under peculiar difficulties.   We could maintain our position awhile, but when Morpheus got the mastery down we would flap into the water, our own discomfort and the strong language of our disturbed comrades assuring us that dreams were false if they had conveyed us to the chambers of Berkshire.   Towards morning it little mattered whether we were lying in or out of the water so we got some sleep.   With my usual good fortune I secured a bed on the roots of a tree with only *one* foot in the water ; and if the old tempter in seducing our grandmother Eve had but given to her posterity his own vertebræ I could have wound myself around those roots and passed a pleasant night.   Sleep some I did, and though the huge 32-pounders, not fifty feet distant, sounded the alarm every fifteen minutes, I heard but two or three of them.   About daybreak you could see the moist, dirty soldiers rising up, and with some grumbling, labor to get the kinks out of their aching bodies.   The light thickened and the coffee came, and soon cheerfulness reigned again.   Since then we put down our rubber blankets (life-preservers they may well be called) on the inside margin of the pits, and, though conscious that a shower of bullets or grape would acquaint some of us with that sleep that knows no waking, we rest in all the luxury of expansion.   "Headquarters" used to mean a fine tent and a pacing sentinel.

Now it brings up before the mind an elevated bed of rails (a long bed it is, for the "tall major" is the presiding genius), thinly covered with some rubbish and an awning of two pieces of a shelter-tent. There the major and adjutant enjoy their *otium cum dignitate* with the help of the rebel weed, which they burn so assiduously as to lead us to imagine that their earnest Union hearts yearned to destroy one of the great staples of the South, almost forgetting that it costs somewhere in the neighborhood of two dollars per pound. Living in such a conspicuous place, I should not be surprised to hear that their home had been entered by secesh bullets, and we as a regiment consigned to the tender mercies of Senior Captain Weller. I do not disparage that officer, for a braver and better and kinder we have not, nor one that could handle the regiment so well; but as the major is in command and doing finely, I want him to have the honor of leading us to a glorious termination of this campaign and a successful raid on Berkshire. Bartlett used to endure torture wearing that cork leg day after day (he put it on much too soon), torture which an iron man only would endure. I know not how he would get along *here*, and the reserve we always felt in his presence might become oppressive, as we would necessarily be in that presence all the time. I never saw him meet an occasion without adapting himself to it, and I fancy we would like him as well in the pits as in camp or battle, though I presume there would be fewer loungers about headquarters. The major shows good sense in maintaining the dignity of his office without trying to imitate that of the colonel. David in Saul's armor never pleased himself or others.

Sutlers have followed us to the front and at fabulous prices supply us with tobacco, ginger bread, cheese, and

other articles considered superfluous by our providers.
They are well patronized. This is neither time nor
place for economy. We are often regaled with fresh
beef, of the quantity of which I can speak more favorably than of the quality. You can judge somewhat of
the pleasure of living in this climate. A few days since
a squad killed some cattle, and in less than two hours
the meat was so fly-blown that we could not use it. For
the first time in our history we have had wormy bread.
Knocking worms out before eating enlarges our experience more than our comfort.

Some of our nights have been grand. I know nothing
more fascinating than lying in these grand woods in the
moonlight. It makes one shudder to think of a future
of roofed chambers; and it will be some time before
we can be reconciled to the effeminacy of feather-beds.
Our experience will enable us to dispense *home* hospitality on a larger scale, by giving to the guest (if sexes
agree) our unnecessary bed, and retiring to what we
would now consider luxurious accommodations, a pil-
low on a carpeted floor. We are generally rocked to
sleep by the music of artillery, and the other night
heaven and earth joined in the concert of awful sounds.
The long peals of thunder mingled with the roar of
cannon and the flashing of artillery blended with the
dull, continuous lightning. Often we could not tell
which was the voice of God and which the voice of
man. At times we would hear the report of one of the
mammoth guns of the fleet; then the heavy, rumbling
thunder would unite with that noise, and again the roar
of cannon, followed quickly by another peal from on
high would keep up an unbroken but awful harmony.
Occasionally the lightning would flash vividly as at
home, and the thunder gather into a fearful crash, re-

vealing the pettiness of man, as if from heaven were sounded "*Power* belongeth unto *God.*" It was a time of solemnity, of awe. The shells shrieked and burst and the great mortars moaned and groaned as if the soul of Freedom was travailing in agonizing desire to reach the heart of Slavery. All night long the mingled storm continued, waxing yet more fearful, till morning, ushering in the light and quietness, was a grateful relief. 'Tis worth a few months' separation from home to enjoy some of our experiences.

Our straw hats were found to be too conspicuous marks, so we have had to return to caps, which leave the back of the head all exposed to the rays of the sun. Recently a major was shot by our own pickets. He passed out the line at one place, and was about returning through at another place without halting to give the countersign, perchance thinking it was the beat he had passed through first, when a sentinel killed him. In one of my wood rambles I got lost, and the remembrance of that incident made me more fearful of friends than I have ever been of foes. "Shot by mistake" is a poor epitaph for a soldier's tomb.

The enemy lose nearly fifty per day by desertion. Eighteen stationed at an outpost killed their officer and escaped to our lines. Some found their way to the works manned by the negroes, and, though the rebel brutality of the 27th was still fresh in their minds, were treated by them with great kindness. We greet these deserters. They may be scaly patriots, but each counts one less rifle to march up against.

I give you a little incident to illustrate the honor of the position of color sergeant and the pride we take in our colors. Major Burt, of the One Hundred and Fifty-ninth New York, led four hundred men in a desperate charge, but met a cross-fire so fearful that almost in the twinkling of an eye one hundred were laid low and the rest had to fall back. The color bearer had planted the flag on the ramparts before he was slain, so it was left behind. A corporal dashed forward, seized the sacred emblem, and was bearing it away, when a bullet through his heart stopped his career The major himself then went for it and came off with it in safety, leaving a part of the staff sticking in the ground where the brave bearer had placed it. You must be a soldier before you can *really* sing " Rally round the *flag!* boys." Oh! 'tis grand thus to rally and at the same time "Ring out the battle-cry of Freedom."

This has been an eventful week to us. Another assault was decided on. It is again said Banks adopts this plan against the advice of all his generals. He looks like a man of much self-reliance. Such men may, by trusting to their own judgments, commit mistakes, but they generally get through. Through we *must* get, and that soon, for rebel attacks in our rear are becoming annoyingly frequent and increasingly alarming. A few days since they captured over fifty of our teams. They waited till we had substituted nice army wagons for our lumbering plantation carts. Almost under General Grover's nose they seized an ambulance with its load of sick. The fact that the time of service of several of the regiments has almost expired suggests haste. Persuasion and threat may keep *them* in the ranks after that time, but their efficiency will be materially lessened. Last Monday lots were drawn for fascine-bearers. That time the fascines were cotton-bags about three feet long which could be carried as shields. No chance was offered for volunteering. Captain Chaffee was appointed to lead them. I had made up my mind to accompany them. A bridge-party was also formed, whose duty it is to bridge a way over the ditch for the artillery; then the pioneers, under Captain Garlick, are to dig down the parapet that we may run our guns inside. *Inside!* what *that* means we know not. Once inside and we may find stronger works and graves. "Do or die" seems to be Banks's motto. Daily the bridge-party practice forming and laying down the bridge, all the timbers being nicely adjusted together; and daily, also, Garlick drills his pioneers. I suppose hundreds of skirmishers will be sent out to keep the walls clear while these forlorn hopes do their work. That will lessen their danger, but they have an appalling task before them. Though they did not *volunteer*, and doubtlessly hope that this cup, aye, this cup of trembling, may pass from them, yet there are no signs of flinching. God bless the dear fellows! I never knew my courage fail me when the hour came, but welcome a dozen assaults rather than those fearful days of waiting and suspense. Some one has said—

"The brave man dies but once;
 The coward dies a thousand deaths in fearing one."

Good poetry, only it is lacking in truth. The brave man is he who *will* do his duty though before and in doing it he may suffer the mental pangs of a thousand deaths. I wish Berkshire, knowing the work before them, could see these men, her sons; and if pride and tears did not mingle together she would be unworthy of them. I often visit them, and as I notice their quiet manner, their calm blue eyes, their undaunted deportment, I am glad I belong to the same regiment. Whether by accident or th'nking them inconsistent with the solemnities of battle-life, cards have been left behind, but few failed to bring their pocket-Testaments;

and I frequently saw some of *them* reading the inspiring truths, and knew they were gathering more than earthly courage for a heavenly duty. I take back my wish that Berkshire could see these men. Ere this, there is enough soul-wearing anxiety there. Hearts are sorrowing for their distant dead, or suffering with their unwatched wounded, or asking for news of their periled living ones, trying to hope for the best, yet fearing the worst, and we mourn with the bereaved and sympathize with the anxiety of those who are as yet only affected in imagination. Weary weeks will roll away before we leave the presence of danger, and yet more weeks before homes are gladdened with the assurance of the safety of our remnant. Knowing this, I can not wish that the mothers and wives of these men should daily pass them as they wait the dread moment; but I would like the many who could not *afford* to serve their country to see what *their* privileges cost.

Last Thursday night earthworks were to be thrown up and rifle-pits dug that Holcomb's battery could be located within forty rods of the foe. A large detail from our regiment was to do the work. Roll cotton-bales over ground almost covered with felled trees and limbs in the face of a foe, and you may be excused if you often think and tremble at the probable consequences of a few discharges of grape, canister, railroad iron, screw-heads, nails, and such other articles as the rebels draw from their armory of death. Those bales were to be our only protection. Thinking that any help might not be unacceptable I went down to the rifle-pit to join the detail. We waited the order to move, the night was very dark and gloomy, and we were far from jubilant. One fine soldier, an Irishman, gave vent to his apprehensions by damning the niggers, and denouncing the whole contest as a "nigger war." The words had scarcely left his lips when Captain Chaffee came to tell us we were excused from the duty. Colonel Hodges's (*negro*) engineers having *volunteered* for the task. Well, there was no more "damning the niggers" that night, and I guess that good Irishman was instantaneously converted to abolitionism. From more than one heart came the fervent "God bless the negroes!" and the resolve to nobly fight that every one of the race may look upon our flag as the emblem of *their* freedom. The night passed on; we, so much farther from those engineers than the rebels, could hear their voices and the noise of their spades, and momentarily expected the sound that would tell that for *us* they had worked and *died*. But not a shot broke the stillness.

In the darkness of the following evening we started to occupy the works they had erected. We were told to maintain the strictest silence, so we walked as if on eggs and with suppressed breath. Nothing will make a man feel quite so timid as to be among hundreds marching in the dark up to loaded guns, treading as softly as if you know you are doing wrong, and *whispering* out your apprehensions to your comrade. I was placed in the *rear* rank, and was glad of it, and half scanned the size of the man before me to be assured that I was safe till he fell : and *then*, then we quickened our pace, and began to speak a little louder, and the tremor was over. 'Tis said a rapid walk on a frosty morning will clear up the evidence of a doubting Christian : I know it will bring out the courage of the wavering soldier. We reached some cotton-bags, and then rested till the major led us to our places, two companies at a time. So near the foe, we hugged our pits pretty closely that

night, but again the rebels gave no signs of life.   This
was the first really forward move we had made since
the command of the regiment devolved on the major,
and he was determined we should not be surprised and
his own name sullied : so he spent the night in the
road considerably in advance of our line of earthworks.
I laid me down to sleep behind a stump, and woke up
to find that my bed fellow was a stalwart darkey.   Prejudices are often stronger than principles, and though
I was willing to *fight*, that under our flag all (negroes
included) should enjoy the rights of humanity, I had
hardly advanced far enough towards miscegenation to
sleep with " God's image carved in ebony."   Involun-
tarily I gave my blanket an extra shake that morning.
He was white when I laid down there ; of that I am
quite sure ; the origin of the first negro is only less of
a puzzle than how my sleeping with him converted him
into an unmistakable darkey.

Not caring to spend the *day* idly basking in a sum-
mer sun, I returned to camp in the morning, meeting
hundreds of negroes carrying shells and kegs of powder
in full view of the enemy, who seemed to care no more
for them and their hostile preparations than an elephant
for a fly.   The cooks and musicians were bringing out
our food.   Carrying the blessings of this life over an
almost open field to within a few hundred yards of thousands of angry weapons is acting the Good Samaritan
to some purpose, and is not a bad school for volunteers
of future forlorn hopes.

About 11 A. M. of the 13th inst., nearly all our batteries opened on the enemy, and for an hour there was
an almost uninterrupted roar of artillery as we gave
rebeldom a specimen of every kind of death-dealing
missile.   Then General Banks sent in a flag of truce

demanding the surrender of the place, which looked to us like boys' play. Every shot is a summons to surrender, and if *they* do not bring out the white flag, certainly a *verbal* demand will not. Perchance, the bombardment and flag of truce were merely intended to give deserters a chance to escape, for soon after several hundreds came into our lines. General Gardner said duty required him to defend the place. Though the morrow was the Sabbath day, we knew that truth would then be preached with cannon and impressed with bayonets, and attended with such sacrificial blood as will bring the Mount of Ascension nearer to Calvary. The afternoon was occupied with preparing for the assault. Night came, making no alteration in the affairs of *our* regiment; so we concluded that the troops of the centre were to be idle spectators of the engagement, or kept back as reserves; but about midnight we were called into line, and knew that our Sabbath meant blood, and wounds, and death. After breakfast the surgeon sent a ration of whisky, but he had been anticipated. I reached the regiment about 1 A. M., and found a man *urging* the boys to fill their canteens with liquor, they having drunk what they thought necessary. I knew that on comparatively empty stomachs much whisky would produce drunkenness, so I told him the men had enough and he had better leave. Perchance, he thought I was an officer, for he left, but soon returned, saying the surgeon had sent him back to get rid of the rest of his stock. Most of our boys refused to take any more, and I did not hear of half a dozen who were in anywise intoxicated. The Second Louisiana were nearly all drunk. We found that out afterwards to our sorrow.

In excellent order the Major placed us very much nearer the fort than we had ever been before. Some

companies had no protection save a few bushes.   The
rebels were so quiet, so seemingly unconscious of our
presence, that then we could have laid the bridge, crossed
the ditch, and in comparative safety the pioneers might
have made a breach in the parapet.   I say in *"comparative* safety," for earthworks are so built that an enfilad-
ing fire will sweep the *ditches*, as some men found to their
cost, fourteen having gotten in in one place, of whom
only three came out alive.   I located myself behind a
stump, with others, but the Major thought it was not
far enough front, so we made an advance, glad to do
so, for that stump was in exact range of our thirty-two
pounders, which went less than three feet over our heads.
Considering that shells often fall short or burst before
their time, some other locality was preferable.   With
the Major and some of Company H, I rested behind a
felled tree.   It was a mammoth one, but, unfortunately,
it had a mammoth bend in it, and the rebels had so laid
it that the bend gracefully curved upwards, leaving the
lower parts of our bodies about as well protected as if
we had sought shelter behind a ladder.   An unexploded
shell, weighing over a hundred pounds, had ceased its
labors right under this bend.   With it and some brush,
we closed up the aperture, so that we were impervious
to the eyes but not to the bullets of the foe.   A signal-
rocket went up from the right, the Major discharged
his pistol, and then we all began to fire as rapidly as
possible.   It was too dark to see the parapet, but understanding that our move was only a feint, to confuse the
enemy while the real attack was being made right and
left, we scattered our cartridges with a perfect looseness.
This was about 3 o'clock in the morning, and we kept
up quite a continuous fire for four or five hours.   Some
ten minutes elapsed before we were answered, and then

in a manner that convinced us that they knew *we* were only feigning. Bullets rattled round us in sufficient numbers and with such accuracy as to send poor Parker (C) to his long home, to wound others, and to disagreeably bring up the contrast between that and the quietness of a New England Sabbath. As we lay there we learned that no exciting work was before *us:* but rapid musketry and wild cheering on the right told us that *there* the valor of the 27th was being repeated Alas! again in vain. Were it not for the occasional bullets that found their way under our tree, we would have felt quite safe, had we not been alarmed by a fire from our rear. We had been at work several hours, when, with a cry of "Forward!" some of the Second Louisiana came up, leaving the great majority of their drunken comrades fifteen or twenty rods behind. As their bullets would come unpleasantly near, we would raise the shout, "Fire higher!" and that shout was carried all along the front. The miserable fellows thought, in their drunken valor, that they were the nearest regiment to the foe, or caring little and seeing no chance to hit rebels, concluded to do *some* kind of execution. Who gave them liquor so freely is answerable for the killing and wounding of many loyal soldiers. So imminent was the danger from their guns, that it became a questionable matter which was the safer side of the logs.

A shell, we thought from one of our gunboats, bursted over our heads. There was a sudden bringing of limbs into the smallest compass possible. The second elapsing between the bursting of a shell and the falling of its fragments, with the mental inquiry, "Who will be hit? will *I?*" is far from pleasurable. The emotions of the battle-field are peculiar and varying. Seeing that young Thompson (H), who had gone gallantly through the scenes of the 27th, did not fire for some time after the order. I asked him the reason. He said: "Oh! I am too frightened." I advised him to pitch in, and in a few minutes he was as free from fear as any of us. To his left was N. Taylor (II), one of our best and bravest, yet, every time a shot passed by him, he would start and shrink, whether it came from friend or foe. We tried to reform him, but it was no use, his nerves were more powerful than his will; yet he kept steadily to work. He may have started just so in the fierce battle of last month, but the Christian determination to do his duty bore him onward despite shrinking nerves. Such men are the really brave. While lying there, a white rabbit sought shelter under our tree and gazed at us with his brown eyes in the most beseeching manner.

I have no incidents of peculiar heroism to record. We did what we were ordered to do, nothing more, nothing less. Bach, our color-sergeant, in carrying messages to different parts of the field, and some who brought cartridge-boxes to us, had better opportunities of showing their disregard for danger than any others, and they did so. Let me assure you that roaming over such a field at such a time is not the pleasantest work you can imagine. You run from stump to stump, followed by bullets, not knowing when you will be hit; or you go through brush that balls regard no more than paper. We started with eighty rounds of cartridges to each man, and some consumed, *wasted*, I might say, over a hundred Having fired twenty times, I became economical and rested. While using that number, my gun got so foul that I had to stop and clean it. Lying there, we became connoisseurs of bullets A partially-spent ball passes by you with a sound like the buzzing of a mad bee, while one in full speed says, "Zip!" Some of our shells would strike the parapet, and, exploding, send fragments back to wound *us*. If a shell bursts after it stops, it scatters the iron hail all around ; but if, in consequence of the fuse being too short, it bursts right over your head soon after leaving the gun, you will be unscathed, for the momentum of the ball, inhering to all its particles, will carry the fragments far ahead of you. Grape and canister are the most deadly of all the munitions of war. They are fired from guns of almost every calibre. Grape-shot, varying in size from two ounces to two pounds each, are put up, about a dozen together, in an iron-wire, which, bursting by the force of the powder, scatters them in every direction. Canister shot is made of tin canisters, holding from a pint to half a peck, filled with bullets. When the gun is fired, these canisters burst, sending their contents about like a fiery spray.

The most unpleasant part of the 14th of June was the fierce heat. It was one of our sultriest days, a day, too, without a cloud. By 7 A. M. the sun scorched us, and we had to shade the barrels of our guns to keep them from becoming too hot to handle. There we lay, right on the ground, where we could not get a breath of air, the sun all the time drawing the blood to our brains. I thought I would go crazy. With my gun and ramrod and blouse I made an awning, which added to our comfort ; but the rebel riflemen in the trees seeing us, and perchance thinking it was designed for the benefit of some officer, paid us so many leaden compliments that I had to pull it down. I bore it till about noon, and could bear it no longer ; so, thinking "a living dog is better than a dead lion," I started for the shade. The firing had greatly ceased, being devoted only to those who exposed themselves. I ran in a zigzag course to divert the aim of those friends who were forcibly urging me to stay on the field to the nearest tree or stump, and down I would fall. I suppose my erratic movements then attracted some attention, for, as I dropped down behind one stump, a ball entered on the ground on either side of me. I got so weak in getting up and down that my strength was failing me, so I bid farewell to all dodging and stumps and struck a bee-line for the woods, almost careless whether I was hit or not. I reached the edge of the woods and threw myself down and slept, how long I know not, but when I woke, as fresh as a lark, the sun was away in the west, broiling down on me. About a week before the fight, and in anticipation thereof, I got half a pint of poor whiskey. It was on hand that Sunday. Before starting to run back I drank it all, and that, I believe, saved me from sun-stroke.

About dark the regiment returned to their rifle-pits, and tired men were sent out on the field as pickets. It was a day of fearful slaughter, poorly recompensed by the few rods we gained. History records no grander fighting than was witnessed on our right. The 31st Massachusetts filled part of the ditch with their cotton-bags, and some unstrapped their guns from their backs, crossed, and mounted the parapets. There they found two lines of earth-works, so ranged that certain death was the reward of that valor that mounted the outer walls. Three small companies of the 8th Vermont lost fifty-eight men by one volley; 338 men were cut down of Weitzel's brigade. It is thought that the loss of the right wing is not less than 1,500. It was an awful day, relieved only by the grand heroism of the sons of New York and New England. Some of our best blood has saturated this *Slaughter's* field General Paine was severely wounded, and lay all the day exposed to the fearful fire. J. V. Woods, Company E, 31st Massachusetts, got a bottle of cordial and carried it to the General, but unfortunately he did not throw it near enough for him to reach it. Getting some lemons and water, he tried to return, but, within five feet of his commander, he rolled over and never moved again. John Williams, Company D, 31st Massachusetts, also went to the relief with lemons and water, but never returned. A 4th Wisconsin man fell in an exposed place, and a sharp-shooter fired at him once or twice afterwards, when a Connecticut boy crawled after him, took him on his back, and carried him safely to a place where the stretcher-bearers could reach him. War is horrid, but not altogether in vain when it shows to us what noble qualities lie dormant in human nature. Representatives of the Christian and Sanitary Commission are here, doing all that men can do for the souls and bodies of the suffering.

I hardly think our surgeons keep near enough to us. That evening we went to support Holcomb's battery, a poor fellow was left all alone in the delirium of fever, and was not found till next day. He had been kept at work too long. I pity the surgeons. Fallible men, they have to decide who are really sick and who are shirking; and they make mistakes, and receive many curses not their due. Dr. Winsor is not as popular as he deserves to be. Many of his own dollars has he expended for the comfort of the sick, but his *apparent* coldness of nature does not allow him to minister that sympathy of *manner* which attracts men's hearts more than gifts. Were there no shirkers, he would be more popular. His earnest love for the cause, and his conscientious desire to give to that cause every man capable of advancing it, may lead him to remand to duty those who should be excused. God have mercy on them who thus throw their burdens on weak and failing comrades? They may carry whole carcasses back to Berkshire, but for all the good they will ever do, they might just as well rot and die in one of these ditches. It seems to me, if manhood has not died out, the sound of battle would bring before them visions of brothers dying whom they might save, that would crowd their future days and nights with unavailing remorse.

I send you a list of our casualties on the 14th inst., being one killed and seventeen wounded:

Company A—M. F. Dailey, hand, slightly; T. Rairdon, hand, slightly.

Company B—E. M. Martin, shoulder; I. Nourse, leg.

Company C—Killed: T. F. Parker. Wounded: W. E. Loomis, hand, slightly; J. E. Downs, hand, slightly.

Company D—H. C. Winters, arm and chin; P. Devanny, shoulder.

Company E—W. Amstead, hand, slightly; A. E. Ferry, finger, amputated.

Company F—J. B. Downs, shoulder and chin, slightly.

Company I—Lieutenant W. E. Nichols, ankle; E. McDonald, finger, amputated; G. L. Geer, hand, slightly; C. E. Wink, hand, slightly; H. Vosburgh, hip, slightly.

Company K—D. Funk, head and shoulder.

Theron F. Parker (C), aged nineteen years, was one of our nicest farmer boys from Lenox, and an excellent, quiet, reliable soldier. He was shot in the head while in the act of firing, and must have died immediately. He remained in that kneeling position some time after his death. His company was so far advanced that they had no shelter but bushes. A good boy, we miss him; a brave boy, his loss is a nation's loss, and his country's glory gilds his lonely grave.

Norman Hollenbeck (E), aged twenty-one years, died at Baton Rouge, June 12th. He was a young farmer from Egremont. A good soldier, in young manhood, has gone to his grave; and far off, in Massachusetts, a widowed mother yearns for the boy she is no more to see.

Christopher Rhoades (E) also died June 12th, in the hospital at Baton Rouge. He was a New Marlboro farmer and a nice man, but had not strength to endure the exposure of a soldier's life. Consumption ended his life in his twenty-sixth year. Of many I have but little to say, for young men, if quiet and moral, go through life attracting but little attention. You know they quietly did life's duties, and that is all. Their many private excellencies are known mainly to loved ones, who mourn them proudly. Of our comrade, all I know is, he was much esteemed, and closed a steady life on the battle-field of the hospital, and that he is mourned for, not only by his brother, who is with us, but also by the members of his company.

David S. Bliss (K), was a farmer from Florida, aged twenty-four years. He was wounded in the battle of the 27th, and taken to Baton Rouge, where he died on the 13th inst. He was a steady, quiet, kind man, and where courage was needed, proved himself a reliable soldier. He leaves a family to mourn for him while they remember the glory and the grief of a day that brought darkness to so many New England homes.

Lieutenant Isaac Eugene Judd is dead. The sad news reached us on Saturday night, illy fitting us for the stern duties of the morrow. Sadness settled on every heart, for we loved and were proud of him. I have seen no profounder sorrow than was caused among us by the melancholy intelligence. In the charge of the 27th he was wounded in the groin in front, just at the joint of the thigh. The doctor said that the bullet narrowly missed the femoral artery, and that had it gone an inch to one side of where it did he would have bled to death instantly. We all thought at that time, with him, that the wound was not serious; and on being brought from the field he answered, when asked if he was badly hurt, "Not so badly but that I shall get another lick at them yet." His true soldier nature thought more about winning the victory than about himself. The wound was in the nature of a slit, causing the surgeon to think the ball might have dropped out. If it remained in his body it would not hurt him for a while, perchance never; and as the wound was so near the main artery, probing was not deemed advisable. Two days after the battle he was removed to the hospital at Baton Rouge, and there, with other officers, received the most excellent care and attention. The doctors and nurses took a special interest in his welfare, as if conscious his was no ordinary life. Some one of Co. K was nearly always in attendance on him; so in hope and cheerfulness he passed the days till on the 10th of June the wound started to bleed and he had spasms of pain at intervals of about five minutes. The doctor would stop the bleeding for the time being, but he grew no better, and it became evident the artery was ruptured by the process of suppuration of the wound. At last he told the surgeon he wanted the wound examined and something done, as matters could not be worse and might be bettered; besides, the spasms of pain were becoming very agonizing. On the 12th instant the medical director of this department, an eminently skillful surgeon, extracted the ball and tied up the artery, the lieutenant being under the influence of chloroform and ether. It was the only chance of saving his life, and a doubtful one at best. He may have realized his condition, but said nothing about it. As late as 1 o'clock he was quiet and his voice clear and strong, but towards night the fatal hour came. As was feared, the artery burst. The doctor delayed the approach of death by keeping his thumb pressed on the artery, but very soon he breathed his last calmly and peacefully. His brother officers, to whom he was endeared by the associations of private life, of the camp, of the battle-field, and of the hospital, gathered around his death-bed. With brave men he had bravely fought; it was fitting that brave men should go with him as far as possible into the dark valley. His last words were, "Doctor, I can't see."

Lieutenant Kellogg, who was going home, was immediately apprised of his death by telegraph. He replied, "Send the body down to New Orleans." That was impossible, for there was no boat, and no metallic case or suitable coffin could be had. The surgeons allowed the body to be kept as long as possible, but it changed so rapidly that he was buried the next day in the cemetery at Baton Rouge. At sunset of June 13th, Lieutenant Judd sank to his rest, while on the field of his young renown graves were yawning for fresh victims.

> " I am weary pining
> Brothers red with brothers' gore ;
> Only that the wrong we're righting,
> Truth and honor's battle fighting,
> I would draw my sword no more."

It *is* "truth and honor's battle" we are fighting. Only this assurance enables us to yield up such lives, and feel that even *this* cost is not too great if *only* thus God's truth can be maintained. Because the cause is so much more sacred than this life, aye, than a hecatomb of such lives, we put away our dead in silence and gird ourselves to follow his brilliant example though it leads us to kindred graves. "Doctor, I can't see," said our dying comrade. We trust that now, in the purer light of eternity, at the touch of the heavenly physician, he can clearly recognize that his death was not in vain. We thank God that battle strikes down not alone the unworthy but also those o'er whom we weep bitter tears, so that the profoundest hopes of our country become as enduring as the profoundest sorrows of our hearts. Martyr's blood is holy seed, from which springs up a posterity careless of death if only they may tread the path rendered glorious by their ancestors' deeds. Around the tombs that crowd the cemetery at Baton Rouge some of the holiest associations of our nation gather; and at the grave of the gallant and much-loved Judd we drink such draughts of patriotism, albeit intermingled is the fennel's bitter leaf, that our moral vision is cleared, and we no longer say, "Doctor, I can't see," but as in a vision of light we see the Genius of Liberty, her "garments rolled in blood," leading America through seas of gore and over mountains of slain to the promised land, the breezes of which unfurl a banner whose stars, hiding its stripes, reflect the glory of that God who is now training us to "proclaim liberty throughout all the land' unto all the inhabitants thereof." Noble, gifted comrade! he has not died in vain or prematurely. His young life counts more for God and humanity than scores of those who are ignobly deaf to a country's call though they may fill up the full measure of *their* years. The warrior sleeps well, having by noble deeds done something to right great wrongs, and to prepare a nation to fulfill the grandest mission ever intrusted to any people.

"I can't see!" Yes, there are hearts in Berkshire which will take up that dying cry. For a while they will not be able to see why *their* only boy should fall in manly prime. A father's pride will struggle hard to get the mastery over his sorrow and loneliness, while the aching heart of a mother, like Rachel, "may refuse to be comforted because her children are not." A many-voiced wailing goes up to God from ten thousand aching hearts in lonely homes, from which life's life love has gone out. They may yet "see" a brightness gilding their sorrow as a nation sheds its tears of pride and joy over the graves of them whose blood turned away a Divine wrath. I sadden as I think of the to be bereaved hearts that clung so fondly about Eugene Judd, but there are parents who would give all their wealth could they mourn as proudly over the tombs of their children as can the parents of the hero we've buried.

Lieutenant Judd was born in the State of New York, March 7th, 1840. He was the only son of A. G. Judd, formerly of South Lee. He had received an excellent education, was a splendid penman, and a very superior business man. For a season he was a popular teacher of the public schools of Great Barrington. At the time of his enlistment he was engaged in the store of S. B. Goodale, South Egremont, of whose family he was a member, and by them loved and cherished as a brother. Though occupied in nothing but a small country store, he gave to *it* all his energy, and manifested business

qualifications that promised a brilliant future. His
social nature was of a rare order. He made friends
readily, and kept them. Gentlemanly, genial, kind,
and sacrificing, "to know him was to love him." He
joined Co. E and was appointed sergeant, having declined a lieutenancy in favor of his tried friend, Lieutenant R. T. Sherman, who has nobly proved his fitness
to lead brave men into the jaws of death, from which
he himself so narrowly escaped with severe wounds.
For a man like young Judd the sacrifice was no light
one. Proud-spirited and gifted, a subordinate position
was not his proper place. He felt within himself the
capacity to *command* men. Faithfully he did the duties of a sergeant in Co. E till Captain Weston (K)
secured his services in raising his company, of which he
was elected second lieutenant. On the resignation of
Lieutenant Taft, Colonel Bartlett appointed him first
lieutenant.

His military qualifications were of a marked character. He had not his superior in the regiment, considering his experience. With a natural fondness for military pursuits, he mastered the details of his profession
with great readiness ; and, had his life been spared, he
intended to remain in the army till the close of the
war. He doubtlessly would have risen to distinction.
He was much of a favorite with the field and staff officers. The colonel saw in him a brother-spirit, and
gave him more than an ordinary share of his notice.
Petted, yet he did not become self-conceited and vain.
Not obsequious to his superiors in rank, he was not
arrogant to his temporary inferiors. None mourn him
more sincerely than the privates of that choice and intelligent company (K.) To his immediate superior,
Captain Weston, he united the respectful kindness of a

brother to the submission of a subordinate, and together they lived in confidence and happiness. I have lingered long at his grave, longer than at any other grave, not because he was morally superior or more patriotic than many others of our "fallen brave," but because he was a marked character in a position where that character could become known and appreciated. I now leave that grave, hoping that it may never be disturbed, but that his remains shall continue to lie here to teach the future freemen, white and black, of this State how costly the price paid for their enfranchisement. He was buried in his military dress; and his sword, so nobly worn, the gift of an appreciating friend, was sent home to his bereaved father.

> "They have sent me the sword that my brave boy wore
>   On the field of his young renown;
> On the last red field, where his faith was sealed,
>   And the sun of his days went down.
>   Away with the tears
>   That are blinding me so;
>   There is joy in his years,
>   Though his young head be low;
> And I'll gaze with a solemn delight evermore
> On the sword that my brave boy wore.
>
> "'Twas for freedom and home that I gave him away,
>   Like the sons of his race of old;
> And though, aged and gray, I am sonless this day,
>   He is dearer a thousand-fold.
>   There's a glory above him
>   To hallow his name,
>   A land that will love him
>   Who died for its fame;
> And a solace will shine, when my old heart is sore,
> Round the sword that my brave boy wore.

" It was kind of his comrades, ye know not how kind,
 It was more than the Indies to me ;
 Ye know not how kind and how steadfast of mind
  The soldier to sorrow can be.
   They know well how lonely,
    How grievously wrung,
   Is the heart that its only
    Love loses so young ;
And they closed his blue eyes when the battle was o'er,
And sent his old father the sword that he wore."

LETTER XXXI.

MY DEAR L.:

I am sick of hearing the cry, "Time's out," as if
our country's claims on us expired with the 19th of
June. A Pennsylvania regiment refused to fight at
the first Bull Run battle because their term of service
expired the day before. We scorned them, and now
the honor of Massachusetts is somewhat stained, for
the Fourth refused to do duty, and, on stern measures
being threatened, one hundred still remained disobedi-
ent, and are now under arrest, as also are some of the
Forty-eighth for a similar offence. The Fiftieth were
about to follow suit when Banks informed them it
would be a death or Dry Tortugas affair, and so they
volunteered to stay two weeks longer, and were publicly
thanked for it. The Major went to headquarters on
the 19th ult., and though he keeps his own counsel, I
guess he learned there that if we refused duty we would
have to measure arms with the power of the United
States Government. He did not tell us so, in so many
words, but we have clearly inferred it. General Banks
said it was not his province to decide when the respective
terms of service ended, but that of the Secretary of War.
Troops were put under his command to do a certain
work, and he meant to keep them till their term was
out, according to the decision of the authorities at
Washington. I believe the *whole* of the Fiftieth have
served out their time of service; and if Banks refuses

to let *them* go, *we* might as well submit quietly, for there
is no help for us.   To do our boys credit, they have
been quite quiet about it, and have only rebelled in
private murmurs.   They say that Banks should give
us the opportunity of *volunteering* till Port Hudson
surrenders.   They forget that that, unless previously
asked for by us, would make him the decider of the
time the claims of the Government cease.   One of Company A, at Baton Rouge, refused to do duty, and was
sent to prison as his reward.   Since it is decided that
the nine months' men can not be drafted till all between
twenty and forty-five years shall have been exhausted,
it would be wiser to send us home, and so secure our
re-enlisting.   If Government can keep us a month longer
than we agreed to serve, why not a year or three years?
We have the letter of the law on our side, but patriotism
demands our continued service.   I would go through a
dozen May 27ths rather than *now* leave the field ; aye,
if I was *certain* of *death*.   I can see no reason why I
should fail my country, merely because the 19th of June
has come and gone.   It may be true, as some say, that
we are poorly led and uselessly slaughtered, and that
the brains are all *within* and not "*before* Port Hudson;"
but *that* should only make the voice of our bleeding
country sink more deeply into our hearts, and bring
out the firmer valor to counteract the inefficiency of our
leaders.

We are *not* poorly led.   An iron man, with a sagacious
head on his shoulders, is holding the reins.   Artillery
failing, assault or abandonment of the siege is our alter-
native.   Assaults have as yet failed, but we are preparing
for another on a grander scale.   Only fourteen thousand
men now draw rations.   That is our whole force, and
includes the sick not in hospitals, cooks, teamsters,

cavalry, artillerists, and others, who count nothing in a
charge. We have not this day 10,000 fighting men before Port Hudson. Small but frequent battles at our
rear, the alarm at Baton Rouge, the raid on Springfield
Landing, the gathering of the foe near Donaldsonville
(where they attacked Fort Butler) by thousands, all
make us doubt whether we will not go home vanquished
rather than victors. Give the rebels another week and
they will gather men enough in our rear to compel the
abandonment of the siege. We must get *into* Port Hudson. Then we could defy the mighty arm of Johnston,
which, if the report be true, is rushing down on us,
unless they closed the river below, of which we have no
fears. A rebel uprising in New Orleans is not improbable. Orders forbidding gatherings of more than six
in the streets have been issued, Guerrillas fire at our
river boats. No wonder that Banks is sick, yet his will
fails not, and God have mercy on those Massachusetts
men who fail him and the nation in *this* hour of peril,
for I am sure they will get no mercy at home, save from
doting mothers, in whose bosoms patriotism never lived
or has died out.

Escaped soldiers say the enemy has but 2,500 men,
no inside works, provisions for one week, and forty
rounds of cartridges. Be assured of that, and that
that week would not bring up their friends, and an assault were better postponed. But how can *prisoners*
know these things? *I* go everywhere and *know* nothing. Guesses are all. I suppose General Banks is in
constant communication by water with Grant, and
knows all about the movements of Johnston, and that
he gives some credence to these stories about short rations within the fort, for the long-expected assault has
been deferred. Immediately after the direful 14th of

June he issued orders to secure, if possible, 1,000 volunteers to storm the enemy's works. A silver medal was to be given to each volunteer. The Forty-ninth furnished no *volunteers*. I do not blame them. Had I been present when the call was made I would not have volunteered. The history of previous assaults rises up as warnings. We will go where *ordered*, not with former enthusiasm, but with no less of *will*, but we will not *thrust* ourselves into the valley of death. Our quota was obtained by drafting. The elected afterwards *volunteered*. They wanted to be robed in that name of honor. Lieutenant Smith (H) was chosen their leader, but being sick, another sick man, Lieutenant Dresser (F), *volunteered* to take his place. We have no nobler than that Dresser. Prostrate with the popular disease, jaundice, and exhausted, he looks better fitted for the hospital than the "forlorn hope;" but Lieutenant Doolittle is sick at Baton Rouge, where Captain Morey is also, unable to carry out his desire to join his company, and so Dresser clings to his men and to duty. On hearing of his step, Morey tried to get up here, but he could not get a pass. Baton Rouge was threatened; nightly the troops were under arms; cannon were posted everywhere; the sick and convalescents were its main defense; thousands of wounded crowded its hospitals; it was one of our bases of supplies, and at all hazards must be held. Badly as we needed men, so valuable an officer as Captain Morey could not be spared. Failing to come up he sent a written protest against Dresser's leaving his company, which his fall would make officerless. On Sunday, the 21st, the stormers from the centre reported at General Augur's quarters, and because our boys were not *volunteers* they were sent back. The work demands men who would throw their whole souls into it. Perchance he feared that those who claimed that their time had expired could not do so. He may have been right, but J doubt whether Colonel Birge will have any men in his choice band who will go further than they would have done.

The assault will be on the right and on the left, where the ambulances have been collected. Daily have we been expecting it. The boats are not allowed to leave the landing, but they tarry there to bear the wounded to Baton Rouge. Preparations are being made to undermine the enemy's works. The frames we watched so closely have been taken away, so the hour is near at hand. On the right and left we are within a few yards of the foe. This time there will be no marching hundreds of rods under a galling fire to reach the ditch and parapet, half dispirited by our loss, and almost totally exhausted by our labor. Gallantly have the negroes held the most exposed part of our lines, advancing rod by rod till not a rebel dare show his head. Frequent sorties have been successfully met by black hands, who dyed their glittering bayonets and their budding hopes in the blood of many a former master. *They have not once flinched.* Protecting *us* and carving out for themselves a name and a nationality, they have shown the world that manhood, crushed for centuries, answers to the call of God and Freedom. We may leave our dead and leave this place in rebel hands, but we will also leave memories that will make the name of "Port Hudson" as dreadful as the sound of a "fire-bell in the night" to those who shall attempt the re-enslavement of the African. For the privilege of commanding a negro company I would be almost willing to endure for years the monotony, the mental stagnation, the *ennui* of a soldier's life. I might fall, and a demand for my body

might be answered, " We've buried him with his niggers," and to my children I could leave no richer
legacy.   To die for one's race, and that the dominant
race of the world, is noble indeed, but nobler yet to
link your life and death with the elevation of your own
land, and of a people, the despised and rejected of
earth.

What we will meet when we get *inside* the parapet we
know not.   Batteries may open cross-fires on us ; exploding mines may mingle our mangled remains with
the torn bodies of desperate foes, but if there be nothing
but bayonet work *we* will be victors.   To stand cold
steel requires the firm nerves, the fixed will, heirlooms
of Northern freemen.   It would require whole chapters
to describe the immense amount of engineering work
that has been done on our right and left.   Scores of
miles of road have been made, mainly at night ; ravines
hundreds of feet deep have been bridged for the passage of guns weighing ten thousand pounds each.   Hundreds on hundreds of miles of rifle-pits unite the different batteries.   On the left we have erected a battery of
twenty guns within fifty rods of the foe, who scarcely
interrupted us by a shot.   For a week an informal truce
preserved quiet on both sides.   Within a few yards
mutual enemies worked to prepare agencies of destruction and preservation, and not a single gun indicated
that they were foes.   Often the laugh and the jest would
be interchanged, and, like our own boys on the centre,
they would mutually throw down their guns, meet as
friends, exchange papers, receive tobacco for bread or
beef, and then go back to their lines awaiting the order
to exchange missiles of death.   Frequently we see rebels
come outside the parapet to get muddy water from the
ditch, but we do not molest them.   On the left we have

dug under their citadel, which we had previously battered almost down since the informal truce was suspended, and have also silenced their river batteries that the boats could come nearer. On their battered citadel floats a flag which again and again has been shot away, replacing which has cost them many a brave life. We are far *beneath* them, and through troughs they roll down thirty-two pound shells, the bursting of which is by no means pleasant though seldom fatal. Hand-grenades, or small shells, are thrown at the foe, and not unfrequently the enemy catch them up before exploding and hurl them into our ranks to do the work of death. "Curses coming home to roost," we say.

The Forty-ninth are located far in front in rifle-pits supporting two large batteries. A, B, F, and D are on the verge of a *woods*, and are comparatively comfortable, but the rest of the companies are many rods ahead, exposed to the unbroken rays of the sun. In going from one part of the regiment to the other it is necessary, after passing through a ravine, to go along pits which are nearly at right angles with the rebel lines, affording them a fine chance to hit us, which they occasionally improve. For three weeks has our left been thus exposed, nearly every night of which has been marked with rain, making their sleeping apartments far from comfortable, for now that they are so much exposed, sleeping *in* the pits is a matter of necessity. When matters are too quiet our boys get up on the works to invite the fire of their foes. By watching carefully the smoke they can jump down before the bullet comes. The danger is some fellow whom they are not watching may show *his* skill. The rebs don't fire at all of these chances, for it occasionally happens that one or two thus make targets of their bodies so that their comrades may

fire when the enemy exposes himself to fire at us. This
kind of life is pleasant for a few days, but three weeks
of burning sun, of rainy nights, and wet beds take all
the fun out of it. Near our works we have found springs
of good, cool water. I have my doubts whether it
would pass muster at home, but to us it is a highly-
prized luxury.

With good sense the major allows the boys much
liberty, and they roam about, regaling themselves with
the novel sights and scenes and the abundant blackberries that crowd and adorn our hedges. I was sorry
to see one poor fellow tied to a tree for insulting his
captain, especially as he was in an exposed place, but I
was glad that the major in his leniency was determined
to enforce discipline, though "time *be* out." He must
do it or nothing but our good sense would keep us from
degenerating into an armed rabble.

Speaking of raids and scares reminds me that the raid
on Springfield Landing was a serious matter. A body
of rebels scattered the few troops that were there, fired
a storehouse, and then retreated at the hoarse voice of
a gunboat. Several hundred contrabands were living
there in mud huts, and at the first alarm rushed on
board the steamboats, twenty-one being drowned in
their frantic efforts to secure their safety. That panic
spread to our cook-stands, a mile to the rear of the
regiment, and to see our butcher pick up his small
demijohn of whiskey, which he sells at two dollars a pint
bottle, and rush for the before carefully avoided rifle-
pits, followed by some of the cooks, who hastily upset
their coffee and beans, resolved that the rebels should
not breakfast thereon, was one of those rich incidents
that need to be seen to be fully appreciated.

I offended a colored woman by calling her a "contraband." Be it understood that "contrabands" are

supported by the Government. *She* supported herself.
A sergeant at the landing, in charge of some colored
workmen, was telling one of them that he would be tied
up by the thumbs and whipped at sunset. I asked him
by what right he would inflict that punishment on a
negro more than on a white citizen. He said it was Lieutenant-Colonel Benedict's order. I replied that no
officer had a right to transform a soldier into a whipper
of poor darkeys, and as for me I would die rather than
so lower my manhood. He shrugged his shoulders,
adding that soldiers' feelings are not much respected.
They can demand respect being paid to those feelings,
or, if nothing else, can scornfully and proudly suffer
for violation of such orders. Send a man into a charge
on Slaughter's field for God and Freedom and then ask
him to aid in tying up a poor negro by the thumbs and
to apply the lash! Like Rossiter, when told to "buck"
one of the "mackerels" at Snedeker's, he asked Captain Garlick if duty required him to do *that;* so a man's
self-respect would put to his conscience the same question, and, receiving the emphatic "No," he would tell
Colonel Benedict, or General Banks himself, that he
was a soldier not a plantation overseer, and abide the
consequences. If he did not his meanness would prove
him a coward. Let contrabands be treated as white
workmen. If they will not duly serve the Government
that feeds them send them off to shift for themselves,
but God forbid that *our* Government, in full view of
Port Hudson, shall take up the abandoned slave whip.

I have made a flying visit to Baton Rouge, and was
surprised to see how sickness improved the appearance
of some of our comrades, and only of *some*. Not a few
would tremblingly ask me, "When will the regiment
return, that we can go home?" Poor fellows! some

of them have seen home for the last time. Arrangements are being made to send our sick North. The loudest complainers have secured their tickets, while noble spirits, like G. C. Ray (D), are destined to tarry. *They* should go ; for a few weeks longer, and they will be past hope of recovery. Mr. Ray has gotten some writing to do for the medical department, that his mind may be employed, hoping thus to counteract the killing monotony of camp-life. His life is too valuable to be lost to his family and his country. Leaving a luxurious home, in middle life, earnestly devoted to the great *principles* of the war, he came to *fight* for Freedom and his native land ; and sad is it that the battle hour finds him utterly unable to do a soldier's part where brave hearts are needed. This, as much as disease, is eating out his life, and, I much fear, his will be one of the graves that swallow up those gallant spirits who yearned to do or die, but are ordained to learn life's hardest lesson, "*suffer* and be strong." It is heart-rending to watch these brave fellows sinking into death. Knowing they can by no possibility serve their country, their one prayer is, to be spared to die at home. The ambition of the patriot is swallowed up in the yearnings of the husband, the father, the son. " Victory, and then home," wells up as a prayer from *our* hearts. God only knows with what intensity and what agony *they* unite in the same petition ; and, if weak, *almost gone*, they emphasize "*home*," who is so much the patriot, so little the man, as to censure them ? The dullness of the camp is fearful, and walks through the city are not much more cheering. The streets are crowded with pale, emaciated, maimed soldiers. Hobbling about on crutches, arms in slings, or with " empty sleeves," you see the dear fellows, and, with moistened eyes, think

of their proud but dependent futures. Most of the
wounded are in good spirits, while the merely sick look
very despondent. The hospitals are crowded, and they
are making arrangements for the victims of the coming
battle. Our privileges are costly. The hospitals are
in excellent order, and many of their stricken inmates
are really jolly. The few loyal women of the place
minister unto them ; and some, whose sympathies rise
above sectional animosity, unite with them in these offices of human kindness. Colonel Bartlett's arm gets
no better. Colonel Sumner goes home on a furlough
on account of his wound. I am sorry for it, for a
regiment ever needs the presence of a cool head and a
brave heart. He will be accompanied by his servant,
without whose aid he can not dress himself. It is better that he should go, for in his present condition he
can not be of any service to us. His wound is sup-
purating since extraction of the bullet, and in this
infernal climate there is always danger of gangrene
setting in, and then death almost surely follows, as we
have sadly learned from the loss of several of our boys
who were reported as only slightly wounded.

Lieutenant Kniffin, who, to his wound, has had fever
superadded, also leaves. We had few Kniffins. Happy
the regiment that has many such ! No officer was more
really loved than he. A good judge says that Company B is the best disciplined company of the Forty-
ninth, and I know that its business account has been
kept in an unsurpassed manner. Garlick and Kniffin
are a strong team, and would have made Company B
one of the best companies, if it had originally been the
worst, instead of being A No. 1 from the beginning.
We begin to hope that the brave Siggins (though minus
an eye) and Sherman will recover. Our effective men

form a company in the convalescent regiment, under the command of Captain Morey. If the hour of their trial shall come, Morey will show that necessity, not a lack of courage, alone kept him from receiving his share of the glory that gathers round Port Hudson.

Independence Day passed without the expected assault. Though long deferred, certainly *that* would be the day. We wanted to connect the surrender of this place with the hallowed memories of the 4th of July. It seemed that the miserable traitors had forgotten the very existence of our National Anniversary, for when a salute of thirty-four *unshotted* guns announced its advent, they noticed no death tokens following the report, and thought we were firing at Johnston, who had at last come to their help. They mounted the walls and cheered lustily, but some guns that *were* shotted showed them the propriety of not "hallooing till they get out of the woods." No wonder they forgot that the nation's birthday had again rolled round, for they are doing what they can to blot out the day, and to give the lie to those great truths that alone separate it from common days. The thirty-four guns rang out to them our proud assertion that every State was yet *in* the Union, and while we had a cannon or a man left, all should stay there. The noon salute was fired from Captain Holcomb's Second Vermont Battery, and he showed his aversion to traitors by crowding his guns with shells, so that the national salute might ring out the guilty souls of some who were doing their best to prevent that day from becoming a world's holiday. A few days before, Banks made stirring speeches to the forlorn hope, and to those who are to follow them on the right, in which he alluded to our flag floating in triumph over Port Hudson on the 4th of July. As that day passed without any general movement on our side, we conclude that he believes the enemy has eaten nearly all his mules, and that he can safely wait a few days for starvation to do the work of an assault. I hope he is right. There are full enough precious graves here, full enough loyal hearts whose saddest recollection will twine about these graves.

Henry E. Grippen (B), a farmer from Lanesboro, aged thirty-five years, was killed by a sharpshooter on Sunday, the 21st of June. He was one of the number who were chosen to represent our regiment in the grand storming party. General Augur dismissed them, and perchance, congratulating himself on being snatched from the fiery furnace, he wended his way to the rifle-pits, where he was suddenly struck down by a ball crashing through his brain. How little man knows where lies the path of safety! Of this only are we assured, that the path of *duty* is the path of *eternal* safety. Wounded about sundown, he died about 11 P. M. A good soldier was thus lost to Company B; and wife and children, so near, as they imagined, to the happy reunion, will see but his vacant place in our ranks "when the boys come home."

Conratt Heins (B), a good, diligent soldier, was wounded in the back by the bursting of one of our own shells, June 22d, and died at Springfield Landing. He was on duty in Slaughter's field in advance of our battery. A shell exploding too soon deprived us of a worthy comrade and a family of its head and protection. He was aged thirty-eight years, and like his brother soldier (Grippen) was a farmer from Lanesboro. His German blood has given this land a new right to the title, the world's asylum. The composite blood that is restoring our national purity sweeps away the heresy that "America belongs to Americans." By "life and blood surrender" of many of the foreign-born it belongs to the world. We are battling for the *world's* triumph.

Joseph B. Wolcott, orderly sergeant of Co. H, was shot by a sharpshooter on the morning of June 23. It was a beautiful morning, and as he sat near the edge of the rifle-pits and saw the sun gilding the majestic trees, he said to a friend, "What a lovely morning this would be to die!" Soon after that a bullet passed through his arm into his lung. Seeing that his arm was bleeding a comrade said, "Joe! it is only your arm; you are safe yet;" but his reply convinced them that the "lovely morning" would witness the close of his young life. For a while he suffered fearfully. The news soon spread, "Wolcott is shot!" and many of his associates gathered round him. To Rising, who joined church at the same time and place, he said, "Ned! they have killed me." Rev. J. H. Wood (E) came, talked with him about the world, on whose verge he was trembling, and received the comforting assurance that a Christian soldier was laying off his armor. At the dying man's request he led in prayer. It was an hour long to be remembered. Giving to his friends for his young wife some blood-stained tokens of his death and love, he tenderly reproved his comrades for their sins, and affectionately exhorted them to turn to Jesus. The moral sublimity of that hour rose high above the grandeur and heroism that marked our battles in which he always bore so honorable a part. Those who had thought but little of the claims of religion, who had almost believed it was an encumbrance to a soldier, there learned the source from which the quiet young Sandisfield farmer drew his unwavering courage. Before leaving his home he had, by will, disposed of his earthly effects, and now, pointing his comrades to his Saviour, he sweetly fell asleep in Jesus. We buried him by the side of his intimate friend, Lieutenant Deming, with prayer and exhortation, and sadly returned to the scene of duty and of death. Mrs. Deming and Mrs. Wolcott have been living together since their husbands left for the war. Seeing those graves, where the soldier-friends lie side by side, we could but think of a home in Berkshire where their wives are living—one mourning and the other comforting. Alas! the latter knows not that a message will soon reach her that will make her a sister in sorrow, and, by the sacredness of her own grief, more fully prepare her to sympathize with the bereaved. A mutual agony now seals their solemn sisterhood. Sandisfield, stricken as she is, will add to her mourning on hearing of the death of Joseph B. Wolcott. Rich must she be if she has better sons left. Falling in his early manhood, for he was only twenty-five years of age, he yet lived long enough to benefit his race, and to twine round his memory the undying gratitude of a free nation. His fellow-soldiers knew him, and they prized him as a comrade and loved him as a man. None, *none* of our "fallen brave" has sunk to rest round whom gathered more of respect, confidence, and affection.

> "Shot through the lungs, how he lay, how he lay,
> At Port Hudson all that fearful day,
> Slowly bleeding his life away!
>
> Yet why our life but to spend it free,
> As the snow that falls on the angry lea,
> For the Right, for the Truth, for Liberty?

" And the brave heart knows, with a quiet content,
   When treason and murder their shafts have sent,
   That the time is at hand for which it was lent.

" But oh ! Fatherland, that we love so well,
   Shall the future annals shuddering tell
   It was all in vain that our heroes fell ?

" We give them up at thy bitter cry,
   We say no word when they go to die—
   Is it Freedom's dawn that reddens the sky ?

" **Ah**, comrade, sleep well in thy soldier's bed
   At Port Hudson, in the field of our dead,
   Who knows who watcheth overhead ?"

Charles H. Cook (B), farmer **boy,** from West Stockbridge, aged twenty, was severely wounded in the **chest,**
in the battle of May 27th, and died on **the 2d inst.,** at
Baton Rouge. Bravely fighting, he met his **death-**
wound, and now sleeps among strangers. **Peace to his**
ashes !

The day following the battle of June **14th, General**
Banks sent in wines, medicines, and other necessaries
for our wounded. As a so-called "honor" sometimes
survives the burial of patriotism, these supplies may
fulfill their mission. While the flag of truce under
which this kind action was done was flying, an officer,
stooping down to pick up some trophies, was reminded
by a bullet that he was abusing that flag. The rebels
have been seen working, when honor thus demanded
rest, so we think our poor sufferers will hardly get *all*
the luxuries we have sent them. Many of our dead and
some of our wounded remained on the field from Sunday
to Wednesday, when Gardner, finding their decomposing
bodies were working pestilence, requested General Banks
to bury them. One hundred and fourteen were found,

two of whom were still alive, almost eaten up with maggots. The enemy says we could have buried them on Monday, but would not ask the favor, and left the putrid bodies to annoy and disable them. I hope they lie, for that is too horrible even for war. Captain Garlick, after that battle, led out the pioneers to act as pickets, and until 10 o'clock of the next night they were not relieved, all of which time they were without food or water. *They* suffered, but who can describe the sufferings of those wounded ones during the awful four days between their fall and recovery!

Governor Andrew having refused to commission **Brooks** (C), Siggins (D). and Gleason (K), (whom Colonel Bartlett appointed second lieutenants in their respective companies) on the ground that in nine months' regiments officers must be *elected* by the men, elections to fill these vacancies were held June 24th, at the rifle-pits. That part of the regiment which is before the foe is the regiment proper, though not one-tenth of the men are present. The veterans were to express their preference. · **In** Co. K. Sergeant Rising had a majority on the first ballot, but thinking that the office properly belonged to the wounded Gleason, he generously declined the proffered honor, and Gleason was elected. In Co. D, the *appointment* of Lieutenant Siggins was confirmed by the *unanimous* vote of the members thereof. Had all of that company been present, I doubt not that the result would have been just the same. In Co. C. Sergeant Strong led Sergeant Nash one vote, and was, consequently, elected. To choose between Strong and Nash was **not easy work.** Both are brave soldiers and both have fully done their duty, and we were sorry that we could not elect both. Perchance Strong's being one of the "forlorn hope" turned the scale in his favor. In the first election for second lieutenant, next to Wells, the then successful candidate, *they* had the greatest number of votes.   Lieutenant Strong deserves this compliment. No man was ever more faithful and reliable.   The honor is much greater than if he had been elected at the first. We have tried him for more than nine months as sergeant, as acting orderly, and as commander, and this election is our mature verdict of "Well done!"   Captain Lingenfelter, though still complaining, has returned to duty.   Lieutenant Foster has been sick for a few days.   *He* now occupies and merits a warm place in our confidence.   Prejudices, honestly entertained, have been swept away, and since we have been in this department, and especially since we have been fighting and facing the foe, we recognize in Lieutenant D. B. Foster a man whom we can trust, a friend who sympathizes with us, and an officer prompt and fearless in the discharge of duty.   Fortunately, good sense and patriotism kept him from throwing up his commission when the authorities refused him promotion, and preserved him to us and to the working out for himself a place in the respect and confidence of the whole regiment. May he long live to preserve and enjoy what he has so fairly gained is the unanimous wish of the members of Co. C.

I see that Orderly Tuttle has again stolen away from the hospital to take his place in the presence of danger, though his wound of the 27th is scarcely healed.   We who charged under his lead on that fatal day ask no better leader if we are destined to form another "forlorn hope."   Some of the convalescents came up to guard an ammunition train, expecting to return the next day, but they find themselves in for the remainder of the campaign.   Night and day have Ordnance Sergeants Cowles and Hulet gone with wagons to Baton

Rouge, running the gauntlet of guerrillas. They are safe as yet, but it is quite probable that death or imprisonment will prevent their returning with us to Berkshire. These trips have none of the excitement of the battle-field, but are accompanied with danger and suspense very far from being agreeable.

Mules and darkeys are so abundant that nearly every man rides and keeps his waiter. Dave takes care of Mr. Brewster's horse and has a contraband to do the work for him. Several wait on our department, and as we are as lazy as those "to the manner born," it is in perfect harmony to have your coffee brought to you before rising. Food, with a little tobacco, is considered by them an ample equivalent for their services. A recent order commanding the turning over of mules and contrabands to Colonel Hodge will throw us back on our own dignity and muscles or lead to explorations of the adjacent plantations. An army is a great cormorant. We have swallowed up all the green corn for fodder, and rails are becoming as scarce as Union men in Charleston.

Nearly every evening Uncle Sam gets up on the left for our benefit a pyrotechnic display that puts to shame every former specimen of that art we have ever seen. Sitting on the top of the earthworths that conceal and protect our batteries, we spend many of our evening hours watching the course and bursting of the shells. At night we can see the path of a shell through all its journey, lighted as it is by the burning fuze. When the range is two miles the track of a shell from a mortar describes very nearly half the arc of a circle. On leaving the mortar it gracefully moves on, climbing up and up into the heavens till it is quite a mile above the earth, and then it glides along for a moment apparently in a horizontal line ; but quickly you see that the little fiery orb is on the home-stretch, describing the other sedgment of the circle.   A shell from a mortar will travel two miles in thirty seconds, and from a Parrott gun in half that time.   The flash of the gun at night and the white smoke by day indicate the moment of discharge, giving from ten to twenty seconds to seek shelter. Though occasionally driven from our posts of observation by stray bullets, we return to gaze on the fascinating scene.   The other evening there was a large fire in rebeldom, which drew a number of Holcomb's men to the walls, when they were greeted by the balls of the rebels, sending some to the hospital and some to the burial.

R. H. Wilcox, whose Testament saved his life at the battle of Plain's Store, has been less fortunate here, having received a bullet in the fleshy part of his leg. Binding the sacred word on our hearts is Scriptural, and Wilcox obeyed *that;* but this time the rebels aimed lower, so the good fellow will have to limp for a few days, regretting that the Bible Society did not give him more than one shield.   On picket one man is detailed to spend two hours up a tree, and then he must needs report to Colonel Paine.   Billy Hogan, a waggish Irishman, of Co. H, spent his two hours in the tree, and on coming down went to sleep.   The officer of the picket waked him, asking, "Have you made your report yet?"

"Report, is it! and sure I saw nothing to report."

"No matter about that," said the officer, "go and report to Colonel Paine;" and Billy drew up before headquarters in the position of the soldier saluting the colonel, and told him his business.

"Well, go ahead, report!" gruffly responded the Acting Brigadier.

" Well, sir, I was over in the tree fornenst and I saw, I saw, sir, two birds fly into the fort, and soon after, I saw two fly out. I think, sir, the two that flew out were pigeons, and I am not certain, sir, that the two that flew in were pigeons or hawks, but I think they was hawks."

" You need not make any further report," said his excellency, and Billy left him. He often says, " By jabers, they didn't report any more from that tree." To *see* and hear Billy describe this scene would drive the blues and dyspepsia from you for one long day at least.

The rebels are gathering in large force near Donaldsonville, and have made considerable progress. On the 28th ult. they attacked Fort Butler, near that village, in overpowering numbers, but were gallantly repulsed by the small garrison, even the sick lending their feeble help. It was one of the most heroic actions of the war, and resulted in the killing, wounding, and capturing of twice as many rebels as there were soldiers in the fort. The appearance of two gunboats effectually secured us the victory. Unless we take Port Hudson soon, these men under General Taylor will appear at our rear, and compel the abandonment of the siege. The Lafourche and Teche countries are full of gathering foes. Some sneered at Banks's generalship, asking why overrun the Teche country only to leave it? Suppose he had allowed General Taylor to remain there undisturbed, how could we have invested Port Hudson? Banks's generalship is that of genius and common sense united.

I close this with a list of those who have died away from the scene of strife.

George W. Babbitt (B), aged thirty-one years, a farmer from New Ashford, died of heart disease at the General Hospital, Baton Rouge, June 18th. He was an intelligent man, and, understanding the duties of a soldier, performed them well.

George Campbell (K), aged eighteen years, from Mount Washington, died of diarrhœa at Baton Rouge, June 19th. He leaves a brother in Company E. George was too weak to do all the duties of a soldier, but he was a steady, pleasant, willing boy.

Thomas Mallaly (E), a farmer boy from Egremont, died in New Orleans, June 26th, aged eighteen years. I know not the cause of his death, nor aught concerning him as a man or soldier.

W. Joyner (A), a stone-cutter from Savoy, aged eighteen years, died of diarrhœa at Baton Rouge, June 30th. As he was sick much, he had not the opportunity to win distinction as a soldier.

William W. Stowell (C) was a farmer lad from Peru. Early on reaching Secessia, diarrhœa claimed him for a victim, and clung to its prey till death released him at Baton Rouge, June 30th. A fine, steady lad he was, willing to do what his strength would permit. He only wanted health and strength to prove, as many of our living and our dead *have* proved, that on our battle-fields the farmer boys of Berkshire are worthy sons of noble sires. His long, weary struggle with the great enemy is ended, and he sleeps with his brother soldiers who, like him, fought back disease that they might die at home. A mother's care was not his solace, but amid comrades too sick to think of aught but themselves he closed the weary round of life.

Charles Videtto (A) died of quick consumption at the camp in Baton Rouge July 6th. His captain says, "he was one of the nicest boys," (he had seen but eighteen years), "and one of my best soldiers." Charlie was very popular with his comrades, and steady and reliable. How many mothers and sisters in Berkshire are anxiously awaiting for their Charlies to come, knowing not that brother soldiers have laid their remains in distant graves. Who can tell the anxiety, the hopes battling with fears, of our homes? Some who expect to see no more their Charlies are to be joyously disappointed, while about others, who are now full of hope, a great darkness is gathering.

" Charlie has come!
Who says that the times are weary,
That the graves of our fallen ones
Cast a shadow deep and dreary
Around our hearts and homes?
The sunshine floating around us
Makes e'en the shadows bright ;
We can not dream of sorrow,
For Charlie came last night.

" Charlie has come!
Has come from the field of battle
Where death-bolts quickly fly,
Led by a mighty Sovereign,
Who heeds a sparrow's cry.
One noble arm is shattered,
A deep scar seams the brow ;
We loved our Charlie always,
But we adore him now.
We fain would praise the blessed,
But our lips with joy are dumb !
God pity the mothers and sisters
Whose Charlies never come!"

LETTER XXXII.

CAMP BANKS, BATON ROUGE, LA., *July* 13, 1863.

MY DEAR L.:

Glory! Hallelujah! Amen! Port Hudson is ours, and the Mississippi is open. The Confederacy is split in two; the backbone of the rebellion is broken: Secessia generally is in a squeamish condition. Hunger, not assault, finished the work, after forty-six days' siege. On the morning of the 7th the fleets above and below opened a joyous fire; cheers began on the right and rolled in increasing volume to the centre, telling us that on the glorious 4th General Grant victoriously entered Vicksburg. Billows of rejoicing surged to and fro over our whole army, awakening the curiosity of the rebels, who refused to believe our report till General Banks, complying with the request of General Gardner, sent in on the morning of the 8th an official copy of Grant's dispatch, which informed them that Vicksburg and 31,000 prisoners, 19 generals, 60,000 new English rifled muskets, besides many pieces of artillery and considerable ammunition had fallen into our hands. On learning this Gardner asked in vain for twenty-four hours' cessation of hostilities, and then requested the appointment of commissioners to arrange the terms of the unconditional surrender. This was granted, and by the middle of that afternoon the matter was settled. The men, but not the officers, are to be paroled. The commissioners met outside of the parapet under the fly of a tent, and several hampers of sparkling Bordeaux kept them in good spirits. A basket was sent to General Gardner within the fort, containing such refreshments as rumor said were not plentiful in that beleaguered place.

Notwithstanding our troops did not formally enter the place until the 8th inst., yet the garrison fully understood that they were to be surrendered, and accordingly they came over the parapet in large numbers to converse with our men. All along the right and centre crowds of them gathered without the works to converse with and see the persevering Yankees, who had at last forced them to surrender.

They examined with the deepest curiosity the guns our men had, and their ammunition, which they averred they had feared much more than the artillery brought to bear against them. Now and then they would seek out a particular stump or log from which they had been worried by our sharpshooters. "This cussed hole," said a keen-eyed, roughly dressed hunter from the wilds of Arkansas, "I have been aiming at for the last two weeks to split the Yankee's head who was always peeping out of it." Somebody had quite evidently been watching that hole rather closely, for the two logs, which were a little apart and formed the aperture, were riddled with bullets.

They were not aware that the place was to be surrendered until after it was known by our own men. They allowed that it was better to be well fed and prisoners than to hold out and starve. Several of the soldiers went within the rebel works on the first day. This was not prohibited. Those who went in returned with numerous trophies of their visit, such as blankets, canteens, belts with the Confederate States plate upon them, pistols, and the like. One beverage was served out with the utmost freedom by the garrison, as they had it in large quantities. It was a light beer made from corn, and really much more palatable than the river water.

Quite early in the morning preparations were made for the ceremony, at which all seemed deeply gratified.

It may be said with truthfulness that all were really gratified at the state of affairs. Certainly our own men were, who had so triumphantly ended a vigorous and shrewdly planned campaign. The half-famished, dilapidated-looking rebels most certainly were, for they never gave heartier cheers than when told by General Beale and Colonel Miles that soon they should see their homes.

They appeared deeply interested in the ceremony of surrender, which was conducted by Brigadier-General Andrew, General Banks's chief of staff. The spot chosen for the ceremony was an open area, near the flag-staff, opposite the centre of the river batteries, and very near the bank.

Along the main street the soldiers composing the garrison were drawn up in line, having all their personal baggage, arms, and equipments with them.

General Gardner and staff, with a numerous escort, occupied a position at the right of the line.

By 7 o'clock our troops marched into the works, headed by the brigade which had volunteered, a thousand strong, to storm the place in the next assault. Colonel Birge, of the Thirteenth Connecticut regiment, was in command of this storming party. It was fitting that they should lead the way with the flag of bloodless victory who had volunteered to do so with bayonet and sabre. Artillery closed in with the infantry, and as the grand cortege swept through the broad streets of

Port Hudson, with the grand old national airs for the first time in many months breaking the morning stillness, the scene was most impressive and soul-stirring. Never did music sound sweeter, never did men march with lighter step or greater rejoicing than our troops as they came into the place which had cost the lives of many of their gallant comrades. All the sorrow for their losses and all the joy for their present victory came to the mind at once. But every private bereavement was instantly forgotten in the nation's great gain, and every man justly seemed proud to have had a part in one of the greatest triumphs of the war.

Passing directly across from the breastworks on the land side to the river batteries the column then marched by the right flank, and afterwards halted and fronted opposite the rebel line. General Andrew and staff then rode up to receive the sword of the rebel commander. It was proffered to General Andrew by General Gardner, with the brief words: "Having thoroughly defended this position as long as I deemed it necessary, I now surrender to you my sword, and with it this post and its garrison."

To which General Andrew replied: "I return your sword as a proper compliment to the gallant commander of such gallant troops—conduct that would be heroic in another cause."

To which General Gardner replied, as he returned his sword with emphasis into the scabbard: "This is neither time nor place to discuss the cause."

The men then grounded their arms, not being able to stack them, since hardly one in ten of their pieces had a bayonet attached. They were mostly very rusty and of old style. Quite a number of the old Queen Bess pattern were included among them, having a bore half as large again as the ordinary musket. Most of the cartridge boxes were well filled, but the scarcity of percussion caps was universal.

An officer of the garrison, in explanation of this fact, remarked that this very scarcity of caps was the reason that the men were allowed to cease firing on the right and left for several days.

The number of men surrendered is over five thousand. Of these nearly four thousand are ready for duty. The remainder are in the hospital from sickness or wounds. There were six thousand stand of arms, with full equipments.

The troops are some of the best in the Confederate service; many of them were at Fort Donelson, and all have been at Port Hudson since the battle of Baton Rouge. At the time of the battle of the Plains there were 6,113 men in the fort. Since that time the loss has been 610 in killed and wounded. Our men who were in the place numbered about fifty, and the rebels say they had every facility for escape. Many officers owned fine horses. Among them Colonel Stone, of the Forty-eighth Massachusetts, recognized two which he had lost in the battle of the Plains.

The works about this famous stronghold are not of such a complicated nature as many have supposed, nor yet are they ineffective on account of their simplicity. The principal defences are on the river side.

They comprise seventeen separate embrasures, mostly built in an arc of a circle. They are finely revetted, and command all the approaches by way of the river. In three of them pivot guns were mounted, which were used both for front and rear. Two magazines are above ground, one in the rear of a battery of eight and ten-inch guns, and below the flag-staff, which is raised in the centre of the works on the river front. The rest of the magazines are under ground.

The land breastworks are built in the ordinary manner on the outer side. They extend in a semi-circular direction from river to river for a distance of nearly seven miles.

Inside they have a narrow ditch, with small caves dug out from it, in which the men slept and sheltered themselves from our fire. On the southern extremity they are very well built, but on the northern end they were not built until the recent investment, and hence are are nothing but rifle-pits.

There are a few houses, a church, two or three stores and shops, and a livery stable, and these originally constituted the town of Port Hudson.

These buildings are close up to the river batteries, separated from them by a broad street. The hospitals were in ravines. Everything within the works bears ample proof of the terrific bombardment the place has suffered.

Great trees lie across the roads and in the area, felled by solid shot and shell, buildings are riddled with round shot, dead animals fill the air about some of the ravines with a horrid effluvia, while shot and fragments of shell are strewn everywhere.

The Confederate officers report that all our artillery fire has not killed more than twenty-five men. "One good rifle I considered equal to ten pieces of artillery," said an artillery officer in commenting upon the effect of our fire.

On speaking of the fight on the 27th an officer said that when the attack was made so vigorously on Weitzel's front they all thought that their game was up. But observing no similar movement along other parts of our line, they moved up eleven pieces of artillery and two large battalions of their best troops so that they were able to offer effectual resistance in that quarter. These movements were seen by our men at the time.

After the ceremony was over General Weitzel was presented with a fine chestnut stallion by a rebel officer who was formerly his pupil at West Point.

The general had several classmates and pupils among the officers of the garrison, and they all seemed glad to revive the days long gone by when they enjoyed that union of hearts and hands which a strange fanaticism has now severed.

And not only between a few classmates but between whole regiments on the day of the surrender there was a constant interchange of good feeling. Perhaps they have crossed bayonets for the last time. That is not certain. But no fears for the future seemed to trouble these heroes of many battles as they talked of the scenes in which they all had borne a part. Ere this day closed many hearts were knit together in friendly bonds, which a few hours before were severed by the deepest enmity.

On the night of the 8th General Banks sent in a liberal supply of provisions for the garrison, and early the next morning they enjoyed the first good meal they had partaken of for a long time. On the 29th of June they issued their last quarter-ration of beef. On the 1st of July some officers partook of a dish of mule meat, which, they say, has a flavor between beef and venison. Horses were found to be good eating, though inferior to mules. Rats were eaten, and declared better than spring chickens. We had fired their mills, so they could not grind the few ears of corn left. They had plenty of peas, but starving men could not use *them*, so to save the corn they fed their horses and mules on the peas, by which many were killed. At the time of the surrender they had eaten their last mule.

Port Hudson is a natural fortification, *in* which one man should keep at bay ten men assaulting from without. It is one net-work of ditches and ravines. The ground is strewed with such hardware as we poured into it for two months from the 8th of May when the fleet commenced the bombardment. The ravages made by shells is fearful. Houses are gutted and mammoth trees broken off. In roads hardened by years of travel you can see caverns twelve or fifteen feet deep, wider and larger than ordinary cellars. One of these descending thunderbolts struck an artillerist about the neck, and drove him through the wooden floor of the battery into the ground beneath, leaving only his feet sticking out. Another killed three men, and soon after their burial still another burst in the cemetery and exploded among their coffins. One afternoon a shell exploded in the river causing seventy or eighty fishes to rise to the surface completely stunned. The rebs put out after them, many of which were the largest sized catfishes. Ten pounds is called a small fish, so that was a lucky shell for them. Many of our projectiles would strike the trees laterally instead of with their percussion-caps, and consequently failed to explode.

Grant is sending troops here from Vicksburg, and and many regiments have gone down to Donaldsonville to drive back Taylor and his horde. The Forty-ninth went on Friday night, the 10th inst. This place, it is said, is to be garrisoned with negro troops.

As it is more fully studied, the siege of Port Hudson will stand out as one of the most remarkable events of the war. It was not a mere adjunct to that of Vicksburg, yet the magnitude of Vicksburg and Gettysburg will measurably cast it into the shade. Had the rebels compelled Banks to retire, an event at one time not improbable, Grant's position would have been a perilous one. There were many points of similarity in the conduct of the two sieges. Each of them was begun by a terrible and terribly unwise assault, and each surrendered to the pressure of hunger. That of Vicksburg lasted forty-six days, and that of Port Hudson forty-seven days. In killed and wounded Grant lost thirteen per cent. of his force, and Banks nineteen per cent. If slaughter of men be the test of generalship or gallantry, we have a bloody pre-eminence. In romantic features, in fierce assaults, in conspicuous bravery, the siege of Port Hudson has not been surpassed. It was well that the "forlorn hope" of June 15th was never called into action, for a glance at the enemy's works convinced me that few of them would have returned alive. Though they did not charge and we did, yet it seems to me that it required greater courage for men to volunteer on the 15th of June than it did on the 26th of May. When *our* "forlorn hope" was formed, our confidence in ourselves and our generals had not been rudely shaken by the futile assaults and unnecessary slaughter of May 27th and June 14th. Despite those disheartening events, Colonel Birge's thousand volunteered to enter the valley of death, and though never called into action, they fully deserve the medal that Gen. Banks has promised them.

We now bid farewell to Port Hudson, with its fields of blood and graves of our comrades. When peace, of which this surrender is a speedy precursor, shall settle on the Sunny South, it will be a proud yet sad pleasure to revisit that place, and roam over Slaughter's field,

and rest by what remains of the burial-places of our
brother soldiers.   Though we think of the slain, and of
the hopes interred with them, we can but be jubilant.
We are victors, and mingling with our shouts are the
hosannas from the gory field of Gettysburg, telling
that the God of battles has at last crowned the merited
valor of the Army of the Potomac with victory.   This
has been a grand year.   It was commenced right.   We
put God and humanity on our side and have gone on
from triumph to triumph.   The 4th of July has been
resurrected.   Again its inspired truths, all undiluted,
fall from the lips of America on the ears of an expectant
world.   The world's sympathies answer in prayers for
our success.   1863 is proving its kindredship to 1776.
The child is nobler than the parent.   The glory of the
latter day is above that of the former.   We are inter-
preting the Declaration of Independence, so that mankind, fearing or hoping, believe that "God hath created
all men free and equal."   The sun of victory, so gilding
our graves that the glory hides the grief, reveals to the
world that our flag is the standard of freedom, imbued
with power from on high to wave triumphantly over
every foe.   Despairing patriots dash away their tears,
and exultingly exclaim, "Liberty *is* man's birthright;
tyrants have *no* divine right to rule; man *is* capable of
self-government."

> "The dwellers in the vales and on the rocks
>   Shout to each other, and the mountain tops,
>   From distant mountains, catch the flying joy ;
>   Till nation after nation taught the strain,
>   Earth rolls the rapturous hosanna round."

It is fitting that black hands should hold Port Hudson.   There those hands signed the charter of the free-

dom of their race.   In the future of the Africans, as
Ethiopia, who has so long stretched out her manacled
hands to God, outrivals the splendor of Egypt and
Carthage, gifted orators will kindle a nation's patriotism by allusions to Port Hudson, even as *we* gather inspiration from the recollections of Bunker Hill.   The
American eagle now watches her shores, that no vessels
enter her harbors, save those freighted with the blessings of civilization, or with the missionaries of the
Gospel of Christ.   Africa, who has so long had her
Calvary, now sees an angel at the grave of her former
renown rolling away the stone and preparing her for
the joy and glory of the resurrection.   *Blood*, all-pow-
erful *blood*, purifies and prepares for greatness.   The
beginning of the ransom price has been paid, and in
that purer light, revealing God's future to our "fallen
brave," they see no shame, but only high honor in having fought, not only for their country, but also for the
rejected *negro*.   Could they speak to loving friends they
would say, "Let our bodies lie on the field of our renown, and let the guardians of our remains be the *un-
fettered* children of them whose fathers mingled their
blood with ours, and thus bought the propitiation of
our national sin and the freedom of *their* race.   Loving,
sad, perchance disconsolate memories gather round the
graves of the comrades we are leaving; but the time
will come when the possessors of such memories will
proudly claim to be the aristocracy of our land.   Children, now too young to know aught but that "father"
will never return to them, will walk more erectly
through the splendor and purity of our future as they
recognize that that splendor is based on their father's
graves.

Since my return to this place I have attended negro meetings. They were jubilant meetings. Old hunkers might have thought that politics had entered into and vitiated their religion, but they felt that the Gospel really means, "Glad tidings of great joy which shall be unto all people." From pulpits where they had often submissively, despairingly, heard the old refrain, "Servants! obey your masters," rang out the grand truths of man's equality, which were answered by shouts and tears of joy. Now they feel that they are safe, and proudly recognize that negro valor materially aided in the purchase of that safety. Respectful to them who "knew that Port Hudson could never be taken," and who had often threatened them with vengeance when Southern bravery had scattered our armies to the wind, yet they firmly and openly consecrate themselves to our service, and in their sanctuary take up the mingled song of piety and joy, as did the Israelites when God had led them through the Red Sea. "The enemy said, I will pursue, I will overtake, I will divide the spoil; my *lust* shall be satisfied upon them; I will draw my sword, my hand shall destroy them. Thou stretchedst out thy right hand, the earth swallowed them. Thou, in thy mercy, hast led forth the people which thou hast redeemed. Sing ye to the Lord, for he hath triumphed gloriously: the horse and his rider hath he thrown into the sea."

Soon we come home, and may meet those cradled in the shadow of Bunker Hill who will call all this only the outpourings of a fanatical heart; but if this letter shall be read fifty years from now, the only surprise and mortification will be that ever any of the sons of Massachusetts were so untrue to their ancestry as to fail in doing all they could to make our *hopes* the world's fruition. If nothing more, we have gained the right to boldly speak of Freedom. The war is not yet over, and the hungry cemeteries will swallow up more of our brothers and sons, but we are moving on to a peace in which we may *abide*. Fresh demands on our patriotism will be made; and we can make them, being assured that we or our race shall receive therefor a hundred-fold. We have fallen on grand times: The days of heroism, of Christian chivalry, have returned.

> " We are living, we are dwelling
>   In a grand and awful time !
> In an age on ages telling,
>   To be living is sublime !
>
> " Will ye play, then, will ye dally
>   With your music and your wine ?
> Up ! It is Jehovah's rally !
>   God's own arm hath need of thine !
>
> " Worlds are charging, heaven beholding,
>   Thou hast but an hour to fight ;
> Now the blazoned cross unfolding,
>   On, right onward, for the right !
>
> "On ! let all the soul within you,
>   For the truth's sake go abroad ;
> Strike ! let every nerve and sinew
>   Tell on ages, tell for God !"

Samuel H. Rossiter (B) died at the hospital in this place July 9th. He was severely wounded in the lungs in the first charge at Port Hudson. For a while we indulged the fond hope of his recovery. Though only a corporal, he was qualified for and worthy of a high position. The man, the Christian, in him was so noble that rank would have been but gilding gold. Tall in stature, he was taller in worth; and in our estimation a purer, better soldier never enlisted. Duty led him to the field. "What does duty require at my hand?" was his life-question. There were but three sons in his father's house. Two of then joined the Forty-ninth. Samuel felt that then he *must* enlist. His country needed his services, and he wanted to watch over his younger brothers. He saw the bright, genial Willie laid in his lonely grave at Carrollton, and for months the other brother has been fighting a doubtful battle with disease. Really unable to travel, he yet marched with us to Port Hudson. Advised, almost commanded, to remain behind, yet he went. Duty called him, and that was enough. A part of our terribly-shattered left, he charged on the foe, and there received his death wound. On coming from the field I saw him walking towards the hospital, supported by two of his comrades, and thought he was one of the "slightly wounded." He was conveyed to the hospital at Baton Rouge, where his remaining brother lay sick. The love his fellow-soldiers bore him secured for him especial attention. He met his death as a Christian. I saw him a few days before he died, when the wound recommenced bleeding. A sweet smile, mingled with the look of pain, assured me that for him death had no terrors. A *disarmed* conqueror was approaching. It was a sad scene. Willie was gone, Abraham was sick, and he was dying. Perchance the old homestead was to be desolate indeed, and the aged parents were to go down to the grave with no sons to lean upon. I was glad then that before going he had married the woman of his affections. A stranger, I had no right to intermeddle with *that* grief, but I prized for her the melancholy pleasure of a sorrow that would be respected. As his weeping comrades gathered about his death-bed. he said, "Mourn not. I shall be home in a few moments;" and in his twenty-seventh year he was not, for God took him. Placed in a decent coffin, he was followed to his grave by a long procession. No regiment is privileged to boast of many Samuel Rossiters. Cheerful and amiable, he was also an earnest Christian. Richmond, in temporal and spiritual affairs, will long miss him. Though young, even God's people had learned to lean and rely on him. He is dead! Home, the church, the Sunday school, his company will greet him no more nor receive from him the genial smile. We mourn him, yet are richer in his death than in the lives of many. He was one of the untitled brave, a Christian man. It is superfluous to say he was one of our best soldiers. Duty, though ever so dangerous or repugnant, he never shunned. A wealth of precious memories gather round his life and death. "Faithful unto death, he has received the crown of life." May we imitate him. God and our country will then say, "Well done!"

LETTER XXXIII.

DONALDSONVILLE, *July* 20, 1863.

MY DEAR L.:

On Friday morning following the surrender of Port Hudson, we reached this place, which was once one of some beauty and importance, but now it is war-wrecked. That same day our brigade went up the river about five miles, on a reconnoissance, arresting all overseers and such persons as would be likely to give us information of the strength and whereabouts of the enemy. On the following Sunday, with the Second Louisiana, we went up to McCall's plantation, about three miles distant, and secured a boat-load of corn. Our associates, the Second Louisiana, well acquainted with the neighborhood, pilfered a considerable quantity of jewelry.

On the morning of the 13th several brigades marched along the Bayou Lafourche into the interior. It is a beautiful and rich country. We proceeded on the upper side of the Bayou for three miles, and then bivouaced and dined. It was the hottest, sultriest day we had experienced in Louisiana. After dinner we went down the Bayou, on the other side of which there was some firing and much confusion. We jumped on the levee to survey the scene, but the blasphemous commands of Colonel Paine drove us down. Horses, teams, ambulances, fugitives, passed by as rapidly as fear could move them, ejaculating, "The rebs! the rebs!" Our friends across the Bayou were evidently flanked, and retreating, as best they could, before a superior force.

Soon the battery accompanying our brigade opened fire, telling us that the enemy was not confined to the other side of the stream. We were drawn up in battle-line on a road running from the Bayou, and thence our regiment was sent diagonally through a cane-field. Co. F was thrown out as skirmishers, and found that, instead of a friendly battery, located at an adjacent sugar-house, there was a large collection of rebels, mounted and on foot. While making these movements we could hear the roar of artillery, the rushing tramp of many fugitives, while around us bullets were flying with much disregard of life and limb. Through the rows of cane could be seen squads of enemies, how many we could not tell, save that they were on three sides of us. Amid all the confusion, only one thing was certain, we were flanked on nearly every hand. There we were alone, and of our own regiment we could see but few at a time, as it was impossible to keep a good line. We returned the fire as best we could till ordered to fall back to the road. There we found that our brigade had fallen back to the Bayou road, and crossing the fence, we formed three times, when Adjutant-General Webber ordered us to retreat. This we did for some rods, when we again formed a line, and, for a short distance, fell back in tolerable order. In the meantime the enemy was pressing yet closer on our lone regiment and pouring scattered volleys into our ranks. The road on either side of the Bayou was crowded with fugitives, and we were convinced that we could do nothing but secure our own safety. When the final order to retreat came, every man started for the river. Confusion became worse confounded. Every attempt to keep in line failed, and in squads or alone we pressed to the rear. It was a day of utter exhaustion. Pressing through corn ten feet high, the sun pouring down on us, unable to catch a mouthful of air, was bad enough, but we found scratching our way through the cane-fields ten-fold worse. Cane grows about seven feet high, and is planted, not like corn, in hills, but in rows, presenting, when grown, an almost impenetrable jungle. Four miles, measured by rods; forty, as computed by discomfort and fatigue, passed over, and we reached the river, some near the fort at Donaldsonville and the rest scattered over miles. Bradley (F) was killed, Adjutant Francis wounded in the leg, many were slightly wounded, some sun-struck, and not a few are recorded as "missing." Whether they are prisoners, or lying in some of the deep ditches that surround and intersect those large fields, we know not.

It was a sad day. Surprised and flanked, we could do nothing but retreat. I do not know that any one was to blame. Dudley's brigade had felt the ground but the day before, and found but few enemies. We have since learned the foe was a part of General Taylor's army, gathered in Western Louisiana and Texas, some 12,000 strong, for the relief of Port Hudson. Since the fight we have heard nothing of them, save that they captured Brashear City, with most of its defenders, and destroyed a vast quantity of stores, which the sudden appearance of a part of our army prevented them from removing. Considering all the circumstances, the Forty-ninth did well. For coolness, for obedience of orders, for forming again and again when left alone, they deserve much credit. That officers got separated from their men, and that nearly all returned in utter confusion, might be expected as the result of being flanked on all sides in a strange country, and was unavoidable when retreating through the luxuriant

cane and corn fields of the Lafourche country. Great
credit is given to Chaffee, Sissons, and Dresser for coolness and steadiness in managing and keeping together
their men. I mention them especially because, though
they did well in the battle of June 14th, they, being
absent from the field of May 27th, had not before had
an opportunity to show their command over men, when
personal influence was nearly everything. They are
earnest lovers of Freedom. Had they flinched, they
would have been the first recreants of that class in the
Forty-ninth.

Since the battle we have had nothing more exciting
than picket duty, unenlivened by the presence of a foe.
We are encamped in an open field, and to the discomforts of actual war we have now superadded the monotony of camp life. The continued mugginess of the
weather has quickened mosquitoes into life, and having
no other enemy to fight we battle with *them*, wondering
why we are not sent home, thereby comforting us and
relieving Uncle Sam of the expense of our mainte-
nance. The camp at Baton Rouge is characterized by
a dreary monotony and a heat even worse than that
that assails our boys at Donaldsonville, for they do get
an occasional breeze from off the river. Our sick are
failing rapidly. "Hope deferred maketh the heart
sick." About the only question of interest is, "When
will we start for home?" and how—by sea or up the
the river? Curiosity desires the latter, health the
former.

Our total loss on the 13th instant stands one killed,
five wounded, and sixteen missing. Among the latter
are some of our very best soldiers. Where are they?
we often ask with painful solicitude.

Alone among the dead stands the name of *Edward R. Bradley* (F), of Stockbridge. He was a farmer, and twenty-seven years of age. He leaves parents and wife to mourn him. We might have lost scores, whose united loss would have been less of a calamity than that of him who lies here in the lonely grave where his comrades buried him. He was an educated, Christian soldier. "Death loves a shining mark." He found that mark in Edward R. Bradley. At home he was known as the beloved son, the affectionate husband, the friend of the poor, the earnest member of the church of Christ. In the army we knew him as a soldier ever faithful, one to be relied on in camp or in field—one who everywhere showed that he was "not ashamed of the gospel of Christ." Oh, for legions of just such men! He wore the armor of his country; beneath that he was clothed in the panoply of God. Richer blood has not dyed this soil. Earthly home will know him no more forever. "In my Father's house are many mansions. I go to prepare a place for you, that where *I* am *there* ye may be also." From the field of strife, fighting for God and Freedom, he has been ushered into those mansions. The Prince of Peace has received him, and, resting on His bosom, he sees how his dying blood was necessary to that hour when wars and rumors of war shall forever cease. We leave him alone with his glory.

Samuel G. Noble (A), aged twenty-three years, clerk from Pittsfield, died in the hospital at Baton Rouge, of congestive fever, on the 14th inst. Illy prepared were we to hear this sad news. Young Noble looked so well and fleshy but a few days before that we had no doubts but that he would be one of those who should soon return to glad, expectant hearts. Even in the freshness of sorrow those hearts will be comforted by knowing that "their loss is his eternal gain." I knew him well, and never saw or heard anything inconsistent with his Christian profession. His happy face carried sunshine with him, and no doubt comforted many of the sick and wounded with whom his duties, as a member of the ambulance corps, brought him in contact. That face was but the exponent of a kind heart and genial spirit, which led him to easily win the love and esteem of his comrades. Carefully tended, death met him, and we leave his grave to the care of strangers, believing that the All-Father has received him into *his* home.

David Winchell (I), aged nineteen years, of Lanesboro', was drowned in the Mississippi River while bathing on the 15th inst. He could not swim, and getting beyond his depth, where there was none to help him, found his last battle-field in the treacherous waters. His body was recovered and decently interred. He was a genial, kind boy, prompt and efficient as a soldier, and as a comrade liked by all. His captain places him among the very best of his company. The bravehearted lad joined the "forlorn hope" of May 27th, but by his company being ordered to the rear before that battle commenced, he was not allowed to share its danger and its glory. He was an only son. Spared by shot and shell, the river, opened to the world by his toil and exposure, folded him in the embrace of death, and by its banks the daily-expected son sleeps his last sleep. There will be weary waiting for *him*.

Artemus R. Comstock (D), aged nineteen years, a farmer boy from Barrington, died on the 18th inst., at Baton Rouge, after a long illness of diarrhœa. A fine boy he was, and while well, a faithful soldier. He came from a good stock, and was much of a favorite with officers and men. When I say he was considered one of the most likely of Company D I use strong language, for that is a company to belong to which any man might well be proud. The lad, with his high hopes, his patriotic aspirations, now sleeps in a Southern grave. We will soon leave it, but will carry with us the recollections of the many virtues of our buried comrade.

LETTER XXXIV.

Camp Banks, Baton Rouge, La., *August* 2, 1863.

My Dear L. :

Yesterday about sundown the regiment returned to camp after a campaign of seventy-three days. We have seen more real war-work than some regiments which have been *years* in the service. Eventful days were they. Looking back over them, remembering our slain and wounded, we claim the right to be called "veterans," and mournfully smile at our prophecy that the Forty-ninth would return home an *untried* regiment. We *have* been tried and *not* found wanting. Seventy-three *such* days try soul and body, and give us an experience and crowd us with such memories that we will never feel as young again as before. Living on the verge of the grave, becoming conversant with wounds and death, years were packed in that period. Crowded with exposures and privations, darkened with a cloud that all the brightness of victory can not fully dispel—a cloud that thickens as we think of the sad hour when expectant friends, through tear-blinded eyes, shall behold ominous gaps in ranks where once in the pride of manly strength stood *their* loved ones—we will ever remember that campaign as the brightest and saddest part of our lives. Stepping into the glory of our country's future, made possible by our success, the sadness will depart, and we will reverently thank God for having vouchsafed strength and courage to do our duty that *our* deeds might be a portion of the nation's wealth, of the *world's* pride. Little matters it that our names will be forgotten. Happy we, lured by no meed of fame, to have advanced the world one step nearer to its heavenly bridegroom! Enfranchised humanity, ever mounting higher, will often pause to render thanks to the "unnamed demi-gods" on whose toils and sufferings and deaths the grand temple of universal freedom was based. God has a purpose in this war, and when *hastened by it* heaven and earth shall vibrate to the jubilant strain, "Hallelujah! the kingdoms of this world are become the Kingdoms of our Lord and of his Christ," "honor shall be given to whom honor is due."

Do you call this egotism? Be it so, though I speak of myself as only one of the multitude; yet personally I am prouder of the last seventy-three days than of any other part of my existence, and of my pride no one shall bereave me. It is worth much to meet friends again, conscious that for them you took your life in your hands and as *their* representative stood in the valley of death. It is yet true, "*all* that a man hath will he give for his *life*." Duty at home seemed so safe and conducive to prosperity that many knew not it was the outworking of a higher power; duty done, where death barred the way and where in doing it life was to be valued only as an empty bubble, reaches man's heart and brings him to realize that there is something stronger, sweeter than the love of life. To count myself out in speaking of our just pride would be only an affectation of humility you would despise. That I might *not* be counted out in the joyous consciousness of having done something to advance the world's best interests I left home, friends, all: and now, danger past, as I think of returning to home and loved ones, I magnify the grace that enabled me to do my duty.

Proudly we will return.   Rich are they who have garments torn by shot and shell ; yet richer they who bear in their bodies honorable but not disabling or disfiguring scars.   The former will cherish their mementoes of this campaign, even as war-tattered banners are cherished, and from the fringed bullet edges impress on the rising race lessons of patriotism, while from the latter much gold could not purchase the sacred evidences of their fealty to God and Freedom.   Some will bear through life heavy mortgages on future independence.   Such *might* have been their fate had they remained at home ; and between being crippled in fighting for money and fighting for a nation's glory, there is an infinite difference.   Come back how we may, it will be with an increased self-respect, an increased claim on the respect of others that will cause many to mourn that *they* selfishly absented themselves from the post of duty and of honor.   The time is coming when posterity will summon such to its bar and demand why they allowed others to beat back unhelped by them the waves that would have desolated all.   If they stand without excuse the honors of the future will not be for them.   Returned soldiers will have the ears of the young for the next thirty years.   Whatever else they may teach they will certainly teach that to the defenders of the land belong its honors and emoluments.   Even the dissipated return with joy, believing that their baptism of fire has purified their record, and will enable them to start afresh in the pursuit of respect and prosperity.

Nothing of interest transpired at Donaldsonville after the date of my last letter.   Picket duty, a daily drill of an hour, fighting bugs and mosquitoes, sweating in the sun by day, absorbing fever at night, watching the passing boats, and wondering *when* we would leave for home is a summary of our last weeks at that God-for-saken place. There was nearly as much of disagreeable monotony here. When will the regiment return? was the great question. Of course, that must antedate starting for home. Some little excitement was created by ordering the light-duty men down the river, awakening the fear that the authorities intend to hold us till the 19th of August. This is now the report, and it comes so straight that we fear it is true. The Major has gone to New Orleans to see about it. On the 19th the Colonel and many of our sick started for the North by the way of the Atlantic. His arm begins to mend. George Burbank made a neat box for it so that he can carry it with some ease. His wound in the right heel has ceased to trouble him.

There are sick here who should have gone. Poor fellows! some will die if they stay here another fortnight! Send them home up the river and by cars, and death will intercept them. This climate grows more infernal daily. We are now enjoying the second crop of flies, and as for mosquitoes, they crop often enough to keep us afflicted day and night. This muggy weather, with mercury at 96°, is their carnival. Were it not for our bars we would succumb. When we came here in February many said they would ultimately settle here. Angels of purity in Hades are not scarcer than those who *now* cherish that idea. We consign the whole of "Lousyana" to negroes and alligators.

T. M. Judd (F) has had the bodies of Lieutenant Deming and Sergeant Wolcott disinterred, and they, with the body of Corporal Case (F), now await cooler weather to bear them to their burial in Sandisfield. Stricken as she has been, it is fitting that some of her slain should be brought home to hallow her soil with their remains. Deming, Wolcott, Case! three Christian soldiers, members of the same church! a sad, yet proud day, when Sandisfield that gave them birth shall give them graves. Let her other dead remain where they fell. The distant tombs will be joined together, and teach the cost and sacredness of the *reunited* Union. Remove all our dead from the South and we seem to yield that soil to the enemy.

Our getting ready to come home makes the three years' troops feel badly, even savage. They are down on the nine months' men, and not unfrequently insult us. The whole grievance is, "we are going home while they must stay in the graveyard." Glad as we are to leave, we pity them, our gallant comrades, but love them no better for the sneering question: "Are you a nine months' man or a *soldier?*" After battling as we have, staying weeks beyond our term of service, doing *everything* required at our hands, this sneer almost makes a man anxious to pitch into brother blue-coats and show them that we can *fight* even if we are not soldiers. The sneer generally comes from those who have heard, not seen the enemy. The commissary sergeant of the Fifty-third Massachusetts, a regiment that is covered all over with honors, went to the bakery after soft bread. The baker, who had never seen fire save in his oven, told him he had no bread for nine monthlings; he baked for *soldiers.* Query: Would pitching him into one of his ovens for a few minutes have been an unpardonable sin? Though the nine months' children are sneered at, tell them you belong to the Forty-ninth and they are proud to recognize you as comrades indeed. Regimental pride is almost as strong as family pride, and I straightened up to my full height the other day at the ordnance office. I was there making arrangements to turn over our guns, and was asked what regiment I belonged to. I replied, "The *Forty-ninth* Massachusetts," emphasizing the number, for it bears emphasis here, when the officer, a three years' man, said, "*That* is a noble regiment." On the bridge across the bayou, at Donaldsonville, two officers were censuring the nine months' soldiers when one, seeing some of our boys, said, "There are those brown-breeches fellows (our dark-blue pants are a dingy brown now), you can never scare them." He perchance had seen us under fire and knew that whether we had enlisted for a long or short period we were worthy of the term "soldiers."

We are not unappreciated; some of our officers and men have been proffered higher positions if they will remain or return after a furlough of sixty days. T. M. Judd (F), one of General Banks's clerks, has been offered a clerkship of $100 per month. He deserves the compliment, but home, wife, child, turn the scale in favor of Berkshire. The extravagant bounty, $402, is leading some to re-enlist. Is there no bottom to our Treasury? Pay (considered as an equivalent for services rendered) the soldier, and you must needs coin national hopes and glory, aye, and some of the beatitude of heaven; so I do not think the bounty too high; but can we, can any nation, afford it?

At the orders of the officers, we threw away some of our clothing on going into battle. We expected the Government to reimburse us. That expectation fails us. Here is a wrong that should be righted. We had "Dress-parade" this evening, and I could not keep back the tears as I gazed down the line. Nearly all were present. Brown as Indians looked the veterans, deathly pale the sick; but where are Deming, Judd, Sherman, Sissons, Rossiter, Wolcott, Warner, Pratt,

and a host of others, good and true? Dead, dying,
wounded. Sad contrast with our last dress-parade,
May 19th. Broken ranks testify to duty done, and rewarded with mutilation, dependence, death. There
were but few of our stalwart giants left. Battle and
sickness swept them away first. Washed and reclothed,
the boys looked well, but nothing becomes them so
much as their bronzed features and their wounds.

We are in receipt of New York papers of July 10th.
They have no account of the surrender of Port Hudson.
They do us injustice who claim the surrender of Port
Hudson as a mere incident of the fall of Vicksburg.
True, that discouraged the rebels, but they knew that
our next assault would be successful, and so yielded,
while they could with honor. I have not heard of a
single negro prisoner being found in Port Hudson.
Were *they* all so wounded that they died? Many of the
whites were living. Were they *murdered?*

The anti-draft riots of the North make us eager to be
at home to put down rebellion in New York. Better
defeats on the Potomac than that mobs should triumph.
Returned soldiers will cheerfully administer allopathic
doses of grape and canister which proved so effectual
in Boston. Fortunately *our* Governor did not recognize
the rioters as "my friends." At the very hour brutal
Irishmen were slaughtering unarmed negroes in New
York the Fifty-fourth Massachusetts was pressing
against the walls of Fort Wagner. Better such negroes
for citizens, aye, for *rulers*, than such foreigners.
America has more to fear from the latter class. I was
always opposed to "Native-Americanism," but a few
riots of the New York kind, and love of country will
make me adopt that system which I once thought so
narrow and bigoted. All honor to our negro soldiers.

They deserve citizenship. They will secure it. When Sergeant Carney held the emblem of liberty over the walls of Fort Wagner, refusing to yield the sacred standard though twice severely wounded, and was carried to the hospital saying to his cheering comrades, "Boys, the old flag never touched the ground," he gave better proof of loyalty to this land than ever did any son of Green Erin. Irishmen fight because fight is in them, but not for freedom. They have but little appreciation of that. Germans, though half infidelized, understand *its* inspiration, and accordingly make better American citizens. I have written much about the negro, and now I bid him adieu. His future here is safe and free. In the transition state thousands will suffer and die. A nation is not born without pangs. The life will fully pay for the sufferings. "Bring me," said a desolate slave-mother, "the ashes of the last auction-block for my sold daughter." What matters that mother's pangs to her joy in seeing the evidence of slavery's death. I have seen much of slavery and no good unless you call this good : proportionately there are fewer *white* prostitutes in the South than in the North. Before Him, who is "no respector of person," call you this "good?"

Berkshire is preparing to receive the Forty-ninth. She will give us a reception expressive of her pride and joy. We are her sons, and have not disgraced her. "When the boys come home" is now her refrain. We fear her cakes will grow stale while waiting. No need of that, for our brothers are even now on the road home, and to *them*, favors shown will be written down in *our* hearts of gratitude. If we return through the loyal North with appetites quickened by seeing delicacies we can not purchase we only hope that short the speeches,

not long the grace, before we are conducted to the
flesh-pots of Berkshire. Ever so fully fed, an angel's
eloquence would tire us till we had clasped wives and
little ones to our hearts. Speed the slow hours till the
boys get home is our prayer. But

> " They come not back though all be won,
> Whose young hearts leaped so high."

Benedict Niles (G), aged twenty-nine, farmer, of
Clarksburgh, died July 22d at this place of heart disease. He leaves wife and family. Weakly, he did
what he could. Spared as was his company from
danger and exposures, he has yet given to this soil his
remains.

Augustine Aldrich (G), also from Clarksburgh, died
July 23d. He, too, leaves a family to expect his speedy
return. Alas! they will come to greet him, but sad
news will change the joy into wailing. He was twenty-
three years of age. His death was caused by an abscess
in the side.

Elijah M. Morse (F), merchant, from Otis, died of
diarrhœa, July 24th, aged twenty-seven years, leaving
a large family to mourn for the husband, the father,
they are no more to see. He was a good soldier, quiet,
faithful, and respected by his comrades.

A. H. Maranville (B), farmer, from Savoy, died here
July 26th, aged thirty-eight years. He was a ready,
prompt soldier and a faithful Christian man. Sad to
die just as we expect to leave; sad, that an anxious
wife shall receive tidings of a dead, instead of the embrace of a living husband; yet the consolation survives
that the weary soldier has been ushered into his heavenly

home, and that God's own peace surrounds and fills him.   There is life in *his* death.

In the hurry of the march on Port Hudson I did not apprise you of two deaths that occurred in Co. G.

Charles G. Courtwright (G), spinner, of South Adams, aged twenty years, died at Baton Rouge, May 15th, of congestion of the bowels.   His sickness was short, but severe, and closed a valuable life, for he was a good soldier, and as a man much respected.

Thomas J. Sweet (G) died in New Orleans, May 19th, of diarrhœa.   He was a farmer, from Hancock, aged twenty-six years ; always sickly, but faithful, according to his strength.

LETTER XXXV.

MISSISSIPPI RIVER, ABOVE NEW ORLEANS, *August* 9, 1863.

MY DEAR L.:

On the 5th inst. the major returned from New Orleans, and informed us that the authorities recognized our term of service as having expired on the 28th of July, and would send us home as soon as they could obtain the needed vessels. That same afternoon we were ordered to prepare for leaving, and a joyous activity reigned in every street.

August 6th Co. G was relieved from provost duty, and returned to camp. Though they have had no share in the honors of the *field* they are not without their laurels. They gave complete satisfaction to the provost-marshal, and the citizens were loth to give them up. Many and delicate were their duties. Not one abused his privileges without this cutting joke were an abuse. Some of the natives are darker than many of the negroes, who are required to be furnished with passes. You can imagine the scene when a guard stops one of these dark citizens requiring to show a pass on the ground that no negroes are allowed to go by without that authority, and the humble apology when citizen angrily asserts his Circassian blood. Company G kept Baton Rouge as quiet as Pittsfield. You would not have imagined there were many thousands of soldiers within a few miles. The negro troops were as orderly as church-wardens. While we were at Port Hudson provost-guards had to do picket work, and were frequently ordered to "fall in" to beat back a foe who threatened often, but never attacked. The citizens of Baton Rouge will forget the Forty-ninth Massachusetts, but will long remember Co. G, whose faithful discharge of duty gave them all the quiet and security of peace amid the turmoils and lawlessness of war. That company enjoyed almost as good health as if they had remained in Berkshire. They realized many of the comforts of home, to which we were strangers. Dismissed with the earnest " Well done, good and faithful guards !" they rejoined us.

The return of nearly all our "missing" on the 7th inst. put us in good spirits. Between their capture, July 13 and July 15, they were marched forty-two miles and then paroled, fed in the meantime on a cup of meal each per day. They were robbed of nearly everything. Most of them found their way to the river and were carried to New Orleans, thence to Ship Island, and thence to Baton Rouge. They suffered much, and H. P. Wood (F), a noble soldier, almost laid down and died. Only the unremitting kindness of his comrades enabled him to find his way into our lines. Poor fellow! I fear an early grave is yawning for him. I hope he may, at least, be spared to die at home. On reaching New Orleans, they were ragged and dirty, but they fell into the hands of Captain W. W. Rockwell (called Willie Rockwell at home), of Pittsfield. He deserves the affectionate abbreviation, for he tenderly cared for them, securing good clothes (at whose expense I know not, certainly not at theirs), and freely furnishing them with money from his own purse. Many of them were strangers to him, but they were Massachusetts soldiers, Berkshire boys. His generous heart cared to know no more.

Of Fuller (F) and Bull (A) we can gather no tidings. There is but little doubt that they are lying in some of the ditches near the battle-field of Donaldsonville. Perchance, wounded, they sought shelter there from the foe, knowing not a fiercer foe was on their track. It may be that, like the lamented Bradley, death mercifully shortened their sufferings. To know this would be easier for friends to bear than the harrowing suspense. Compelled to relinquish all hopes of seeing them again, I give you their brief obituaries.

Wells Fuller was a Stockbridge farmer, aged thirty years. He leaves a wife and several children. In camp, he was ever steady, faithful, and reliable. He was one of our pioneers, and did his duty intelligently and fully. He made a fine appearance, *looking* the soldier. For long days he waited for the signal to batter down the walls of Port Hudson. It came not, and he was spared to pioneer us amid the cane-brakes of Bayou Lafourche. Doing his duty he met the unconquerable enemy. We know not the spot of his burial, but we record him among our "fallen brave."

James B. Bull was an excellent soldier and an intelligent man. He was a corporal in Company A. Unwell, he did not go up to Port Hudson till near the close of that siege. Spared those scenes of slaughter, he yielded up his life in an hour of comparative safety. The land of stern devotion to duty, Scotland, gave him birth; Louisiana gives him a burial. 'Twere worth the death-struggle to plant in that morally barren soil the love of religious freedom that has lifted Scotland so high among the races of men. "Missing!" who knows how much of agony gathers round that word. A soldier missing. The world hears and heeds but little, but some hear, and sorrowing echoes ring through the chambers of their souls. "When thousands fall, and are massed into trenches together, when thousands of homes are darkened, and thousands of hearts bereft forever, we weep over the magnificent sacrifice which entirely fills our imagination. But when a single life is offered, a solitary home desolated for the sake of country, why, it is of such small account we can not come down from our splendid grief, we who have bewept the stupendous carnage of Fredericksburg, Gettysburg and Port Hudson—to bewail the loss of 'only a man.' He died for his country, yet who will pronounce his eulogy, who print his name in the newspapers, and 'cover it with glory?' It is of no account to the great world, mad for her crowned heroes, that waiting their nameless brave—

> " 'Mother or maiden stand
> Within a lonely home,
> And say: " When will he come
> Out from the returning ranks? How long he lingers
> With his victorious band!"
> Tender loving lips have kissed
> Their last; and never more shall thrill white fingers
> For that one soldier missed!' "

Ralph E. Phelps (K), aged thirty-six years, farmer, from Florida, was wounded in the leg May 27th, so that amputation became necessary He died in the hospital at Baton Rouge the day we left. The brave corporal reached his home first. He leaves a family to mourn his loss. Florida sent ten good men with the Fortyninth; only one half return. She may well sadden at their loss, but pride also gathers round the grave of such dauntless heroes as Ralph E. Phelps.

We left Baton Rouge August 8th, 5 P. M., by the steamer J. Raymond. Our rejuvenated band played, a fine breeze quickened our blood, and, passing the State House and General Hospital, we sailed down the river "homeward bound." True, some of our wounded comrades were looking at our receding forms with sadness ; true, we were much crowded on deck and in cabin, but everything was forgotten in the joyous thought. "duty done, and we're homeward bound." Saturday afternoon it was, and, of course, the negroes' holiday. Their toil over, a toil *our* toil has mingled with hope, it was fitting that they should wave us their adieus. Cheerfully the night passed, and the morning found us at New Orleans.

Lo! the T. A. Scott had left us. A Connecticut regiment played a Yankee trick, and stole an earlier passage. We embarked on the steamboat Tempest about 2:30 P. M. August 9th, and are now retracing our weary steps. A long, discomforting, exhausting trip is before us. The well will bear it, for each revolution of the wheels brings us nearer home. I fear me the very anxiety of our sick to reach Berkshire will exhaust them and open intervening graves.

LETTER XXXVI.

CAIRO, ILLINOIS, *August* 18, 1863.

MY DEAR L.:

Sunday night, the 16th inst., at 11 P. M., we reached this gloomy place, and are yet waiting for transportation. We have had a dull trip. The river is beautiful, but monotonous. Above Baton Rouge, which we re-left on the 10th, 9 A. M., there are few houses to be seen on the banks of the stream. We gazed on the dear old flag we had followed into battle, floating in triumph over Port Hudson and Vicksburg, with emotions of mingled sorrow and pride. The numerous boats descending the river eloquently proclaim that we have not spent our strength for naught. It is free. Its freedom proclaims the death of slavery and rebellion. It was fitting we should sail over the scene of our triumphs, yet but few of us have any desire to renew the triumphal march. Coming up this river in August, under the most favorable circumstances, is not a matter of pleasure; to us it was crowded with discomforts. Lying on the damp, cinder-covered decks at night was positive comfort to enduring the rays of the sun by day. On the unsheltered deck we must be, or seek shade in the suffocating hold, in close proximity to the fires. Too crowded to be benefited by circulation of air, which Heaven gave grudgingly, we panted through the days and hailed the nights with their dampness and mosquitoes as friends indeed. Cooking was performed under difficulties only inferior to those we encountered on the Illinois. All was borne cheerfully, for, are we not "homeward bound?" You can imagine how the sick fared. They are failing rapidly. Some have died.

We had to go slowly up this tortuous river because new bars form so rapidly that constant travel is necessary to understand their location. After two years' rest it was almost a strange channel to our pilot. Getting on a bar would not only have delayed us, but might have brought us into disagreeable proximity to the prowling guerrillas, who amuse themselves by firing into passing boats, and by capturing those who get " stuck." Twenty-five unloaded rifles may enable us to do guard duty as we return, but would hardly keep back a horde of rebels. To men who are in a hurry, whose friends are awaiting them, it is provoking to look over a jet of land, not a mile wide, and learn that you have to travel thirty miles to reach that spot. All that belongs to the trip " up the river."

The officers tried to make up their accounts while on the boat, so as not to delay our being mustered out and paid off, but our craft was rightly named "Tempest," and after specimens of chirography that would have appalled the Departments at Washington, the attempt was abandoned.

We leave some of our sick at this place, among whom is William E. Clark (A), of Pittsfield, a tip-top soldier. I hope we do not leave him to die among strangers. As we were near Donaldsonville, on the night of the 9th inst., Ezra Van Dusen (E) walked, while asleep, into the river and was drowned. His body could not be recovered. He was a farmer, from Egremont, aged twenty-seven years, and is spoken of as a nice man. He was mainly employed in the cooking department, where he gave general satisfaction. He leaves a wife and children. Perchance they will come to Pittsfield, to greet the returning husband and father. God pity them in that hour.

Daniel Owens (1) died on the 13th inst., aged thirty-one years. His brother, Nelson, who disappeared when we were encamped at Bayou Montecino, died among the rebels, at Jackson, Mississippi. I had no acquaintance with either of them.

Levi Proutt (I), farmer, from Cummington, aged forty-four years, died of diarrhœa, August 14th.

Egbert Smith (II), a Sandisfield farmer, aged twenty-six years, died on the same day. His health was poor, but he was always willing to do his duty. A good soldier he was, one on whom you could always depend. He started with us when we moved on Port Hudson, but was too weak for service, so had to return. A good man and a faithful comrade, we buried him in Arkansas, as we did the others who died on the boat. Sad interruptions were these stoppages. Death demanded additional tribute almost on the confines of our eagerly-sought homes. Thank God, the weary trip, with its suspense and exhaustion and death, is over. Soon we will be on our homeward road again; soon reach the desired haven. Has death been as remorseless *there?*

LETTER XXXVII.

PITTSFIELD, MASS., *August* 24, 1865.

MY DEAR L.:

Home again! and now I sit down to finish the account of our trip.   Officers in passenger-cars and "enlisted men" in cattle-cars, we left Cairo on the evening of the 18th.   Cattle-cars awakened our indignation at first, but we learned they were more comfortable for a four days' journey than those occupied by the officers, for, occasionally, we could enjoy the luxury of expansion, and, albeit, they were hard and springless, get some sleep.   Clean straw was given to the sick for bedding.   Passing through fever-cursed Southern Illinois, we reached Mattoon the next morning, where we were furnished, gratuitously, by the ladies with an excellent breakfast.   Fresh from hard-tack and salt-beef, we did that breakfast such justice as left our providers no doubts as to our appetite or their capacity to cater for hungry men.   I tell you, the mother rose to our eyes as we overfilled our craving stomachs.   Despite the wretched Copperheads, who held a meeting there a few days before, at which cheers for Davis and groans for Lincoln were intermingled, we knew we were in the loyal North, and woman's kindness came to us with an unexpected and touching power.   God bless them! they were not handsome, but they were earnestly good, and, with their comforts, we received fresh draughts of patriotism for future sacrifices.   We had been worrying ourselves about the emptiness of our purses; we knew

not that the great heart of the North was alive to our
coming. After we had penetrated a few miles into
Illinois apple-peddlers offered their wares at what
seemed to us marvelously low prices, but still beyond
our reach; anon, some kind souls would throw apples
into the passing cars; then, at small stations, we would
see miniatures of the "dear old flag" flying, and whole
baskets of fruit would be handed in, and at times those
who had money would rush out and get a little milk or
a few eggs, and return with the purses no lighter,
which, being published, would lead scores to the friendly
doors, from which none came away empty-handed, and
then we exclaimed, "This is *our* land; God bless it
forever and ever!" At Mattoon we began to learn that
returning soldiers had coin more precious than gold;
coin that secured not only all needed blessings, but the
affectionate attention of men too old to be in the army,
and of women who so loved their country that they had
given to its defense husbands, brothers, sons, lovers,
all. Our trip was one continued ovation. So many
regiments had preceded us that their benevolence had
become systematized, and from station to station the
lightning flashed the news, "The boys are coming!"
and great hearts, knowing that they are "our boys,"
no matter whether they hail from Illinois or Massachusetts, met us with so many luxuries that money seemed
a thing too sordid to connect with such a triumphal
march.

Everything substantial was offered, and a good
woman, perchance thinking of her "old man," who
liked his tobacco after meals, would supply us with
some "fine-cut," and another would pass round a little
of the "ardent," concluding it would not do to be too
strict, and the change of water might make it beneficial

to the boys; while others presented us with bottles of
blackberry brandy or little vials of medicine for diarrhœa. God bless them! It was worth much of our
privations to be the recipients of such loving and grateful attentions. No one gave because we were moneyless : they knew not *that*, but their hearts said, "These
are *our* boys; they have been fighting for us; can't we
do yet more for them?" At first they did not complain
of our appetites, but after two or three gorgings we
necessarily came down to human standards, and really
saddened some because we could not eat all they offered. "Take it along with you, you may need it on
the road;" and filling up haversacks we would pass on.
Bless their dear souls! they forgot that there were many
stations on the road, and we must leave some vacant
corners for future benefactors.

Cold will be our hearts before we forget Mattoon,
Indianapolis, Bellefontaine, Cleveland, Buffalo, Utica.
We had sick with us, for whom *we* cared, but with such
rough manner that they thought of home by a tenderness which was lacking; but, stop where we would,
strong men and earnest-eyed women sought out the
sick, pressing dainties upon them till our good surgeon
had to interfere to prevent any illustrations of being
killed with kindness. What loving hearts could devise
or loving skill prepare was furnished with an accompanying tenderness that brought *home* vividly before
our almost despairing, aye, dying comrades. Refined,
delicate women would sit down in the dirty cars, take
the heads of the poor fellows on their laps, and tenderly bathe their brows and wash hands and feet that
had long been guiltless of water. Like angels they
hovered over these wrecks of human strength, and,
like angels, wept not, lest the tears welling up from

overcharged hearts should hinder them in the discharge of their loving, but hurried duties.

At Cleveland we left Lieutenant Reed, Charley French (D), and others. I fear they will return to Berkshire only as corpses. Reed is a noble fellow. Had he been willing to leave his company sooner than he did he might now be well. To go to Port Hudson he left the hospital, and only returned thither when his shrinking flesh could no longer submit to the earnest, patriotic will. If he dies he is a battle-victim as surely as if he had fallen in the thickest of the strife.

It would take up too much of your time to read of all our receptions, but you must pause a while at the followlowing extract from the Utica *Herald:*

"THE FORTY-NINTH MASSACHUSETTS.—It was about fifteen minutes before eight o'clock last evening when the Forty-ninth Massachusetts regiment arrived at the depot on a train of twenty cars. The vigilant committee and their vigilant aids had made their preparations on a more extensive scale than heretofore. in order that the large regiment of seven, hundred and fifteen men might be suitably accommodated and refreshed. Besides the usual complement of coffee, biscuits, sandwiches, cakes, and meats, there were platters heaped with warm boiled potatoes, a good supply of different varieties of pickles, pies, and other niceties—a feast fit to make all who looked upon it hungry. The ladies who lent their assistance never looked more kind and smiling, and many of them stood ready to wait on the sick, with wines and cordials and such other delicacies as were needed.

"Such a crowd as was at the depot to see and greet the Forty-ninth has not been there since the reception of the Fourteenth and Twenty-sixth regiments. The people began to gather before 7 o'clock, and continued to flock depot-ward until the number was estimated at five or six thousand.

"The regiment was greeted with cheers and thunders from Dunn and Morrison's battery on its arrival, and responded with other cheers and martial music. It was pleasant to see the soldiers' faces light up as they looked over the well-spread tables and smelt the fragrance of the coffee cups. They had had nothing to eat since morning, at Buffalo. As they filed out of the cars and into position it was remarked by many that a finer-appearing body of soldiers had not been seen in Utica. A much more stalwart regiment physically than most others, it appears to have considerably more than its share of intelligence; and as to their faces, the ladies were charmed. And such cheery prattle and bustle as these good ladies distributed among the handsome soldier faces can not be outdone by any other ladies of any other town; of this we are absolutely certain; and the owners of the handsome faces will remember them to the everlasting honor of Utica—we heard them say they would. They had received handsome treatment, they said, at Buffalo, Cleveland, and other places along their route, but Utica was ahead—Utica ladies did beat all. And so it is no wonder that they went off cheering vociferously for the ladies of Utica. Some of the ladies had prepared pretty bouquets, and did not forget to distribute them.

"Citizens who looked after the sick inform us that they were all very comfortable and better cared for than those of the previous regiments have been. They say that Surgeons Winsor and Rice are evidently just the men for their position, and deserving of the highest credit."

The editor of the *Eagle* truthfully and happily says:
"And let us add that they still keep on cheering for
Utica. By every Berkshire fireside the patriotic kindness of those Utica ladies is told, and warm hearts expand with gratitude to hear it. Tens of thousands of
Berkshire hearts will beat with a kindlier feeling whenever hereafter they hear or see the name of a city which
so nobly cheered the wayfaring of those we were impatient to welcome home. God bless the glorious city
of Utica."

On the 22d, at 1:30 A. M., we reached Albany, where
some received sandwiches and coffee, and where all
washed up and put on their best toggery, so as to look
as well as possible under the gaze of Berkshire. To
have marched into Pittsfield in all our dirt and rags
would only have been an affectation of heroism. We
knew that "mother," wife, sister, would be better
pleased to have us look presentable, and the nearer
home we got the gentler and softer were our feelings.
In comfortable passenger cars we left Albany about 7
A. M., and cheerily sped on our way. Never did any
country look so beautiful as did the rich counties of
Albany and Columbia. We crossed the State line, and,
with a joy too deep for cheers, felt we were again in the
dear old Commonwealth whose principles we had gone
forth to uphold and extend. The booming cannon and
the deep cheers at last told us we were at *home*. Berkshire was there to greet us. Her proudest day had
dawned. The long-expected Forty-ninth had come.
She was there to give us an ovation as honorable to her
as it was grateful to us. In that ovation pride for our
victories mingled with joy for our return. It was the
expression of a patriotism wedded to domestic happiness. The "oldest inhabitant" never before saw such

a crowd in Pittsfield. From early light extra trains had poured in their thousands. It was a lovely morning, and "The boys had come home!" We were to keep in order, fall into line, and, after a short march and a short speech, repair to the tables of feasting. A nice programme, but a mother's eyes met those of her child, and must they wait an hour for the fond embrace? The husband, the father, saw the wife, the little ones, and Heaven prompted one glad greeting before the formal reception. Robed in mourning the bereaved parent could poorly wait to shed her tears on the breast of her last boy, while she sadly thought of the other lying in his lonely Southern grave.

The following extracts from the Pittsfield *Sun* will give you a good view of " Reception Day :"

"The regiment was received at the depot and escorted to the Park in the following order : Cavalcade of citizens ; Stewart's Band, of N. Adams ; Housatonic Engine Company ; Greylock Hook and Ladder Company : Taconic Engine Company ; Lee Cornet Band ; Water-Witch Fire Engine Company, of Lee; St. Joseph's Mutual Aid Society ; the Pittsfield Liederkranz ; Schreiber's Band, of Albany ; Forty-ninth Regiment Massachusetts Volunteers.

"The line of march was from the Western Railroad Depot, through Depot street, North street, and South street, to East Housatonic street ; through East Housatonic street to Maple street ; through Maple to East street ; up East street to the north side of the Park.

"At the front of the regiment rode its heroic commander, Colonel Bartlett, mounted upon a splendid horse, which he took with him to Port Hudson, having but one arm at liberty, the other not yet being recovered from the wound received early in the attack upon the fort. His soldier-like bearing, and the enthusiasm of the regiment upon meeting him again, added to the record of his deeds and the silent testimony of his wounds, prove him to be one of the few of our many officers who honor their positions more than their positions honor them. When the history of the present war shall be written, Massachusetts, in her long train of heroes, shall write high upon the scroll of fame the name of the gallant Colonel of the Forty-ninth.

"A little to the rear of the Colonel rode Lieutenant-Colonel Sumner, on whom the command of the regiment devolved upon the fall of the Colonel, and who also fell, wounded, while gallantly leading on the charge. Farther down the regiment rode Major Plunkett, who commanded the regiment after his two superior officers were wounded, until their arrival in Pittsfield. The enthusiasm of the men for this tried and true officer knew no bounds. As in stature he *fully sustains the reputation of his family*, he was especially a mark for the sharpshooters of the enemy, and fears were entertained for him by his friends on this account. But through all the exposure and trials which the regiment has been compelled to undergo he has passed unharmed, faithfully discharging his duties upon every occasion, winning the admiration of friend and foe by his courageous bearing in battle, and bravely leading the regiment at Port Hudson and Donaldsonville. It will be remembered by our readers that a rebel sharpshooter, taken prisoner from a rifle-pit at Port Hudson, inquired (pointing to the Major) who that officer was, and stated that 'he'd fired five times at the critter and couldn't hit him once.' Rarely do we see a corps of officers so well deserving a gallant regiment, rarely a regiment reflecting such honor upon their officers.

"The streets through which the procession passed were all beautifully decorated, and the town appeared in its gayest colors in honor of the occasion. Near the depot was suspended a banner bearing the inscription so familiar to all, ' How are *you*, Forty-ninth?' Large flags were suspended across North street, from Goodrich, Geer's, Root's, and Burbank Blocks, and smaller ones were displayed from the various stores. There were also banners with the mottoes, ' Welcome Home, Gallant Forty-ninth,' and 'Ain't you glad you've come?' Farther down the street, a little above the corner of East street, stood the triumphal arch, the framework of which was first covered with cloth of the national colors—red, white, and blue—and afterwards tastefully ornamented with wreaths of evergreens and decorated with flags. Upon the north side was the inscription, ' Welcome,' the truth of which was verified in the hearty cheers and joyous countenances of the vast throng assembled to receive these brave and loyal sons of Berkshire. Upon the south side were the following: 'Plain's Store, May 21st,' 'Port Hudson, May 27th, June 14th,' ' Donaldsonville, July 13th.' There were also upon the north side two beautiful stars of roses, above which, respectively, were the words ' Berkshire' and '49th.' Between the Pittsfield Bank and Backus's Block were suspended flags, on one of which was the motto, 'In God is our trust,' and also a large banner trimmed with black, containing the inscription, '*In Memoriam—The Fallen Brave.*' As the regiment passed beneath it, every cap was raised. It was a beautiful and affecting sight—those hardened, sun-burned men, happy at regaining once again their native hills, turning from the cheers and congratulations of the crowd to heave a sigh or drop a silent tear to the memory of 'the fallen brave' who went forth from among us to return no more.

"From the Sanitary Rooms was suspended the inscription, 'Know them which labor among you. Esteem them very highly in love for their works' sake.' Between the Rooms and the Park a Louisiana State flag waved, taken from the Custom House, New Orleans. Over the Pittsfield Bank, and under the national colors, hung a Confederate flag, reversed, which was taken from the enemy by our troops. On the Old Elm in the Park was a sentiment, prepared by Miss R——, which was worthy of the old tree itself: 'Only the brave deserve the FAIR.' Nearly all the private dwellings and entrances on the line of march were tastefully ornamented, but we have neither space to particularize nor ability to discriminate between these various evidences of patriotism and good will.

"The procession arrived at the Park about 11:30 A. M., where the regiment, drawn up with closed ranks opposite the First Congregational Church, was addressed by the Hon. James D. Colt, as the Hon. S. W. Bowerman, previously selected for that purpose on account of his efforts in raising the regiment and the interest he has always felt in it, being unable through sickness to fulfill his appointment.

"Mr. Colt's address of welcome was not written out by himself, as was supposed, and does not appear in this report. We took no notes. The speaker alluded very eloquently and appropriately to 'the fallen brave;' to the gallant colonel, lieutenant-colonel, and major, and soldiers of the regiment; the heroic and patriotic services they have rendered the country; to the heartfelt regard entertained for them by their fellow-citizens, which was evidenced in the immense gathering on the occasion; in the triumphal arches that had been erected; the expressive mottoes that greeted them; the national flags that floated in the breeze, and the liberal provisions that fair hands had made to give them a sumptuous repast.

".At the conclusion of the address the regiment was invited by the Marshal, Graham A. Root, Esq., on behalf of the ladies of Berkshire, to enter the Park and partake of the refreshments provided. After the soldiers had done ample justice to the viands set before them, the tables were thrown open to all who wished to avail themselves of this opportunity to appease the cravings of the inner man, and a large number accepted the invitation. It is an evidence of the unexampled generosity of the ladies in preparing the entertainment, that after all had finished at the tables, there remained large quantities of refreshments, part of which were reserved for the regiment expected in the evening, and the remainder distributed among the poor.

"The entire reception was a magnificent ovation, and may be regarded in every respect as a complete success. The morning trains into Pittsfield, both regular and extra, brought from every direction large numbers of the citizens of Berkshire to do honor to the regiment, representing, as it did, every town in the county, and it is, we think, a fair estimate to say that the number present was about 10,000. A more orderly celebration we have rarely seen.

"'Toward the close of the afternoon, the trains departed on the various railroads, bearing with them their loads of strangers, and the town sank into comparative quiet. Only the occasional passing of some soldier with, by his side, a fine matronly countenance beaming with satisfaction at the safe return of her 'boy,' or with some younger member of the softer sex, whose rosy cheeks and downcast eyes betokened a nearer tie, told us that 'Our happy jubilee was o'er,' and the gallant Forty-ninth at home in old Berkshire.

"Great praise is due to the Chief Marshal, Graham A. Root, and the Assistant Marshals, for the admirable manner in which they discharged their duties.

"To the ladies of the several committees who arranged the contributions of our citizens for the collation, who spread the tables, arranged the flowers, and dispensed the bounties of the repast, too much credit can not be given.

"The music by the Pittsfield Liederkranz, in the Park, was listened to with great satisfaction.

"The arduous labors of the gentlemen who arranged the triumphal arch, and whose efforts were unceasing to meet the expectations of the public, and make the reception of the Forty-ninth such as would reflect honor upon the county and town, have elicited warm commendation. We perform an act of simple justice in mentioning the names of Messrs. Wm. R. Plunkett, R. W. Adam, A. E. Goodrich, Wm. II. Teeling, D. J. Dodge, and J. D. Adams, Jr., in this connection."

It was a happy and a *sad* day. Friends with joy came to greet friends, yet many saw, in the first embrace, that the only joy left them was to hand them tenderly down to early graves. A comrade whose strength had never failed him in the day of battle found himself but a babe when from his stricken wife he first learned that Death had snatched away his last "household jewel." Wives came to receive their husbands, only to learn that they were dead and buried. Three little children, clad in mourning for a recently deceased mother, instead of meeting a father's embrace, were told that that father was one of our dead—our "fallen brave." As we marched, with uncovered heads, beneath the banner bearing the inscription, "*In Memoriam— The Fallen Brave*," so near the triumphal arch, and thought of those who had so fondly looked forward to that hour, when they should see *their* loved ones proudly returning from the war, but who, through tear-darkened eyes, now saw naught but their vacant places in the ranks, sorrow mingled with our gladness, and our joy, though sincere, was quiet and subdued.

Next to our pleasure in seeing relatives was that of once more looking into the face of our cherished Colonel. We greeted him with such cheers as convinced him that, way down in the depths of our heart, among our proudest and holiest remembrances, may be found his name. "Boys," said he, as we entered Slaughter's field, on the 27th of May, "do nothing that you will be ashamed of when you meet your friends in Berkshire." The record of that day shows how well we obeyed him, how well we merited

"THE HEROES' RECEPTION.

"Them have I seen! Oh, sight to cheer
    The patriot, when he bleeding lies;
To kindle hope and scatter fear,
    And light new fire in dying eyes!

"Their way with banners waved and burned,
    The welkin rang with patriot cheers,
From every window fondly yearned
    Bright eyes that spoke their joy in tears.

"And music round their pathway flung
    Its gladness in a silver shower,
And over all the great bells swung,
    Shouting their joy from every tower."

" The war-horse their colonel bestrode
  Stepped conscious with a soul of flame,
As if he knew his master rode
  Straight to the glorious gates of Fame.

" The coldest gazer's heart grew warm,
  And felt no more its indecision ;
For every soul which saw that form
  Grew larger to contain the vision."

The papers inform us that Bartlett has been appointed Colonel of a veteran regiment, to be raised in Western Massachusetts. His wrist may be a little stiff, as the result of his Port Hudson wound ; otherwise he is as competent to lead a new regiment as he was to lead the "Forty-ninth." *They* will say, "No troops need a more capable leader." Though he is young, I hope he will soon become a Brigadier. He should have a wider field of usefulness than that of Colonel.

Too much praise can not be awarded to that excellent lady, Mrs. C. T. Fenn, and her effective coadjutors, for their care of our sick and wounded. About fifty were taken to the hospital, where they received all the attentions that patriotism allied to Christianity, working out through women's hearts and hands, could inspire. None made question of rank or residence, nothing but the measure of illness and necessity. Of Mrs. C. T. Fenn, Mrs. L. F. Sperry, Mrs. W. Carpenter, Mrs. M. V. Lee and daughters, Mrs. P. Allen, Mrs. D. J. Dodge, Mrs. H. Melville, Mrs. J. P. Rockwell, Mrs. J. Gregory, Mrs. D. Wilson, and Miss Sandford, many a stricken soldier will ever think with gratitude, and many a soldier's widow will, in her loneliness, invoke Heaven's blessings on them who so tenderly handed *their* loved ones to God and His mercy.

The sick sent home by sea were landed at Fort Schuyler, New York, and, by the workings of red-tape, were dragged to Pittsfield by the way of Stonington and Boston, though their friends were on hand to conduct them gently home. I conclude this "Reception" letter with brief memoirs of our dead. Do you wonder that reception day was marked with sombreness?

Edward N. French (C), a farmer boy, from Peru, aged eighteen, died at home, of consumption, July 17th. He was one of the very finest boys of his company. Had there been any of the "shirk" in his composition his life might have been prolonged, for he clung to duty long after he was fit for the hospital. Discharged after we had commenced the siege of Port Hudson, God mercifully spared him to hear the news of our success, and to die at home.

George W. Clark (E), of Sheffield aged twenty years, died August 8th, in the hospital at New Haven, Ct. For months he lay prostrate with fever, and was sent North with the Colonel. The day before his death his father went to see him, hoping to be able to remove him to his home, but God ordered otherwise. He was a good soldier, and a young man of more than ordinary promise, loved and respected by all who knew him. On leaving, with another son, he said, "Mother, one of us will be returned to you again, and one will not." Not "will *return*," but "will *be returned*." He realized that God, not man, was the disposer of such events. Of five from Sheffield who died, George alone was buried in his native soil. Duty done and suffered, he rests well.

William Funk, jr (K), also from Sheffield, was buried at sea, August 10th, from the ship St. Mary, which was bearing him and other sick homeward. He was a steady, reliable farmer, aged forty-four years.

The remains of *Henry D. Rhoades* (E) were deposited in the sea, August 12th. His brother sleeps in his soldier's grave at Baton Rouge. Henry was but twenty-one years of age ; and in his death, so near home, New Marlboro' loses a fine, steady boy. "After life's fitful *fever*, he sleeps well."

On the same day, from the same fever-ship, the body of *Moseley Pomeroy* (F), of Monterey, was buried in the Atlantic to await that day when "the sea shall give up its dead." He was sick a long while, and in his nineteenth year found rest.

The greedy deep swallowed up all that was mortal of *Sylvester Burrows* (I), on the 13th inst., at the age of forty-four years. He was a farmer, from Mount Washington, and was a nice, moral man. Diarrhœa, which closed his career, alone prevented him from mingling in the glory and the grief that surround the name of Port Hudson. A family mourns his loss.

George Yager (D), a large, strong farmer, from Alford, was taken with diarrhœa soon after we reached Baton Rouge, and was buried at sea on the 13th inst. He was a German, aged thirty-six years, and leaves quite a large family, to whom our return brought only blighted hopes and blasted anticipations. A very fine soldier was given to consecrate the ocean to the rights of mankind.

John M. Tuller (I), aged thirty-five years, of Lee, was buried at home, having died of diarrhœa in New Haven the 14th inst. He was a good, moral man, and a faithful, reliable soldier.

Charles Turgeon (E), aged twenty-seven years, farmer from New Marlboro', was sent home in the hope of sparing his life, but fever closed his career about the time we reached Pittsfield.   As a man and a soldier he bore a good name.

Myron Nichols, orderly sergeant of Co. F, fell from the cars, near Little Falls, N. Y., as we were returning on the 21st inst., and when found, was dead.   He was a farmer, from Otis, aged twenty-six years, and leaves a wife and child.   We were telegraphed that a member of Co. *I* was found dead.   Owing to the mistake in the letter we were not aware of our real loss till we reached Albany.   Our comrade was an excellent soldier, and bore well his part in the toils and dangers of the bloody campaign, out of which he came uninjured, to meet death when his wife and child, of whom he often spoke, were almost within sight.   He said on the trip home he had a presentiment that he would never live to see Berkshire.   He was a *steady* man and a reliable soldier. We mourn for him, but who may enter into the sacredness of the grief of her who came to meet a husband's embrace, and received only his corpse !   Has death **no** relentings?

Ozro P. Brown (K), aged eighteen years, one of the best farmer boys of Florida, yielded to diarrhœa after we had left him at New Orleans.   He begged hard to come home with us, but his young life was too valuable to be risked, and we left him, but not alone.   His comrade, J. Tinney, though eager to see his family, stayed with him.   Captain Weston, with his usual kindness, left him money to secure all comforts, and now we are apprised that the noble lad tenants one of the nameless graves that crowd and sanctify the shores of the Mississippi.

Zebulon Beebe (G), a carpenter, from Williamstown, aged forty-four years, died in the hospital at New

Haven, on the 18th inst. He leaves a large family. Our comrade was steady, but too weakly for a soldier's duties ; yet he did his part well as hospital cook. Consumption, which ended his life, was not of Southern birth. He took it with him.

Hosea Wheeler (B) died this day at his home in West Stockbridge, of diarrhœa, aged forty-seven years. He was spared to die among the friends for whom he went forth as a soldier, and as such contracted the disease that has carried desolation and sorrow to so many hearts.

John A. Francis (B) was one of our best soldiers. He did his part nobly as a member of our left wing, which met the fiercest surges of the wave of fire that on the 27th of May covered so many homes with honor and sadness. He had recovered from a wound in the head received then, and, in good health, started for home, but was taken sick in the cars, and to-day yielded up a well-spent life at his home in Windsor, aged twenty-six years. He was faithful as a soldier ; could we expect less of one who was faithful as a man and a Christian ?

I can not more fittingly close this letter than with these choice verses from the pen of the pastor of the M. E. Church in this place :

IN MEMORIA.

THE FALLEN BRAVE OF THE FORTY-NINTH

BY J. WESLEY CARHART, D. D.

" Sleep, ye fallen, sweetly sleep,
     Your work was nobly done ;
Your names are written with the bra
     Who fadeless laurels won.
Ye saw the vaunting foe advance,
     With banners floating high—
Ye struck for freedom and the right
     Resolved to win, or die.

"Sleep, ye gallant fallen, sleep
     Where winds your requiems sigh ;
Your memory lives in many a heart
     And moistens many an eye.
No monuments of marble mark
     Your places of repose ;
Ye sleep where Southern violets bloom,
     Or tangled sea-weed grows.

" Sleep, ye sons of Freedom, sleep,
     Where bugles never sound,
Nor clash of steel nor cannon's boom
     Disturb your rest profound !
The glorious flag of fadeless hues,
     ' Neath which we fought and fell,
Shall ever proudly wave on high
     And of your valor tell."

LETTER XXXVIII.

PITTSFIELD, MASS., *September* 1, 1863.

MY DEAR L.:

This day we were mustered out of the service of the United States. There is now no more a "Forty-ninth Regiment Massachusetts Volunteers." Our corporate life is extinct. The soldier is merged in the citizen. We step to the duties of private life with a prouder tread. We have done something to make that life more secure, something to make American citizenship a holier title. Our toils, our sufferings, our deaths, have advanced the finger on the dial of Time. Earth feels more the attraction of the great sacrifice and is nearer Jesus. We have had a part in the grandest movements of the race. Clothed in the livery of the nation, we have stood as Heaven's soldiers. Consciously or unconsciously, we have been "workers together with God." Our names, but not the results of our deeds, will be forgotten on earth. If duty really prompted us they will be enshrined in eternity as of them who counted life less valuable than man's welfare. Great upward strides this nation has taken since we were mustered in as soldiers. Animated by a holy idea, God has given us his "mercies of reoccupation." We reoccupy territory wrenched from us, principles buried beneath party and prosperity, and the hope and sympathy of the world. Death, anticipating the tardy officer, has mustered out many of our number. What reck we of that? Life is given to advance truth. Have not our dead, in their

brief lives and noble endings, further advanced truth
than will the fourscore years of them who now sneer-
ingly ask, as if their coward hearts had taught them
aright in refusing to defend common privileges, "I
suppose you have got enough of war?" Yes, we have
had enough of war. We have seen its horrors, and
would not willingly gaze on them again; but only those
who bring home *blurred* memories will fail to draw
from our past fresh incentives to deeds of patriotic self-
sacrifice.

Writing my last letter, I will close the list of our
dead. Southern foes have followed many to their peaceful homes, and some have already closed their campaign
in the quiet of Berkshire graves. Over others, and not
a few, the drawn sword hangs. I fear in vain are the
prayers and loving services. That sword must fall again
and again. Freedom's full ransom price has not been
paid. New graves yawn for failing comrades. Berkshire must see the dying agonies to enter into fuller
sympathy with the struggle that is not only to restore
our *Union* but to complete our liberty. I may revise
these letters for the press. If so, my great regret will
be that I have had such limited materials for the obituaries. I have done none of our dead *more* than justice.
Ignorance has prevented me *doing* justice to many.
Uniform goodness presents few salient points for the
biographer; so of some all I could gather was they were
good men and true.

Franklin W. Harmon (D), farmer, from Monterey,
aged twenty-one years, died at the house of G. Robinson, in Pittsfield, August 27th, of diarrhœa. Though
away from home, his last hours were surrounded with
tender care. I had no personal acquaintance with him,
but Lieutenant Tucker responded to my query, "What

kind of a man and soldier was F. W. Harmon, of your company?" "None *better* in the regiment."

Henry R. Clark (B), of Becket, aged twenty-six years, died at New Orleans, of diarrhœa, August 22d. He was wounded in the side, May 27th. He leaves a family behind him.

Levi H. Gilmore (F), a farmer boy from Monterey, aged eighteen years, died at home August 30th. I believe he was taken sick after his return.

John W. Burghardt (D), aged twenty-four years, farmer, from Barrington, was taken with fever at Cairo, and died at this place, at the house of H. Webster, who was, I believe, a stranger to our comrade, but watched over him as a brother.

Patrick Downing (I), aged eighteen, from MittenEaque, died yesterday of diarrhœa. He was a steady, moral man and a first-rate soldier.

William F. Burnett (K), a Florida farmer, aged thirty years, died in Louisiana, after we left, of diarrhœa. His captain speaks of him as a "splendid fellow," a steady man, a good soldier, and a Christian. On our leaving, he said, "If I can only get home!" God was even then opening to him the gates of an eternal home. The head of a family, he yearned once more to see that family before entering into rest. The loving Master ordered otherwise. Oh! how often that cry has gone up from our crowded hospitals, "If I can only get home!" Now that *I* am at home it rings in my ears as if in reproach for having left the dying.

I turn from our graves to the living. Receptions, in the form of suppers, picnics, &c., have greeted our boys all over the county. It seems as if the heart of Berkshire, wrapped up as it was in the Forty-ninth, yearned to burst forth, that her returned sons might *see* how

proud she is of them.   The citizens of Barrington are
very justly attached to Company D, and Mrs. Bigelow's
bountiful and tasty supper, so characteristic of that
lady, did not satisfy them ; so they selected Lieutenants
Tucker and Siggins, as true representatives of a choice
company, to receive further expressions of their grateful appreciation.   The former gentleman, too proud of
the evidence of his being deemed worthy to suffer in the
cause of freedom to mourn that the hard chances of war
fell on *him*, received a handsome service of plate.

The following letter will explain itself.   I know not
its author, but the happiness of its composition is only
equalled by the munificence of the favor inclosed.   Unexpectedly the gallant, maimed leader of our forlorn
hope reached home ; so this epistle, with its rich burden
of near a thousand dollars and its richer burden of a
thousand sympathies, was placed in his hands instead
of in the mail :

"GREAT BARRINGTON, *August* 10, 1863.

"Lieut. SIGGINS, Co. D, Forty-ninth Reg. Mass.Vols.:

"DEAR SIR: Your friends here have watched with
intense interest the conduct of the Forty-ninth during
the recent campaign in Louisiana.   Naturally they have
thought more particularly of Company D ; and they are
proud to say that their hopes and highest aspirations
have been most nobly realized by the heroic gallantry
of that company.   We have learned with feelings of
deep sadness that the hard fortunes of battle have fallen
heavily upon yourself.   Your courageous and stern devotion to duty as an American citizen-soldier during
that terrible conflict of the 27th of May last we can never
forget.   You are far from us ; we can not nurse you, we
can not give you the cheering word or grasp of friend-
ship and heartfelt sympathy.   We must do something

for you and yours. Do accept the inclosed as a token, though a very inadequate one, of our pride in your conduct and sympathy in your misfortune as frankly and heartily as we tender it. Hoping for your speedy return to your friends at home, we remain, most respectfully and sincerely, YOUR FRIENDS."

We find it pleasant to be at home. We can go to bed when we please, and, what is far more pleasurable, get up when we please. Who has not learned the luxury of the little cat-naps between daybreak and sunrise, when you are just enough awake to know that you are asleep, has not drunk the elixir of life. In those most witching hours we have been so used to the disturbance of the *reveille* as to be tempted to begin that word with a "D" instead of 'an "R." Prudence leading wealth in her train says get up at once, but now we "don't see it." Draining the goblet of sleep at one swallow will do for the soldier, but the returned veteran has heard that sipping lengthens enjoyment, and he means to give it a trial. Away in Dixie we used to get up much pathos over the "little ones," but when they crawl over their mother early in the morning to your side of the bed, and having satisfied themselves that you have a right there, that you are really "papa," begin to beat a "reveille" of pats and kisses, accompanied with experiments on your beard, you think it very funny the first time ; but it soon loses its novelty, and you are in doubt whether it is any improvement on the "Dooty, dooty, dooty calls you" of our *quondam* chief bugler, Baker, of Company H. After lying on planks and Mother Earth for near a year, feathers were so hard to be borne that divorces "*a mensa*," if not "*et toro*," were only forestalled by the forthcoming of mattresses.

The officers, with your humble servant, have had a busy week of it fixing up our accounts and trying to make two and one count four, or three and five count seven. The latter is just as desirable as the former, for the authorities care about exactness of figures and accuracy of accounts more than a few hundred garments or cartridges. Mr. Brewster has justly deserved the name of "Honest Quartermaster," but sickness has compelled him to shirk the work on me; and for a like reason Howard and Northup, who never deserted the post of duty, have failed to aid in overcoming this Sebastopol of "Abstracts and Vouchers." Dashes failed at Port Hudson; this, also, can only be reduced by siege. The happy *Lieutenants* roam round the streets, hob-nobbing with friends, thanking Fortune that bullets did not promote them to captaincies and settling of accounts. Kangaroo-like, we find the "tail of the business" the most troublesome part. Patriotism might allow us a little rest, but a big pile of "greenbacks" is at the end, and *only* at the end of the job.

In concluding this series of letters I send you an abstract of our statistics:

No. of men brought home	652	Men missing	2
No of officers brought home	24	Men died of disease	82
Men discharged	56	Men died of wounds	32
Men left sick at New Orleans	12	Casualties in battle	132
Men left sick at Cairo	1	Commissioned officers killed	2
Men left sick at Cleveland, O.	7	" " wounded	12
Men sent home sick	51		

Free now to do what other citizens may, to obey only what our judgment or conscience approves, we take our unobtrusive places in life. Our privileges will never

again seem common. We have been where the price
was paid. One additional privilege we have secured—
I value it more than gold—we have the right to say before all, aye, in the very centre of the bereaved : "This
war pays. The victory, as sure to come as that the
God of Justice lives, will be worth *more* than all it will
cost."

> " For whether on the gallows high,
>   Or in the battle's van,
>   The noblest place for man to die
>   Is where he dies for man."

APPENDIX.

ROLL OF FIELD AND STAFF OFFICERS OF THE FORTY-
NINTH MASSACHUSETTS VOLUNTEERS.

September 1, 1863.

‡WILLIAM F. BARTLETT,	Colonel.
SAMUEL B. SUMNER,	Lieutenant-Colonel.
CHARLES T. PLUNKETT,	Major.
‡FREDERICK WINSOR,	Surgeon.
ALBERT R. RICE,	Assistant Surgeon,
‡JOSEPH B. REYNOLDS,	" "
*‡BENJAMIN C. MIFFLIN,	Adjutant.
FREDERICK A. FRANCIS,	Acting Adjutant.
‡HENRY B. BREWSTER,	Quartermaster.

NON-COMMISSIONED STAFF.

‡ALBERT J. MOREY,	Hospital Steward.
HENRY J. WYLIE,	Sergeant-Major.
GEORGE E. HOWARD,	Quartermaster-Sergeant.
HENRY H. NORTHUP,	Commissary-Sergeant.
‡EDWARD W. STEADMAN,	Drum-Major.

* Detached.   ‡ Died since discharge.

ROLL OF COMPANY A. FORTY-NINTH MASS. VOLUNTEERS.

September 1, 1863.

Weller, Israel C.,	Captain.	Biety, Thomas,	Corporal.
Clark, George W.,	First Lieut.	*Bull, James B.,	"
Francis, Frederick A.,	" "	Priestly, John,	"
‡Reed, George,	Second Lieut.	Barnes, Erastus D.,	"
Howe, Albert C.,	Sergeant.	Kearn, George H.,	"
Adams, Charles P.,	"	Read, Lyman J.,	"
‡Greber, David,	"	Daily, Michael F.,	"
Hazard, Charles J.,	"	Seace, John B.,	"
Rodgers, Judson B.,	"		

PRIVATES.

Allen, Joseph H.	Grant, Aleander A.	†Platt, Charles E.
Abbe, Merrick L.	Hanley, Michael	‡Packard, John K.
‡Aldrich, Cornelius S.	Holland, George A.	Reed, William
‡Bassett, James W.	Hall, Thomas E.	Rucktashell, Henry
‡Bailey, Julius F.	Hubbard, Lewis F.	Reehl, Henry
Bills, Henry	‡Hufneagle, Frederick	‡Rairdon, Hugh
‡Bryce, John, jr.	Horton, Manly H.	Rairdon, Timothy
Blake, Frank V.	‡Joyner, Daniel M.	Rogers, John
‡Bayne, Wm. H.	‡Jones, Seth R.	Robbins, Henry M.
‡Burkett, Willard L.	Jones, William	Root, Henry L.
Bogard, Robert	Kittle, James	Russell, Edwin F.
Bailey, William H.	Kendall, Chauncey E.	Stupka, William
Burbank, George W.	Kimple, John	Smart, John
Brockway, Albert C.	Landon, Edwin A.	Swart, John W.
Burt, Orville D.	Lathrop, Frank B.	‡Shaw, William
Brooks, Franklin	Le Barnes, George E.	Schmidt, John
‡Coleman, Charles A.	Lewis, Alanson	‡Taylor, William
Cleman, William	Merry, John C.	Tuggey, William
Clark, William E.	Marshall, Joseph	Tillottson, William E.
Clark, John B.	Malcolm, Joseph	Vandeburgh, Charles B
Colt, Merrick R.	Miller, Henry	‡Videtto, Charles
*Davis, Luther M.	McCoy, Martin	Watkins, Charles B.
‡Daniels, Peter	‡Merriem, Andrew	Warner, Henry C.
Drew, Timothy	Merriem, Louis	Watkins, Willard H.
Dunlap, Thomas	Maxwell, John	‡Wiedman, John
‡Ende, Emile	‡Noble, Samuel G.	Wells, Charles H.
Fuller, George W.	‡Nicholas, William	Weisse, August
Grawe, Henry	Neuber, Emile	
Green, Robert A.	O'Brien, William	

* Killed.   † Died of wounds.   ‡ Died of disease.   § Died since discharge.

ROLL OF COMPANY B, FORTY-NINTH MASS. VOLUNTEERS.

September 1, 1863.

‡Garlick, Charles R., Captain.
Kniffin, Charles W., First Lieutenant.
Noble, Robert R., Second "
Jennings, Orton W., Sergeant.
Arnold, Josiah "
‡Bliss, Alvin F., "
Burbank, Henry S., "
‡Boynton, Charles S., "

‡Pierce, Eugene W., Corporal.
†Rossiter, Samuel H., "
Phelps, Henry P. "
‡Nourse, Isaac, "
‡Gamwell, John M., "
‡Burlingham, Hiram "
‡Wood, George M., "
Wood, Oliver L., "
Davis, Henry H., "

PRIVATES.

Adams, William K.
‡Arnold, John A.
‡Arnold, Samuel, jr.
‡Ashburn, William
Belcher, Arnold
†Belcher, Frederick
‡Barrett, George N.
Barnes, Charles H.
Billings, Almond M.
‡Bliss, William D.
Bliss, Robbins K.
Brown, George W.
Barnes, Araid V.
Bennett, Samuel H.
‡Babbitt, George W.
Bailey, William W.
‡Babbitt, William S.
Broga, Charles T.
Brown, Edwin
Boice, Wildman
Beckwith, Charles B.
Cole, Russell
Cadwell, George
Chapman, Araid L.
Carey, John B.
Codding, Ebenezer
Collier, John
Collyer, Charles
Cornell, James A.

Carter, George G.
†Cook, Charles H.
‡Codding, Abner D.
‡Clark, Henry R.
‡Denslow, Isaac
Darley, George
Fuller, Charles R.
Furrow, Walter A.
Fillio, Edmund
*Fitzgerald, Garrett
‡Francis, John A.
Gannon, Thomas
*Grippen, Henry E.
‡Green, Thomas
Goodell, Myron
‡Glead, William J.
*Heins, Conratt
Hamilton, Chester E.
Hinman, William H.
‡Hinman, Caleb C.
Hathaway, Alvin H.
Hofmeyer, Samuel
‡Jordan, James A.
Lynch, Charles D.
Lynch, Edwin E.
Lennon, William
Lee, Henry E.
Lyman, John
Middlebrook, Anson L.

Merchant, William
Markham, Charles
‡Markham, Alfred
Moore, James S.
‡Maranville, Araid H.
‡Morgan, Wells B.
Martin, Ezra M.
Noonan, Thomas
Nichols, Henry C.
Rossiter, Abram N.
‡Rossiter, William W.
Simmons, Ensign J.
Stevens, John A.
Sherman, Dwight
Smith, Nathan B.
Stearns, Edward A.
Sturtevant, Samuel S.
Soule, E. A.
Slosson, Frank
‡Thayer, Rufus L.
Van Bramer, Albert
Van Volkenburgh, Alex.
‡Wilson, Frank
Whipple, James L.
Werden, Gilbert, jr.
‡Wheeler, Allen H.
*Wentworth, Henry D.

* Killed. † Died of wounds. ‡ Died of disease. ‡ Died since discharge.

ROLL OF COMPANY C, FORTY-NINTH MASS. VOLUNTEERS.

September 1, 1863.

Lingenfelter, Geo. R., Captain.
‡Foster, Daniel B., First Lieutenant.
Wells, William M., Second "
Strong, James N., " "
Goddard, Lewis W., Sergeant.
Brooks, Crowell H., "
Temple, Edwin L., "
‡Dwyer, John, "
Nash, Edward P., "

Cranston, William H., Corporal
Haskins, Frank H., "
*Griswold, Albert, "
King, Emory, "
‡French, Edward N., "
Wade, Warren W., "
Warren, Francis E., "
Phillips, Truman G., "
‡Dewey, Allen M., "

PRIVATES.

‡Baker, Robert H.
Bastianello, James E.
‡Bowles, John W.
Braunwalder, Daniel
Bristol, Gilbert A.
Brown, Addison W.
‡Brown, John L.
Burnham, Orastes E.
Campbell, Henry J.
‡Camp, John R.
Carrissey, Eugene
Clark, Alvin L.
Connors, Timothy
Cook, John L.
Cummings, Norman
Downs, Edson
Dudley, Charles F.
Edwards, Albert L.
Farley, Matthew
Farling, Hiram
Farrall, Lawrence
Fay, Sedgwick N.
Field, George W.
Gallup, Henry C.
Hodge, George H.

‡Hummell, John W.
Jacques, Wm. S.
Johns, Henry T.
‡Jones, Abel
Kelley, Henry
Kittredge, Frederick C.
Kittredge, William C.
Kendall, H. J.
Knight, John N.
‡Knox, Francis M.
Lee, John H.
Leland, Waldo C.
Loomis, William E.
Mack, Lyman
Mason, Homer O.
Mallaly, James
Mattison, Micah G.
‡McCann, Peter
McCarty, John
McDonald, John
Merry, Edward F.
Merry, Henry N.
Moore, Henry
Murray, Octave
Noble, John

Newton, Isaac J.
Olin, John H.
Ollinger, Charles
*Parker, Theron F.
‡Parsons, Harlan P.
Pierce, Benjamin F.
Root, Erastus P.
Scott, Thos. A.
Silk, Michael
‡Smith, Alexander
Smith, Henry
*Stelfax, William
‡Stowell, William W.
‡Stowell, Harvey E.
Stetson, Norman W.
‡Sturtevant, Hezekiah W.
Stevens, Joseph H.
Tift, Samuel W.
Tilton, Thurston
Tower, Cyrus R.
Tucker, Edward A.
Wade, Benjamin D.
‡Wells, Albert W.
‡Wilcox, Rensselaer H.
Wells, John H.

* Killed. † Died of wounds. ‡ Died of disease. ‡ Died since discharge.

ROLL OF COMPANY D, FORTY-NINTH MASS. VOLUNTEERS.

September 1, 1863.

Chaffee, Samuel J.,	Captain.	Odenwalt, William,	Corporal.
Tucker, Joseph,	First Lieutenant.	Fowler, Henry R.,	"
Morey, Henry G.,	Second Lieutenant.	Tucker, Henry R.,	"
¿Siggins, Thomas,	" "	Dresser, John A.,	"
¿Gilbert, William S.,	Sergeant.	Evans, John W.,	"
Parker, James K.,	"	¿Toby, Edward,	"
¿Mansir, Henry W.,	"	Bristol, Henry A.,	"
¿Murray, Elias H.,	"	Hughes, Thomas H.,	"
¿Ray, Guy C.,	"		

PRIVATES.

Adams, James H.	Decker, Milo	McGrath, James
Andrews, George A.	¿Devaney, Patrick	Neumaster, Henry
Broderick, Michael	‡French, Charles H.	Nettleton, Dwight S.
Broderick, Morris	‡Fitzgerald, John W.	Parsons, Edwin W.
Bangs, Charles G.	‡Godson, John	¿Parsons, William H.
Barry, Morris	*Hensey, Thomas	Phillips, James P.
*Bracken, Mark	Hubbard, Edwin N.	Ramsey, Legrand
Bailey, Alpheus H.	‡Harmon, Franklin W.	*Reynolds, Mills S.
Bump, William E.	Heacox, David	Ryan, John
‡Bills, Samuel C.	Hunt, Henry W.	Steinhardt, Antoine
‡Burghardt, John W.	¿Luddington, Charles B.	Seymour, James A.
¿Beach, Mills S.	¿Lewis, Horace H.	Shook, Edwin H.
Brett, Charles W.	Luka, Henry	Seymour, Enos
Brainard, Albert M.	Luddington, Henry W.	Shelly, Benjamin
Bills, George	Latham, Sydney H.	Shutts, Clarence W.
Come, Peter	Latham, Almon S.	Thomas, John
Curtis, James H.	Loring, Lyman A.	Van Deusen, James
Conners, Thomas	Loop, Arthur A.	¿Warner, Albert S.
‡Colby, George	Luddington, Edwin C.	Weyants, Charles
Chapin, Clarence C.	Lewis, Ward	¿Wilcox, Bradford B.
¿Coffing, Charles F.	Luddington, James H.	Wilcox, Henry F.
‡Comstock, Artemas H.	Moore, Richard H.	‡Wilcox, Isaac V.
Church, Charles C.	McGowen, James	Winchell, John
Campion, John	Murray, Horatio E.	Winters, Henry
Dearing, Marcus H.	Morse, Benjamin F.	‡Yager, George
Donahue, John	¿Mullany, James	
Deland, Frederick N.	McCurdy, Robert F.	

* Killed.   † Died of wounds.   ‡ Died of disease.   ¿ Died since discharge.

ROLL OF COMPANY E. FORTY-NINTH MASS. VOLUNTEERS.

September 1, 1863.

‡Train, Horace D.,   Captain.
Sherman, Robert T., First Lieutenant.
Sissons, H. Dwight, Second   "
Tuttle, Moses H.,   First Sergeant.
Stanard, David K.,   "
Schutt, Marcus M.,   "
Keyes, Loren P.,   "
Parsons, George L.,

Kainer, William J., Corporal.
Booth, Edwin L.,   "
Boardman, Dwight,   "
Kamer, Warren G.,   "
‡Wood, Joseph H.,   "
Dewey, Charles O.,   "
‡Palmentier, George H.,   "
Arnold, Frederick K.,   "
Taft, Robert S.,   "

PRIVATES.

‡Adams, Harvey D.
Amstead, William
Bignal, Claudius E.
Brauan, Luke
Brayne, Jonathan
Brennison, Charles H.
Brett, Alonzo W.
Callender, George E.
‡Campbell, Levi
Carroll, Henry M.
Chapin, Alva W.
Chapin, Norman C.
‡Chapin, Edwin W.
Clark, Amos W.
‡Clark, George W.
Clark, Wilbur J.
Collins, Thomas
‡Cowles, Albert N.
Decker, George W.
‡Ensign, Edward E.
‡Ferry, Albert
Fogarty, William
Foley, Dennis
‡Foote, Bradford C.
‡Ford, John J.
‡Gorham, Lyman
Garland, Owen
Harford, Nicholas
‡Hatch, William H.

Hedger, Libbens
*Hewins, Horatio S.
‡Hewins, Sylvester J.
‡Hinman, Ebenezer S.
‡Hinton, John E.
‡Hollenbeck, Norman H.
‡Holmes, Henry L.
Hyde, Henry D.
‡Jackson, John
Joyner, Elbert S.
Joyner, Herbert C.
Lampson, Horace W.
Lawrence, William H.
Lee, Curtis
‡Lindsey, Lyman
Little, Asahel M.
Little, Frank
Loomis, Albert K.
‡Loring, James B.
McCarty, Michael
McCormick, John
‡Mallaly, Thomas
Maxwell, William H.
Moore, Joseph H.
Miller, Jeremiah
Murphy, William
‡O'Brien, John
‡Palmer, George W.
Palmer, Henry W.

Parsons, Albert H.
Patterson, David C.
Platz, John
Reapy, John
‡Rhoades, Christopher.
‡Rhoades, Henry D.
‡Root, Gideon
Roraback, Milton
Sage, George W.
Seeley, Dwight
‡Slater, Samuel
Smith, Alva M.
Smith, Maloy J.
Stanard, Edwin R.
‡Stevens, George H.
‡Stevens, John J.
Thatcher, Charles F.
‡Turgeon, Charles
Van Deusen, Levi
*Van Deusen, Ezra
Ward, Jabez C.
Webb, Daniel G.
Webb, James L.
‡Webster, Nelson
Wilber, William L.
Williams, Charles K.
Winters, William E.
Winchell, Norman C.

* Killed.   † Died of wounds.   ‡ Died of disease.   ‡ Died since discharge.

ROLL OF COMPANY F, FORTY-NINTH MASS. VOLUNTEERS.

September 1, 1863.

⸸Morey, Benjamin A., Captain.
⸸Dresser, Edson T., First Lieutenant.
⸸Sweet, George H., Second "
  Doolittle, John, " "
*Nichols, Myron, Sergeant.
  Silva, Albert P., "
  Nettleton, C. Luther, "
  Back, Thomas, "
⸸Judd, Thomas M. "

  Palmer, William H., Corporal.
⸸Case, Nelson M., "
  Flint, Andrew J., "
⸸May, Henry S., "
  Wright, Lucius W. "
  Videtto, Charles A.,
  Bradley, George T
  Steadman, Thomas, "
⸸Townsend, Charles J., "

PRIVATES.

⸸Alexander, George W.
  Blake, Horace W.
⸸Bigelow, Alfred S.
  Barnes, George L.
⸸Barnes, Theodore
⸸Babcock, Collins H.
*Bradley, Edward R.
  Comstock, George H.
  Cooper, George W.
⸸Crosby, John
  Curtis, Miles H.
⸸Caffrey, James
  Clary, Robert E.
  Curtin, Carl
  Day, Henry A.
  Dambose, Henry
  Downs, Isaac B.
*Fuller, Wells
‡Fargo, Waldo R.
  Fay, Linas S.
  Gay, Charles A.
  Gardner, Henry J.
‡Gilmore, Levi H.
‡Gibbs, Sheldon E.
  Green, Henry C.
  Harmon, Moses
  Hall, Peter
⸸Hunt, Rufus

  Heath, Franklin
  Heath, Addison B.
  Horton, Benjamin J.
  Horton, Charles H.
  Haskell, David
  Harrington, Henry R.
  Harris, Addison J.
  Hulet, Orrin
  Hugins, Merritt S.
  Johnson, Albert
⸸Jones, Henry R.
  Knapp, Henry A.
  Kellogg, Lucian F.
  Latham, Watson C.
  Lawless, John
  Lynch Charles L.
  Lynch, John D.
⸸Lamont, Daniel
  May, George T.
  Morgan, William
‡Morse, Elijah M.
⸸Morey, Albert J.
  Norton, Willis K.
  Nettleton, Albert C.
⸸O'Neill, John
⸸O'Brien, Dennis
‡Olds, Morton
  Pearl, William N.

⸸Perry, Edward F.
‡Pomeroy, Mosely
  Pomeroy, Curtis
  Peck, Solomon E.
⸸Potter, George B.
  Palmer, Franklin A.
  Street, Oscar D.
  Spoor, Albert J.
⸸Sperry, Harmon
  Sergeant, John E.
  Sprague, Charles
  Steadman, Henry C.
⸸Steadman, Edward W.
⸸Steadman, James L.
  Thompson, Marcus A.
⸸Twing, Eleazer
  Twing, Silas
⸸Townsend, Charles J.
  Underwood, Henry M.
  Wilson, Scott W.
  Woods, William
  Wood, Harlan P.
⸸Wright, Henry W.
  Williams, George R.
  Whipple, Edgar O.
  Wheelock, Harlan A.
⸸Young, James S.

* Killed. ‡ Died of disease. § Died since discharge.

ROLL OF COMPANY G, FORTY-NINTH MASS. VOLUNTEERS.

September 1, 1863.

‡Parker, Francis W., Captain.
Harvie, Robert B., First Lieutenant.
Lyons, Henry M., Second "
‡Southwick, Geo. T., Sergeant.
Torrey, David W., "
Lyons, George M., "
Noyes, Dana W., "
‡Nordaby, Robert T., "

‡Glasier, Henry A., Corpora'.
Waters, Charles A., "
‡Marsh, Oscar H., "
Garlick, Erwin W., "
Davis, Edward J., "
Crandall, Henry C., "
‡Upton, Albert H., "
Fowler, Subreski, "

PRIVATES.

‡Aldrich, Augustine
§Adams, John W.
Avy, Joseph
Babcock, Henry W.
‡Beebe, Zebulon
Brown, Henry N.
Bennett, Samuel B.
Briggs, Jerome N.
§Brown, Walter S.
Crosier, William L.
§Cox, Seymour W.
Clark, George S.
Courtney, John E.
‡Courtwright, Charles G.
Carde, Franklin
Colwell, Riley
§Curley, Patrick
§Clark, Daniel D.
§Cobleigh, Edward H.
§Clegg, Jerome S.
Cheesboro, Dwight
Cheesboro, Chadwick B.
Cheesboro, Albert W.
Cheesboro, Alfred H.
§Daniels, Lucien H.
Dodge, George W.
§Dorman, Wallace B.
Dalrymple, Orson

§Dillworth, Dennis
Estes, Benjamin C.
Fenn, B. H.
Fern, Patrick H.
Gray, Walter F.
Gallusha, John M.
Gove, Franklin B.
§Green, William
Hussey, James
Herman, Chas. B.
Hillard, John
Hekox, Samuel
Howland, Edmund J.
Ingraham, Edwin
Leonard, John M.
§McGee, John
Montgomery, Wm. H. H.
Miller, William C.
Murphy, Thomas
May, Henry H.
Martindale, Merritt M.
§Maynard, Wells G.
‡Niles, Benedict
Nelson, John W.
Noyes, John W.
Ormsby, Almon F.
Porter, Levi M.
§Parsons, Warren

Quackenbush, John
Reed, Albert W.
Ryan, Michael
Rosevelt, Isaac
Robinson, Stephen P.
Raymond, Edwin H.
§Robertson, Francis G.
Read, William T.
Reynolds, Michael J.
Reynolds, John F.
Ray, Daniel
Sampson, Whitcomb
Sweet, Elijah B.
‡Sweet, Thomas J.
Smith, Albert N.
§Smedley, Edward G.
Southwick, Daniel W.
Sheldon, Horace M.
Smith, George
§Snooks, James D.
Stocking, James
§Tower, Edwin O.
Torrey, Chauncey E.
Welton, William A.
Wood, Ira H.
Weeks, George
Wilbur, Charles A.
White, Harrison

‡ Died of disease.   § Died since discharge.

ROLL OF COMPANY H, FORTY-NINTH MASS. VOLUNTEERS.

September 1, 1863.

Shannon, Augustus V.,	Captain	§Taylor, Nathan,	Sergeant.
*Deming, Burton D.,	First Lieut nt.	Whittaker, Amos,	Corporal.
Smith, DeWitt S.,	Second "	Bliss, Elizur	"
*Wolcott, Joseph B.,	Sergeant.	Couch, Julius P.,	"
Bosworth, Mills J.,	"	Sears, Porter H.,	"
Phelps, Gustavus A.,	"	Hess, William,	"
Hitchcock, Albert V.,	"	‡Deming, William,	"

PRIVATES.

*Allen, Albert	Fosdick, James H.	Pratt, George F.
Allen, Franklin	Gregory, George	Rathbone, David
Alexander, Austin A.	§Heath, Alvin	Richardson, Charles N.
Baker, George S.	Hills, John F.	‡Richardson, Henry
Belden, Alfred	Hogan, William	Richards, James M.
†Beach, Henry L.	*Ingersoll, Eugene	Rowe, Homer
Bliss, Chauncey T.	Keough, Michael	Seymour, Sidney
Bliss, Henry J.	Knickerbocker, George	‡Seymour, Frederick P.
Bowen, Laurence	Loomis, Harvey	‡Smith, Egbert
Brown, Walter S.	Madden, James	‡Smith, James J.
Brown, A. W.	Maxfield, Samuel A.	‡Smith, Milton
Burke, Dennis	Merrill, Samuel B.	Snow, Anson
§Calkins, Jesse H.	McNamara, Andrew	Spring, Henry
Cline, George	McGinty, John	Stone, George H.
Carroll, John	Munson, Miles	Sturgess, George E.
Cady, George	Northway, John A.	Sariner, John
Daniels, Michael	Norton, Thomas	Thompson, Sheridan W.
Dennison, Luke L.	Obey, Alexander	Vincent, John
Earles, Frederick	O'Donnell, Michael S.	Wood, John
Fuller, William F.	Osborne, George	Ward, James
Foote, Alphonzo	Parsons, Harvey	Wright, Charles

* Killed. † Died of wounds. ‡ Died of disease. § Died since discharge.

ROLL OF COMPANY I FORTY-NINTH MASS. VOLUNTEERS.

September 1, 1863.

Rennie, Zenas C., Captain.
Kellogg, Le Roy S., First Lieutenant.
Nichols, William A., Second "
Marsh, Warner A., Sergeant.
Plank, Ogden H., "
McDonald, Edward, "
Geer, George L., "
Beeher, John, "
Rockwell, Charles A., "

‡Fuller, John M., Corporal.
Abbott, Charles V., "
Smith, Andrew, "
Kelly, John, "
§Ingall, Cheney L., "
§Spring, Milo, "
§Van Denburgh, Richard, "
*Winchell, David "

PRIVATES.

Avery, Peter
Allen, Daniel B.
§Allen, Isaac N.
Barnum, Zera
Bastion, Frederick
‡Burrows, Sylvester
Beckley, James
Brown, Ezra
Chamberlain, Wallace
Calaghan, John
Crozier, Lewis
Carpenter, Seneca A.
Carpenter, Alden
‡Cressor, James
Collins, Henry A.
‡Downing, Patrick
Deland, Edmund
Dresser, Gilbert W.
Farnam, Albert S.
Farnam, Alfred
Foster, Orestes R.
Gallipeaux, Joseph
Groat, Rufus
Hizler, Caspar J.

Hatch, Edmund
Haskell, Nathan W.
§Higgins, Ira
Howard, Albigence W.
Jeffers, Lewis W.
‡Joray, Francis
Kettell, Samuel S.
Knell, Christopher
Loveland, Francis E.
Leeman, Daniel
§Morgan, Ambrose
McDonough, Thomas
McKenna, James
Mettis, Joseph
McDaniel, William M.
Mason, Elisha L.
Merrills, John W.
Mallison, Martin
Mason, John
Noble, Jerry
‡Nea, Francis
‡Owens, David
‡Owens, Nelson
Proud, William
‡Proutt, L.

Powers, John*
§Perkins, William S.
Packard, William H.
Rogers, James B.
Seagers, Henry M.
Sedgwick, Daniel A.
Smith, Andrew C.
§Staples, Stillman S.
Seeman, Daniel
Swett, Levi
Turner, Edmund B.
Thayer, Edward C.
Tobin, David
Vautriene, Peter
Vosburgh, Herman
Walker, Philemon
Wilcox, George W.
Wilcox, Edward H.
Winters, Jacob
‡Wheldon, Wells E.
Wilson, Ephraim
§Wilson, William
Wink, Charles E.
Wilson, Ezra A. D.

* Killed. † Died of wounds. ‡ Died of disease. § Died since discharge.

ROLL OF COMPANY K, FORTY-NINTH MASS. VOLUNTEERS.

September 1, 1863.

Weston, Byron,   **Captain.**
Taft, Roscoe C.,   **First Lieutenant.**
§Judd, Isaac E.,   "   "
Gleason, Sanford B.,   **Second**   "
Rising, Edward J.,   **Sergeant.**
White, James L.,   "
*Warner, Henry E.,   "
§Clark, Charles B.,   "
Dalzell, David G., jr.,   "

Welton, Edson A.,   Corporal.
†Phelps, Ralph E.,   "
§Carey, Thomas,   "
Bunce, Edwin,   "
Robbins, Dwight M.,   "
Wheeler, George H.,   "
Parmerlee, Homer M.,   "
†Stetson, Nelson B.,   "

PRIVATES.

Ashley, Henry J.
Allen, George W.
†Bliss, David S.
Bradley, Ira
‡Burnett, William F.
Bartlett, Seth C.
Brazer, John
‡Brown, Ozro P.
‡Bartholomew, Charles
Bicknell, Oscar A.
§Beach, DeWitt C.
Burlingame, Zelotas M.
Brocha, Stephen
Bidwell, John W.
‡Cain, Henry W.
§Carman, Benjamin
Curtiss, James
‡Campbell, George
Campbell, David
§Carley, Stever W.
Chadwick, Philander B.
§Culver, Philander
Chapin, George B.
Clark, Hamlin F.
§Chapin, Henry B.

Decker, Harvey
§Decker, John
*Dowd, Solomon
Devine, Barney
Doton, John L.
Decker, Morris
Dunham, James E.
De Forrest, John C.
Decker, John, jr.
Funk, David
*Funk, Luther
‡Funk, William, jr.
§Fullerton, Stewart M. G.
§Fairfield, John H.
Graham, John A.
Hathaway, Lyman
§Hanalon, Timothy
Hennessey, William
Hart, Charles W.
Hollister, Gilbert
Hunt, Henry
Johnston, Israel H.
Johnston, William A.
§Leonard, William D.
Moseley, Lorenzo

Moseley, Lewis
Mahoney, James
Maloney, Thomas
Morrison, Henry
Noteware, Franklin
Powell, Stephen
Roys, John M.
Sears, John S.
Sheldon, Gilbert L.
*Shaw, Theron C.
Thompson, Albert F.
Tenney, Josiah
Tower, Chester L.
Taft, Lorenzo D.
Tower, Sedate T.
Thompson, George E.
Torrey, Rodney W.
Van Tassell, Henry
‡Van Deusen, David
Van Deusen, Nicholas
Wolfinger, John J.
‡Wolfinger, Godfrey
‡Webster, Seth R.
Wheaton, W. R.

* Killed.   †Died of wounds.   ‡ Died of disease.   § Died since discharge.

www.ingramcontent.com/pod-product-compliance
Lightning Source LLC
Chambersburg PA
CBHW030947110726
47900CB00004B/1159